BEHIND THE WINDOW

For Trieu

Behind The Window

HARRISON HICKMAN

Harrison James Frank Hickman

Contents

Initiation

Chipping Norton

Tuesday 1st August 1989

One moment was all it took. A glance, just a quick glance.

He knew straightaway that it was love. Pure, simple love.

Five minutes beforehand, he was sitting in his father's study, probably shitting himself about the move to university in a few weeks. Five minutes beforehand, he was going over the university paperwork that he needed to review. Five minutes beforehand, he wondered whether he would truly be great. All he knew was computers. The things of the future.

In five minutes, everything would change.

Peter 'Petey' McGough, flexed back in the leather chair, wiping sweat from the back of his neck.

Outside, the summer sun sparkled against the grass, a glittering green jewel. Tarmac shimmered in the heat.

Mrs Lyons had walked past earlier, on her way to the shops, her ever-grim face the same as usual: devoid of empathy. Now, *empathy*, that was a word, one that Petey had taken to using since his sixteenth birthday. Mrs Lyons had found it "inappropriate" for him to be doing so, calling him "too posh for his own good." Not that it mattered. Who gave a hoot what that old bag thought? She'd known him since he was a child, always putting him down. *"You haven't tied your laces properly." "There's a stain down your shirt." "You should stand up when a lady walks in the room."*

But Petey was a man now, just turned eighteen. They'd had a party here, in this house: wine, soft music, champagne, cakes, rolls. Alan had been there, his best friend since nursery. Various family members too. And to cap everything off: fireworks.

He went through to the kitchen, making his fourth cup of coffee that day, trying to calm himself. University was still weeks away, but it opened in his mind like a great chasm. After pouring the milk into the blackness, so gently, a mother's touch, he sidled back through to his father's study.

Sitting down, looking at the paperwork. How these things typically start.

He sipped his coffee.

Looked up. Through the other side of the window.

A woman. Thick, ginger hair, plaited. Her clothes were mere simplicity: thin blue vest, red shorts, a small dirty white backpack. Her face: an intense look of concentration.

Petey stepped up, launching himself out of the study, down the hallway, yanking the front door open. He burst into the light like a dark ghost. And he went to the woman with the thick, ginger hair.

"I love you," he blurted.

She stopped in her tracks, hands on her hips, her look speculative.

Somewhere, in the distance, a man shouted, vulgar language piercing the humid summer air. A plane flew overhead, engines growling. A flock of birds shot up from a grand oak.

"Excuse me?" she gasped.

"Um, sorry, I just –"

"Who the hell are you?"

He became aware, quite suddenly, of the true parameters: there they were, standing in the middle of a country road, he looking like a complete idiot, dressed in a cotton shirt, jeans and slippers. She, whoever she was, standing bemused, sweat glistening on her neck and shoulders.

"Petey," he stammered. "No – Peter, Peter Mc-Gough."

"Well, Peter, go back inside. I've had a long day, alright. Could do without this."

"Where are you from? Your accent..."

"Seriously, go away, you strange little boy."

"Okay, I'm sorry." He still couldn't believe the words *I love you* had come from his lips, directed to a total stranger! He turned to go.

"Oh, for fuck's sake." The woman nudged into him. "Look, is there any chance of a cup of tea?"

"The name's Sarah, by the way," said the woman, as Petey placed the tea in front of her.

"It's good to meet you." Petey sat the other side of the kitchen table, his heart still fluttering.

They shared a nervous first handshake.

"So, what brings you to Chipping Norton? I mean –" He felt the words swirl around his tongue. "I mean, if that's not a rude question or anything."

"It's okay, don't worry. I'm travelling. Thought I'd spend the summer going across the U.K. Always wanted to come here. What about you?"

"Oh, I'm a school leaver. Heading off to university in a few weeks."

"Which one?"

"Edinburgh. I'm going to read computing."

"Sounds wonderful. Wish I was as organised in life like you." Sarah slurped the tea, eyes pointed to the base of his chin.

"What you're doing sounds wonderful. Travelling. I'd love to do that someday. Never really been any-where, apart from the United States, France, Spain, West Germany, a few other places."

"Beats me." Sarah's eyes flashed with jealousy. "I've only been to West Germany with my school, and to France. Just at the start of my travelling adventures."

"The world's a big place."

"You're right in that." She tipped the cup to her lips and drank. "Lovely hot tea you have here. Where are your parents?"

"They're down in Kent visiting my Aunt Janine. They're coming back tomorrow."

"Must be nice having the house to yourself." She flashed a devilish smile at him.

"Well, I've got a lot of work to do in preparation for uni. There's hardly any time for partying."

"You seem to have found time for me though."

"Well..." Words failed him again. "I just had to..."

"You told me that you love me." Her words were sharp, the gentle intimacy between them gone. "Why did you do it?"

"I don't know."

"Well, I'm going to be brutally honest with you. I'm not looking for a boyfriend or anything. I'm trying to enjoy the single life at the moment. Sorry."

"It's okay." Petey's tea had turned cold. "I just got a little impulsive. I should be the one apologising."

"Tell you what, how about you cook me dinner and we'll forget about it?"

"Really nice garden you have here," remarked Sarah.

The two of them stood on the rough stone patio, gazing down the long, thin stretch of grass mixed with trees, shrubs, multicoloured fruits and a greenhouse. Each of them had a glass of red wine in their hand.

"Thanks," Petey replied. "Dad's a big fan of small trees."

"Trees are very important. I'm very passionate about our natural world."

"You're not a tree-hugger, are you?" He meant the words as a joke, but offence clearly crossed her vision.

"Maybe I am. You got a problem with that?"

"Of course not! I didn't mean to upset you. It was just a joke!"

"Sure it fucking was."

"Oh, come on!" he spluttered. "Honestly, I didn't mean to push things! I was just having a joke!"

"Oh, don't lie to me!"

He saw straightaway that *she* had been the one joking. Her lips curled into a smile and she snorted with laughter.

"You're so easy to wind up! Look at you!"

He sipped his wine, shyness coming on again. The evening was warm. Insects fluttered around. Leaves shifted around in the gentle breeze. A bird sang in the distance. A car swished down a far-off road, the faintest blare of its stereo swimming across the fields.

"When I was five years old, the doctors told my mother to give me up." Sarah's statement was random, so out of place with the tranquil scene. She moved over to one of the deckchairs that Petey had set up for them and sat down with a huff.

He dropped down on the other, listening with all his might.

"Teachers as well," she continued. "They said I was too disruptive in school, that I would never get any grades. They had a big meeting with my mother, a really gigantic one. Doctors, social workers, psychiatrists, you name it. They portrayed me as a troublesome little girl. They said that I would never go on to achieve anything. They told my mother that I was worthless, that she should hand me over to adoption and never see me again." She stopped, placing the wineglass on the floor, placing her head in her hands.

"Well, that's illegal, isn't it? What they did?"

"None of it makes sense. My mother didn't listen to them. She kept hold of me. Over the years, I behaved as they predicted: causing trouble, failing in class. They were right. My mother eventually cut me loose. I have a tiny flat somewhere, that's about it. I support myself on tiny jobs, barely eating, saving up for travelling. That's all I am, Petey, that's all I am. I've never achieved anything."

Without thinking, he reached out and stroked her hair. She didn't pull away.

"You achieved one thing today," he whispered. "I know it might not seem like anything, but... you made a new friend. And you're sipping wine on a beautiful summer's evening."

"Thanks." She raised her head, her cheeks moist. "I'm... feeling a little tired. I think maybe I should be heading back to the hostel."

"I thought you were going to stay for dinner."

"You know what, I'm not that hungry."

"Stay for dinner." He knew he was being pushy, but he couldn't help it.

"You really don't want my company."

"Maybe I do."

"Why? So you can try to fuck me later?"

"No, because you're quite simply the most fascinating person I've ever met. And because I meant what I said earlier. I love you."

"Lasagne," Petey announced with some glee. "Not my best effort, but I've been taking some cooking lessons off Mum. According to her, it's a necessary skill if I'm going to 'impress any young ladies' at university."

"I think it's fucking tasty," Sarah said, wolfing it down.

"Glad you like it." Petey flexed his fingers and dug his fork in.

They were in the dining room: a huge candlelit affair with cupboards full to the brim of cut glass. The dark table stretched from one end of the room to the other, so many empty seats representative of the many guests from across the country (and the world) who has come here over the years. The two of them were sat opposite to each other at the (very carefully) denoted head of the table, just below the master chair. Petey's dad had bought the set from an antique dealer in Kensington many years ago. Still shiny and sparkly, it was a suitable metaphor for rich diplomacy.

"It's like being royalty," remarked Sarah. "How do your parents afford this?" She fingered the silver cutlery.

"They manage."

"What do your parents do?"

"They both work in finance. Boring stuff really."

"Not so, if they're able to have all this stuff. I mean, look at what you've got here! Shite, Petey!"

"Well..."

"Let me ask you a question." She licked some sauce

from her lips. "What do you want to do? What is your ultimate ambition?"

"Well, I want to build a computing empire. A massive company."

"Wow, that's some ambition. Why you into computers? I'm hopeless with them."

"They take some getting used to, but once you do get the hang of them, they're amazing. Honestly, they're really cool." He poured them some more wine.

"Your family big wine drinkers?" she asked.

"Yeah. My parents like French stuff in particular. We had a good bottle of French red a few weeks ago. Succulent."

"I'll show you what succulent is, boy!" Sarah jumped up from her seat, strode around the table and planted her lips on Petey's.

"Oh my," he stuttered. "I –"

"That was for making my day." She went back to her seat and continued eating.

The lasagne tasted cold and clammy now, its authentic touch lost to the chaos of romance.

The truth was, Petey didn't have a single idea as to what to say next. Best keep his mouth shut and let the moment be savoured.

"Well, I'd better start thinking about heading back to the hostel," she said, face drooping. "I don't know if they have a curfew or not."

"Where are you staying?"

"Banbury."

"Can I take you to the bus stop?"

"Not necessary. I'm walking."

"You can't be serious!" he snapped.

"I'm being perfectly serious. I like walking. Unless you have something against walkers, like you do tree-huggers."

"I don't –" In his frustration, he knocked over his glass. "Damn it! Blast!" He reached for a tissue in his pocket, a feeble little thing. "Oh, Christ, this is going to stain!"

"Oh, you're such a ponce." Sarah was next to him, dabbing the table with an even larger tissue. "You probably never turn on the lights in here anyway, so I doubt anyone will notice."

He could sense her closeness, her warmth. His hand was on hers. "Don't go," he whispered. "Please."

"Do you have any whiskies in the house?"

"There's a decanter in the lounge."

"I'll finish mopping up this spill, if you'll go and pour us both a large measure."

As the sun finished its cycle, disappearing over the fields, Petey and Sarah clinked their glasses and drank.

"Now, this *is* posh," she said, gazing around at the leather armchairs, oil paintings (including one of a knight with his hands folded over his sword), a fireplace with original carvings dug into the stone, a bookshelf with authentic leather-bound books, a chunky cathode-ray television...

"I'd say we're a modest family..."

"*Modest*?!" She nearly spat out her whisky. "Fuck

that, you live like a king here! Look at your bookshelf. A whole herd of cows must have died for those fucking books!"

"I'm not sure what an entire herd of cows dying has to do with me being vaguely wealthier than others."

"Okay." She put her glass down, shutting her eyes and pressing her hands together as if in prayer. "Okay. You have a lot to learn." Sarah was trying to hold in that laughter, quite clearly struggling to do so. "I'm sorry, you're just so funny, Mr Posh." In a crude impersonation of his accent, she said, "*Vaguely wealthier than others.*"

"So, what are you planning to teach me?" It sounded cornier than he intended.

"That was about the worst joke anyone could ever make." She took her glass up again, downed the rest of the liquid in one gulp and came forward. "The first thing I'm going to teach you is how to be a better kisser. 'Cos that last effort was terrible. Seriously terrible."

Petey realised, all too late, that he'd lowered his whisky hand; the stuff was dribbling onto the floor. "Shit, not again," he muttered. "I'll have to get a dishcloth."

"Or we could clean it up tomorrow..."

He looked into her multicoloured, multi-layered, multi-everything eyes, and felt her thick hair run over the pale skin of his hands. Around them the house was completely silent. No radio, no T.V., no voices, no birdsong, no Mrs Lyons shouting criticism.

The realisation dawned on him.

"You're staying the night?" he asked scarcely louder than a whisper.

"Of course."

"Well, that's us well and truly fucked."

"How was I to know? I didn't exactly expect anything like this when I woke up this morning?"

"You mean you don't carry condoms around? You know, with the AIDS crisis and stuff?"

"I don't have AIDS."

"Never said you did."

It was indeed an extremely awkward moment between the two of them. Semi-naked, standing on either side of Petey's bed. He'd turned the lights off before they undressed, so all he could see of her body was from the silvery glare from the moonlight shining through the sky window.

"I'm just never good with these situations," he confessed.

"That, I can tell, Mr Posh."

"Will you stop calling me that?"

"What, 'Mr Posh'?"

"Yes."

"Why?"

"Because," he said, his voice beginning to show signs of strain, "Peter is my name."

"Fuck, you're such a pretentious little twerp. Now, what are we going to do about the present situation?"

"Well, I could maybe..." He looked down, embarrassed at himself. "Well, maybe I could perform... perform... oral sex on you?"

"Okay, you're seriously fucking weird. I've just thought of a better idea. Where's your parents' room?"

"On the first floor. We're not doing it in there! If they find out, they'll kill me!"

"That's not what I'm saying, you stupid idiot!" She burst out in a fit of laughter. "For fuck's sake, come with me."

Bounding down the stairs like rabbits, they descended to the first floor. Petey reluctantly pointed out his parents' room and she leapt straight inside. Straightaway, without asking, she rummaged in his parents' bedside tables, pulling out watches, boxes containing jewellery, books, notebooks, a figurine of a ballet dancer that Petey's mother had been given for her tenth birthday by her very frail grandmother (who, by the way, had been one of the thousands waving the *Titanic* off on its disastrous voyage), a signed copy of a Beatles record... and a ball of very old, brown string.

"What are you looking for?" he asked.

"What do you think?!" She stood up, slapping her hands on her thighs. "Okay, your parents are close, right?"

"Of course –"

"They love each other, right? Til death do us part. You know what I mean? Surely, as a close intimate couple, they're bound to do certain things together, right?"

"I don't understand –"

"For the sake of Jesus, I'm looking for your parents' *condoms*!"

"Ah, in that case we'd better check their bathroom." Cheeks flushing, he led her along the corridor to the next room. He flicked on the light and straightaway she started digging through the white cupboard, flinging out toiletries that had been building up over the past ten or so years.

"That's us fucked then," she said. "Fuck. I was looking forward to getting laid with my first upper-class Englishman."

"But –"

"No, seriously, I don't want to hear it. I mean, you tell me you love me, take me into your house, try to have sex with me... all without the decency of having protection." She stormed out of the bathroom, heading back up the stairs. "I need you to help me find a couple of things!" she called down. "It's the least you can do!"

After climbing, very defeatedly, up the tight carpeted stairs to his room, he stopped in a heavy gasp before the doorway. Sarah was standing there with her arms folded, blocking his way in.

"I know you're angry," he said. "If you want, I can get the spare room ready for you. Or I could call you a taxi."

"Will you just shut up for a minute?" She cursed silently with her lips. "I make sure that I have everything I need with me at all times, clearly unlike you.

It's a good job I brought this with me." She held up a silver packet.

"But, we've, no *you've* just churned up my parents' room *and* their bathroom!"

"Yeah, but it was fun." She broke into a smile. "Come on, let's see what you've got."

"Where have you always wanted to go to?"

"What?" Petey murmured, dreary with sleep. He gazed at the clock on his wall: 11:30.

"What country do you most want to go to?"

"I've always fancied Argentina."

"What, seriously? Britain and Argentina aren't exactly on friendly terms right now."

"Well, there was a bit of disagreement."

"Christ, you were shooting the hell out of one another. Thatcher went and kicked the shite out of them." She stroked his chin. "Typical British. Getting involved in things that don't concern you."

"So, where do you want to go?" Petey said, yawning.

"Not sure yet. World's a big place. When I get back home, I'll have a think. I'm thinking New Zealand, but I'm not too sure."

"Can I ask you something? I don't know how to ask it, I just have to."

It was almost as if she knew every detail of his mind. She planted a kiss on his neck and whispered, "Can you see me again?"

"Can I?"

"No." Her voice was flight, like it had been hours

earlier, when he'd approached her on the street. The coldness was back.

"Why not?"

"Because we both need to live our lives. We're both eighteen. You're about to head off to university, I'm going to travel the world... hopefully. I can't keep pausing just to visit you in Edinburgh."

"Stay in touch?" he pleaded.

"No, babe. No. This is a passing moment for us. A single day. We should enjoy this moment." She held onto him tighter. "But I'll make you a promise. I was reading a book on Edinburgh a few months ago, so I know a bit of its geography. North Bridge. It's apparently really amazing. Stupendous, as you English would say. Well, you can't miss it. You'll find it when you get there. I will meet you on that bridge on the Nineteenth of May, Nineteen-Ninety-Three, at two o'clock in the afternoon. Got that?"

"Yeah." He reached across the table to where he kept his diary and noted the details down, struggling to see in the moonlight.

"Wow, didn't expect you to have to write it down. Such a romantic turn-off." She coughed. "Christ, come here." She pulled him back down, kissing him on the neck and shoulders.

"I will miss you." His measly little voice just like a mouse's.

"Let's not talk about that. Let's enjoy tonight. You still got any energy?"

"A little. Why?"

"Well, let's have another... session."

"Thought you only had one condom."

"First rule of travelling. Double up on everything."

"You mean you have two condoms?"

"I've got twenty."

"Well, we'd better get busy then, hadn't we?"

Wednesday 2nd August 1989

Breakfast: a rush of fried bacon, fried eggs, fried toast, fried mushrooms, black pudding, buttered toast, black coffee and fresh orange juice. Bright sunlight filtered through the kitchen windows, turning the coffeemaker, worksurfaces, white cooker, silver cutlery, tiled floor and ceramic mugs into a sky of jewels.

"Fuck, I haven't eaten like this in ages," she said, with eyes as wide as the sun. "You certainly know how to cook a fry-up, don't you?"

"It's one of the rare things I'm talented at. Eat up, don't let it go cold." Petey had finished his, the plate already in the sink.

"Oh, you're talented, believe me. Last night..."

"Yes, well *I even* didn't know I could do that."

"Yeah, yeah, yeah. So, what are you up to today?"

"Well, I've got some more stuff to get ready for university. I'll have to do a bit of tidying up before my parents get home; actually, quite a lot of tidying, particularly with regards to their bedroom."

"Ha, ha, ha. But I thought it was funny."

"You would do, wouldn't you? So, what are you doing with yourself today?"

"Well, I'm getting the train down to London. I'm staying there for a few days and then I head up north to Glasgow. See what's up there."

"That's really cool. I shall miss you, a great deal."

"I will too."

There was a solemn deep loss between them, a void which would forever burn in his heart.

"Listen," she said, pushing her plate to the side, "how do you fancy walking me to the bus stop?"

It was certainly a lot cooler today. The wind was picking up, swirling around their feet. Several times, they had to stop to let cars past, but eventually they were walking on a small gravel path, just wide enough for them to hold hands.

"It's a beautiful day," Petey said. "I think it might get warm later too."

"Well, in a few hours, I'll be in London – not much scenery there."

"Yeah, you can say that."

They walked slowly and clumsily. Petey knew which bus stop she was talking about. It was by a junction, where the small road they were on opened onto a larger one that led to Banbury. He could see the junction up ahead. The knowledge that every footstep brought them closer to parting ways was painful. Mortifying. Unthinkable.

He only realised he was crying when she wrapped him in a big hug.

"God, you're like a lovesick thirteen-year-old," she hissed. "Listen, I know this hurts, but it's not the end. As I said, Nineteen-Ninety-Three. Less than four years. You'll more than likely have met someone by then, a lady or something from Buckinghamshire probably. You'll forget all about me. Honestly. I'll probably be standing waiting for you and you won't turn up."

"I promise I will!" he declared.

"And I promise I'll be there," she said, kissing him on the forehead. "Come on, hurry up, the bus'll be along any moment now."

When they reached the bus stop, she put her rucksack down and checked the timetable on the post. "Okay, a couple of minutes," she muttered. "So, you gonna be all right?"

"Yeah, I'll be fine." He fought back tears. "I really enjoyed last night, being with you."

"Me too. When you burst out of your house, I thought you were some sort of idiot. Really, I thought you were. A fucking imbecile. But you're cute."

"Thanks."

"That wasn't necessarily a compliment," she said, sniggering.

A growling sounded in the distance, followed swiftly by a white shape. The bus trundled along, pulling up to the stop.

"Be strong, okay?" She kissed him, squeezing his hands, then climbed aboard the bus.

It moved off as soon as the fare had been paid. He

waved at her and she waved back, their eyes locked for the briefest moment. But soon the bus was gaining speed and that moment of true intimacy was gone.

Petey stood alone, passing a hand through the space in which she'd once stood. It was empty now, as though she had never existed. But he could still smell her on him. He started walking, back to the house.

He knew what he had to do: wait. Wait for that day: 19th May 1993. He would see her again. In the three and a half years before then, he would study, make friends, date... and travel. The world was big. And he would see her again.

"What was I thinking?" Sarah muttered to herself as she got off the bus in Banbury. "Christ, you stupid bitch!"

Shoppers were out in the masses and she nearly swore at an old lady who pushed into her. A driver honked their horn at someone. A group of men were gathering for an afternoon drinking session outside a pub.

She looked at her watch: the train departed in less than two hours. That might have seemed lengthy to most people, but she had business to conduct in this little market town. Her hostel was near the station, but still she would need to hurry up.

Nothing hid the truth though. The truth that she had very little money on her. It was in a traveller's nature to have very little money, but damn it felt awful. Maybe she shouldn't have used that condom madness to steal a couple of pearls from that boy's mother. But she had to survive somehow! There would be a pawn shop in London where she could sell them with an extremely guilty conscience. But right now, she needed money, a lot of it. She turned towards the pub.

One hundred pounds richer, she set off in the direction of the train station. Feeling on top of the world!

Her mouth didn't taste too good though. How old was he? Sixty? At least! But she had money. And her belly was still full from the breakfast earlier.

She still had an hour before her train, but it would be a good idea to hurry.

She found a small café, grabbed a coffee and sat in a dark corner, going over plan for London. She would find a place to stay, no doubt. London was full of hostels. Even if she didn't find one, a rich man would offer her a place to stay and she would earn some more money. She wrote down a few potential sites to visit in her tiny pink notebook (using her last remaining pencil that had worn down so much it was like writing ghosts onto the paper).

The smell of cigarette smoke alerted her that she was no longer alone. She looked up, folding her arms with annoyance.

"What do you want?" she snapped. "I told you I wasn't interested at all!"

"You and I need to talk," Nick said angrily. "I mean it. You humiliated me yesterday."

"How did I humiliate you?" Sarah said, puffing her lips.

"That stupid little wanker rushed out of his house and you immediately followed him in! You didn't think of coming to me instead."

"Considering you'd been following me all day, trying to get my knickers off, it seemed a logical thing to do. Why the hell do you think I went all the way to that shithole town, Chipping Norton or whatever the hell it's called?"

"You humiliated me!" Nick repeated, folding his arms. His leather jacket crinkled under the stress.

"I know, I heard you shouting your head off and swearing. Christ, Nick, I was trying to get away from you!" She put away her notebook, aware that people were staring at them. An elderly couple were whispering, the husband turning around every few moments for a glance in their direction. "Look, Nick, I know it hurts, but I'm just not into you."

"When we met in that pub, you were totally chatting to me, listening to everything I said. Then you completely ignore me the next day when I asked if you wanted lunch."

"First," she told him, her voice turning into a nun's harsh tone, "when I met you in the pub, I was celebrating the fact that I'd arrived safely in England. I was a bit flirty, maybe I got a little pushy."

"You *were* pushy!" he shouted. "Fuck you!"

"But, and let me stress this, I *wasn't* in to you. Secondly, when you came to ask me out for lunch, you came to my hostel and wouldn't leave the manager alone until I'd come down from my dorm to speak to you. Then you got angry when I refused your date offer. You kicked a hole in the reception desk!"

"Look, I apologise for that."

"After you were ejected, I decided to get away from Banbury, at least for a few hours. I was desperate to get away from you. Now, I've had enough, Nick. I'm getting on a train soon. I'm leaving here and I'm not coming back. Go away."

"You have no idea what I'm about to do," said Nick, calmly now. "You have no idea." He turned to go, his crinkly jacket making horrid rubbing noises as he moved. He turned around at the last moment, yelling, "You have no fucking idea!"

Sarah waited for a few minutes, making sure the man had gone, before she started packing up. She'd only been in Banbury for a few days and she'd had two doomed love affairs! Smirking, she waved for the bill. It was time to leave. After making sure she had everything, that's what she did. Heading straight for the hostel like a bullet, she didn't stop to talk to anyone. Only when she was safely on the train, did she let herself relax. Calm down. Calm.

When Sarah arrived in London, she was greeted by an unusual guest for this time of year: rain.

The streets were as she'd imagined them to be: choked with cars, harsh accents, red buses, flaring tempters. Since she was a little girl, she had dreamed of coming here. Now that dream was a damp reality.

Her stomach growling, she set off in search of a hostel. She wanted nothing more than a juicy hot meal and a cold beer. Yet there was an even more un-settling feeling in her stomach than fear: the feeling of longing.

Something had happened with that boy. It had triggered an unbalance with her. She found that she craved rich men, not because of their money, but because there was an insidious desire, one that simply could not be quelled.

The Jaguar pulled up just after Eight O'Clock that evening. Petey's dad was the first out, rushing to the boot to get the cases. Mum sidled out, her face contorted. She stretched on the driveway, then followed Dad into the house.

"Thanks for looking after the place, Petey," Dad said, putting the cases down in the hallway. "Your mother and I really appreciate what you've done. We'll go out for a meal tomorrow night, the three of us."

"Thanks, Dad, I'd love that." Petey's emotions were tearing at his brain, but he held himself together.

"How did your university stuff go?" asked Mum.

"Oh, fine. Got everything done I needed to." In reality, he hadn't. He'd spent most of the afternoon crying in his bed, before finally summoning the strength to tidy the house up. Every time he'd put a disturbed object back, he felt like he was driving a knife into the existence of Sarah. Soon that memory would bleed out and nothing would be left.

"Your Aunt Janine is doing well," Dad informed. "Got a bit of a brutal summer cold, but she's getting through it. She sends her love. She's very excited for you going off to university."

"I'm pleased she's coping. I will definitely write to her when I'm in Edinburgh." Petey tried to thrust himself into the conversation, anything to avoid thinking about Sarah.

"Her son is planning to spend a year abroad," said Mum chirpily. "America."

"That sounds incredible."

"Just needs to get the money together, and I do wonder what his source for that will be," Dad joked. "Right, now, let's get a bottle of red opened!" He led them all into the kitchen and retrieved a bottle from one of the cupboards. He uncorked it, smelled the rim and took three glasses from the glass cabinet. After pouring it out, he raised his glass. "To good health," he toasted.

"To good health," Petey and his mum said in unison.

The doorbell rang. Mum went for it. Petey thought for a moment, just a moment, a pathetic excuse of a moment, that it might be Sarah. But before he could put his glass down, Alan, red-faced, exhausted and panicky, came through to the kitchen.

"Is everything okay?" asked Dad.

"Something's happened." Alan took a deep breath "It's about Nick."

"I don't want to hear about it!" Dad shouted. "Nick is a bully. He's nothing but a pathetic little bully! He's tormented Petey since he was a kid! He's a vile little creature!"

"Is everything okay?" Petey's Mum asked, as she tiptoed into the kitchen.

"No, things aren't good. Things are very bad, actually."

"Slow down." She steadied Petey's best friend by the shoulders. "What's happened?"

"He was hit by a car outside his house," said Alan, beginning to pant like a dog. "Neck broken!" A long pause as he took several deep breaths. "He's dead."

Glasgow

Tuesday 8th August 1989

Sarah's arrival in Glasgow was marked by the train guard shouting for her to wake up.

"Come on, it's not a hotel!" shouted the moustached, brisk man, checking his watch.

"Sorry," she replied, voice thick with sleep. She picked up her bags and followed the straggling passengers off the platform and into Glasgow Central Station.

She knew quite a bit about Glasgow Central, from what she'd read in guides. During both world wars, it was used to transport soldiers. She imagined that, for just a moment, the many troops departing, saying goodbye to their families. Many would never come home.

There was a decent hostel situated near the station, a couple of streets away. Someone she'd met in London had told her about it, recommending it as a cheap place to stay for a bit. They'd also told her to be wary of this city. Knife crime, drugs, that sort of stuff. It was a haven for the desolate.

The station was full, she guessed, because it was just past Five O'Clock and the commuters were out in full force. Someday, she would be joining the grey suits, living a normal life. She had to make the most of what she had now, to live free and happy and ecstatic. That was one of the reasons she'd abandoned Petey. She had to let him go, forget about him.

As she left the station, a man with deep-set blue eyes and wavy blonde hair waved at her, grinning with perfectly set white teeth. She ignored him and pushed on into the evening.

She found the hostel with no difficulty. The manager, it could be supposed, was a pleasant enough guy. With a semi-bald head and a cardigan, he had the caring grandfather look. He gave her a key, took her payment (of £50) for five nights, and wished her an enjoyable stay.

She shared her room with four others, though only one of the other beds was occupied. (The other two, she presumed, judging from the ruffled sheets and half-opened bags, were out somewhere.) The man currently occupying Bed 2 was a severely overweight guy with a bushy, grey beard. He lay back, staring at the ceiling, flabs hanging out from underneath his t-shirt.

Sarah dumped her things, slipped off her shoes, and lay down on her allotted bunk. She stayed there for a few hours, trying to fall asleep, but it wasn't working. Eventually, she sat up and put her shoes back on.

"You going somewhere?" said the fat man. He sounded drunk.

"As a matter of fact, I am. Don't be so nosy." She left before he could reply.

Why was she so angry? She didn't know, but she was storming out of the hostel like a poltergeist. She was fuming so much that she didn't hear footsteps behind her.

Something caught hold of her and began dragging her by her hair. She was shoved hard into a small alleyway. No one was around. She tried to yell, but no sound came out. Her elbows smacked into the tarmac. Sharp daggers and splinters travelled up through her arms.

"Give me every single penny on you," a voice said calmly, a flick-knife glinting in the streetlight. He was on top of her, bleach teeth twisted in a smile. His blonde hair bounced around like a badly run basketball game.

"It's all back in the hostel," she whimpered.

"Why would a girl like you be going out without a single penny on her?" The man let out a snort of laughter. "Just give me your fucking purse and we'll call it quits, how 'bout that?"

"Fuck, you're that guy from the station, aren't

you?" Why she said the next few words, she would never fully understand: "Thought you were a bit weird."

"That I am. You should have reported me then and there. Then I wouldn't have followed you to that pathetic shithole hostel you're staying in." The man reached down, curling his fingers around her collar. "Come on, give me your fucking money."

She felt something sharp in her hand. Something wet. Glass. She slashed like a cat swiping at a mouse. A small spray of blood jetted from the man's cheek, as he screamed in shock and pain. She kicked him away from her, rising to her feet, nearly falling again.

The man was crying, babbling like a child.

Sarah legged it out of the alleyway, dashing back to the hostel in a cartoon of stumbles. Bounding to her room, she tried to stop the waterfalls of tears. The dorm was completely empty, its occupants out in the dying day. Perfect. She gathered her things, doing a quick check, before dashing back out to the streets.

It was the second time on this trip that she'd been forced to flee. But this time, it seemed like she didn't have anywhere to run. Her best bet was going back to the station, get a train to London. But it seemed futile now. In the distance, police sirens wailed.

Millennium

Bangkok

Thursday 30th December 1999

The fasten seatbelt sign came on, just as he left the bathroom.

"Please return to your seat, sir," said a smiling Thai hostess.

"Just on my way."

Her smile got even bigger. Why did all air hostesses act with the same sense of sarcasm wherever you went in the world? Bizarre.

Everyone in the business class cabin was half-asleep, or half-drunk. They stirred as the plane began to drop.

Alan Stanley raised his eyebrows as Petey sat down next to him.

"How many people are coming to this bloody conference?" asked Alan.

"A lot," said Petey.

"And how many protesters are we expecting?"

"Alan, I hired you as my lawyer. I didn't expect you to be asking questions every five minutes."

"As your lawyer, that's my job."

"Well, let's focus on the positives." Petey picked up

the leaflet for the conference: *A New Millennium: New Frontiers and No Boundaries. Guidebook.* "We have a really good chance of making some excellent deals here. Greg Yirrell, no less, is going to be there."

"You've already got a successful company, Peter. Your computers are in every school in Britain."

"Yeah, but I want them in every school in *the world.*"

"Are you two going to have another argument?" said Nicola, stirring from her sleep.

"Great, you've woken her," grumbled Petey.

The two men shared what appeared to be a moment of hostility, a second of anger, an attosecond of bitterness. Then they broke into smiles, clapping each other on the shoulder.

Nicola yawned and leaned out from her seat. "Hey, babe," she whispered to Petey.

"Hi." He snapped his fingers. "Fasten your safety belts."

"Oh, you're such a stickler for the rules," she teased.

Other passengers were starting to wake now, rumbling from their slumbering.

The pilot's voice, dreary and tired (no doubt from the fact that he was probably going to be working New Year's Eve) came on, informing them that they would be landing in ten minutes.

"What are we doing for dinner tonight?" asked Alan. "I hope we –" He switched to a whisper. "– don't have to go for fucking noodles."

"I'm sure we won't." Petey put the programme away in his satchel and straightened up his seat. "Your wife usually has good ideas in this area. Ask her."

"You can tell she's enthusiastic about it." Alan nodded to the seat next to Nicola: his wife, the always bright Irene, was snoring away.

The plane descended through the clouds and Petey caught a glimpse of the sprawling mass of Bangkok. He'd thought about moving there once, but now, as the buildings got bigger and the suffocating fingers of the traffic curled around his neck, he realised that not coming anywhere near the place had been a bloody good idea.

The plane landed with a stiff jolt. The fuselage shuddered. The other passengers, many no doubt glad to be home for the festivities, were only too happy to let out a small cheer. But Petey didn't feel happy. He had his fists clenched like he was looking for a fight.

The four of them emerge into the arrivals hall, jaded, legs like rubber. Irene, in particular, really looked like she didn't want to be there.

"Is there someone picking us up?" she asked in her hard Liverpudlian accent.

"No, I thought it would be quicker if we just got a taxi," said Petey. He quickly scanned about him: the travellers, tourists, bored-to-tears businessmen, cleaners, lost souls, bitter losers-in-life. "Okay, I think it's this way to the taxi rank."

"I had hoped we'd be picked up," Irene complained. "My feet are sore."

"And she's only been sitting down," Alan muttered in Petey's ear, "in a seat that our fucking company paid for."

"Come on, let's get moving, you lot," jeered Nicola. "You guys need to pick your feet up!"

The party emerged into the horn-blaring air, stressed-looking taxi directors pointing half-dazed tourists in any particular direction.

Petey, having gained a special confidence in hailing taxis from his various trips around the globe, had no trouble finding them one. After a bit of angry debating (on the part of Irene) with the driver on the cleanliness of the taxi (which ended with Alan nearly losing his temper and forcing his wife into an extremely embarrassed silence), they were on their way to their five-star hotel (paid for, very generously, by the company).

"Thought we'd never get away," said Alan, letting out a long sigh.

"I'll tell you one thing that I've learned on my travels. Even if you have the worst complainer in the group, the absolute worst, take them to a swimming pool in a very posh hotel, and it'll sort them no bother."

"Well, I'll take that onboard."

The two men had taken a short walk from the hotel, eventually giving up on exploring and settling for a small, lowkey bar. They looked mildly conspicuous, in their white shirts and black trousers, contrasting with the locals dressed in shorts and vests. A man was fixing his bike at the entrance, a cigarette smouldering away between his lips.

"How was your Christmas?" asked Alan. "Sorry, I never really got much of a chance to ask you."

"It was okay. Nicola and I went to her parents. Turkey dinner, the usual." Petey took a sip of beer.

"Are you going to propose?"

"I don't know. She hasn't even met my parents yet."

"Why not?" The realisation quickly sprung up on Alan's face. "Oh, don't tell me…"

"Yes, Mum still blames me for those pearls going missing." Petey pressed the heels of his hands into his cheeks. "I mean, for Christ's sake, I have *no* idea where they went. You know something, Alan? She genuinely believed I took them to uni with me to sell for drugs!"

"Yeah, I remember you telling me about that."

"It wouldn't have been such a big deal if it had been something else. It's just, those pearls belonged to her great-grandmother." Petey downed the last of his beer. "Listen, mate, I don't want to talk about this anymore. Let's just have a great time, okay? Do you fancy another drink?"

"Yeah sure." Alan flexed his fingers as Petey ordered more drinks. "You know, I'm pleased with what you've achieved, particularly in the past two years."

"Alan, you're my lawyer, not my psychic."

"I'm being serious, mate. You know, that whole business with Georgina. I mean, the… suicide."

"Honestly, I'm fine about it. It was a long time ago.

I was a young man then. Young and foolish, as they say."

"You're young now!" Alan said. "We're both young!"

"But you act like a forty-year-old professional. Alan, let me remind you, you've only been a qualified lawyer for a year."

"But you were impressed enough with my credentials to hire me to your company."

"Alan, I hired you for the simple reason that you've been my best friend since nursery. You know how I tick. You know my thinking process. You know what I'm going to do, *before* I go and do it."

"You're right, I know how you tick. And I know that there's something up with you. Ever since Sarah."

"For Christ's sake, Alan!" Petey realised he'd raised his voice a little bit too high and backed down. "That was a long time ago. It's dead and buried."

"Sorry, mate, I pushed it a bit too far." The lawyer threw a glance at his watch. "Right –" The motorbike roared into life. The owner cast an apologetic *I don't give a shit* look at them, before riding off into the day. "Right, I think we'd best be getting back. Our respective other halves will be wondering what we've gotten up to."

They did indeed go for noodles that night, much to Alan's dismay. He looked repulsively at a bowl on another table like it was a bowl of worms.

The restaurant was pretty good. Just half a kilometre away from the hotel. No taxi needed. The tables were covered with silky cloths, trussed up with the latest in the Asian cutlery scene, a proper bloody good decanter of wine, brutal wooden seats that made you sit up straight (good, in Petey's opinion, as slouching during dinner gave you terrible indigestion later), and an excellent view from the balcony (of which they were seated quite near to) of the busy street below.

"To good fortunes!" said Petey, after a waiter had filled their glasses.

"And," stressed Nicola, "*and*, a Happy New Year!"

"Happy New Millennium!" said Irene, raising her glass and drinking it straight down. Alan gave her a scolding look.

"Aren't you drinking?" asked Petey, noticing that his girlfriend hadn't touched her wine.

"I think I'll give the alcohol a miss tonight," said Nicola.

"Don't tell me you're not in the mood for drinking." Irene dug a fork into the table cover.

"I'm not feeling too well. Anyway, we're going to be drinking a lot tomorrow night."

"Well, if she's not going to drink perfectly good wine," said Irene, "I will." She snatched Nicola's glass. Irene's makeup, mixed with sweat, dazzled in the dim lights of the restaurant.

The waiter came over. "Everything okay so far?" he asked timidly.

"Very good," said Petey.

"Your meal will be along soon."

"Take your time. No rush."

"What do you mean, no rush?" snapped Irene. "Maybe I want my meal now!"

"Well, I'm sure it won't be too long," said Alan.

Petey, seated across from his friend, could see the strain in his eyes. He flashed Alan a concerned look and then reached his hand for Nicola's.

"You remember our wedding?" said Irene, stroking her hand over Alan's cheek. "Castle in Scotland? Bagpipes? All sorts of shit?"

"It was a great day," said Nicola. "I remember you, Alan, dressed in that kilt."

"Even though I'm not bloody Scottish!" Alan chuckled. "Damn, I felt like a wally."

"He was so clumsy, it was like watching a spastic crossed with Basil Brush go around and try to act like a gentleman!" Irene stifled a laugh so hard that wine dribbled down her chin onto her blue dress.

"Yeah, I remember." Nicola ran a finger over her spoon. "I remember."

"And I remember how Peter bored my dad to death with his talk on computers, even though my dad is the most boring fucking person on the planet." She signalled to the waiter. "Another bottle please. Mr McGough is paying."

"Maybe you should go easy on the wine," said Nicola gently. "We've got an early start tomorrow."

"Don't tell me to go easy," Irene responded.

Just then, the waiter brought over the four steaming bowls of noodles. He placed them down, neatly, not a care in the world, then went back and brought over the wine, placing it next to the decanter. "Let me know when you want the decanter refilled," he said.

"Are you okay?" asked Nicola.

Alan was clearly trying to find things to distract himself, looking around like he was searching for a wasp.

"Nicola, you come from a nice family, a good family." Irene filled her glass up. "If you guys want me to serve you some wine, let me know – I don't know how much longer I'll be able to do it."

"You come from a good family as well," said Nicola, reaching a hand over to Irene. Alan's wife quickly pulled her hand back.

"I thought I did, until just before Christmas." Tears were shimmering on the edge of Irene's eyes. "Fuck. I don't know how to say it."

"Do you want to go back to the hotel?" asked Petey. "Alan, why don't you guys head back? We'll take care of the bill."

"No, I want to tell you what happened, before I'm too bladdered." She was crying openly. Alan quickly took the glass off her. "I just... My parents took me out for a meal a few weeks ago for my birthday."

"Look, if this is about me not being able to make it, I'm truly sorry." Alan was doing that ever-mildly-just-so-familiar dance of waving his hands and lowering his eyes: a patronising display of him trying to prove that he had a fair idea of what was going on. "As I said, I was stuck up in Aberdeen with my flight being cancelled.

There was genuinely nothing I could do to get down any sooner."

"Alan, that's not what it's about!" Irene's makeup was running down her face, like a dam containing emotion after emotion after emotion had been hit by a bouncing bomb. "My parents took me to a pub in Ormskirk. A stupid little place. Dad got drunk, horribly drunk, and he started saying things. He was swearing, really fucking aggressively. Making threats to guys at the bar. Saying he was going to burn the place down. Of course, the landlord called the police. They handcuffed my dad. You should have seen the threats he'd made. Nothing like this has ever happened before. He is not this sort of man! He's always been kind, gentle, dedicated. As the police dragged him out, he told my mum how he'd fucked a prostitute in London in the late Eighties. He told her really graphically; I mean, to the level where he talked about how much his cock hurt after it was over."

"Jesus Christ," said Nicola, again reaching out for Irene's hand. This time the offer wasn't rebuffed. "Is your dad being taken to court?"

"No, thankfully the landlord doesn't want to press charges. The police have let him off with a warning. Though –" She cast her eyes upwards. "– Mum's divorcing him."

"I'm so sorry," said Petey.

"It's okay. None of you are responsible for this. It's just, my whole life I've always believed Dad was right. He was always calm and respectful. Always held the door open for ladies. It is not him to lash out the way he did. Everything's fucked, isn't it?"

"Why didn't you tell us earlier?" said Alan, wrapping an arm around his wife's shoulders. "Why didn't you tell me? We could have gone away, just the two of us. Italy or somewhere."

"Your conference means a lot, to both of you. I didn't want to get in the way."

"Don't say that! I would have understood!"

"Let's be positive guys." Petey refilled all their glasses (with the exception of Nicola's). "A new millennium is about to start. I'm here, in Thailand, with my girlfriend and my two best friends. That's what's important. That's what matters. Let's drink to the future."

"To the Year Two-Thousand!" said Nicola, raising a glass of water.

"The new millennium!" Alan cheered.

"A bright future!" Irene cried out.

"And to a successful computing empire," said Petey. His joke was well received.

Friday 31st December 1999

"Right, the conference finishes at Five O'Clock, so that should give us enough time to jet back to the hotel and change into our party clothes. Plus, go for a drink."

"Dear, the party kicks off at seven. Believe me, we'll have plenty of time. And I think, we can schedule more than a drink..." Nicola pushed her hands into his neck. Her dark hair, tied into a ponytail, swished from side to side. "And, and, I think you need another shave."

"And, and," he said, trying (and bloody-well failing) to mock her, "I think you need to let a man take care of his hygiene. Do I tell you how to operate a hair straightener?"

"You wouldn't know how," she said, running to the bathroom.

"You're talking to a guy who owns one of the biggest computing companies on the planet. I built it up from scratch. With a little help, of course, from certain benefactors."

"Namely my father!" she shouted.

"Yeah, yeah, yeah. But, don't forget, he got his investment back. Let me tell you, I have been referred to –"

"– as the new Bill Gates. I know. You've told me a hundred times."

"And how long are you going to be? We need to meet the others downstairs for breakfast."

"If Irene's not hungover." Nicola came out of the bathroom, adjusting her jacket. "Petey, is she going to be okay? I'm pretty worried about her."

"Oh, she'll be fine. She's strong. She'll pull through. Her mum's probably trying to make her dad uncomfortable, then she'll take him back."

"I don't think so, dear." Nicola handed him his

briefcase. "Now, are you going to take me to breakfast or what?"

The protesters had gathered like a throng of bees outside the conference centre. Numerous placards read:

Computers Are Polluters!

Down with the Processing Systems

BAN A.I.

The usual rubbish that Petey was used to at these sorts of events. He wasn't even surprised to see a bearded man with thick George Smiley glasses waving a poster that proclaimed: *Newton-M-Wren Computers KILL BABIES.*

"Don't they have anything better to do?" said Alan, as he helped his wife out of the taxi.

A banner announcing the title of the conference was hanging above the great glass entrance doors.

"Come on, homies," said Irene. It was clear she was okay now: her savagely bad sense of humour was back.

Nicola took her boyfriend's hand, kissing him on the earlobe. The four of them walked up the steps to the entrance, a few boos coming in their direction.

"It's not like we're selling guns to Africa!" joked Alan. "These people really need to get a life!" He fished out the formal invites and handed them over to one of the security guards. The guard studied the papers and opened one of the glass doors.

The group entered a small lobby, where their invites were checked again and they were given official passes. They entered a tight corridor filled with other excited attendees, all wanting to be discovered, all wanting a hand in the honeypot of fame.

"Very nice," remarked Alan. "Oh, Petey, are you ready for your speech?"

"Oh yeah, I'm ready, don't you worry." Petey had his speech ready in his mind. Simple. Perfect. Not needing any adjusting.

"Ah, you're here!" said a booming, larger-than-life voice.

"Anton!" Petey spluttered, exchanging a hard handshake with one of his former lecturers.

"It's so good to see you!" said Anton, brushing crumbs off his shirt. "You have created such a brilliant company! Seems like yesterday you were a fresher, looking scared beyond belief."

"Nicola, this is one of my lecturers from university, Professor Anton Newcombe." Petey cleared his throat. "Anton, this is my partner Nicola, my lawyer Alan, and his wife Irene."

"Good to meet you all," said Anton. "My grandson has one of your computers in his school. He's completely obsessed by it. Teachers have had to pull him off it on numerous occasions."

"What brings you to the conference?" Nicola asked.

"I'm an adviser." Anton folded his arms. "A colleague of a colleague mentioned my name and my background to the head honcho and... abracadabra... I'm here. Right, must be off guys. I need to meet with a few people before the conference kicks off. See you all later."

"Well, that was short and sweet," said Nicola.

They followed the other guests to the conference room, well, rather a large dining hall. Tables, set up with coffee and biscuits, with bright white chairs, were spread out across the floor. A raised table with five seats (presumably for the very important computer people) was situated at the front, before a gold and pink curtain that reminded Petey of Japanese martial arts films.

"Where the hell do we sit?" stammered Alan.

"It's on the pass," said Petey, but his voice was lost. The room was too big, way too big, bigger than anyone of his position could possibly imagine.

Kick-off was at nine o'clock sharp. Greg Yirrell, in a pitch-black suit and tie, stood up from his seat at the high table and came forward to a small lectern.

"Good morning everyone," he said in his chirpy little voice. "I would like to welcome you all to *A New Millennium: New Frontiers and No Boundaries*. Despite what the protesters are saying about us killing the planet, the core theme of this conference is the exact opposite."

Applause.

"I have been accused of all sorts of nasty things. They seriously believe that I want to destroy the environment and the ozone layer. Why would I do that? I have two children!"

Applause.

"But, let us not be distracted anymore. This conference is about progress. Like it says in the title, it is about new frontiers. It is about pushing forward and not letting anything define us."

Applause.

"It is the last day of this millennium and the beginning of another. Computers will have a big role to play in the years to come. Before the conference properly starts, I want you to take a few moments, each and every one of you, to think about what computers mean to you. Some of you own companies, some of you are scientists, a few of you are science journalists. But all of you are driven by the core desire to see what is around the corner. Today, there will be many talks; a lot of scientific vocabulary. But I want you to think about what *you* want. What your *heart* wants. Ladies and gentlemen, welcome."

Grand applause.

"You all set?" asked Alan, nudging Petey on the shoulder.

They were watching Mike Heckle from Harvard University deliver a speech entitled *The Intrinsic Value of the Small*. It was all about the benefits of smaller and smaller computers. Petey thought it was a waste of time. All Professor Heckle had talked about so far was the benefit of having a laptop that fitted so smugly inside a case that it had a practically unnoticeable weight.

"I'm good to go," whispered Petey. "As soon as this prat's finished."

"Shh!" someone on a neighbouring table hissed.

"...and I'll certainly tell you," Heckle went on, his droning Texan accent even beginning to annoy fellow Americans in the room, "that a small computer makes a great companion. Y'all should know that! Microprocessors, what the hell?! The thing that needs to be small is the darn computer itself!"

Nicola was fidgeting. Very unlike her. She was always relaxed, always patient. A trickle of sweat snaked down her cheekbone. She took a sip of water and then looked across to Petey, rolling her eyes. He smiled back.

A group of young Asian businessmen were seated at a table on the far left of the hall. They stared at the podium, eyes devoid of distraction and packed to the brim with concentration. Beside them was a larger table with a collection of young men and women, all wearing the latest in business attire. Several of them were frantically taking notes. Two others had laptops out, typing away. At a table nearer to him, a woman in a short skirt and grey blouse was chewing gum. Petey was entranced by her, sucked in. She was turning to look. If he could keep eye contact on her for just one more moment, just one more moment...

"Thank you, Professor Heckle, for that very interesting talk," said a youngish Thai man who was the host, his three-piece suit so ill-fitting. "I'm sure that we all aspire to have smaller things, downsize our lives, so to speak."

Mike Heckle waved his hands in a friendly gesture

from his table. A woman, presumably his wife, hair tied into a bun too bloody tight, stroked his arm.

"Now," said the announcer, "I would like to introduce our next guest. Peter McGough is the founder of Newton-M-Wren, which, since its inception in Nineteen-Ninety-Six, has already been nominated for many business awards worldwide. Producers of state-of-the-art computers, they have received praise from a number of business leaders. They recently acquired a contract to put a computer in every British school, a contract that they have fulfilled to the letter. As for Mr McGough himself, he is, according to numerous marks from numerous professionals, 'one of the most important figures in computing today'. Ladies and gentlemen, please welcome Peter McGough."

"Bon Chance," Nicola mimed at him (a signal they had developed over the years).

"Merci," he mimed back. He strode up to the stage, shook hands with the announcer and exchanged a wink with Anton (currently munching through another croissant, leaving crumbs all over the immaculate surface of his at-the-back-of-the-hall-because-he's-merely-a-scientific-adviser table).

The applause was great. No doubt everyone in this room had heard of him. He had the mark of a true businessman, someone at the top of his game.

"Thank you, ladies and gentlemen," Petey said, nearly stammering but righting himself just in time. "Thank you." He waited for the clapping to die down.

"When I was sixteen, I had the dream of launching my own computing company someday. Yes, I'll admit, I even dreamed of an empire. Well, I'm pretty bloody close."

Laughter and applause.

"I'd like to tell you about the challenges Newton-M-Wren has faced and how we've overcome some of the technical and monetary difficulties. I then want to describe to you the aims of Newton-M-Wren in the new millennium. There are many key challenges that we have to tackle, but…"

Now commenced the boring bit of the speech. He discussed financing, intricacies of computers, distribution issues. But all the while, the icing on the cake (with the cherry on top) danced in his mind. When his speech was done, he forced himself to slow down:

"Since forming Newton-M-Wren in Nineteen-Ninety-Six, I will admit that there have been big struggles. But I succeeded. And there's a single reason why. Not because of funding, not because of diplomatic support. Quite simply, because of one special person: my wonderful girlfriend, Nicola."

Massive applause. Very massive applause.

He could see the glint of happiness in her eyes. It gave him the courage to proceed. "I never really thank her enough, I never really show my appreciation." He reached his hand into his trouser pocket, slyly, casually. The small box was there. The wonderful fuzzy feeling of its outside tickled his fingertips. "I have a very important question to ask her today. Will she –"

"Baby killer!" howled a voice.

The protestor, the one with the George Smiley glasses, stood at the entrance to the hall, jabbing and pointing at Petey.

"Excuse me," said the Thai announcer, flashing with anger, "can you please leave?"

"That man kills babies!" shouted the protestor. "*He* needs to leave!" Two security guards grasped hold of him, dragging him back out. "Baby killer!"

The room rang loud with applause and muffled laughter.

"Can I just say," muttered an embarrassed Petey, "that Newton-M-Wren has never killed any babies. I hate to state the obvious."

"Of course you haven't," said the announcer. "Okay, I think it's time to move to our next speaker. Thank you, Peter McGough, for that very inspirational speech. Please accept my apologies for what has just happened."

"It's okay," said Petey, returning to his seat.

"Are you okay?" asked Nicola.

"Yeah, I'm fine. Just a little surprised."

"What was it you were going to ask me?"

"Hmm?"

"You know, what you said at the end of your speech."

"Oh, that! I was going to ask you to come up to the stage, so I could thank you in front of everybody." Petey faked a chuckle. He reached for his glass of water, groaning when he saw it empty, and huffing at the sight of the empty jug. "I'm just going to nip out for a few minutes. Get some more water."

"Sure, not to worry."

Crouching, he fumbled his way past the table, patting Alan on the elbow, and made his way into the corridor outside. He looked about him for a water dispenser.

"Excuse me," he asked a security guard, "do you know where I might get some water?"

"There is a machine at the end of the corridor," the stoic man said. "I also advise you to be careful. We have a security breach."

"Yes, I've just seen. What a prick."

"There is another protestor who came in with the man. They're hiding somewhere in the building. We have security looking for them."

"Well, I'll be on the lookout." Petey smiled and started down the corridor.

"Hey!" the guard yelled.

Petey turned.

The man smiled. "Be careful," he said. "I think they're dangerous."

"I will." Petey walked away, smirking. But inside he was shaking. Suddenly the whole conference centre seemed small, very small, cold.

True to the guard's word, at the end of the corridor, there the machine was, nestled underneath a window Petey took one of the small cone-shaped cups and filled it two thirds of the way up. He was thirstier than he imagined and ended up having several cups of the icy water.

Something moved behind him. Footsteps.

He spun around, heart pounding.

"Hello?" he said. Then, realising what a tit he was making of himself, he slapped his cheek. "Christ sakes, man. Cool it." He tossed the cup in a nearby bin.

Something smashed beyond the walls. A glass of some sort. A voice swore. The noise came from behind a door marked *Maintenance*. He tiptoed over to it, a surprising bravado pulling a shield over him. He gripped the silver handle and turned it as hard as he could, ramming his shoulder into the door.

It was a broken glass vase, scattered like diamonds. Water spread like a pool of peaceful blood. An over-head light flickered. A workbench filled with tools was the only other thing occupying the small room. No sign of any intruder. And, more seriously, there were no other doors leading from here.

He walked, as quickly as he dared, over to the work-bench, picking up a rusty hammer.

"You may as well come out!" he shouted. "Security's looking for you! I'm armed! Where are you?!" He began to head back to the door, the horrific knowl-edge of his mistake becoming apparent when he heard someone drop down behind him. A strong arm wrapped around his neck, pulling him down. The hammer fell from his grip. He threw a weak punch be-hind him and yanked himself free. He turned to face his attacker, ready to throw another, much stronger punch.

He stopped. He fell back, half in shock, half in... well, he didn't know. It was inexplicable.

"Sarah?!" he blurted.

"Peter?!" came the reply.

Two security guards burst into the room, jumping on Sarah, pinning her arms behind her. The stoic man came in next and informed her – rather calmly, it must be said – that she was going to be handed over to the police.

"No!" Petey said. "It's okay!"

"She's an intruder," said the stoic guy, taking out his radio.

"She's not. She's a journalist."

"Does she have any identification?"

"No, she doesn't. She left it all at the hotel. She's clumsy, but she's no threat. She's employed by my company, so I signed her in."

"I will have to check the records."

"No, you will not!" Petey bellowed. "You will do this: You will go back to your stations and forget about all this, or I will instruct my lawyer, who is currently seated in the conference hall, to bring the full legal power that Newton-M-Wren has against three security guards who viciously manhandled one of my journalists! Is that clear?!"

"Guys," said Mr Stoic, seemingly accepting defeat, "let's leave."

"Best decision you've made all day. Now beat it!"

When they were gone, Sarah burst into laughter. Petey soon joined in. Before either of them knew it, they were enveloped in each other's arms.

"Can't believe I'd find you here!" said Sarah. "Where the hell… How the hell are you?"

"I'm okay. I've missed you. A lot, I should say."

"I've heard so much about you. Your company and stuff. Really pleased for you. Well done!"

"Thank you!"

"I'm not keeping you, am I?"

"It's okay, I've delivered my speech. I'm just listening to other people's now. Listen, do you want to head out? I'll just deliver an excuse to my girlfriend and colleague's that I have to make an urgent conference call."

"Your girlfriend?"

He realised he'd said too much too soon. But it was the truth. "Yeah, my girlfriend. We've been together for several years now. But, anyway, let me go back to the hall for a few minutes, then I'll come back here and pick you up."

"Are you sure?"

"Sarah, I haven't seen you in over ten years. I think the world of computing can spare me for a few hours."

"So, how have you been?" he asked finally, when they'd left the centre. By now, the protesters had been largely hoarded away by the police, but a few stragglers remained, determined to fight to the bitter end, whatever that may be.

"I've been busy, you could say. Been doing a lot

of travelling. Borneo, Vietnam, United States, Mozambique, many other places."

"Wow, that's incredible."

"What about you?"

"Oh, been doing a bit, but mainly business travel, what with the company and everything. I spent two months in Mexico last year as part of a research project."

"That's good." She linked arms with him. He felt her warmth next to him, like that night many years ago.

They found a small bar a few streets away and ordered beer and some local cuisine neither of them could pronounce. The streets were quiet and the bar was near-empty. They looked at each other, Petey feeling his emotions swell up. He couldn't contain it any longer. He just couldn't. He had to say it.

"That day, the Nineteenth of May, Nineteen-Ninety-Three, you never turned up. I showed up at One O'Clock, just to be on the safe side. Two hours I waited. You never showed."

"You seriously expected me to?"

"What?"

"Babe, that night. It meant so much to me. I enjoyed our brief time together. But I make promises all the time. Babe, I genuinely expected you to move on with your life, find someone."

"I didn't realise. Why did you make it?"

"Because, you looked an absolute fucking mess. Honestly, you were crying your eyes out. I thought you were going to hang yourself or something. So, I gave you a bullshit promise, just to keep you happy. Then, a few years later, I knew that the truth wouldn't hurt so much. Sorry, but that's... that's what I had to do."

"I understand. Totally. But, that's water under the bridge. We've both moved on with our lives. So, Mozambique, tell me all about it."

"What do you want to know?"

"Well, where did you go, how long were you there for? What was it like?"

"I thought a rich posh boy like you would've already been there three times over."

"Not necessarily."

"If you want to know, I stayed there for over a year. Part of an environmental protest thing."

"It took you over a year to do an environmental protest?"

"Yup."

"And I take it that's where you hooked up with those guys who called me a baby killer?"

"Yup."

"Why the hell do they do that? Where did they get that idea from?"

"I dunno."

"You think it's funny, don't you?"

"A little bit."

First, Sarah sniggered, then Petey joined in. She touched his arm.

"It's good to see you again," she whispered, fiddling with her glass with her free hand. "I have missed you."

"I've missed you too."

After their meal, Petey led the way out of the bar, paying a small tip to the very grateful manager.

"Well," he said, feeling bitter, "I'd best be getting back to the others."

"What, so you can spend your New Year's Eve with a bunch of nerdy morons?" There was an aggressive stance in her voice.

"I am the CEO of Newton-M-Wren," he countered. "What do you expect me to do? Join your fellow pro-testers for a big showdown into the new millennium?"

"Not really. I thought you might like to come out with me for a party."

"It's just..."

"Just what?"

"Alan's – that's my lawyer – his wife is having a few issues."

"Which I'm sure Alan can take care of...?"

"I can't exactly make another feeble excuse. I can't tell them I've been called to another emergency con-ference call. The three of them would know some-thing's up."

"Well, my dear, well then." She folded her arms and pinched his chin. "You're the genius here. You've built a massive fucking empire. I'm sure you can work something out."

"Wait, wait, wait," he said, clasping her hands, "I might just have an idea."

Security let them past, no problem. Mr Stoic evidently didn't want another legal confrontation.

Nicola was the first to see them. It was the lunch break and everyone mingling around the hall. She pushed through a thick group, glued together near her table, and, very mystified, approached Petey and Sarah.

"Hi," she said, holding her hand out to Sarah. "I don't believe we've met. I'm Nicola."

"Nicola, this is Sarah," Petey said, feeling deep relief as the two of them shook hands. "Sarah, this is my partner, Nicola. Sarah's a writer working for this big magazine in New York. She wants to do an interview with me. This could potentially be a very big opportunity."

"When is it?" Alan asked, coming into the picture, his forefinger locked around his wife's wrist. Irene looked mildly fed up.

"It's actually going to be for several hours. She's going to watch the conference for a bit, then we're going to do a big... I don't know how to say it..."

"Basically, I'm going to spend several hours with Mr McGough, talking about his career. You're welcome to come with us, Nicola, in fact, I'd love for you to come with us." Sarah indicated Alan and Irene. "The two of you as well."

"I think it would be a good idea," said Petey. "I mean, this conference is great, but an interview with this magazine... Bloody hell, guys."

"Can I borrow you for a couple of minutes, Petey?" said Nicola.

"Sure." He followed his girlfriend out of the conference hall, his feet like floppy kippers.

When they were alone, she leaned back against the wall, eyes down at the floor. This posture she held for a few seconds.

"What the hell is this about?" she snapped. "Are you drunk?"

"Of course I'm not drunk! Christ, do you think...?" He lowered his voice, placing his hands on her shoulders. "Do you think I'm having an affair?"

"No, I don't. But I don't like the way you're acting. We've had this trip planned for months. This is very important. You could make a great many connections here."

"But this is an opportunity to be interviewed for a major magazine. Do you realise what this means? Excellent worldwide promotion! Christ, to be interviewed in Bangkok at the dawn of the new millennium, that's an opportunity not to be wasted. You know I'm right, don't you?"

She briefly hummed to herself and scratched behind her ear. A team of four security guards passing by gave them suspicious looks. She pushed herself against the wall, as if trying to relieve a thousand strains of tension. Eventually, she wrapped her arms around him. "Yeah," she said, kissing his neck. "This is a good opportunity."

"Right, she wants to watch the next talk, and then we'll all head off."

"No, I'll stay here. Alan and Irene will stay too. We need to have a presence here."

"You sure? We've stayed for the most important bits."

"No, it's okay. You go and do your thing. I guess I'll see you in the early hours of the new millennium."

"I guess I will. Happy New Year."

"Happy New Year." She kissed his lips. "Right, troublemaker, let's get back to the conference and see what the next CEO has to tell us."

His fortunes for the new millennium were already on the up, he thought, pushing back the urge to let a smile break out. He felt like a Cold War spy who had successfully arranged a trap for an enemy agent. His plan had worked. He and Sarah would definitely be alone.

"I told you I'd do it."

"Haha, you're just rubbing it in now." Sarah punched him gently in the ribs. "Come on, Mr CEO, let's see what Bangkok has to offer us."

"You still haven't told me about Mozambique."

"And I will! Fuck, you're so impatient!"

"I've really enjoyed today," said Petey, stretching his arms above his head.

"It's not even started yet, believe me."

He suddenly felt clammy. Sweat patches hung on his shirt. "Mind if I go back to the hotel and freshen up?"

"Sure, if I can come with you."

"Now, try not to disturb any of her stuff." Petey shut the door quietly and went over to his suitcase, pulling out a casual shirt and jeans (and accidentally some of Nicola's clothes (he always insisted on ensuring they had their own clothes in each other's bags in case one of the bags was misplaced by an underpaid-poverty-stricken-(not-likely)-beating-around-the-bush baggage handler)). "She'll know."

"Wow, you've gone really posh here." Sarah fingered a crystal ornament on the desk. "Shit, this place is the posh of all posh places."

"Yeah, it is." He pulled off his jacket and tossed it on the bed.

"What the...?" She was holding something.

Oh no. A small green box. It must have fallen out of his jacket pocket.

"Give that back, please," he said, reaching for it. She held it away from his grip. "Please," he insisted.

"You guys must be serious then," she said, bully-ingly.

"I haven't popped the question yet."

"Should I leave?" She looked offended. Really upset. Hurt. Broken. Feverish. "Fuck you," she snarled. She shoved past him, tossing the box in the air. It landed on the bed, bouncing like a broken dream that was fading into nothing.

"Don't go!" he shouted. "Please! I still love you!"

"Hmm, I'll stay on one condition."

"What's that?"

"You live a little."

"What do you mean?"

"Christ! I mean, take a risk, one hell of a risk. Feel a buzz. Feel alive."

"Let's go and get hilariously drunk," he said ponderingly. "Find a ladyboy and have a threesome."

"Not extreme enough. Come on, think of something more imaginative."

"Um, let's find a cheap motel and massage each other with lube."

"You're so disappointing." She licked her lips. "How about we fuck, right here, right now."

"What if Nicola comes back?"

"Exactly. Put everything at risk. Everything you have. That's feeling alive."

"No time like the present," he said, running up to her and touching her hot, sweet lips with his. "I've missed you. So much."

"God, you're such a wimp."

"Look, I'm sorry!" she called from outside the bathroom.

Petey finished drying himself off and began to put on his clothes. What was she talking about? Presumably not the fact that she'd pressured him into performing cunnilingus on his girlfriend's side of the bed.

"I should've turned up, at least to say hello." She couldn't make eye contact with him. It was as though he were a vicious demon.

"What do you mean?"

"Nineteen-Ninety-Three.

"Oh, for Heaven's sakes, woman, stop fretting. I thought we'd both pretty much agreed that it was in the past. Come on, let's enjoy ourselves." *And get out of this room before my totally fuckable girlfriend comes back and finds I've been an unfaithful, backstabbing, malicious, borderline-nuisance-borderline-mischievous-borderline-totally-being-a-prick, loser-in-life... prick,* he wanted to add.

"But I feel bad."

"That's why you're buying the first round." He grinned, pressing his lips against hers. "Oops, nearly forgot." He nipped over to the bed and picked up the little box. "Better put this away." He stashed it back in his jacket which he proceeded to hang in the closet. "Let's hope she doesn't go through my things... or sends it to be cleaned."

They left the hotel, not daring to link hands. Thankfully, none of the reception staff gave them dodgy looks as they made their way out of the foyer. But once they were on the street, Sarah grabbed his cock and kissed him hard.

"God, I've missed that," he moaned. "Ah, fuck."

"I'll grip you hard into the new millennium."

"Oh, yeah?"

"Oh yeah."

Their first stop was the bar he'd been to with Alan the previous day. The mechanic wasn't there this time, an absence of conscience. They ordered a beer each, which they both duly drank, gulping them down like medicine.

"Shit, the local stuff's good," she blubbered. "I wish I could drink this shit all day."

"I bet."

Did she notice something was wrong with him? She must have. Because she asked the question, that one question, one he didn't want to hear. It came short, it came sharp. Amidst the drinkers celebrating the end of this millennium and the beginning of the next in complete silence, the question came:

"Why are you so angry?"

"Excuse me?" he responded.

"Let's be honest, you're still pissed at me not turning up that day. Why?" She slammed her glass down on the table.

"Tell you what, let's have a few more drinks. Then I'll tell you."

So, off they went. To another bar. Another round of drinks. Then another.

He finally emptied his words (and thankfully not his stomach) onto the table between them.

They were in a bar that was quite literally a work-surface with a few fridges (containing beers of course). The floor was composed of black and white tiles, arranged in the typical quite boring formation, like a giant, never-ending chessboard. A photograph of the owner and his family hung on the wall, a Collie nestled between them. Six tables, scatted like fallen dominoes, barely filled the place. It seemed an empty tomb for the dispossessed.

"Her name was Georgina," he said, trying to keep

the emotion out. "We were at uni together. We were close. She loved me. I just suppose I didn't love her as much. There was something wrong with her."

"You perhaps?" Sarah joked. Her face immediately flashed with guilt.

"The doctors thought she had depression. She got clingy to me. She needed my support. We'd met in freshers week during First Year. By the time Nineteen-Ninety-Three came, she was completely dependent on me. On that day in May, when I was going to meet you, I told her the truth. That I was in love with you. She took it hard."

"What happened?"

"When I got back to campus after you'd failed to show, I tried to find her, to talk to her. I couldn't find her."

"She run away or something?"

"No. Do you know Blairhill station?"

"No."

"It's in the east end of Glasgow. Really nice little station. On the Nineteenth of May, in the Year of Our Lord Nineteen-Hundred-And-Ninety-Three, at around Two O'Clock in the afternoon, Georgina threw herself off the platform in front of a fast train. Cut to pieces."

"I'm sorry." She bowed her head.

"No, you're not." The anger welled in him, like a wave at the edge of a pier on a stormy day In a year long forgotten in a century only dreamed about in the minds of small children who had too much imagination stemming from an upbringing that lacked good parenting. "You don't fucking care. Not a fucking fig. You were too busy fucking travelling."

"Let's get out of here. I think you need some more alcohol."

The next bar was packed to the brim with drinkers. Golden lager, a treasure sometimes so underrated, flowed down throats like a fluid of the rich. Except they weren't rich. The drinkers were coated in sweat; three-day-old clothes (no doubt (well, it was obvious they were all in some sort of mild poverty)) hung from their bodies like rags. Yes, rags you could say.

"How long are you staying in Thailand?" she asked, putting a hand on his neck, stroking at the perspiration beginning to form there.

They were standing near the door, the thick throng of borderline alcoholics full to the brim with vulgar conversation.

"We leave on the Second of January," he replied. "What about you?"

"Not sure yet. There aren't any further protests scheduled, so I'm planning to do a bit of travelling around Thailand. Maybe see if I can get a visa or something to stay for a year or so. Actually really like it here."

"Listen, I'm sorry about earlier, speaking to you like that." His speech was slurred, bubbling, falling all over the place. "I haven't really dealt with what happened."

"No, I'm sorry. If I'd known about that, I wouldn't

have said all that shit about me making that promise to you. You know, mocking you for waiting for me."

"It's okay." He took another swig of beer, letting it slosh around his mouth before swallowing. "I never stopped loving you," he said, trying to be sincere. "Every day, I always thought about you."

"Maybe you won't get hurt this time."

"What do you mean?"

She drew him closer, prising his beer glass away and placing it on the floor. After she had planted yet another kiss on his lips, she said, "We don't have to part ways this time. We could go off together."

"What you mean?"

"It's a big world. Maybe we could go and explore it together."

"You mean, run off together?"

"Yes. Are you afraid of that?"

A trillion thoughts bashing his brain. "A little. I mean, you're talking about me leaving my girlfriend."

"I'm not just talking about that. You would have to drop everything. I mean, everything. You would have to abandon that company of yours. Cut yourself off from all family and friends. Go off the grid. Would you be willing to do that? For me?"

"Wow." He shuffled on his feet. She dragged him even closer, her hot breath pummelling against his mouth. "I need to think about this."

"I'm going to make you an offer, and I suggest you take it." She tapped hard against his right temple. "Tomorrow, at One O'Clock, I will be waiting outside the conference centre. If you want to come with me, turn up at that time, in that place. We'll head north and we won't look back. If you don't turn up, I'll understand."

"You make it sound so big."

"That's because it *is* big. Think about what I've said. Think very hard."

A horrible familiar voice suddenly burst into the conversation: "What are you doing here, baby killer?"

Petey and Sarah spent the final hour of the Twentieth Century in an open-air bar. They weren't alone. The baby killer protester (whose real name was, quite unimaginably, Clive) gave a long monologue on his opinion of the scientific progress (and its consequent environmental impact) of the twentieth century. They were also joined by two New Zealander women who had abandoned plans for millennial celebrations with their respective parents and travelled to Thailand to join the protest.

"Fine group we've got here," said Megan, one of the New Zealanders. She patted her friend, Trudy, hard on the shoulder. "Can't find a better way to end the Twentieth Century."

"Well, technically the twentieth century ends on December Thirty-First, Two-Thousand-And-One, and so does the Second Millennium," Petey corrected.

"Are you drunk or just a boring fucking cunt?" Trudy told him. "Well, you're English, that definitely makes you a cunt."

"No, it doesn't!" Sarah shouted at her.

"Let's look at it this way." Clive stood up from the

table, knocking nearly knocking Megan's drink over. "We're a bunch of travellers."

"I'm not," corrected Petey. "I'm just here for a fucking conference." The New Zealander girls sniggered.

"We're all travellers. All of us." Clive was very insistent. "We're all on our own journeys, to wherever we may end up. Whether that's deep Africa, or the remote Pacific, or the middle of the Amazon, we're all on our own little trips in this life. But, but we all believe in something greater. Fate. Now, fate, fate has brought us all together."

"Sit down, you great oaf!" Sarah yanked the man back to his seat. He missed, sliding to the floor.

Laughter spread over all of them like a common cold. Clive tried to get up, stumbled again. Eventually Megan grabbed him under the armpit, heaving him back to his seat.

"You're fucking strong, Megan!" Sarah boomed. "Fuck you! I can't even lift my fucking suitcase sometimes."

"I work out," she retorted; then, adding a vicious New York accent: "Bitch."

"Oh, I'm a bitch?"

"Christ, girl, I'm taking the piss!"

"I know! Not stupid, you know. Wouldn't mind if you called me a bitch. I really can be one sometimes. When I get pissed."

"How drunk are we going to get tonight?" asked Clive.

"As drunk as you want to get," said Trudy.

"I need to get more beer in my system," Petey remarked.

"That was one hell of a statement!" Sarah threw her hands in the air. "Fucking hell, Petey boy."

"Petey boy?" Trudy keeled over in hysterics. "Where'd you get that name from?"

"Oh, that's not the worst name I have for him."

"We have to know!" said Megan.

"Please, babe, please." Petey hid his face in his hands. "Don't tell them."

"Mr Posh," Sarah said eventually.

All of them, in that moment of pure pleasure, of pure ecstasy, nearly collapsed. Other drinkers stared, but this small group, at the mercy of the unpredictable, couldn't care less. They weren't to be controlled. They weren't to be governed. In that moment, like it or not, they were free.

The chanting began like an old holy prayer.

"*Twenty... Nineteen... Eighteen...*"

"Raise your glasses!" Megan commanded.

"*Five...* Four... Three... Two... One! Happy New Year!"

Saturday 1^{*st*} *January 2000*

Fireworks, chants, car horn blares, music, tasteless random kissing. The new millennium was in.

Petey and Sarah, eyes solely on one another, kissed. They pulled apart and kissed again.

"Put it away, you two," said Trudy, just as a crowd

of drinkers emptied out of a bar across the street and shouted at the top of their lungs. In a true moment – one that only comes from embracing the sheer icy cliff face of the unknown – she kissed Clive and then Megan, right on the lips, both of them.

"Ooh, you pervert!" jeered Petey. He was trying so hard not to look at Sarah, knowing if he did, he would be transfixed, sucked in. But her warm presence seemed to burn away the humidity, like a firework exploding and cracking the air. She made him invincible. She made him immortal.

"I love you." Those words. Words which meant so much. Which could be so true and yet so untrue. Something that should shatter the very fabric of what binds us together. Those words. They came from her.

"I love you too."

Everything in that moment was perfect. Stupendously beautiful.

They didn't notice that the others had gone, stumbling off into the night like some hideous six-legged fiend. They didn't notice a group of angry, aggressive young men steal the empty seats, making sick gestures (using fingers).

"Wanna get out of here?" she said, kissing him, holding him there, releasing her lips.

"Yeah."

The first rays of sunlight peeped through the mouldy curtain of the hostel dorm, stabbing Petey right in the eye. And bloody hell, it was painful. He shifted his head, feeling her damp torso shift against his. He was well aware, thank you very much, that there were other snoring guests in the room, happily comatose on their bunks.

Her tongue licked his ear. No accident. No careless tongue-hanging-out. It tickled. She moved from his neck up to his ear.

"Hey," he whispered. "Didn't think you'd be awake."

"Course I am." She yawned. "Fuck, that was some party, eh?"

"It was. I have to say, I much preferred the after-party..."

"You really are dirty, aren't you? Not even funny dirty. *Dirty* dirty. Yeah, you know it." She was doing his accent again.

"More than ten years and you're still doing imper-sonations of me."

"Haha."

He became silent and sombre, almost as quickly as he'd turned joyous and party-animal-like last night. "I'm ready for this." He stroked her hair, moving a fin-ger past her ear, maintaining eye contact. "For you, I am prepared to do anything."

"After we meet at the centre, we'll get the hell out of the city. Then we'll work out a plan for the next few months."

"Sounds good."

"Of course it does. It's a plan that will work better than anything."

"We're about to start new lives."

"Yep."

His heart beat faster as she squeezed his cock. "I don't care what happens. The first month, I am going to fuck you all day every day."

"I hope you've got the stamina for that." She began rubbing. Her fingers were coarse and rough, nails nipping at his foreskin. "I hope things aren't too hard for us in the first few months."

"Hard? I like a challenge."

"Bet you do."

He nearly cried out when he came. Luckily, she pushed her hand over his mouth. His moan came out as a muffled grunt. He let himself relax. He would have fallen asleep if he hadn't seen the time on his watch (a crowning stone on the top of his pile of clothes): nearly ten o'clock.

"Shit!" he growled. "Fuck!"

"What is it?"

"I need to get back to the hotel. Nicola will be worried sick."

"Okay, sure." She rolled onto his chest. "Right, get what you need done. I won't wait for you. If you're five minutes late, it's bye-bye. Understand?"

"Yes."

There was indeed a lot of damage from last night's party. Beer cans, beer bottles, beer spills. A few stragglers, still scurrying about like dying squirrels, still in the throes of the big party.

Petey took a taxi from Sarah's hostel (a really dismal shithole: the *very* bare essentials, nothing more) to the hotel. Looking like a disgusting tramp, reeking of stale beer and already graced with a five o'clock shadow, he darted into the hotel.

Nicola, the past few years have been wonderful for me. They've meant the world to me. But there's someone else. I'm sorry I didn't tell you the truth earlier. The truth is, I was afraid. But I love this woman. I love her with all my heart. I don't want to hurt you. But I have to do what I believe is right.

Those were the words he told himself as he ascended in the elevator. His justification to destroy this stable relationship he was in – and blow up a number of friendships. While he was at it, he could say that he would be slashing a sword across Newton-M-Wren, leaving it to the wolves of insanity.

When he arrived at the floor, he took the key out, ready to make his case. He marched to his room. This was the right thing to do. This was the dutiful thing to do. This was the only thing to do. He entered his room, head held high.

Nicola stood by the television.

"We need to talk," were the first words out of her mouth. Followed by: "Where the fuck were you last night?"

"That journalist thing."

"Are you drunk?"

"Of course I am: it was one hell of a party. Sarah brought a number of her colleagues along. We all drank quite a lot."

"Okay. Well, I trust you didn't go overboard. Anyways, that's not what I wanted you to chat about." She motioned for him to sit on the bed. "We need to talk about our future."

"Actually, there's something I need to talk to you about. I feel I need to be honest."

"Me first. Sit."

He was finding this rather inconvenient. It was already nearly eleven. It would take him a good half hour to pack his things; even longer to ensure that Nicola was all right before he walked out of her life.

When they were both perched on the bed, she took his hands. "You may or may not have noticed I've been behaving a little oddly. It was for a reason. I've also been abstaining from alcohol. I wanted to tell you sooner, but I needed some time to think about how I was going to say it." She took his hands. Sarah had done that hours earlier. For a moment, they were one and the same person. Nicola smiled, kissing his forehead. "Petey, I'm pregnant."

"Oh my God." He kissed her. "Oh my, I don't know what to say."

"Well, why don't you phone reception and order us breakfast in bed?"

"Sounds like a plan to me!" He leapt up, pacing around the room.

He genuinely didn't know how to think. He had to make a decision, what seemed like an impossible one; yet it was so simple: Sarah or Nicola? He went over to his jacket and took out the box, keeping it concealed from Nicola's view. What should he do? He flipped it open. The ring was not there. He knew it had been stolen, and he knew who had done it. His decision was made. He put the box back in his jacket and rushed back to Nicola. He held her tightly, so close, like someone afraid of letting go.

Positronic

Edinburgh

Monday 20th August 2007

The festival was in full swing. Coloured streamers, dancing, drumbeats, violins, singing choirs, food stalls, chip vans, stand-up comedians, circus acts, death-defying stunts filled the pavements of Princes Street. The rest, billowing onto North Bridge and butting its way into the Old Town, was a multi-coloured, dimension-splitting rainbow of intrigue, mystery, true/false love, and desire.

Petey pushed past a trio of demonstrators (thankfully not protesting against him, but against nuclear weapons) and took a right turn off Princes Street. He felt mildly exhausted and had a horrid knot in the pit of his stomach. Airline food, most probably: the bacon and eggs the plastic-faced stewardess had served him on the flight yesterday (due to depart at 08:30, but delayed to 10:30 due to mechanical issues, or so they claimed).

Not that it had mattered to Petey. He wasn't late for anything. Actually, the only reason his publisher had organised the early flight was due to it being a little bit cheaper than the later ones.

But he was here, about to do his first book festival. The Edinburgh International Book Festival. What had his agent said about it last week? *"You'll love it, Peter, this book festival is the expensive stuff."* Well, he was about to find out the truth.

He kept walking, the shoes really beginning to pinch. They were new, a birthday present from Nicola. All that inspecting of his shoes – he'd thought she was trying to make sure his hygiene was up to standards (her standards).

His favourite present had been from his daughter: a gold-coloured chain for his reading glasses. Nicola had told him later that Mary had been making it in secret for a month, putting it together link by link.

He put his hand to his chest, checking for the fiftieth time that his reading glasses case was still there, that it hadn't been stolen by some pickpocket with an agenda.

Up ahead, he saw the large banner, proclaiming for all the world to see: *EDINBURGH INTERNATIONAL BOOK FESTIVAL. My, it looked a welcome sight*, he thought, striding up the street, across perhaps the worst pedestrian junction he'd ever encountered, and through the entrance into a fairly grandiose lobby. Why the area was called Charlotte Square, he didn't know, but they should have renamed it Annoyance Square, given the level of traffic and noisy kids with balloons.

He waited, back straight. According to his agent, he was supposed to be met by the bloke interviewing him, the writer Donny Bell. Petey had never heard of him, but the man had apparently sold thousands of copies of his latest novel, *The Clapping of Fate*, in which a computer virus spreads throughout the world and a group of mismatched agents have to stop it. Some sort of crap like that anyway.

After five minutes (carefully counting the seconds on his watch), he grew restless and approached one of the festival volunteers, a vacant-looking young woman (student-type) with long brown hair. Her name badge read *Olga*.

"Excuse me," he said, "I'm here for the event *A.I.: Friend or Foe?* It starts at Three O'Clock."

"Have you got a ticket?" she asked in a thick Eastern European accent.

"Excuse me?"

"I'm afraid the event sold out."

"No, I'm Peter McGough. I'm the guy being interviewed."

"I'm sorry?"

"I wrote *A Big Paradox: The Humanity of A.I.* Do you know it?"

"Oh, yes. We have copies of it in our bookshop, if you would like to purchase one."

"Is there someone else I can speak to?" he asked, beginning to fume. He was already getting tired of her sad bulging eyes failing to make contact with his. "I'm Peter McGough, I was supposed to meet Donny Bell here, right now. It's One O'Clock. I'm scheduled to meet Donny Bell. Right here, right now."

"Ah, yes!" Recognition flashed across the girl's face. "One moment please." She signalled another woman over, a senior official by the looks of her. Face grim, too little makeup applied, summer flower top, fading blue jeans.

"Peter McGough?" the woman asked.

"Yes, that would be me," he said, trying to keep his cool.

"I'm Jeanette, the festival director," she said. "Donny said to let you know that he'll be a little late."

"Why, is he writing?" His attempt at making a joke didn't work.

"He'll be along in half an hour, maybe a little more. Why don't you go on in to the festival garden? There's coffee and food. If you fancy, there's beer or wine."

"Thank you."

"I'll let him know you're here."

"Thank you." He strode off, entering the garden in a daze. Well, it couldn't exactly be called a garden: a glorified outdoor café was a better description. He saw a small bar selling drinks, the barman an un-shaven lout, the only thing keeping him anchored to this world the promise of a drink-fuelled night in the near future. Petey ordered a half-pint of ale and took a seat on a small plastic chair that faced Prince Albert proud on his horse.

His mobile rang. Grunting, he put down the plastic cup and answered.

"Hi babe." Nicola.

"Oh, hiya, things okay?"

"Yeah, they're good. Mary's at school. She's really excited for you. I am as well, don't forget."

"I know. Listen, I was thinking, do you want to take a trip somewhere after this?"

"Babe, we can't keep taking holidays in term time. Mary needs to be at school. We've really pushed them on this. We're already over the limit on the number of days she can be away this year."

"No, I was thinking just the two of us. Go off to Los Angeles or something."

"I really don't want to go there, you know that. It's full of gangs and drugs."

"Well, we'll go to the nice parts. Come on, Nicola, the best hotels. You can't turn me down! And I'd hate to go on my own..."

"I'll have a think. Anyway, I just called to wish you the best of luck for today. I know you won't need it."

"Thanks. Also, we need to talk about Mary's birthday. It's not long now. What are you planning to get her?"

"I'm not sure. What do you think of a doll's house?"

"I honestly don't think that's the best idea. Why don't we take her out for the day?"

"Where to?"

"Oh, I don't know. We're London-dwellers now. I'm sure we can think of something."

"We'll have a chat about it when you get home. What time are you back tomorrow?"

"I'm due to get back at Half-Past Six in the evening. Assuming, of course, the bloody flight isn't delayed."

"You shouldn't be stressing about these things, I've told you that."

"I know, but it really gets me pissed off some-times."

"Well, don't get pissed off. Now, Mr Writer, I'd better let you get off. Text me later?"

"I will."

"Oh, I know you won't. You'll have had a few drinks with your writer friends."

"I'm sure I'll remember to give you a text."

"And remember to let me know if you're flight's arriving late! Don't forget, it's a hell of a drive for me. I'm going to bring Mary as well and I don't want to keep her up too late."

"Okay, sure thing. I'll message you later. I love you, Nicola."

"I love you too." She hung up.

Petey flexed his muscles and took a deep drink of the ale (which was starting to go – much to his dismay – flat). He stared up at the statue, part of him wanting to stay here, another part desiring to nip into the bookshop and see copies of his project stacked up on the shelves.

A Big Paradox was the result of two years of research and one year of solid writing. It had been Alan who'd egged him into writing it, over a drink during a Christmas night out for the senior staff of Newton-M-Wren. Petey had been reluctant, but he'd agreed to give it a go. To his surprise, doing research into artificial intelligence had proved very interesting. In the end, he had produced a book that had sold over a hundred thousand copies worldwide in its first month. With the paperback edition being launched soon, he was going to make – to put it bluntly – easy cash. Suddenly, Newton-M-Wren (which had already done extremely well, with over three quarters of schools in the United States equipped with one of their computers) got celebrity status. Petey had done several radio interviews (before the book was even published!) and had had an appearance on *BBC Breakfast*. News articles, the front cover of *The Guardian*, these were just two of the other things that had come his way. Essentially, Petey was, well, a celebrity.

His daze of self-pride was interrupted by a hard-spoken Scottish male voice. "Excuse me, Peter McGough, right?"

"Yes, that's me."

"Hi, I'm Donny." The man shook Petey's hand with surprisingly violent strength. "Sorry for being a bit late. I had some issues with the trains. Have you had lunch?"

"Not yet."

"Well, that's no problem. There's a small café just down the road. We can go and have some lunch and talk a little about today's event. Unless, you'd rather eat here? I'm not bothered."

"The café sounds great. I'm pretty peckish actually."

"Excellent, follow me."

In truth, Petey was slightly alarmed by this Donny

Bell. It wasn't his wavy blonde hair, nor his snakeskin boots, nor the skull ring wrapped around the middle finger of his left hand. It was a scar that ran the length of his left cheek, a deep gorge in the flesh.

"So, how did you get into writing?" Petey asked him, after they'd both placed their orders.

"It's a long story," said Donny. "No pun intended, of course."

The café, quite surprisingly empty for a busy festival season, was near empty; the only other company they had were two old ladies sitting at the back, bickering over a novel both of them were reading. Scottish techno-bagpipe music played from concealed speakers. In the background, two loudmouthed chefs barked commands at each other. A tartan quilt hung from the window, casting a shadow over the waitress: yet another student-type occupier of the city, this one with dyed red hair and pale skin; she looked half-dead, but she wasn't quite a goth.

"Well, I had a rough childhood," Donny began. "My mother and father were both alcoholics. I spent a lot of time playing at being a gangster on the streets of Glasgow. Little shithead I was. Pardon my French. Eventually, I realised that this wasn't good for me. I got into writing, did the MLitt at the University of Glasgow and... well, here I am. What about you?"

"Nothing as dramatic as yours. I hardly get the time for anything as CEO of Newton-M-Wren." He hated lying. Guiltily, he thought about his last trip: jetting off in first class to the Bahamas. Very guilty. "I've always had an interest in artificial intelligence; my friend and lawyer, Alan Stanley, put me up to writing a book on it."

"How did you get an agent?"

"Alan Stanley's very resourceful."

"He sounds like a great guy. Must be really smart."

"Oh, he is," Petey responded, almost defensively. Actually, the man wasn't as clever as he used to be. Not since his divorce from Irene anyway.

"How many books have you written?" he asked.

"Well, *The Clapping of Fate* is my eighth book," said Donny. "Jesus, can't believe it's been that number already."

"That's really cool. Forgive me, I haven't read any of your works. Is it a science fiction novel or something?"

"Well, it's a mixture of sci-fi and crime. My other books have either been sci-fi *or* crime."

"Wow."

They continued chatting. Petey found that he was beginning to like Donny. The writer seemed to have a unique perspective on everything, from Gordon Brown to Louisiana highways to the best kinds of brass instrument.

After his lunch of fresh lasagne, Petey was anxious to get started. But, as he watched Donny finish the remains of his mushroom soup, there was a fear ticking in the back of his mind. He had to get out of here. Edinburgh was full of painful memories. Georgina and

Sarah, two women who truly broken him; one, a suicide case, the other, a self-centred thief.

On the way back to the forest of tents, he felt apprehensive. Deeply disturbed.

"We're in the Prince Theatre," said Donny.

But Petey was feeling very unsettled right now. He could almost feel her next to him, an invisible effigy of broken promises, death, and regret.

"You all miked up?" enquired the sound engineer.

"Yes." Petey flinched as an author pushed past him.

Damn, this 'authors area' was crowded. They were all like an excited bag of jumping beans. A PA was desperately trying to manage her charge: a big bearded man with a loud, booming voice. "I must be getting ready!" the man shouted, his lungs seeming to make the tent vibrate. "There is no time!"

"Right, you all set?" said Donny.

"Yeah, I'm ready to go. I'm ready."

"Good, let's get out of this... nest."

"Ah, that's what you call it!"

They entered the afternoon air, walking along the wooden decking to the Prince Theatre. A volunteer held the door open for them, smiling at Donny, but opening her mouth and baring her teeth for Petey. Like two soldiers going into enemy territory, they entered the tent and were welcomed by cheering.

Donny led the way up to the small platform (complete with two white plastic chairs, a white plastic table, and wonderfully transparent plastic cups and a jug). He motioned for them both to sit down whilst he drew out a collection of papers from his jacket pocket and beamed at the audience.

Petey glanced behind him, seeing the title of their event projected onto a screen.

The second the doors closed, Donny started: "Well, ladies and gentlemen, welcome to the Edinburgh International Book Festival. I've particularly enjoyed it so far. My name is Donny Bell, and I'm a writer specialising in crime fiction and science fiction.

"I'd like to welcome you all to this event, which I'm sure is going to be spectacular: *A.I.: Friend or Foe?* It is my particular honour to introduce Peter McGough. He is the CEO of Newton-M-Wren, which is, as I'm sure you all know, an internationally recognised software company. Their computers can be found in every school in Britain and a good proportion of the rest of the world.

"Peter has written a book, *A Big Paradox: The Humanity of A.I.*" Donny held a copy up for all the audience to see, like a Roman gladiator proudly showing a baying crowd the head of his opponent. "Not only has it received praise from a variety of news outlets and magazines, but it has even made it into the hands of the U.N. Secretary General, so I'm told..."

"I don't know about that," Petey said laughingly.

"Well, there are always surprises. I'm going to talk to Peter for the next forty-five minutes or so, then we'll open it up to the audience for questions. Ladies and gentlemen, without further ado, please welcome Peter McGough."

There was a long round of clapping. Petey waved at them. Well, he'd never been to a book festival before, not even as an audience member. Was this the right thing to do, waving like an imbecile?

"So..." Donny folded his arms. "Peter, well, first of all, congratulations on the book."

"Why, thank you."

"What made you write it?"

Petey had to give a professional answer this time: "Well, I've had a vested interest in artificial intelligence for a number of years. In fact, I'd go so far as to say I've had it since I launched Newton-M-Wren. I think artificial intelligence, or A.I. if you like, isn't something you can get away from. I think it's engrained into the human psyche."

"Absolutely," said Donny. "Whether it's your microwave, your television, or your computer at work, A.I. is a guest, whether you like it or not."

"I'd be interested in asking you how A.I. translates into fiction."

"There's not really that much excitement unfortunately." Donny paused to take a sip of water. "There's a bit of research involved."

"Haha. I'd have just watched the movie." Petey relaxed his hands as the audience laughed. "How much research do you do?"

"Actually, I've found, as a writer, that it's a case of not spending too much time on the research. You can spend weeks researching CPUs. What's the point?"

"First of all, CPUs are bloody interesting. Secondly, you can't fault a good few weeks of research."

"Not when you're trying to meet the next deadline for your publisher," Donny retorted.

Both men laughed, along with the audience.

Things went smoothly. Donny prodded him about his book, trying to get "behind the scenes", wanting to know his "writing process". The literary world was an alien world, something he'd only just discovered. There were many strange terms: *ecstatic, the power of writing, genre, ambiance.* Though he knew what they were, here they seemed to have different meanings, different characteristics, different personalities.

Too soon, way too soon, Donny wrapped up: "I think it's time that we opened it up to the audience. Does anyone have any questions for Peter? Or myself?" A long halt in the proceedings as the brains whirred. "Ah yes, the gentleman in the blue shirt. Hold on, sir, there's a mike coming your way."

"Thank you," said a deep American voice, frighteningly amplified. "A very interesting discussion, if I may say so. If I could ask Mr McGough, how do you feel about the threat posed by other largescale computer corporations?"

A question Petey had been asked many times before. He knew exactly how to answer: "I'll be clear with you, there *aren't* any threats to Newton-M-Wren. Newton-M-Wren is invincible. I can guarantee that no other, similar companies will put it out of business, quite simply because there *are no* similar companies."

"Okay, next question," said Donny, scanning around, hand levelled over his eyes like a sailor departing on an epic voyage. "Yes, the man with the red sweater. Hand him the mike, please."

"Thank you," said a bright, chirpy, posh English voice. "I'd like to ask you, Peter, your views on whether the government is investing enough into computing science. I'm a student here in Edinburgh. I'm doing the course I believe you did."

"Glad to know I'm not alone in that department. I felt bloody lonely studying on that course." Petey breathed in deeply. The audience hadn't laughed this time. "You know, I think the government's doing what it can. With the really bad floods we've had this summer, I think their priorities are elsewhere at the moment. But I don't think government funding's all that important. I mean, Newton-M-Wren is far better at investing into computing than the government. We also have more money to give than they do. I know that's not a clear-cut response, but I hope that answers your question."

"Well, ladies and gentlemen, we have time for one last question," said Donny. "Yes, the lady with the spectacles."

"I have a small question for a small man," said a hoarse voice. "Peter, do you enjoy delving into writing?"

"Yes, I do. It's a fascinating pursuit." He wasn't sure of where this question was going.

"That's all I wanted to ask." The mike screamed.

"Ow, interference." Donny clenched his ear playfully. "Okay, ladies and gentlemen, I'm afraid that's all the time for questions. However, there will be a book signing next door, where I'm sure Peter will be happy to answer any further questions that you may have. Follow the directions of the festival staff. Finally, please join me in thanking Peter McGough for coming along today."

The queue snaked its way out of the signing tent and along the decking. As a volunteer proceeded to disconnect Petey, he felt a little dismayed that nearly everyone from his event was carrying a copy of the book. His hand was going to hurt like hell by the end of the day. He followed the volunteer into the tent, where he was promptly directed to a table on a raised platform. No sooner had he sat down, when Donny took the seat next to him.

"I hate getting the mike removed," remarked the writer, filling both his and Petey's plastic cups from the jug (just delivered by a smiling elderly woman). "It feels like you're being physically disconnected from fame."

The elderly volunteer placed a pen in front of each of them and stepped back.

"Well, fame's about to come on full force," said Petey, as the first audience member was gestured forward by another volunteer. He signed her copy of *A Big Paradox*.

Next to come was the American man. "Thank you very much," he said, as Petey handed back his copy, freshly soaked with a signature. "I apologise if I put you on the spot back there."

"It's okay," Petey told him. "Believe me, I got a lot worse at last year's AGM."

Donny signed a copy of *The Clapping of Fate* and passed it back.

"Thank you, gentlemen, both of you," said the American, promptly walking off.

"You're doing well so far," said Donny. "Keep up the smiling."

"Indeed." Petey took a sip of water as the next person came forward. The student.

"That was a very interesting talk you gave," said the young man, placing his copies of *The Clapping of Fate* and *Mr Integral* in front of Donny. The novelist quickly signed them and shoved them back over.

"Glad you enjoyed it. You want that signed?" Petey nodded at the copy of *A Big Paradox* the student had clenched under his armpit.

"Oh, sorry, I'd love that!" Such a young, ambitious, high-pitched voice! The student twiddled his glasses and pulled at his wispy, brown hair. Poverty-stricken, he wore a white t-shirt with a band of some sort emblazoned on the front and black jeans with sneakers. He took the signed books back, nodded at them both, and half-walked, half-skipped away.

Soon, it became routine: someone would come forward; Petey (and often Donny) would sign books; the customer would maybe ask a question; and then the customer would simply walk away.

Petey was jolted from his near-slumber when *A Big Paradox* hit the table hard. He glanced up: the woman who had asked him the awkward question at the end.

"Hi," she said. "Remember me?"

"Don't think I do," he said. "Have we met?"

"You tell me." Her accent was familiar. So were the eyes and the hair.

"Did we meet at my headquarters?"

"No." She leaned forward, folding her arms on the table.

"I still don't recognise you. Have you visited my office before?"

"No – we met in Bangkok. Dawn of the new millennium."

"Oh my God. Megan?" Petey didn't know whether to smile or sigh. Yeah, it was definitely her, no question.

"You remember now, don't you?"

"Is everything okay?" Donny interjected.

"I'll tell you something!" Megan shouted, standing up straight. Her denim skirt, tightfitting, exposed her pale legs and platform shoes. "Everyone, listen in! You know what this guy did? December Thirty-First, Nineteen-Ninety-Nine, this man ruined me!"

"I'm sorry, I really don't know what this is about." Petey was once again a protester.

"Do you remember me, Trudy and that fat prick walking off into the night, leaving you with your whore girlfriend? The protest movement found out we'd been drinking with you. They didn't expel fatso, or Trudy. They kicked *me* out! I lost friends, a lifestyle I loved, a community. Being part of that movement was my life!"

"Well, why didn't you put up a fight?" Donny said, sniggering.

"Because Trudy and fatso conspired against me. Said I was the one who invited you."

"Not surprised. You're a drunk." Donny nodded to one of the volunteers. "Please get security. Remove this woman."

Speed, in all honesty, had never been Petey's strong point. Megan yelled, "Now it's fucking pay-back!", and yanked something out of her skirt. He threw himself back, just as a knife slashed down. His chair hit the poster marked *Author Signing Area* and he went straight through, sprawled out like Jesus on the cross.

Helpless. Shit-scared. Waiting for the final blow.

Megan tore the table to the side and went for him. Quick as a heartbeat, Donny lunged at her, knocking the knife away, pinning her to the floor. "Security!" he yelled. Suddenly Megan kicked his foot and wriggled free. He went to stop her, trying to grab her waist, but she smacked her elbow right into his nose.

The crowd had broken free from the line, yelling abuse at the fleeing Megan. Someone helped Petey up.

Donny was lying on the floor, bleeding profusely from his nose. Someone was yelling for a medic.

"Are you okay?" Petey asked the novelist. "Shit, your nose!"

"Get the fuck away from me!" Donny yelled with such fierceness that everyone tending to him winced. "Go and write about fucking computers!"

"I'm sorry. Help is on the way."

"It'd better be! Seriously, you little prick, fuck off!"

A medic arrived a few moments later and set about tending to Donny's injuries. But she couldn't fix his eyes. They were locked on Petey, full of rage, as though something in the Glaswegian writer had finally broken free.

The police arrived less than an hour later and interviewed Petey and Donny separately, as well as a number of festival volunteers and people in the book signing queue. The book signing area had taken on a sombre, joyless tone. But the book fair continued outside.

Just before the police left, the officer in charge informed the both of them that Megan had been tracked down and arrested a few streets away.

"I don't want to press charges," said Petey. "I'd rather just let this go."

"Well, I do," said Donny. "That bitch broke my fucking nose."

"We'll be in touch with both of you to let you know of any developments," said the officer, before following in the footsteps of his colleagues.

Of course, the book signing had been stopped.

Where there had once been a queue, there was empty space.

"Listen, I'm sorry for yelling at you earlier," said Donny, as the medic began leading him away. "No hard feelings, eh mate?"

"It's okay. Don't worry about it."

Donny didn't have the chance to reply: the medic, like a father giving away his daughter, led him out of view.

Petey stood in the signing tent, his heart hammering. Alone. The table was still where Megan had thrown it. The poster, ripped like a threaded sweater, lay in a pile of paper and metal poles. The whole place had an uncomfortable stillness to it.

He headed for the bar. "One solid pint, please," he ordered.

"What would you like?"

"Whatever you recommend."

He walked out of the festival an hour later, slightly lightheaded. Early evening was approaching. Traffic was building up.

A drink always solved things. A good pint of ale.

Surprisingly, it was a bit chilly. He was only wearing a shirt, a jacket and thin black trousers, stupidly thinking that it would be rather warm today.

He was shaking. PTSD? Did it come on that fast?

He wandered back to the hotel, breathing in, breathing out. It didn't feel good. He felt a dangerous bravado of the extremes. The lights were brighter and the car horns louder. When he was back in his room, he paced back and forth. There was no minibar. Hadn't they promised him one?

Why her? She didn't deserve it. No wait, it was his fault. He'd gone chasing after that stupid, unfaithful bitch, instead of looking after Georgina. It was his fault. *He* was responsible for her death.

He stormed out of the room, heading down to the measly bar. "Whisky," he said, when the barman appeared.

"What kind, sir?"

"Oh, I dunno. Give me some of that, what d'ya call it, Grouse or something. Double. No ice."

"Certainly, sir."

When it was placed before him, he gulped it down in one go.

Something was ringing. Oh, fuck, his phone.

"Babe, how did it go?" Nicola asked. She sounded so far away.

"Pretty bad."

"Why, what happened? Are you okay?"

"Considering I just got assaulted, I'm perfect."

"Fuck, are you okay? I'll drive up tonight."

"No, it's all right. I just need to calm down. I'm flying home tomorrow."

"Well, take it easy okay. We'll go for a meal later in the week, okay? Just –"

The phone died. He tapped the keypad furiously. Shit. The battery.

"Another one, sir?" asked the barman.

"Yeah, why not?"

That second whisky had really gone to his head. Fucking hell. He laughed to himself as he walked. He found himself on North Bridge. He had been destined to meet Sarah here, over fourteen years ago. He leaned over the side, looking down at the hissing station.

"Georgina," he whimpered. "Georgina."

"Mate, you okay?" said a nasal Scottish voice.

He turned to face a group of young men, all three of whom had fluff under their lips.

"Yeah, I'm fine," he told them. "Just had a little too much to drink."

"Well, take it easy mate, alright?"

The group set off towards the Old Town. Petey found himself saying after them, "Where are you guys going?"

"Pub up the road," one of them said.

"You're a little young to be drinking, aren't you?"

"We're all eighteen. We're legal."

"How much money you have?"

"Are you trying to be funny, mister?" said a guy with disastrous acne and a ring through his lip.

"I'm being genuine."

"We've each got ten quid on us."

"I've got two-hundred." He staggered towards the group. "First round's on me, what do you say?"

"Yeah, I totally screwed her," said Rick.

"Was she good?" jeered Iain. "Hope she fucking was!"

All of them bellowed in hysterics. Annoyed patrons looked on, some quietly swearing between themselves.

"I'll tell you a little story," said Giz, the one with the ring through his lip. "Couple of weeks ago, got this amazing BJ from this like total slut. Man, she sucked my bell-end like... fucking hell."

"I thought you were going to tell us a story," slurred Petey. "That sounds depressing."

Rick slammed his fists on the table. "Fuck, this guy's so funny!" he shouted. "Let's get him another drink."

"No fucking way, guys." Petey produced his wallet. "Next round is on me."

"You've bought three rounds already," said Iain.

"Yeah, well, I'm feelin' generous."

"Just get the round," said Giz. "Iain doesn't know what he's talking about. He's not a real man yet."

Petey went to the bar and ordered four more pints. He ferried them back to the table like buckets of gold.

"Why's Iain not a real man?" he asked, when everyone had their drink in their hands.

"Well, he's got an embarrassing secret," said Rick. "No girl's found themselves wanting to fuck him yet."

"Come on," said Iain. "Seriously, mate!"

"It's not our fault you haven't done it yet." Rick thumped his friend on the back. "Anyway, cheers guys."

"Cheers!" Petey called out. "Cheers to the end of the fucking world!" He drank his pint in one.

Wow, this was a rush.

Many drinks later, it was all a blur. One of the guys said something along the lines of: "Hey mate, I think you need to go home."

The next thing he knew, he was on the street, trying to find the hotel.

He was yelling. "Fuck you!" "What you fucking looking at?!" "I fucking hate my life!"

He was stumbling. The road was liquid, out to get him.

Did he head back to the book festival? Did a security guard turf him back out?

He was padding along. Was he in a shop? Why was he buying a bottle of wine? Why was he buying a bottle that cost nearly forty quid? Then he was sauntering across a busy road. He was quenching himself with an undying thirst, the bottle to his lips.

"Aye, fuck it!" he yelled to a group of bemused women.

One of them answered back with, "Ignore him, he's just drunk."

Then he was in a taxi. Had he told the driver to go to Blairhill station?

The streetlights flickered by like a drug-fuelled dream of chaos.

The guilt was too much. He was emptying the bottle down his throat. He'd killed Georgina. Her death, it belonged to him. It possessed him.

When the taxi stopped, he realised he didn't have enough money to pay the driver. So, he crawled to a cashpoint, withdrew a hundred, gave it to the stupid wanker who'd driven him all the way to, was it Blairhill? He told the driver to keep the change.

He was on the ground. Someone called him a nasty name. His fingernails scraped the floor.

Up ahead, yes, up ahead. Lights. Blairhill station. That was it. He yanked himself to his feet, ran, full pelt.

He was on the platform, so drunk. He drank the last titbits of wine.

Vomit came, all down his front. Fuck, he was going to feel it tomorrow.

A train was coming. It was time to go. His punishment for letting her die.

Soon, he would pay.

He stood at the edge of the platform, ready to jump.

Strong hands. Pulled him back.

He was down on the floor. The bottle clinked away. The train shot past.

Someone had saved him. He looked into their eyes. Who had dared to interrupt the process of justice? In his drunken stupor, he could just about make out who it was.

Sarah.

Tuesday 21st August 2007

"Ah," his mouth uttered, as the sun tickled the back of his neck. His head was pounding. He rolled over, facing the eternal blue sky. Sitting up, his vision spun. "Shit." He fell, vomiting to his side.

"Are you okay?" boomed a hard Scottish voice. A woman, slightly chubby, wearing a business suit and eyeliner, ventured towards him. He could see her spiky high heels out of the corner of his eye.

"I'm fine," he could barely spit out.

"No, you're not." She put her hands on her hips, her handbag flailing out to the side.

Panicking, he checked himself: wallet and phone were present.

"Listen, I'm phoning for an ambulance," she said, her tone an authority even to him.

"No, please. I have a flight to catch this afternoon. I need to get back to the hotel to freshen up."

"You're not going anywhere. Christ, you're a fucking mess. Look at you."

"Quite frankly, it's none of your business. Anyway, don't you have work to go to? You're all dressed up."

She fished out a mobile from her handbag, typing in a number with her fat thumb. "Hi, Gerry, it's Yvonne." The woman coughed. Smoker, definitely. "Listen, unfortunately I'm not going to be able to make it in today. I've been held up with some personal stuff. It's my mum." She listened to Gerry's reply. "Thanks for your help in this. Really appreciate it. See you later." She snapped the phone shut. "Right, that's that sorted."

"Maybe it's better if I just go."

"Where will you go?"

"I'll head into Glasgow, get a bus or train over to Edinburgh. I'm sure I can work it out."

"I'm sure you could. You've got puke all over yourself."

"I'm fine!" he told her firmly. He stood up. A wave of nausea washed over him. He emptied his stomach again onto the platform.

"Okay, that seals it. You're not going anywhere." Yvonne steadied him.

"Why do you care?"

"I used to be a nurse. Seen plenty of men in your state before."

"Thanks for kind compliment."

"Then I started working for the council." She began escorting him off the platform, holding him steady like he was her child. "And the rest, as they say, is history."

"Where are you taking me?"

"Home."

She lived in a small close, white-mixed-with-grey houses standing in line like troops. Her house was at the end on the left. Blurry glass, lumpy like a rockfall, formed the window on her peeling paint door.

"Welcome to my humble abode," said Yvonne, inserting a key into the lock. She opened up and led him in.

"Nice place you got here." Petey said this by way of a friendly introduction, but it came out in a drunken mishap of the tongue.

And it wasn't a 'nice' place. Well, from his perspective, it was a council house. Near-black carpet, the smell of cigarette smoke, walls that seemed to want to crush you.

"Glad you like it. There's a bathroom upstairs. Get yourself cleaned up. I'll bring you some fresh clothes."

"Thanks." He took out his mobile. "Do you have a charger for this? I need to call the hotel, let them know, and also my agent and lawyer."

"Agent and lawyer?" she said suspiciously.

"I may as well tell you, I was at the Edinburgh Book Festival. Little too much to drink..."

"Sounds to me like you had a more than a 'little too much'." She took the phone from him.

"Haha."

"Okay, you go up and shower. I'll put your phone on charge – I think I've got a suitable cable. Also, bring your used clothes down with you. I'll need to get them in the washing machine."

He found it embarrassing, but what choice was there? Tiptoeing down the steps in clothes (her clothes) that were a size too big for him, he looked like a child who had dressed as his mum for Halloween.

"You look good," Yvonne remarked. "Actually, you look amazing."

"Thanks. I don't suppose you happen to have any male clothes at all..."

"Well, unless you can whizz back in time and cancel my divorce, I can't help you in that area."

"Ah, I'm sorry."

"Don't be." Yvonne let out a mighty yawn. "Damn,

I'm tired. Listen, go into the living room, lie down. I'll bring your phone in. Have you brushed your teeth?"

"Yes, I did. Hope you didn't mind. There was only one toothbrush available."

"It's okay. I need to replace it anyway. And I'll take those..." She removed the bundle from his arms. "Go lie down." Just like a dog.

"Fuck," he moaned, seeing the sixteen missed calls and five voice messages from Nicola. "Fuck." He stretched out on Yvonne's blue, beginning-to-thread sofa, and phoned his wife back.

"*Where the fuck were you last night?*" she screamed. "*I was worried sick!*"

"I'm sorry. My phone ran out of battery."

"*I've had the police over. Been in hysterics! What happened?!*"

"I got drunk. Stupid thing. I'm okay now. An old uni friend has helped me out. I'm staying with him. I'm still planning on flying back today."

"*I hope so. I'm seriously not impressed with you, hun. Christ, you're a father now!*"

"Yeah, I've known that for the past seven years," he snapped back at her.

"*Well, start acting like one. Go and sober up. When you get home tonight, you and I need to have a long chat!*"

"I'm sorry."

"*I've now got to let the police know that you're okay.*"

"We'll talk about it when I get home, I promise."

"Just go and sober up." She hung up.

"You okay?" said Yvonne, two steaming mugs of tea in her hands.

"Not really. Had an argument with the wife." He took the tea off her. "Give me a minute. I need to phone my lawyer and agent, let them know that I got fucked up last night. My agent will need to get in contact with the hotel, just to make sure they keep my belongings secure."

"Why don't you do it yourself? You're a grown man?"

"I could. But, I'm sophisticated."

"You mean you're rich."

"Yes." He sipped his tea.

"Hold on, I recognise you!" Yvonne slumped into the armchair (the same design as the sofa, complete with the beginnings of decomposition). "You're that guy. That bloke who owns Newton-M-Wren."

"That would be me."

"Well, this is my lucky day. Now, Mr Computer Man, I want you to rest."

"Very well. Listen, I need to get home today. I really can't stay. Obviously, you've heard me on the phone to my wife."

"What time do you need to be at the airport? I'm assuming it's Edinburgh...?"

"I need to be there for one o'clock."

She looked at her watch, like a disapproving headmistress as a boy arrived late for school. "It's nearly eight. Make sure you rest, try and grab some sleep. I'll arrange for a taxi to pick you up at ten."

"Thanks. I really appreciate it."

"Now, get some rest."

"Phone calls first," said Petey, holding his phone tauntingly at her.

He dreamed that he was falling. He was on the piss in some city; he didn't know where. He didn't know why he was doing it. He just knew he was falling. So far.

He awoke to find himself staring into the face of the woman. She was ugly, yet oddly pretty as well, the scars of trauma bearing themselves in her eyes.

"It's Half-Nine," she informed. "I put your clothes in my tumble dryer, so they're nice and dry."

"Thanks," he whispered hoarsely.

"How are you feeling?"

"A little better."

"That's good. Do you want a slice of toast or something?"

"Ah, no thanks. I'll eat when I get to the airport. The taxi'll be here at ten, did you say?"

"Yep." She looked hurt. Bruised.

"Thanks a lot. Listen, sorry for being off with you earlier. I wasn't at my best –"

"It's understandable. Totally." She patted his shoulder.

It occurred to him, maybe just a little too late, that she was sitting on the sofa. Her hand moved down, taking his.

"I can't," he protested. "I'm sorry. Yvonne, I'm married."

"You don't think I know that?" Tears were forming in her eyes. "I'm sorry, since my divorce, things have been difficult."

"I really don't know what to say. I mean, I'm a devoted husband and father. Not doing my best right now in that area, I admit."

"You're a better parent than I ever would have made."

"Look, I can't get dragged into this." Petey felt trapped. Pinned down by this lonely woman's existence.

"I don't have children. I'm in my forties now. It's too late."

"I think it's time that I left."

His phone rang. Nicola. "Oh, shit," he murmured.

"I'll get your things ready," said Yvonne.

"Look, I'm sorry about earlier." He could hear Nicola crying on the other end.

"It's okay. This was all my fault."

"You know I love you, Petey, don't you?"

"Yeah, I love you too."

"Well, listen, safe travels, okay? I'll be there to pick you up."

"Listen, babe, I'm still feeling pretty rough. I'm going to phone Alan, get him to change my flight to tomorrow morning."

"That's a good idea. Get some sleep and get some food, okay? I love you, Petey."

"I love you two. Don't worry about picking me up tomorrow. I'll get a taxi from the airport."

"Okay, take it easy, okay?"

"Sure. Chat later, babe." He hung up, then dialled Alan. His lawyer duly rearranged the flight for eight-thirty tomorrow morning.

He located Yvonne in what appeared to be a utility room (very bland, the bare creamy essentials) folding his clothes into a small pile. "Cancel the taxi," he said. "Dinner's on me tonight."

It was a basic pub that served basic food. Nothing special.

He didn't want to say it, but... well, Yvonne ate like an animal. She munched down her fish and chips, barely making any eye contact with him. She drank her cheap lager like a girl with one hell of a crush.

The pub was empty, only two (seemingly) old regulars at the bar. A record from bygone years played in the background.

"It's strange being in a pub without the smell of cigarettes," she said, just as she finished her meal.

"It is a bit." Petey took another bite of his steak pie. "Well, you can't fault the smoking ban."

"I used to love smoking in here," she said sadly. "When I was with the husband. Just the two of us."

"What happened, if you don't mind my asking?"

"We just fell apart. There was a lot wrong in our relationship. From the start I think. I wanted kids, he didn't. I suppose that's how it all broke to pieces. I want kids so much, Peter. I really do. And I'll never have them." She wiped a tear away.

"I wish I could do something." Petey finished the last bite of the pie and took a glug from the cheap lager.

"There is one thing you could do." Her voice was that of a terrified old woman, afraid of the next event in her life.

And he felt scared. It had all been a mistake, staying here like a teenager desperate to get laid. Stupid, stupid, fucking stupid. He could have been home in the arms of his wife. He could have been watching a silly cartoon with Mary. But he was here, in this desolate place, drinking shit beer. And he was alone with this woman.

"I want you to get me pregnant," she said flatly. "Please."

"Can't you go to a sperm bank or something?"

"I could. But I'd prefer to do it properly."

"I don't know. It's –"

Her lips were on his before he could tell her that he was trying his best to be faithful to his wife. He nearly panicked, but something (he would never know) kept him together. She tasted like those sweet cigarettes. He liked it.

And it was amazing how quickly they drank up.

They said a mildly drunk farewell to the barman and the regulars, then rushed outside into the warm summer evening. The streets were quiet catacombs.

"It's a fair walk to your house," he remarked casually.

"It is. Can you go any faster?"

"I was never that much good at running at school."

She gripped his hand, her fingers like cold claws. Faster they went. He struggled to keep up. She was strong.

No sooner were they in her house, when their lips touched. They kissed hard and groped.

"Don't go," she whispered, slamming the front door. "Please don't go."

"I'm not planning to. Listen, do you mind if I get a glass of water first?

"Go ahead. I'll head upstairs and freshen up." She kissed his neck and began her ascent.

Petey softly stomped through to the kitchen. He filled a tall pint glass to the brim with water and drank it deep, so quick that his oesophagus stretched.

What was he doing? He was panicking. He was cheating on his wife. For the sake of sanity, he was pushing things way too far. He couldn't do this. He couldn't ruin things.

Sighing, he trudged upstairs. Yvonne would be disappointed, but she'd understand. But his vision was caught by a most vivid sight.

Yvonne stood in the doorway of her room, not a stitch on her.

If there were any boundaries between them, they collapsed in that moment.

Wednesday 22nd August 2007

"I can't stay any longer," he said, watching the sunlight peeping through the curtains. "Really, I can't."

"Go on," she whispered, hands locked around his waist. "Just another hour."

"My train leaves in thirty minutes."

"Get another train."

"I'd miss my flight."

"Then get another flight."

"I don't want to get home late. Nicola might get suspicious."

"That's her problem then."

He kissed her. "God, I'll miss you."

They were warm underneath the covers, the world outside something that didn't matter. He wanted to stay here, holding this stranger. She'd saved him from himself, picked him up when he'd been in pain. And now, quite simply, he had to leave.

"You gonna be okay?" she asked.

"Yeah, I'll be fine. What about you?"

"I'll be good. Got plenty to keep me busy."

"You know, if you're in the area again, you're more than welcome to visit."

"I doubt that, but thank you." He pulled off the covers and slipped out of the bed. He put on his clothes. The vomit stains were pretty minimal. Not too much damage. Chances were, Nicola wouldn't notice.

"Thanks for a great night," said Yvonne. "I really

enjoyed it. Thanks for making a dream come true as well."

"You'll have to get tested, won't you? When will you know?"

"Don't worry, I'll get everything sorted. And don't worry, you won't hear from me again."

"Thanks, seriously. I'd support you and everything, but..."

"Yes, yes, yes... Nicola. She can't know."

"You up to much today?"

"Not much." She spread out on the bed, arms like tree trunks. She yawned like a cat. "Got work later. Then when I get home tonight, I'll probably go for a drink or something."

"Thanks for everything. I mean it." He leaned forward and planted a soft kiss on her lips. "Take care of yourself, okay?"

"I will. You too."

He showed himself out. The second the door shut behind him, he kept walking. He didn't once look the other way. He made straight for the station, looking like a drug-addicted tramp.

Blairhill station was exactly the way it had been yesterday. Was that a pool of his vomit? Christ, why had no one cleaned it up?

The train was running five minutes late, but that was no bother. The journey was simple and succinct: train to Glasgow; train to Edinburgh; stop at the hotel to retrieve belongings left behind in a stupid drunk slurry; get to the airport; home.

When the train pulled up, he got on without sparing a single glance at the place he'd spent the night. It was his past now. Nicola and Mary, they were his future; they were his life.

The journey was rickety, grey, opaque.

The only thing of note was an elderly woman giving him disapproving looks, whilst she knitted away like a closet adventurer.

A ticket examiner charged him the full fare and he was too full of questions and distress about his experiences of the past two days to ask for a discount.

When the train pulled into Glasgow Queen Street, he was only too happy to vanish into the morning commuter rush. To think, he could have been one of those suits... Well, he was a suit, but one who could travel the world.

He caught the connection to Edinburgh no bother and was soon on a fast trip back to the capital city. All the while, he thought of his wife and daughter. He was coming home to them. He was coming home.

He arrived in the beginning-to-die-but-not-quite-in-crisis-stage of the Fringe. The performers were only just waking up, no doubt most of them hungover (and probably a few riddled with drugs).

There was a short, quite embarrassing exchange between him and the hotel manager. Having to explain that you got absolutely, unbelievably, irreversibly pissed, so much so that you left your belongings in a hotel that you had no business being in for an extra day (and not forgetting the inconvenience to the next guest(s) whilst they waited for the staff to clean out the wreck-of-a-room and move your belongings to a secure place), is never easy.

But he got it done and was soon in a taxi on the way to the airport.

His flight was on time and he had a good breakfast in the executive lounge. This was the life, he realised. This was the fucking life.

"Boarding pass, sir," the stewardess said politely, as he boarded the plane.

He handed it over and she looked at it with a glint of recognition. It was nice being known! He smiled at her, thanking "her professional service".

He took his assigned business class seat and watched as the baggage handlers finished loading everything up. The engines started with a jerk and the plane pushed back.

He was in a happy comatose state all the way down to London. Suddenly the sun was so bright and the airline coffee sweet and creamy.

When the plane bumped down at Heathrow, he resisted the urge to let out a cheer.

Collecting his case was a slim, perfect mission. He grinned at his disgruntled fellow passengers, picked his wheelie bag up from the conveyer belt, and headed out of the airport.

Like so many times in so many countries, he hailed a taxi and was soon on his way.

Mary and Nicola were less than an hour away – depending on the traffic, of course. Indeed, it did get a little bit busy as they headed into London. But he was thinking, imagining what the taste of Nicola's tea would be like. She always had a way with it, able to make her own unique flavour.

The driver gave him (extremely surprisingly) a good fare when he dropped him off.

"Have a good day, guv," said the thinly man, his East End accent thick. The driver opened the boot and retrieved his bags.

"Cheers mate. Have a good one." Petey waved the driver off and stepped into his driveway.

Nicola's car was gone. Shopping most likely.

A pang of guilt struck his temple and his gut. Last night was stupid. What if Yvonne found a way to get in touch? He would have to get Alan to think of an emergency legal response.

He put the key in the lock and entered his house. Silence. Well, of course it would be quiet! They were both out! He took his wheelie case upstairs to their bedroom and dumped his shoulder bag next to it. The kettle went on next and he was soon seated in the lounge with a hot mug of tea.

A drunken memory came to him like a drunken sailor coming home. Had it been Sarah? There? At Blairhill? No. No, no, no. If she'd been there, she would have looked after him. It was his imagination.

He dozed off, his thoughts money. Then Sarah popped in, like a cancer, eating away at his mind. There was too much pain there; even the knowledge that he'd done the right thing back then didn't comfort his ever-so-tender soul.

Two things happened in quick succession: the doorbell rang and he spilt tea down his lap.

Cursing with near-rage, he ambled to the front door. He forced himself to breathe. In. Out. He didn't want to alarm Mary. She was too young for the stresses of life. He nearly knocked an antique vase (all the way from Zimbabwe (the result of an excellent deal when he'd been there on business three years ago)) off its stand. The doorbell rang again. Why didn't they just come in? Had he left the key in the lock?

The two policemen who stood there seemed to want to fold their arms.

"Are you Peter McGough?" one of them enquired.

"That would be me," he said. "Is this about the incident at the Book Festival?"

"No, sir, we don't know anything about that."

"Is this about me getting drunk? Look, I didn't commit any criminal acts or anything."

"No, sir, we are here on another matter." The other policeman was speaking now. Very young. Evidently new to the job. "I regret to inform you that your wife and daughter have been killed in a car accident."

The next words were blurry verbal vision. Something about a drunk driver. Was there someone they could call? Could they arrange a counsellor to come over?

His knees gave way. At what point, he didn't know. But they gave way like collapsing sandcastles.

The hours and days were an undying fog. Alan was there, so was Irene.

Petey refused any help. He wanted to be alone. He needed loneliness like the desert needs rain. He needed peace.

Phrases were uttered to him, useless things like: "We're here for you."; "It's okay"; "It will heal."; "Time is the best healer."

How long went by? Weeks?

The endless torment was broken by a discovery, as all these things tend to be.

He was sitting in the kitchen, alone and bitter, reaching for his glasses case, still stuffed inside the jacket that he'd kept on. He needed to hold the chain. Mary had made it for him. A part of her with him always. He prised the case open and found only his lenses.

Sarah *had* been there. He hadn't been hallucinating. That thief had stolen from him, taken the most precious thing he had. There was only one thing left to do. He would find Sarah. However long it would take. He would find her. But this time for revenge, not love.

Deception

Glasgow

Sunday 1ˢᵗ June 2014

Mrs Malice, owner of The Cross Name, was used to her regular crowd of regulars. For a Tuesday night, it was bustling; the drinkers were jostling for space at the bar like kids fighting for space on a theme park ride.

Damn, she was stressed. Damn, she wanted out. But the job kept her on a tight leash.

"Hello, Norrie," she grumbled, as one of the most troublesome patrons came over. "Another?"

"Aye, why not?" Norrie grunted in response.

She poured him another pint, which he took with glee. "And when are you going to pay your tab?"

"Soon, don't worry." Norrie shifted away, his stained jacket rubbing against the other patrons.

"I've heard that many times before," Mrs Malice mumbled to herself. She watched the pub scene for a fraction of a moment, wishing that she could be somewhere else. But the arrival of the Lilleys split her daydream like a mini celebrity divorce. "How are youse two?" she asked.

"Aye, fine," said Dan Lilley, thrusting his girl against

the bar, forceful enough to make her makeup twitch, but not enough to get the attention of the tougher men so nearby.

"Your usual?" Mrs Malice asked them.

"Yeah."

She went about pouring Dan a pint of his favourite lager and Gillian a small glass of white wine. "That's a hell of a bruise you've got on your cheek, Dan," she remarked, handing over their drinks.

"Was boxing last week." Dan took a long sip.

"How's things going with work?"

"Fine. Well, you know what personal training's like. Trying to get some of those fat fucks into shape is never easy. Christ, you should see some of the blubbers we get at the gym."

"How are you, Gillian?"

"Aye, I'm all right." Gillian kept her eyes down. "I'm starting a summer placement next week."

"How did your exams go?"

"They went fine," Dan cut in. "She's a right little angel, this one. With the Commonwealth Games coming up, she's going to be very busy keeping our flat in order. You know how busy I'm going to be. I need a woman's touch around my home."

Gillian kept looking at the floor. She pulled at her white shirt and let out a stream of breath.

"Youse guys are coming up to your first anniversary, aren't you?" Mrs Malice's attempt at diverting the wild train of conversation succeeded.

"Aye." Dan slapped the bar. "We're happy and free

at twenty, but she's bound tightly to me like we're fifty."

"Well, do come here for a drink on the big night."

"Of course."

"You know, we could book it out for you. Buffet or something."

"Aye, sounds a plan."

Mrs Malice was about to speak to Gillian, when Shuffles came in, called so because of the fact he was always staggering around drunk. He'd been barred from The Cross Name and most of the other pubs in Glasgow City Centre.

"Pint a lager," blabbed Shuffles.

"Come on, pal, you've been barred." Mrs Malice stood defiant. "Look mate, you need to go."

"Just a pint of somethin'." Shuffles pulled off his fleece. "Please."

"Look, you're drunk. Go home, mate."

"Yeah, go home," Dan butted in. "Go."

"A pint a the heavy."

When Dan moved fast, he moved fast. Pinning the drunk's arms behind his back, he marched him out of the pub, to the cheering of the other punters. "Now stay the fuck away from here!" came Dan's aggressive voice. He came back in, quite proudly fuming. "Finish your drink, darling. Now."

There was no use trying to interfere, Mrs Malice sadly realised. Accusing Dan of sexism would only make things worse. She watched the couple swallow the last of their drinks and then leave in a silent huff.

She would have been condemned to the drab night ahead if it wasn't for the arrival of her (she had to admit) favourite customer, who sat down where Dan had been and, with a sad smile, placed his order.

"How've you been?" she said, placing his regular pint of dark ale before him.

The pub was beginning to thin a little. A hungry crowd of young lads walked out, bellowing laughter.

"I'm okay," said Peter. "Long day." He looked tired, worn down to the nub.

"I finished reading your book last night."

"Yeah, well I'm not in the mood to talk about books."

"You know, if you need anything, I'm here."

"What I need... is for you to let me enjoy my pint in peace."

Monday 2nd June 2014

Sometimes, when the alarm woke him, he would think, just for the tiniest instance, that he was heading to the airport to travel to yet another exotic country for yet another breathless trip into the unknown. When such a lucky (maybe unlucky would be a more appropriate word) moment of clandestine inspiration struck his brain, he would pretend to mentally pack his bags: toothbrush, business notes, camera.

But not this morning. No, no, no. He wondered what was happening in Zambia right now. He'd been there once. 2006, during that glorious summer. Only for three days, mind; but Nicola and Mary had been with him. Such a beautiful little snapshot of a time.

He rolled over in bed, just wishing he didn't have to get up. In the days when he was a giant, he didn't have to drag his arse into the shower. Now he did. It was a strange existence, feeling like you're defined by the drilling alarm clock.

The water was acid rain. He leaned against the wall of the shower, letting it run down his face. It ran so smoothly, trickling like the tears of the forgotten dead.

His short-sleeved shirt, grey trousers, black shoes and red tie wanted to crush him to death. Maybe it was because they showed the drastic nature of his loss. Maybe it was because he was massively over-weight.

Just before leaving his flat, he picked up the photograph of him with his wife and daughter, taken when they were in Zambia. It pained, oh yes it did. But he forced himself to watch it every morning. He had to remember what he'd lost. Or the pain would be too great.

The bus ride (and his fellow passengers) were the same as they always were: a decrepit bunch of losers. He tried not to look at them, fearful that he would get dragged into their sphere of uselessness. He was fed up. He was obese. He just wanted to die.

But another day at work came first. Another day sitting in that grizzly little office. No hope. No future.

He got off the bus in George Square, making

straight for his work: a small software company that he provided technical support to. For a recent start-up, they were doing quite well: in the past year, they had received two grants from the Scottish Government and one from Glasgow City Council. Eight years ago, he would have been officially impressed.

He'd cried all his tears now. He'd cried the lot of them. He would be coming up to the seventh anniversary, just over two months away. But he wouldn't shed a tear that day. Maybe he'd go to The Cross Name for a pint – well, he did that nearly every night. Something more special was in order. Maybe, if he had the money, he would go to Stranraer, go for a walk by the sea.

The morning commuters, shuffling about, silently screaming their moans, were all locked in a trance of nothing-mattered-only-waiting-for-the-weekend. And Petey, he was glad to be part of them.

An old woman carrying a charity bucket approached him, asking if he had any change to spare. There was a time when he would have been more than happy to help. But he didn't have the money. Instead, he flatly told her, "No, sorry", and walked on.

It was a fairly simple story of how he had ended up like this. After losing Mary and Nicola, Petey had taken his eye off Newton-M-Wren. The financial crisis of 2008 had landed a crippling blow to the company; with his interest in it gone, it had practically collapsed overnight. He had lost most of his finances and was tossed headfirst into the world of bankruptcy. With not a penny to his name, he had been forced to apply for any job he could. After a few short-term positions, he had been offered this job here in Glasgow. With very little money, he had bought a small flat in a high-rise in the east end. He was living the life of the lost and the dispossessed.

There was only one thing in his life. Sarah. He would find that bitch, that traitor who had stolen the last relic of his daughter. He would find her and choke her to death with his bare hands.

The morning briefing in the rec room was the same. Mr MacDonald, the CEO, addressed the ragtag bunch of workers like a judge sentencing a gang to life imprisonment. He sat on the small stationary cabinet, watery eyes passing over them, trying to generate some sort of interest.

"There are a lot of things to do today, people," the very clinically obese Mr MacDonald said, clearly not seeing (or caring about) the Africa-shaped coffee stain on his shirt. (It was a wonder how the cabinet (which he used as Arthur's Seat for his briefings) didn't break under his great bulging arse. "First of all, as you all no doubt know, we have the Commonwealth Games coming up. The City Centre is going to be Ground Zero for the massive crowds, so we need to plan ahead. I'm sure you will all agree with that. Who drives in?"

A couple of hands shot up.

"Well, I suggest you try to make alternative arrangements. Very important. I will not tolerate lateness. I don't care whether the athlete of your dreams blocks the road off. Lateness will not be tolerated. Is that clear with everyone?"

There was murmured agreement.

"Good. Okay, in other news, as they say, I've been looking at a number of your reports for this new project we're involved in with the Council. Quite simply, they're not good enough. Two paragraphs is a pretty piss-poor effort. Come on, guys, this isn't college. We are a professional software company. Am I clear on this, folks?"

"Absolutely," said someone.

"Good. I'll take that as a 'yes' from all of you. We've got another project coming up with a school in Edinburgh. Peter, this should interest you. I'll be needing you to provide some expertise."

"Sure, no problem," Petey responded. "I'll get on to that. Who's working on it?"

"Maggie and Hank." Mr MacDonald barked an almighty cough. "Okay, folks, there's also the matter of..."

Petey zoned out. He reminded himself that he'd just been paid and that opened many doors to cheap pleasures. His end-of-the-month treat had been delayed due to Sally being unavailable; but she'd texted him last night to say she'd be happy to see him this evening. He focused on her. What treats did she have for him? What would she do?

When the briefing finished, Maggie, a young woman just out of university, tapped him on the shoulder. "Are you ready to get going on this?"

"Yes." Petey yawned. "I'll come to your desk in five minutes."

"Well, don't be too long. Some of us work hard here." She signalled Hank, a half-asleep intern, to come with her.

As seemed to be the usual way of things these days, Petey was the last man left in the room.

After work, he made his way to Sally's place. It was a bit of a journey. Well, it involved going to Glasgow Central and catching the train to Neilston.

At the entrance to the busy station, he stopped for a couple of minutes to smoke a cigarette. He was trying to cut down, but what was the point? He liked a smoke.

The train ride to Neilston was uneventful, but long. He supposed that was why he liked it. No random changes. Barring any disruption, a fairly consistent journey. He spent this one looking out the window, reflecting.

He had to ask himself, quite seriously, whether he was looking for Nicola and Mary, out there in the countryside somewhere.

When he arrived in Neilston, he went for a drink. Just a half-pint, a sort of tradition. He would have a few more beers later. He sat in the corner of this unremarkable pub, drinking it slowly. He still had half an hour to spare.

Sally's place was at the end of the village. Very unnoticeable. But, when he knocked on her door, and she opened up, her stunning beauty clear for all the world to see, it was clear that there was something amazing here.

"You feeling okay, Petey?" she asked, as she always did, when they were done.

"Yeah." He stretched out, pulling her closer to him. Not that he was in love with her. How could you be in love with an escort, or whore, as he preferred to say?

Sally's house was a semidetached bungalow at the end of a close. It was sparsely decorated: a few DVDs piled beside a plasma television; a tiny kitchenette with dirty plates, cups and cutlery dumped in the sink; a stained carpet (candlewax in some places) that badly needed sticking down properly.

Her bedroom was even more despairing than her house: a small chest of drawers with a bra strung over one of the knobs; a bedside light with a broken shade on the floor; a bed stripped of the sheets.

"You know, I really appreciate you coming to see me," said Sally. "I haven't been getting that many clients lately."

"You should move to the city. This is a commuter town, full of happy, settled families."

"You'd be surprised how many men are willing to cheat on their wives."

"Damn, work was tough today." Peter wanted to change subject from families. He knew how inquisitive she was. He'd told her a little of what happened, but she didn't know the whole story. Like his regular binge drinking episodes that went on for weeks after the accident. Stuff like that.

"How are your colleagues treating you?"

"Pretty shit, to be honest. Remember Maggie, who I mentioned? She's really getting on my fucking nerves. She's such a bitch. Always telling me what a mess I am."

"Why don't you report her?"

Sally (if that was her real name) had lost the fullness of her Spanish accent in the four years he'd been seeing her, but there was still a hint there. He didn't mind. He found it reassuring. Her fake body also gave him a comfort: there was no danger of human intimacy.

"What, to Mr Fat?!" he exclaimed. "He'd probably kick my arse out the building!"

"Would that be so bad?"

"Darling, this job matters to me. All I have is my career." He knew how depressed he sounded. "It's all I've got. My whole world."

"It's not all you've got. We always enjoy our sessions together."

"Of course! I'd see you more often, every day in fact, if I had more money. Don't suppose I could get you to do a cheaper rate?"

"Sorry babe, can't do that." She massaged his face with cool hands.

"I'll tell you, Sally, there was a day when I was on top of everything. I would've been seeing you all day every day. Funny how things change, isn't it?"

"It is."

Sally's phone alarm rang out it in its series of beeps. Time was up.

Saturday 7th June 2014

Petey cuddled his third pint in The Cross Name, trying to pretend the thing was warm. The cold, moist glass nipped at his palms. The atmosphere was good, though that was to be expected for a Saturday night.

He had watched documentaries about Glasgow before, years ago, cuddled up with his family. He used to tell his daughter that this was "a terrible world", as they watched relentless drunks staggering about in the cold, dark night, lost and alone in the never-ending streets. Never did he think he would end up amongst them, trapped.

There was a tickle in his gut, a very strange little voice in his head, telling him to go to Blairhill, to see that woman. He wouldn't though. Even though he lived in Shettleston, not too far away, he didn't dare go. It was like a black hole on the edge of his vision. Always there, always present.

He was lost. He was forgotten about. He had no family. No friends. Alan Stanley had disappeared from his radar. All those business contacts in all those countries... gone.

But worst bit was the guilt. If he hadn't gone and gotten drunk, self-pitying over Georgina, he would have been home much earlier. Nicola wouldn't have taken the car and driven to her friend's house with

Mary to have a cry over him. He shouldn't have touched alcohol that night. He should have had a glass of water and gone to the hotel to sleep. Then he would have been home with his family, snuggled in front of the television, with a takeaway pizza and other little niceties.

Dan and Gillian entered the pub, the disastrous young couple. He watched them, with quite a morbid fascination, as they had the same drinks they always did. And only the one each. Gillian was quite an interesting young woman: her makeup only amplified her shyness.

Mrs Malice, with her pained expression, kept an eye on them. Did she anticipate trouble?

It was definitely time to leave.

He returned to the high-rise in Shettleston just before midnight. A couple of Neds gave him the finger, yelling at him: "Ya fat bastard!" "Get ur fat arse home!" He didn't dare snap back with, "Fuck you!" They would run him down. Instead, he merely smiled and headed on up to his flat.

He sat on his armchair, looking out at the city lights until One A.M. It was funny being so high in the world, yet so low at the same time. When he finally turned in, he thought about Mary, reached out a hand.

How old would she be now? Thirteen – yeah, that sounded right. A teenager. Maybe somewhere, in some parallel universe, they were all a family. He would be meeting her first boyfriend. That old father-meets-daughter's-boyfriend thing... he would never experience that now. Actually, there were a lot of things he would never know: giving his daughter away, having grandchildren, a large family Christmas.

Sometimes, when he was coming home from work, particularly in the festive period, he would see families, all bustling along. It hurt.

Christmas was about families coming together. He didn't have anything like that. That was why he requested access to the office during the holidays, so that he could slave away. No one protested; after all, he was getting work done.

Sunday 8th June 2014

The knocking was harsh. And the mild hangover didn't help.

BANG-BANG-BANG.

"For Christ's sake!" Petey hissed. Then fear came. Neds, drug dealers. They had come for him!

He slipped on his dressing gown and cautiously ventured out into the corridor.

BANG-BANG-BANG. Harder this time. *BANG-BANG-BANG.*

He looked through the peephole, expecting (hoping?) to see a gang of Neds with knives, ready to stab him to death and steal his measly earnings. He opened the door a second later, words hanging lucidly in his throat.

"What the hell are you doing here...?" he spluttered. "How the hell you find me...?"

"Followed you from the pub," said Gillian. "It's Peter, right?"

"Yeah, that's me. Petey, if you want. Is your man with you?"

"No, he doesn't know I'm here."

"You do realise what time it is, don't you? Four in the morning." He crossed his arms. "Dan might be wondering where you are?"

"He went clubbing with his pals. He'll probably be home tomorrow, well, this afternoon." She threw a smile at him. "Listen, Peter, can I come in?"

"Why do you want to come in?"

"I need to talk to you. Something's happened. I don't know who else to turn to."

"It's Dan," she said, when they were sitting at the dining table, each with a cup of cheap supermarket coffee. "I think he's mixed up in some stuff."

"What do you expect me to do about it?" Petey rubbed his cheeks, trying to drum some life into his eyes. "Christ, you don't even know me."

"I wouldn't be here if there was someone else I could go to."

"You're a young woman. Early twenties. Surely you've got plenty of friends."

"Dan would know if I started talking to them. He's just, well, he's a great guy, but he's very controlling."

"Well, go to the police then." He let out a long yawn. "Sorry. Look, the police will help. I'm just a face you see down the pub."

"I can't!" she whimpered. She let out a sob and

wiped her eyes with the back of her wrist. "I really need to talk to you! Please!"

"Okay then. What's the matter?"

"Dan came in the other night after going out with friends. I could smell weed on him. I tried to get him to talk about it, but he shut me out. He actually got very aggressive. I love him. I'm really scared for him."

"And this is exactly the reason you should go to the police. They will help you out. I'm just a software guy. I work five days a week, Nine to Five. I'm nothing special."

"But you once were." She paused to let a bulb of coffee shoot down her throat. "You once ran your own computing empire."

"*Once*. A long time ago. I was a different person back then."

"I'm sorry for what happened."

"It's okay." He stood up and took away their mugs. "Look, I really need to be getting some sleep. I'm serious. You need to go home."

"I understand." She stared at him with her sad, milky eyes. "I need your help, Peter. He's all on his own. He's got mixed up in something terrible. I'm so scared for him. Please help him."

"Okay." He was resigned now. Buggered. "What is it you want me to do?"

"Follow him one night, see where he goes. If he's involved in something very big, if you're able to tell me what it is, I may be able to help him."

"Take my advice." He was getting tired of repeating

this now. "Go to the fucking police. They will help you."

"Dan'd hurt me."

"Then you shouldn't be in a relationship with him. Divorce the prick. Get away."

"I can't."

"Alright, it seems I can't win. Where might I find Dan, apart from The Cross Name?"

"The Gorbals. There's a small pub called The White Drill, it's very lowkey. I heard him on the phone a couple of days ago, talking about meeting someone there. Next Tuesday, around Eight. Maybe, if you go there, follow him when he leaves, you might find out who he's involved with."

"Okay, I'll go and have a look. No promises though. If I think it's too dangerous, I'll walk away and phone the police, got it?"

"Okay."

He yawned again. The cheap plastic clock on the wall seemed to tick louder with every passing second. "Listen, I need some sleep."

"Okay, sure." She took out a scrap of paper and a pen and started scribbling. "Here's my number. Text me when you've done it."

"Okay."

He saw her off at the door, promising that he would do what she requested. When she was gone, he went straight back to bed. Sleep didn't take him this time. Was he excited? Something had come up in his life at last.

Tuesday 10th June 2014

After a long day of Maggie and Hank standing over him, breathing down his neck like he was a pupil in a never-ending boarding school, he was finally away. He stopped at a pub outside Central Station for a couple of drinks, thinking about how he'd approach this task tonight.

It was a bit like a military operation: tag a suspected dealer, follow them, find out as much information as was feasibly possible, get home.

When he'd sorted everything out in his mind, he walked around the streets for a bit, no rush: he had several hours to kill. Eventually, he got bored and decided to head to The White Drill. What harm would it do, to sit inside the pub and have a few drinks? Provided he kept a low profile in a corner, Dan wouldn't see him.

The White Drill was a fairly bland pub. He'd been there a couple of times, when he'd wanted a change of scenery from The Cross Name. The punters there were unfriendly, but other than that, it was a nice place to have a couple of drinks. As they said, this was the non-student-type. The only folk who belonged here were those with no futures. He would fit right in.

He walked over the South Portland Street Suspension Bridge, passing through a tight housing estate, and then into the Gorbals. The traffic was dying down now. The smell of a distillery hung in the air like a beacon. It was a fair stretch, but not too difficult on his feeble fat legs.

A few passers-by gave him pitiful looks. He realised why: summer was dancing its full routine and he was treading the hot pavement with a thick fleece on. At the very least, he looked like an imbecile. At the very most, he must have appeared like a flat fat blob.

Upon arriving at The White Drill, he entered its cool interior, ordered a pint of lager and sat in a small corner booth.

Music was playing. Some American-girl-sounding-like-she's-on-a-mild-dose-of-helium-song. He didn't care... but it sounded so sad.

A young man with a baseball cap came in, yelling down his phone, "For fuck's sake man, screw him. He's no got enough energy to come to this party!"

Petey finished his pint and got another one. He was playing the waiting game now.

The minutes ticked by. Eight O'Clock approached like a freight train, merciless and foreboding.

He had a couple more pints and a shot of whisky. Not the cleverest thing to do.

When the hour came, he waited like a rabbit caught in headlights. Frozen.

Dan came in, in his usual huff, accompanied by a small skinny man with a shaved head. The latter didn't look well: an AIDS victim on cocaine, wearing the typical uniform around here: a white shell suit.

"Two pints of lager please," said Dan.

"It's gonna be a very big thing," said the thin man. "Remus is very proud of you."

"Remus would be proud if we stopped talking about this in public."

"Sure, no worries, pal."

"It's okay." Dan sipped his lager. "How's things anyway, Jez?"

"Aye, all right. Usual stuff. Been back and forth to Edinburgh a few times. You know, this Independence thing's really gathering pace."

"It is indeed. I forgot to ask, how's the family?"

"Aye, they're all right, pal," said Jez, rolling up a cigarette. "They're a bit stressed, but they're okay."

"Stressed? They live like kings, for Christ's sake! How can they be stressed?"

"You'd never guess."

The two of them finished their pints in complete silence. This was no ordinary get-together. Something was awry here.

Petey made sure he kept a good distance when they got up and left. But there was no need. They were too busy murmuring to one another. Like two little fishies waddling through a stream, they walked into the dusky evening. He followed them down a few streets. They had a demeanour that suggested their whole lives had been leading to wherever it was they were going. They stopped before a warehouse the size of a typical high school gym. Jez rapped on a red door and they were admitted.

Very suspicious. And he'd gone far enough. He

went back the way he came, making his way to the city centre. He wound up at The Cross Name, ordered a friendly pint, and texted Gillian on what he'd seen.

She came to his flat that night, just after Ten.

This time, he was only too eager to let her in.

Again, like they were an old married couple, they sat around the table, tea cuddled in their hands.

Gillian kicked off, a rampant outburst: "Well, this is serious, isn't it? Why didn't you go in there, take a look? Christ knows what he's up to!"

"Look at me," he said calmly. "I'm massively over-weight. I'm a borderline alcoholic. I'm not exactly at the peak of my fitness. Did you seriously expect me to infiltrate a fucking criminal headquarters or what-ever it is? Hmm?"

"Nope. Sorry, I get a little pushy."

"Maybe it's time to get the police involved."

"No, we can't do that until we know more. Are you free Saturday night?"

"Don't have anything else on."

"Look, try to take this seriously."

"I am!"

"Okay, I need you to go back to that warehouse. I need you to look inside. I need answers, Peter. I need them now."

Saturday 14th June 2014

This time, he didn't drink before the job. It was an awful sensation, when you're so sick and dizzy you don't know what's happening. But he forced himself forward. Dressed in black, he was a shadow of failure, set perfectly against the orange and dark Gorbals streets. Yes, it was warm and clammy, but the only black top he had was his fleece. His work trousers and shoes did the rest. Fuck, it was hot.

He found his way to the warehouse and hid behind a bin. He watched two men, faces concealed in shadow, walk through the doorway into the building. There was a loud, despairing shout, and the door slammed.

He had to go now.

He raised himself up and, like a terrible SAS commander, made his way over to the warehouse. As he got closer, he began to hear the groaning of machines.

Closer, nearer, whatever description you could use; that's what he was doing.

He remembered the police officer's face, the one who had told him his wife and daughter were no longer on this earth. That face was taunting. A small bully that could easily proclaim innocence. A face that could happily say it was 'just doing its duty'.

He was here! He had made it to the warehouse! It deserved a victory dance of some sort... And there was a bin, a small one, a useless thing to look at, but conveniently right underneath a window. He pulled himself up – so much effort with all the ever-so-inconvenient obesity that clung to him like an old Egyptian curse. He peeped through that window like some desperate American-high-school-prom-failure-desperate-to-fuck-a-desperate-girl loser.

A conveyer belt. Workers, wearing masks. Machinery hissing and clanking and puffing. Why were they handling small vials? An awfully big operation for something like that. Dan was there, talking with that bloke Jez. There was a man at the back, hidden behind a wide hat and overcoat: like a gangster from 1950s America. Then Dan looked up. Their eyes met.

He was falling, peeling off the bin like a seesaw tipped too far the wrong way. And he was running. Feet clapped the ground, punches to the next world. He wasn't obese now. Fear had a surprising effect.

He stopped when he was outside the Gorbals. He was in a park of some kind. No one running after him. Relief was so joyous that it made his chest hurt.

Too much. Fuck. FUCK! No, it wasn't his time.

He smiled. Beaming like a writer at their first book event. He'd been like that... an obnoxious beaming, grinning, affluent toff... seven years ago.

Suddenly he was on the floor, writhing.

Strong hands took hold of him. He was dead. Dan was going to kick him to death. He was ready. Ready to be with Nicola and Mary.

"Are you okay?" said a voice he'd silently prayed he'd never hear again.

Sarah.

He was about to reach for her, but a black curtain fell down in front of his eyes.

Sunday 15th June 2014

The instant he awoke, the vengeance, the rage, was there.

He was in a hospital bed. White sheets strapped him in like he was an astronaut on the way to the moon. Everything around him seemed white: the curtains, floor, nurses; all with a degree of ghost.

And *she* was there. She looked older, yeah, she did, but there was that youthfulness, that spirit of adventure; it clung to her like a swarm.

"Why?" he hissed. "Why'd you fucking do it?"

"What are you talking about?"

"You fucking little thief."

A nurse came in. A plump, red-faced woman, she checked something on a clipboard sandwiched amongst the mounds of fat and whistled a merry tune to herself. "You're okay," she said eventually. "Just a bit of muscle fatigue."

"I thought it was a heart attack," he said.

"No, don't worry. You're reasonably healthy. Though the doctor will probably advise you to lose some weight." The nurse turned to Sarah. "Are you family?"

"No. I'm a friend of his."

"Well, visiting hours are over."

"It's okay, nurse," said Petey, pulling himself out of bed. He disconnected the various little things. "I'm discharging myself. Where're my clothes?"

No sooner were they in the car park, when Petey

grabbed Sarah by the neck and rammed her against a nearby four-wheel drive.

"What the fuck are you doing?" she protested. "Are you out of your fucking mind?"

"Maybe."

A group of pensioners were staring their way, tut-tutting amongst themselves, alarm quivering in their little crowd. Petey gave them a hard stare and squeezed Sarah's neck harder. "Where the fuck is it?" he snarled. "Give it to me."

"I don't know what you're talking about!"

"That's not fucking good enough! Where's the chain?"

"The what?"

"The spectacles chain you stole from me seven years ago?"

"What?" Her eyes were sincere. Tearful.

"You know what I'm talking about. My late daughter made it for me. It was special, a piece of her. Where the fuck is it?"

"Peter, honestly, I'm really sorry. I don't know what you're talking about."

He let her go, the truth smacking his teeth. "I'm sorry. It's just, seven years I've been fucking lost."

"I know. I heard what happened. I'm sorry. That stuff with your wife and daughter. Christ, you look a fucking mess. I just wish there was something I could say. Really, I do."

"There's nothing that could possibly come out of your mouth that would heal those wounds. They're gone. I have nothing. Except my fucking career. That's it. There's nothing else. Nothing more."

"I can't say anything."

"That's the wisest thing you've said all day."

"Well, I'd better get back to the hotel. The protest starts at Ten."

"I'm sorry." He took her by the shoulders. "You didn't steal the chain, did you?"

"Of course I didn't!" She lowered her eyes.

"Then why did you hang over me and not help?"

"Petey, I wasn't there. I wasn't in Scotland. Honestly!"

"So, were my eyes playing tricks on me then? When I was comatose on the floor, drunk as a lord, I could swear you were there."

"Whilst you were drunk..." she hissed. "Fuck, Petey, how about a bit of common sense? Maybe you hallucinated? Look, I'm sorry. I really am. I should go."

"Okay." He took a deep breath. "I'm sorry too. You in the mood for breakfast?"

"Well, I need to be there for this fucking protest. But I'm sure they can wait a little while."

He took her to his favourite breakfast-eat-out-place. Located just outside the University of Glasgow, it was usually packed with students, but today the place was not too busy. He ordered them both a Full Scottish Breakfast with a mug of tea.

"I need to ask you a couple of things," he stated, as they took seats at a table facing the quiet-Sunday-hungover street. He shifted the salt and pepper pots to the right, and the sugar dispenser to the left. "When we met, back in Eighty-Nine, did you steal my mother's pearls? When we saw each other again in Bangkok, ten years later, did you steal the engagement ring I'd bought for Nicola? Be honest with me, Sarah. I need to know those answers."

"Yes and yes."

"Okay, explain."

"In Nineteen-Eighty-Nine, I needed the money. Really desperately. Like you can't imagine."

"I take it you sold them."

"Yes."

"Okay." He undid another button on his shirt. Damn, it was getting stuffy. "Okay. In Bangkok, did you sell the engagement ring?"

"Yes."

Despite all the hatred that had built up over the past seven years, maybe longer, he started sniggering. "Oh, for fuck's sake," he stuttered. "How the fuck are you?"

She was laughing as well, wiping happy tears from her cheeks. "Yeah, I'm good. Been travelling a lot. Seen many countries."

"That's good. That's important."

"You owe me an explanation as well. Why didn't you show up, all those years ago?"

"I take it you mean Bangkok?"

"Yes." She pushed back in her seat and folded her arms. "Tell me. I mean, you've just interrogated me for an hour. Now it's my turn to hear some answers. Explain. Come on."

"After I left the hostel, I went back to the hotel. I was going to be firm with Nicola, tell her I was leaving her. Tell her I was with someone else. But then she dropped the bombshell. She told me she was pregnant. I couldn't leave her, Sarah. Not after that. When I found the engagement ring had gone missing, everything added up. What did you expect me to do?"

"You did what you believed was the right thing to do." Her face grew solemn. "I'm sorry, I really am. About your family. I can't imagine the pain."

"Well, I'm over it." He took a long took out the window. A postal van passed them in a trundle. A group of Japanese tourists argued over a map. A young couple were having an bicker. "I got over things a long time ago."

"You don't look it."

"What, because I've put on a couple of pounds? I'm fine, Sarah. Look, I'm sorry. I want to hear about you. How long are you in town for?"

"A couple of days. It's just for this protest thing. I'm living in Malibu now. I'm really enjoying my life."

"Are you married?" he asked, straightaway dreading the answer.

"No. I'm still single."

He didn't know the appropriate response. No one could possibly know.

She was quick in with her own line: "Well, I thought you'd be relieved."

"Why would I? It's just, the loss that I suffered, it really impacted me..." He changed his tone to a far more aggressive one: "Do you remember when we met? Do you remember?"

"I remember it very much. It was a very important day for me."

Their breakfasts arrived, clunking down on the rickety, metal table.

"It was such a random thing for me to do. Just jumping out like that. Saying those three words. To this day, I have no idea why I did such a spontaneous thing."

"Neither do I. But, let's forget about it." She took his hands, an alien grasp that felt so human. Really human.

"What's the protest for?" he asked her, releasing those cool hands. He picked up a hot sausage with his fingers and bit into it, his mouth beginning to smoulder.

"Oh, there's a small furnace being built out in West Lothian." Her face became puzzled. "I don't know how to say this, but it's not exactly a big thing. Hardly any pollution will occur because of it. So strange."

"How did you get involved with it?"

"Oh, a friend of a friend is part of the protest. They emailed me a few weeks ago to see if I would be interested in coming." She dug into her food. "Couldn't exactly turn them down." She sipped her tea. "What were you up to last night?"

"Oh, me? Actually, it's pretty serious. I don't want to tell you here. Come back to my flat and I'll tell you."

"I've got the protest thing on. Can we meet up after?"

"Okay. Sorry, I didn't realise, I forgot."

"It's okay." Sarah took out a large phone, the casing the colour of the purple that had been between them all those years ago. "Oh, shit." Her face dropped. "Oh, fuck. Protest's been called off." She put the phone down on the table and took his hands again. "Guess I'm coming back to yours then."

If she looked shocked at the depravity of what he lived in, she didn't show it. She wandered around his flat, like a tourist in a foreign land, puzzled at what they were supposed to be looking for. He watched her, his eyes blurring.

He made them both a cup of tea and they sat down on the sofa.

"This isn't easy to explain," he said. But her eyes were drifting to the window, to the great metropolis outside.

"Sorry," she said, coming back to him.

He told her about Gillian and her husband, about Gillian asking him to investigate the bloke, about the warehouse in the Gorbals. When he was done, she looked slightly alarmed. He reassured her that he wasn't in any serious trouble.

"Well, you can't expect me not to be worried for you," was her response. "I mean, you're in a right fucking mess. You should have turned this Gillian away the second she came to your door."

"Will you help me?"

"What is it you want me to do?" she snapped viciously. "Clean up this filthy craphole you live in? Suck your cock?"

"I mean help with my investigation."

"So now you're Poirot or something?"

"I'm just trying to help out." He was trying to stand firm, but failing.

"No, you're not. You're just a sad fuck who needs attention. Christ, look at you! Sorry your wife and kid died, but *fucking get over it*! I've seen things on my travels, Peter, things you wouldn't believe. Poverty. War. Famine. Believe me, it's not pretty. You need to get out of this shithole, go somewhere else." She stood up and grabbed her coat from the armchair. "I'm going. Back to the fucking hostel. See some fucking life for once!"

"Don't go," he said, voice cracking with grief. "Please don't go."

Their arms were around each other seconds later. He knew that there was so much emotion and fear and betrayal between them that a relationship, any future at all between them, was as hopeless as a grain of sand lost in the ocean. Yet, they cuddled.

Their embrace was broken by a sudden rigidness that croaked through Sarah's body. Petey felt it: a silent tremor of fear.

"You okay?" he asked.

"You mentioned a warehouse in the Gorbals?"

"Yeah."

"That's a bit strange." She led him back to the sofa and held onto him. "When I ran into you, I was actually on my way to meet the guy who contacted me about the protest. He told me to meet him outside his work. Said he did shifts in a warehouse in the Gorbals."

"Come on, I think there are definitely a few warehouses in that part," he countered. "Who was this guy?"

"Hold on." She went to her coat and rummaged through the pockets, retrieving her phone. "I'm probably wrong about this, in fact I most likely am, but I have a nasty little feeling. Hold on..." She tapped a few buttons. "In his email, he always has a photo attached. Guess he likes being professional."

Petey gulped – if you can believe such a thing – when he saw the image. Though it was a tiny pinprick at the bottom of an email, the person was unmistakable. Like he'd been picked from a line-up of the damned. It was Jez.

The warehouse was lit up like it was its own miniature city, an island in the metropolis.

"That's it," said Sarah, eyes glistening. "Gosh, we're like spies, aren't we?" She nodded at their improvised black outfits. (She didn't have any black clothes with her, so he'd been forced to lend her some from his wardrobe: the black jacket and trousers he'd worn to the funeral of his wife and daughter.)

The city was quiet, a void. Traffic passed by in the background. Somewhere a lorry groaned. A dog barked.

"We've got a good vantage point here," she whispered, so seductively, in his ear.

"Yeah, but if we stayed we wouldn't get anything done, would we now?"

"Why are you doing this? This isn't your problem. You could come away with me. Come to Malibu with me. I have plenty of money, so we could both start over."

"I want to." He squeezed her hand harder. "As soon as this is done, I'll come with you. We'll put our past issues behind us. But I can't leave this. Gillian needs my help, *our* help. We have to do this."

"Speaking of which, has she replied to you?"

"No. I sent her another text just before we set out. She's probably been held up."

Sarah let out a long yawn. "Sorry." She kissed him. Full on. Sudden. Shock. "Let's go."

"Come on then."

They dashed over to the warehouse like two Cold War spies, heading straight for the bin.

The words *Christ, what am I fucking doing?* ricocheted across his brain as he climbed on top of the bin and peered through the window. The interior was dimly lit by a lamp on the far wall. Empty. The conveyer wasn't running. No workers. But there were those little vials, just a few of them bundled together at the end of the line. He tugged at the window latch. Loose.

"Fancy a little climb?" he joked nervously.

"Are you sure?" Her voice was wavering.

"Come on, where's your sense of adventure?" He grinned.

He went through first. There was a table right below the window, so there was only a two-foot drop. Despite his bulk, he got through okay. Sarah had a little more trouble, totally off-balance, nearly falling back out; but he pulled her safely through.

After giving her a kiss, he rushed over to the vials and examined them. "Strange," he remarked. "What are these?" He tried unscrewing the lid: jammed. "Sarah, can you see if you can find a knife or something?"

"Sure. What do you think's in there?"

"I have no idea."

Suddenly they were shrouded in light, a sadistic sun beating down on them. Heavy boots stomped the ground. Laughter. Cackling. A voice said, "Gotcha!"

Jez came through the doorway, followed by Dan and a bunch of five hard-looking men.

"Our plan worked!" Jez shouted. "Fuckin' hell!"

Sarah was panicking, hyperventilating.

"See, youse guys totally fell for it!" Jez clapped his hands and then directed the consort of hard men to go back outside and take positions around the warehouse. "Got things like a fucking army here."

Dan didn't go with them. He stayed by Jez's side, hands behind his back.

"This was a setup, wasn't it?" said Petey, trying to be confident and firm.

"That it was," said Dan. "I thought Gillian would make a very good ruse, if you catch my drift."

"Yes, well I believed her."

"Just let us go," Sarah whimpered. "Honestly, guys, we didn't mean any harm."

"Youse aren't goin' anywhere," said Jez. "Not til the boss says so."

"Who's this boss of yours?" demanded Petey.

"I think you'll like him." Jez looked at the doorway. "He knows you, Petey, very well."

It was the man from the other night, the one Petey had seen through the window. He wore a long over-coat the colour of cream. With his hat, jet-black trousers and shiny shoes, he looked formidable, or-ganised, psychotic and vengeful.

"Remember me?" said the man, yanking off the hat.

"What the fuck?!" spluttered Petey, voice wobbling. He heard Sarah cry out.

"It's been a long time." The scar on Donny Bell's cheek twitched, a lifeform of its own. "I have missed you so dreadfully."

"You see, it's simple," Donny began, once he, Petey and Sarah had been provided with seats (the latter two with customary rope restraints). Jez and Dan had been ordered to go outside. "In fact, it's more than simple. I never made it to America, Peter. When I was viciously assaulted at the Edinburgh International Posh Coffee-Drinking Festival, things, shall we say, unravelled for me. My whole fucking character changed. Became aggressive, bad-tempered. Regular arguments with the wife. She left me in the end. Divorce is a cunt, let me tell you. Couldn't really go to America, could I? Not with the arts council suddenly cutting their funding. The ex went though. She's having such a great time, last I heard. New husband. New York penthouse. First-class holidays to the Maldives."

"It's not my fault," said Petey. "You can't really blame things on me!"

"Maybe I can. Your girlfriend helped out a little bit as well. But we'll get onto that later. Oh, we will."

"Do you want me to feel sorry for you?"

"No." Donny stood up, paced back and forward, as if trying to summon intelligence itself, and then sat back down. "After I lost my American dream, I came back to Glasgow. Immersed myself back in its crime world. You know, it's funny, when you hear these posh twats at arts festivals saying that you can escape crime. Trust me, you can't. Over the past seven years, I've built up my profile. Now I'm Glasgow's top gangster. You can't fuck with me." He stood up again and went to a small television that had been wheeled in by Dan and Jez.

"You know, it's funny, this place has always been my home," he continued. "My home. I grew up here. Had my first kiss just a few streets away. When I first got involved with organised crime, I was known as the

'Little Bastard'. With my blonde hair, leather clothes, I was everything. Adored by the girls." He smirked. "So strange, how things change."

Donny Bell stepped over to Sarah and stroked her cheek. He looked so tired and done in. His hair had receded quite considerably since 2007; it was peppered with areas of grey. His face was pockmarked with stress and alcohol.

"How did you set this up?" asked Petey.

"What, this?" Donny went to the television. "Well, for you, Peter, Gillian was the key. I knew you wouldn't be able to resist an offer from her. As for you, Sarah, I made up a fake protest movement, got Jez to get in contact with you. He did a good job by the way. Might buy him a pint later."

"Why?" demanded Petey.

"Why? Your girlfriend: Sarah. In Nineteen-Eighty-Nine, she scarred me for life. A little piece of glass. She swung it, slashed open my cheek." Donny pushed a forefinger against the scar like it was a fleshy trophy.

"After you attacked me!" Sarah shouted at him.

"What do you mean, Sarah?" Petey stuttered. "Please tell me."

"After I met you for the first time, when I headed up to Glasgow, I met Donny Bell." She was crying openly. "He assaulted me, dragged me down to the ground. I had no choice!"

"I'm sure you didn't." Donny switched on the television and picked up a remote control. "I'm going to show you something. It may shock you a little bit.

Both of you. You see, Peter, after I had come back to my home, once my empire started building up, I obtained security footage. Strangely enough, I got some from the train station in Blairhill. Do you remember the little incident all those years ago? When you got fucking pissed?"

The television burst into life. A small video of Petey lying on the ground, drunk. Shame hung in his mind. It made him sick to watch this. Then... no, it couldn't be!... Sarah was there, kneeling next to him, rummaging through his pockets.

"You lying bitch!" Petey found himself shrieking.

"I'm sorry," were the only words that came from her. "I'm so sorry."

"Anyways, let's move on." Donny pressed the remote. The image chained to a bustling street full of partygoers. Fireworks boomed in the distance. This wasn't security footage. This was a handheld video recorder. "You should recognise this, both of you. The big millennium party in Bangkok." The crowd cleared and, for a second, there was Petey with Sarah and those three protesters. Then they were gone. Donny rewound the footage and paused it. "Since I returned to crime, after I lost everything, because of *you*, Peter, I have been plotting my revenge. I have criminal contacts all over the world. Let's just say, it was fairly easy to find someone who'd recorded footage of you. With the Bangkok video and the Blairhill video, and a bunch of other stuff, it didn't take me long to find out that you and Sarah are linked. And obviously, in Bangkok,

I can clearly see the bitch who assaulted me at the book festival. The two of you are in love. It's such a shame you drifted apart. But now, the three of us are together. And you're both going to be part of my little plan. I don't want to kill either of you; I want you both to become part of my world. This is my revenge."

"What's your master plan then, Mr Bell?" said Petey. "Come on, tell us."

"We have a little referendum coming up, not sure if you noticed." Donny switched the television off and tossed the remote to the ground. The batteries bounced out, pinging into the darkness. "You see, as much as I love being a proud Scotsman, if we do go independent, that's bad news for me. It means I'll have certain issues transporting certain... *things* between England and Scotland, and vice versa. Of course, it would be nearly impossible to directly sabotage the Independence Referendum. One has to take, shall we say, a more inventive approach." He picked up one of the vials. "You see this? Do you know what's in it? Drugs. Performance-enhancing drugs. A whole fucking mix. We have the Commonwealth Games coming up..."

"And you're going to give it to the athletes," said Petey.

"Not all of them. Just the Scottish athletes. We've paid off a few doctors to help inject them with the stuff under the pretence of medical tests. Then it's simple, an anonymous caller will tip off the police. Athletes will be arrested. Careers ruined. And the

Scottish Government will have serious questions to answer. Their referendum campaign will be in tatters, or at the very least, left with a serious dent in its side."

"Why?" Sarah stuttered. "Why are you fucking doing this to us?"

"Because we are all bound together. The three of us!"

"We're not," said Petey.

"Oh, yes, we are. When this little operation is over, you both are going to be a part of my new empire. You will understand my pain. My agony. My fear. You will be trapped here, with me, like fucking rats. I'll make sure you get involved in the gritty world of drug trafficking, properly stuck in. You'll be buried up to your fucking necks. And you will never escape. If you try and run away, my boys will fucking bury you alive. And don't think of the police for one second. They can't –"

"We will not do anything for you," said Petey, the moment a hard, earth-pounding gunshot rang out.

Boots were clamping the ground. The door burst open and armed police stormed in. "On the ground!" one of them yelled. Donny Bell was in handcuffs a heartbeat later.

Petey smiled. One hell of a risk. And it had worked.

He was with Sarah now, holding her outside the warehouse. He caught a glimpse of a body being wheeled away: Dan.

It hadn't been a complicated plan. When Gillian had first got in contact with him, he'd got in touch with the police. He'd known this was a setup. He may have been broken, but he was no pushover.

"Sorry," she whispered. "I should have told you the truth."

"It's okay."

"But I give you my word, I did not steal that chain."

"I'm sure you didn't."

Monday 16th June 2014

"So, what happens to us now?" said Sarah.

"Well, according to that police officer, we're going to get a massive payoff," said Petey, switching the kettle on. "There's a possibility we'll get a commendation of some sort as well."

The flat was cold and damp, as it had always been. Cold and bitter.

"I meant us." Sarah folded her arms.

"What 'us'?" snapped Petey. "What 'us'? You fucking lied to me! You fucking stabbed me in the back!"

"I didn't lie to you." She was crying hard again.

"Well, you said you weren't even in Scotland that summer. How can you possibly live off that bullshit?"

"Well, I suppose I'd better leave. Thanks for putting me up for the night."

"So, why didn't you help me out? I mean, I was drunk as fuck. All over the place."

"And you blame me for that?"

"Well, yes. I mean, you go off on a fucking bender and you expect me to help you up?" She was snatching her things up, like they were the baggage of her life. Like they were the pain of a thousand pinpricks.

But she calmed down. When she was calm, she always made sense. Just as she did now:

"Okay, I'm going to make this clear. Clear as daylight. You need help. Okay? And I want to help you. I want to be there for you. Get you through this."

"I know."

"No, you don't. So, I'm going to make a little arrangement. I need to head back to the States. But I want you to come with me. I want you to come to the States with me. I want you back in my life. I'll get you sorted out. I'll get you the help you need. What do you want to do? It's totally up to you."

Friday 19th September 2014

He awoke in what he knew would be his final time in this flat. It felt like a prison to him. A prison for his soul.

He showered, dressed, made sure he had everything. The night before, he'd put his bags by the door, a mental preparation for his departure to a new life.

A small breakfast, made up of toast and coffee, constituted his leaving party. He sat alone, knowing that this chapter of his life was nearly at an end.

He'd been out the night before, a farewell drink at The Cross Name, just the one, since he was driving today. It had been full of Scots singing their famous national anthem, quite drunkenly. Petey had disappeared before Nine P.M., walking out of the bar, giving Mrs Malice a glance as long as a nanosecond. Why would he try and say farewell? Why, for that matter, would Mrs Malice want to say goodbye to him?

Gillian had been arrested a few days after the warehouse incident. Grief-stricken, she had been charged alongside Donny Bell, Jez (real name Jeremiah Smith) and the rest of the hard nuts. The offences were as varied as the streets of the Gorbals: drug possession, drug trafficking, drug use, etc.

He and Sarah had each been given £20,000 from the police. The chief investigating officer leading the investigation had called them both, "Courageous." They had both given interviews to the press (Sarah via the phone from the U.S.). They were heroes, apparently. True heroes.

But today, he was going to escape. He'd arranged for a number of his belongings to be shipped to the States. He was going to rendezvous with Sarah in London on the morning of the 20th September. They would fly out that evening. A simple plan.

After finishing breakfast, he washed up, then put the utensils into his small rucksack, one he typically sometimes took to work. Not anymore. He would never work for that wretched organisation again.

He ferried his bags down to the rental car. It took four trips. At long last, he took one final look around the flat. He would leave these painful memories here, a grave for the damned. He locked up and went down to the car (he would post the flat keys back to the council). He drove off from the estate and started heading towards the motorway.

He went to Blairhill. He had never been back in all these seven years, even though it was practically next door to him. He remembered everything about its layout, just like the back of his hand. He would say goodbye to her. No, this was stupid. Turn around. But it was too late. Her house was up ahead. Damn, the place was the same as it had been seven years previously. All the same stuff. A time capsule. He pulled up on the opposite side of the street and watched, transfixed. *Turn around. Drive to London.*

The door opened and his heart stopped. There she was, Yvonne, carrying... the same handbag as she'd been holding all those years before? She'd lost some weight. She seemed happy. Peaceful. A child ran out, nearly stumbling. And he saw that there wasn't a man. And the child seemed... between six and seven? He'd given Yvonne what she wanted. He'd given her what she had dreamt of for so many years. And the child had something around her neck. Yvonne was on her mobile to somebody, remarking how the people of Scotland had voted to reject independence. And the child had something around her neck. No, it couldn't be. Was that a golden necklace?

Yvonne saw him. Alarm flashed.

He switched the engine on, turned the car in the road, stalled, all the while Yvonne approaching him like the fate of inevitability, and he turned the engine off, then on again, and he moved off. Was she scream-ing something at him?

He thought about visiting his woman in Neilston. And he did. Turned up at her door. Asked if he could have one final session. He was leaving, forever. He was never coming back. And she smiled and gave him a free session and fucked him like he'd never been fucked. When they were done, she shook his hand.

Then he was on his way. He was out of the Glasgow area. He was heading south. The road, the car, the traf-fic, all a blur. Suddenly, he was in the Lake District. The past seven years were all a blur. A vicious blur of grief and pain.

Now he was heading home. He was getting there, bit by bit. He was coming home.

Redux

Texas

Friday 5th October 2018

The desert could be so open at times. Dark, foreboding, punctuated by the lights of distant towns and cities.

He drove through it like it was nothing. He wasn't affected by it. He didn't care for any of the pain it inflicted. He just wanted to get there.

The lights of a passing car dazzled him.

Who was she?

He didn't know, fully. She was a loner. Someone looking in the darkness, someone looking for darkness.

She would fit in perfectly here.

It was raining now. Coming on fast.

Petey turned the wipers to maximum. He took a deep breath, feeling his lungs twang.

There was nothing on the radio, no songs, no nothing.

Petey's life was different now.

He'd recovered. He'd changed.

The weight was gone. Lifting bulky things in the gym, running, swimming: all a result of Sarah's unflinching loyalty. She had helped with the grief and the loss. Together, they had rebuilt.

So why was he driving to Houston? Why was he driving to Houston for a one-night stand with a woman he'd met online? And why had he left Sarah, his wife, back home in Malibu, with a careful lie that he was going to meet an old friend?

Over the past four years, Sarah's environmental campaign group, Awareness Of Orange, had grown. She currently employed over three-hundred people worldwide. The sole aim was to make the public aware of the dangers of pollution, etc. But the important thing was this: it made them a hell of a lot of money, which meant that they could both live a comfortable lifestyle.

She was his saviour; there was no doubt of that.

But she also made him uncomfortable, unsettled. She made him feel inferior. After all, what had he done with his life?

When you spend a life not taking chances, something builds up inside you. A horrid feeling of gruesome churning. Sarah had done so much with her life. It seemed like every time he talked to her, she had something new to say, some new corner of the world she'd been to. What did he have to offer: *Yes, I travelled the world frequently... to sell computers.* It was clear: she made him uneasy.

There was a place coming up: Seymour. A city of some sort. He would stop there for the night. Find a motel or something.

There was another thing, too.

There had been a letter, addressed to him. It had arrived… in a pristine envelope… delivered by an unsmiling man only too eager to be gone.

Sarah had been out for lunch with a friend, so Petey had opened it in their luxurious lounge – complete with, of course, glass table, glass ornaments, a photograph on the wall that showed a white sandy beach with overhanging palm trees (a very expensive piece from an art exhibition they'd attended just after he'd moved here), and a number of bottles of wine in a rack. The contents had slid out like the merciless calling of fate.

It had been a notice of legal action from Georgina's younger brother, Trevor, who had become a successful lawyer, complete with the plush car. He, Peter McGough, was being sued for her suicide.

Why had it come now? Well, first, obviously Trevor himself: he was family and he was rich. A case like this needed commitment and money. The second reason – and Petey had found some of this out after a lengthy discussion with Alan Stanley on the phone – was a series of bizarre coincidences and fates, a whole network of improbabilities, that had alerted Trevor to the fact that it was he, Peter McGough, who was responsible for Georgina's tragic, brutal death on the 19th May 1993.

The motel was small, very reclusive.

But he'd managed to get a room.

He went out and got himself a hamburger and fries.

Sitting alone in the fast-food restaurant, he watched the last hour of the day play out like a forgotten Eighties commercial.

He was pleased that he had reconnected with Alan Stanley. They were good together. They were close friends. Shortly after moving to the United States, Alan had visited; they'd met up at a restaurant, sharing food, tears and memories. Petey's childhood friend had remarried: a middle-aged fitness instructor who still had the allure of her twenties. In short, the two men had recovered. Okay, Petey himself had a few 'insecurity' issues, but that was nothing. Unfortunately, it tends to be unclean past mistakes that lead to the unravelling of a beautiful present.

And how had this happened? Why was he in this legal mess with Georgina's brother? A chance meeting between two strangers: Iain and Olga.

Iain Melrose was born on the 10th February 1988. With three older brothers, he quickly learned to show his strength.

He grew up in Airdrie, near Glasgow, just outside the town centre. He did reasonably well at school, obtaining a decent selection of grades. Enough to get him into the University of Edinburgh to study zoology. After a childhood spent mostly alone, Edinburgh – which he'd only visited once during a school trip to Portobello many years before – seemed like another world.

Upon arriving at university, he quickly became

friends with a large number of people, including staff. He was well-spoken, relaxed, but not confident. His ability to interact with girls he liked was, to say the least, pretty poor. It led to him being mocked by his closest friends: Rick and Giz. How they loved to tease him...

In his desperation to appear attractive to the opposite sex, he regularly went drinking with the two of them, constantly trying (and constantly failing) to chat up women.

On the evening of the 22nd August 2007, just prior to starting his second year at university, he met up with Rick and Giz for drinks. Of course, what started as a casual chat over beers quickly escalated into a full-flung night out.

On their way to a pub, they met this guy on the bridge. He was drunk as fuck, but what did it matter? He was offering to buy them rounds! After the embarrassing episode in this pub, the man left. Rick and Giz were only too happy to see the back of him. But Iain was too curious.

He followed the man as he stumbled his way through the streets to the Edinburgh International Book Festival. The man was chucked out by a very angry security guard, falling over onto the road. A car blared its horn, narrowly missing him. Iain immediately rushed over, and so did another person.

She wore the uniform of a festival volunteer.

"It's okay," the woman said, squeezing the man's hand. "You're okay."

"You know him?" Iain asked.

"Yes, he was here earlier today." Her accent was thick Eastern European. Very thick. "I think we should leave him."

"We shouldn't, he might get himself killed."

"No, we leave him. You come with me now. We need to leave." She held out a cold, damp hand. "My name is Olga."

Olga Samson was born on the 15th October 1987.

Her mother, Elena, was Bulgarian, a proud one at that. Her whole life, she had worked as a seamstress. She took a great deal of enjoyment from it, a craft that, in her opinion, everyone should know.

Her father, Rodney, was a Cornishman, born and bred in Truro. He was a doctor, from a big family of doctors. It was often said that anyone who lived in Truro had had at least one drink with one of the Samsons.

The two of them met when the latter was in Sofia for a medical conference in 1985. Olga's mother had been assisting in the hanging up of curtains at the conference centre. Quite a clumsy soul, she hadn't attached one of the curtains properly and it had fallen on Rodney as he walked by. Normally, anger would have flown like a red river; but there was attraction ricocheted between them. After a few lines of apology, he'd invited her to get coffee at the end of the day. Coffee had turned to dinner. Within a few days, they had fallen deeply in love. Within a few months, they were engaged.

Elena came to the U.K. and moved in with Rodney in his grandiose house on the edge of Truro. He swore that he would give her "a proper Cornish experience". After the two of them were married in a lavish ceremony, attended by large numbers of their respective families, they settled down and began the process of starting a family, resulting in the birth of Olga.

Olga attended a nearby primary school and quickly picked up English. Her mother insisted that she spend at least two months a year during the summer in Bulgaria with extended family. This insistence, coupled with Rodney being absent a lot (at work, various conferences around the U.K., and regularly seeing a prostitute in deepest, darkest Devon (who, by the way, was the aunt of the escort Petey had seen during his years in Glasgow)), meant that Olga not only learned Bulgarian, but developed a thick Bulgarian accent.

After primary school, she moved to a prestigious high school, where she achieved good grades in her classes and made strong friends. Her teachers regularly referred to her as "top of her class", "a gold star". She was destined for a brilliant future.

Sadly though, Rodney was murdered by a patient in his practice in 2003. He'd refused to prescribe her antidepressants (sensing she was addicted to them). In response, she had, with a surprising piece of strength, lifted his Newton-M-Wren computer off his desk and smashed it over his head, killing him instantly.

Rodney hadn't quite got around to sorting out life insurance. As a result, Elena and Olga were forced to move to Cardiff. Olga finished her education in a fairly rundown school there. Here, she was frequently bullied. On numerous occasions, she was beaten up by a gang of girls who enjoyed mocking her accent. Her grades suffered. On leaving school, she worked in dead-end jobs for a bit, but was eventually accepted to study engineering at the University of Glasgow.

In the summer of 2007, instead of electing to return to Bulgaria, she decided to volunteer at the Edinburgh International Book Festival, in the hopes that it would advance her CV somewhat.

That night, the 22nd August 2007, these two characters quickly scarpered.

It was Olga's last day at the festival anyway. If those in charge got pissed off, well, what could they do? The next day, she would be heading back to Cardiff to be with her mother for a bit before returning to university.

They spent the night wandering around the city together. They bonded, discussing music, politics, science, the latest movies, literary nonsense. They became attracted to one another, sleeping together.

A relationship quickly blossomed, faster than they could have imagined.

Over the next three years, they made numerous pledges towards each other, becoming engaged in the summer of 2010.

But on the 7th September 2010, whilst they were visiting Dundee to buy a present for Iain's mum's birthday, they were caught up in torrential rain. Despite the fact that businesses were being evacuated, they wandered into Seagate to have a look around. Olga slipped and banged her head on the kerb. She was rushed to hospital, but was sadly pronounced dead later that day.

Iain became a truly broken man. Over the next two years, he entered into a deep depression. He was hospitalised on numerous occasions, much to the dismay of his family, who eventually grew distant from him.

In September 2012, he began to realise that Olga would have wanted for him to keep going with his life. He took the prescribed medication and spent the last few months of 2012 reconnecting with his family.

In January 2013, he took a trip to Budapest. He stayed for five nights in a backpackers' hostel. During his time there, he made a connection with an American student called Herbert Heywood. (He had decided to travel Europe for a bit to get away from his annoying girlfriend (who desperately wanted to be his "forever wife") and to experience something new.)

Coincidences, it seems, tend to run in parallel lines. Herbert happened to be staying in Budapest, in this measly hostel, for the exact same period as Iain. They became good friends and Herbert invited him to visit his family in Cleveland, Ohio, that summer. Iain was only too glad to accept. They swapped details and, after a few days of exploring Budapest, said a sad farewell. Iain flew home, but Herbert continued on his travels.

In June 2013, Iain flew to the United States. They

had a most excellent two weeks, going out for dinners, chilling out with beers, barbeques, swimming. The whole trip was capped with a fine cherry when Iain and Herbert did a sneaky trip to New York for two nights. After returning from the metropolis, they spent the last two days at the Heywood family home.

On the last night, at a big family dinner (thankfully Herbert's obsessed girlfriend had been invited to a movie night with friends (which just showed how much she loved him)), there was a big discussion on the business world, kicked off by Herbert's father, Claude, a prominent investment banker with connections in Wall Street. Claude told the eager family crowd that the 2008 Financial Crisis had impacted every corner of the planet... and then proceeded to list a few examples of businesses that had fallen, like a solemn-faced sheriff naming a list of victims in a massive train crash. When Claude had finished, Herbert's brother, Jens, said to his father that he had forgotten perhaps the most key casualty: Newton-M-Wren. There was a heavy discussion about Newton-M-Wren, everyone with their own little chip to add. The line of conversation moved on to its former CEO, a certain Peter McGough. All the Heywoods agreed that his personal loss (i.e., news of the horrific accident that had made headlines in a number of newspapers and television channels) had affected his ability to govern the company and the Financial Crisis had driven a spear into the company's heart. But it wasn't until Herbert's youngest brother, Ira, showed everyone a picture of Peter McGough on his phone that Iain recognised him. Rekindling the sad memories of the night he met Olga, he told the Heywoods how he and his friends had discovered him drunk on a bridge in Edinburgh. After going to the pub with him, the CEO had brazenly blurted that he still felt guilty over going to meet a girl on North Bridge, instead of looking after his girlfriend, Georgina, who later committed suicide by jumping in front of a train at... Blairhill or something? This really created an interesting line of conversation and for the next hour everyone talked about Peter McGough. Claude had read his book and was most taken aback by these revelations. Eventually, however, the night grew old and everyone retired to their beds.

The next day, Iain went home. But he kept doing return visits. Herbert came to visit him too. Soon they were inseparable friends.

Herbert got engaged in March 2014 (there was a little pressure from his "I wanna be with you" girlfriend). At the wedding in July 2014, Herbert introduced Iain to one of his new wife's friends, Tracy. The two of them clicked instantly, becoming friends within minutes, and lovers within days. In February 2015, Iain and Tracy became engaged and hosted a quiet ceremony at a remote Scottish castle in October 2015.

At Iain's wedding, Claude Heywood was persuaded by his wife, Ursula, to write a book on the 2008 Financial Crisis. In November 2016, after a long year of researching and writing, the book was snapped up by a prominent publisher. In August 2017, at the Edinburgh International Book Festival, he was asked a question by an audience member on Newton-M-Wren (which featured prominently in the book). In that moment, Claude recalled the conversation a number of years before at the family table, something about Mr Peter McGough being a nervous drunk, who had neglected his girlfriend, Georgina. Georgina ended up committing suicide, whilst he, Peter McGough, went to meet a girl on North Bridge.

The lady who asked the question was a Mrs Erica Pollock. Her daughter, Maria, was about to start university in Glasgow, studying law. Mrs Pollock bought a copy of the book *2008: The Year That Everything Changed* and gave it to Maria as a going-away-to-university present. The night before Maria set off, they went out for a mother-and-daughter-tearful-goodbye dinner. Casual chat often takes varied courses and Erica Pollock suddenly related the tale of Georgina to her daughter.

In April 2018, towards the end of her first year, Maria went out for drinks with her friends in The Cross Name. Mrs Malice, ever bitterer, served them cold, white wines. For some reason, their conversation drifted to the pain of leaving the family home. Maria related the story that her mother, most likely in an attempt to ensure that she, Maria, would not succumb to depression at university, told her at the going-away-to-university dinner. The mention of Peter McGough set the nerves of her friends ablaze and the tale spread like an Australian bushfire at the university the next day. Trevor, the brother of Georgina, happened to be doing a guest lecture on their course. And when he found out about it, he made some phone calls and the legal action began.

So that was one of the reasons why Petey was running away.

He went back to the motel in a daze, fairly annoyed about the whole ridiculous legal action nonsense. It was a load of bollocks.

A police car whizzed by, lights dazzling the whole area. Why did they need to be so bloody bright? He nearly tripped over because of their ferocity. Righting himself, he continued in the direction of the motel.

He was nearly there, just a hundred yards or so, when a girl cut across him.

"Watch where you're going, mister!" she snapped.

"Sorry, my mistake," he grumbled.

"I bet!" the girl shot at him, walking off into the night.

When he got back to his room, he stripped off and dashed under his covers. But sleep was hard coming; a very reluctant visitor. At one o'clock in the morning, he still couldn't drift under. He gave up, slipped his clothes back on and wandered off in search of adventure.

Saturday 6th October 2018

The streets of Seymour did have a haunted nature about them. That feeling when you're not quite sure if something is absent, but when you try to think about what it could be, your mind draws a blank.

He walked, hands in pockets, like he was truly lost. Dogs barked, a baby cried, a car screeched, a guitar strummed (somewhere – and on a loudspeaker, of course), a loudmouthed probably-quite-rich couple argued over insurance.

The sky lit up as a firework exploded, multi-coloured stars falling like teardrops.

He started towards the direction of the launch, feeling mildly curious.

There was music booming. It snaked its way to him, wrapping around his throat. He was being drawn into this temptation.

It was clear that it was a high school party of some kind. The parents were away and some rich kid had gotten all his mates to come over. There was dancing, another firework, a swimming pool (with a fat specky kid jumping in), a cocky-looking guy chatting up three girls.

The party was being held in what could be supposed to be your typical American middle-class suburban home. The actual house was basic: two floors, a number of windows (through which it was possible to see a few people drinking various alcoholic substances), and a red door (opened, with a lonely-looking loser hanging from it and puking onto the driveway). But the icing on the cake was the garden. It wasn't at the back, which one would normally expect, but it was situated at the left-hand-side of the house. A wall kept it sealed off from the rest of the world, but a black gate that allowed prompt access was open. Thus, Petey was able to see inside.

He smirked, admiring the cheeky nature of it, and walked off.

"Hey man!" a voice called; even the words were drunk. "Man, come on! Join the party!"

Petey turned around, giving them a curt shake of the head, and then continued on his way. But the thrill of it was too much. He turned about and said that he would be most delighted to join them, and then proceeded to pass through the gate.

"I must be the oldest person here!" Petey said, by means of a joke, as Brett, the athletic son of the couple who owned the house, handed him a beer.

"You're never too old to have some fun!" Brett shouted, slapping him hard on the shoulder.

The two of them were sat on deckchairs, at a dark corner of the garden, watching the revellers stagger around. The fat kid jumped into the pool, probably for the hundredth time, a court jester for the dumb and dim-witted.

"So, you're glad you came along, right?" said Brett. "I know Jordan can be a total jerk, but he's cool."

"Well, he was cool enough to persuade me to come inside." Petey took a sip of the cold stuff. "I'm glad to be here. Life's a total fucker at the moment."

"Tell me about it. It's good to have some different

company for once. We're all in our last year of high school. We're all gonna go different directions soon."

"You don't mind if I just stay here and drink? I'm not fancying jumping around or anything."

"That's cool man. I'm doing the same."

Two guys changed the digital device on a large speaker. Techno music babbled out. A group of girls in miniskirts automatically danced faster, as though their lives were connected to this drunken display. The fat kid picked out another rocket and placed it in the launcher. The fuse was lit and he ran for cover. The firework screamed its way up the heavens and shattered the air.

Petey and Brett chatted for a bit more. It turned out that Brett was on the cusp of being offered a big athletic scholarship in Seattle. The future was big for him. All the girls fancied him, much to the dismay of his girlfriend, Jilly.

Eventually, Petey did feel a little tired and decided to leave. He shook hands with Brett and left the garden party. He'd only had the two beers, but his head did feel a little fuzzy.

He became aware of footsteps behind him and mild sobbing. He turned to see who it was: a blonde girl, from the party; yeah, she'd been one of the dancing miniskirts.

"Are you okay?" he asked.

"I'm fine," she responded.

"Well, unless you're very good at faking things, it's pretty clear you're not."

"What were you even fucking doing at our party?" she said accusingly. "Never mind. Look, unless you can help heal a broken heart, fuck off."

"Maybe I can help."

"In that case, you'd better follow my lead. You're about to meet my ex-boyfriend."

She talked rapidly as they went along, in a voice that suggested insecurity. When Petey had first seen her, he'd thought of her as the cheerleader type, adored by all the guys. But as she went on, muttering about this and that, he increasingly got the impression that she was geeky, covered up by a thin layer of beauty. Her walk, her steps, were that of one of those Eighties high school losers, afraid of everything, afraid of the very nature of their existence. Timid, shaking, barely there.

"Have you ever heard *The Legend of the Redux*?" she asked him.

"Can't say that I have."

They crossed the road. Petey narrowly missed a puddle, his shoes dancing at its edge. The girl linked arms with him, pulling him tight to her.

"My name's Kate," she said. "So, have you heard it?"

"What, this legend?"

"Hmm."

"As I said, I haven't."

"Well, it's a good story." Kate let out a mighty cough. "Sorry, darn cigarettes. Darn things. You'll hear the story later, when we meet my ex."

"Can't wait."

"So, what's your name."

"Peter McGough."

"Wait, aren't you that computer guy?"

"Yeah, that's me."

"Ah, I'm so sorry. Your wife and kid. Really sorry."

"It's okay. It was a long time ago, Kate." Already the flashbacks of the police at his door were springing into his mind like toxic jumping beans. "So, where are we going?"

"My house."

"Cool. I take it your parents aren't home."

"Nope. They're away in France, visiting my grandparents."

"Ooh, France. Lovely place."

"You typical Brits always say shit like that. Just so you can fuck French girls."

"That's not typical for me. I was never very good at picking up girls."

"I don't believe that."

"Believe it or not, that's the truth."

"Same here." Kate stopped, breathed in, then led them both forward again. "Spent my childhood as a bratty little cunt. Parents hated me. Bullied at school. No boys wanted to be seen near me. It'd make them uncool. I spent so much time on my own. The library became my best friend. But I was happy. So long as I had the books, I was okay. Funny how things change, isn't it?"

"What happened?" He suddenly found himself deeply and utterly worried about her, like she was a concealed lover. Now that abnormal existence was about to be exposed.

"It was Thursday, the Twenty-Sixth of February, Two-Thousand-And-Fifteen," she said. "We had a new arrival at our school. Timothy, or Timmy, as he liked to be called. He was this English dude, this geeky little kid, who'd come as part of a foreign exchange. I'd been up late the night before, masturbating to a social media picture of this guy I liked in class. Fuck, I really went for it, you should've seen me. But, anyway, I saw Timothy standing at the back of Mrs Chandler's science class. Didn't notice him at first, until we'd all sat down and Mrs Chandler made Timmy come up to the front. She introduced him. Told us to be nice to him. Treat him with respect. He was only going to be here for three months.

"I didn't talk with him much, at first, just spent the time getting on with my work, trying to make something of myself. You should get to know the American education system, Peter; you either triumph or you fall to oblivion. If you fail, you end up working as a labourer. That's the best-case scenario. The worst is landing up on death row."

"But, anyway, on March the Sixteenth, a Monday, I was heading into school on the bus. There's a girl, Tiffany, who always used to taunt me. She was going for it that day, leaning over me, calling me a whore, dirty little slut, a filthy little cunt. Fuck, she was a nasty little cunt herself. Suddenly, I heard this voice. This English voice. This lovely English voice. So smooth and milky. Timmy told Tiffany to go away. Tiffany got really aggressive with him, told him to mind his own business. But Timmy stood his ground. She backed down. Timmy checked whether I was okay, then returned to his seat. After school that day, I ran into Timmy outside the gates. We ended up walking and talking and he told me his story..."

Petey found himself listening intently. He'd thought Kate was off her head, drunk as anything, but the story she told was intricate, interesting and on the borderline of fanatical...

Timothy Kieran Pike was born on the 12th May 2001 – coincidentally the same day as Kate – in a rough housing estate in the east end of London. He was brought up by kindly parents, but they were in severe poverty, barely able to put food on the table.

Life for Timmy was okay. He was educated at a nearby primary school, where he got on well with his teachers and made good friends with his fellow pupils, though he failed to form any lasting friendships.

His parents struggled to provide for him, but they gave it everything they had. His father, Graham, worked nightshifts at a construction site. His mother, Andrea, cleaned offices around London.

But, as chance would have it, in late 2006 Andrea got a cleaning job in one of Newton-M-Wren's offices in the south of London. The wages were quite decent, enough for the three of them to go on a little two-day holiday to Norfolk.

But in 2008, the Financial Crisis struck. Newton-M-Wren was gone. Andrea not only lost her job there, but her other jobs also vanished. Graham's construction firm became another casualty...

On her last day at Newton-M-Wren, as she was gathering her things, Andrea spotted a lottery ticket on the floor. It had been filled out. For the hell of it, she tried her luck. To say that she was surprised when she got the 5 Million Jackpot would be an understatement.

Life changed very quickly for the Pikes: they moved to a posh house in Kent and sent Timmy to a proper education.

Graham was adamant that Timothy would have a good chance at life. When his son moved up to secondary school, Graham arranged with the headteacher to have him sent on an exchange to the United States. The headteacher, Mr Gordon Elsmere, said that whilst it was an amazing idea, the school didn't operate such a scheme. But when Graham mentioned the word 'legal', Mr Elsmere made a few phone calls and got an exchange for three months organised with a school in Texas. Regretfully, however, Timothy would have to be a bit older before he was able to go.

In February 2015, Timothy Pike set off for America in search of new frontiers.

"We became really good friends, really fast," said Kate, babbling like a chipmunk. "I mean it. We hung out together all the time. Then, one day, we went to the mall for ice-cream and he kissed me. My first kiss. My first tender kiss. We were just so happy. Every day was like a dream. But as the days passed, him leaving came closer. A few nights before he left, in the warm air, we made love in my bedroom. It was so beautiful. It was like the whole world was screaming. When he left, the day he left, the Twenty-Seventh of May, just before he went to the airport, he told me that he loved me and that he would see me again. Then he was gone.

"For two years, I waited. He'd given me his address and phone number. He didn't have social media. For a year, I phoned him, no answer. I wrote letters from the bottom of my heart. No response. Then, exactly two years after his departure, the Twenty-Seventh of May Two-Thousand-And-Seventeen, a letter arrived. From him. It had the words *I love you* written at the top. Immediately below were the words: *Solve the Mystery of the Redux and I shall be forever yours. Timothy.* A week later, I received a package, from him, his address. It was a story, entitled *The Legend of the Redux.*

"Now you, Mr McGough, are going to help me solve it."

Kate's house was much like Brett's: same design of walls, same window layout; but there was no garden wall at the side; no happiness to it; no hope; no future. It was merely a failed and bitter copy of a dream.

They went inside, past numerous bookshelves, depleted ready meal packs, a small stand with several family photos on (some on a beach. Malibu?), a rather disturbing ornament of a two-headed Labrador, and a rather out-of-place packet of super-size condoms. The lounge looked like a drug den: two threadbare armchairs, a broken coffee table, and a plasma television tucked in the corner.

"Where's this ex-boyfriend of yours?" he asked.

"You'll see. Now, sit."

He plonked himself down in one of the armchairs, watching Kate go across the lounge to the television. She removed a small box from behind it, collapsed onto the other chair and slapped the box down on her lab. It was a curious little object: intricate patterns, swirls, vortexes, shapes and colours coated its lid and sides. The box itself was made of black wood, polished over, beautifully; it shone like a black star. She opened it up, the hinge creaking like a billion ages of stories, and removed several A4 sheets of paper stapled together. "*The Legend of the Redux*," she explained. "Have a read."

He took it from her and started at the first page, like an ancient professor about to grade the last of the exam papers before the summer recess.

In 1981, in a small town in southwest Texas called Viewpoint, there was a teenager called John Redux. He attended Viewpoint High School. Barely able to maintain eye contact, he was regularly bullied and had very few friends.

Life would have continued that way if it wasn't for the arrival of a girl called Gertrude...

"Where's the rest of it?" said Petey.

"What?" said Kate.

Both of them sat there like two drug users, unable to contemplate the simplest things.

"The rest of the story." He thumped the bundle with his knuckles. "You've only given me a few lines here."

"Bullshit. Can't you see how John and Gertrude fell in love? Oh, they loved each other so much!" Tears were creeping out of her eyes. "That story's all I've got!"

"Where's your ex-boyfriend?" he asked gently. "There isn't one, is there?"

She shook her head. Somewhere, a truck's brakes screeched.

She was a liar. There was no Timmy. He didn't even have to interrogate her on that. She was a lonely, aggressive teenager. Delusional. She wanted to believe in this so much that it had taken over her like a parasite.

"This isn't even your parents' home, is it?"

Her silence told all.

"What are you, a street child?" Why was he becoming more and more angry at her? As if he had been taken into this wild tale, becoming dependent on it like food? As if this dependency had translated into a vicious equation. A=B=Existence.

His barrage of volcanic anger continued:

"How dare you take me in like this and lie to me!"

He was becoming a father figure.

"I trusted you!"

She was whimpering. Voice low. A shadow. "Don't leave me," she pleaded.

"Listen, you need help," he told her.

"No, I don't. I need Timmy!"

"Timmy isn't real!"

"He is!"

"I'm going to give you some advice and I suggest you listen to it." He stood up and yawned. "Christ, I'm fucking tired." He handed the 'legend' back to her. "Put pen to paper. Write it down."

"What do you mean?"

"What do you think I mean? I'm talking about writing it down, a story. You quite clearly have one hell of an imagination."

"Fuck you!" She wiped her cheeks with a dirty sleeve. "Seriously, man, fuck you!"

"I've given you my advice!"

"Fuck off!"

He was only too pleased to. He left the house, greeting the early hours of the morning by breathing in deeply, tasting that sweet, fresh air with his soul.

He didn't know who this girl was. Some loser who'd never done anything, condemned to spend her life never achieving more than getting a deal on a few bottles of vodka. A lost life. That was the appropriate expression.

When he reached the motel, he was straight under the covers. And this time he slept.

Leaving Seymour with a belly full of pancakes and orange juice, he felt a renewed sense of determination. He would get to Houston and meet this woman. He would live. He would actually feel the buzz of life zap through his blood and muscles.

He stopped at a gas station to fill up his tank. Before departing, he phoned his wife to let her know that his trip was going to plan. It was always a joy to report back to home. There's nothing that can quite beat the feeling of telling your loved ones that you are well, and hearing their soft voice on the other end.

On the highway, he picked up speed. The aircon was at full blast. His cotton shirt billowed like a flag on a clifftop. He turned on the radio; country music leapt out of the speakers. He leaned back, let his muscles relax.

Something caught his eye. Up ahead. A glint. A diamond sparkle.

He swerved, wheel to the left.

"Shit!" he screamed.

The broken bottle missed the left wheels, but scraped the front right one instead. There was an almighty crack as the tyre exploded. He slammed the brakes. The car shuddered. He veered off the highway, into the rough ground beyond: a territory for the damned.

"No, no, no," he groaned, as the car snapped to a halt, a cloud of dust ascending and preparing for its billowing descent. He stepped outside. The air was warm, but his blood was cold. He fished out his phone. No signal. The highway was devoid of cars and trucks.

Nothing moved. He was truly, utterly, without a single shred of doubt, alone.

Morning shifted to afternoon with the grace of a fresh-off-the-line car changing from third to fourth gears. Evening came like the gradual slowing of a rusty, unwanted car to a deathly stop. The stars were beginning to show, hateful little pinpricks enjoying taunting him with their warmth.

Petey waited outside, standing at the edge of the road, praying that someone would come. What he would give for bright, sparkling headlamps... When it got too cold, he climbed back inside the car, huddling beneath his jacket. Apart from a half-empty bottle of water, he had nothing else to drink, and no food.

Night came on in its ever-familiar hug.

He watched the stars twinkle, trying to pick out the constellations. He'd never been very good at it. On a school trip when he was twelve, he and his class had been taken to a remote field in the north of Oxfordshire. Their task had been to try and identify as many constellations as they could. Everyone had succeeded in identifying at least three. But Petey just couldn't do it. He'd tried, he'd really tried; but the images and connections refused to form in his mind. A solid telling-off from the teacher the next day didn't help.

But now, as he looked at the mass above him, he could begin to make a few out. It was like they'd been there all that time, waiting for him, waiting to reveal themselves, secrets in the sky.

He turned on the engine for a few minutes, blasting the car with hot air. He rubbed his arms and shivered.

When had he last been like this, alone beneath the sky? A few weeks after Sarah had loved and left him at the bus stop, he'd gone into the middle of a field nearby and cried up at the stars. Damn, they could be so beautiful at times. Damn, they could make you think of a breaking heart.

Suddenly, he felt an ache in his belly. He needed to be with Sarah. Why did he have the feeling that she would run off? Just the thought of her with some other guy, it was enough to drill him into the ground.

Next year it would be three decades since they had met. He would organise a surprise party. Take them both to Hawaii. Dinner. Wine. A spirit or two afterwards. A walk along the beach.

The loneliness of the night only seemed to amplify his sense of discomfort. He was a failure. He'd travelled the world, but he hadn't seen it. He'd made serious money (and lost it), but he'd never earned the fruits of life. He'd never taken a wrong turn. He'd never tried to get lost. He'd never stood on a mountaintop and just taken in the view. He'd never gone off the beaten path. He'd never taken a leap of faith. He'd never broken out of the pearly cage of luxury.

Tiredness came on like a forgotten memory, one that kicked his mind. His eyelids slipped closed, their last sight that of the blinking, fiery furnaces above.

Sunday 7th October 2018

He mistook, at first, the knocking to be gunfire. Explosions, starbursts, violence. The whole combination.

"What the...?" He sprang awake, head slapping the steering wheel.

"Are you okay, sir?" came a cheesy All-American voice.

A woman, greying hair falling over her freckled face, rapped at the window. She had a large, golden, dangly earing through each earlobe. A bright red scarf was wrapped tightly around her neck, contrasting with the black t-shirt that seemed a size too small for her.

"I'm fine," he told her. "Broke down yesterday."

"Feeling unwell? Get wasted last night?"

"Absolutely not! There was a broken fucking bottle back up the road. Tyre burst open! I've been here for a day now!"

"Come on, get out. I don't believe you."

"I need help." He opened the door and swung his legs out. "Are you a cop?"

"No, I'm a ranch owner." The woman helped him to his feet. "But cops will be on their way. We'd better get you moving."

"A ranch owner?"

"Yeah." She gestured at a small red truck down the road. "I was on my way to a friend's house to return a book, when I saw you out here. Come on, I'll help you out. You got a spare?"

"It's a rental car. I'm presuming so. I fucking hope so anyway."

The woman was actually, in many respects, quite beautiful. Her steely blue eyes struggled to connect with his, but that made her more attractive. She seemed shy, reluctant to engage with the world. She wasn't quite there, an echo.

He decided to cheer up. She'd only come to help, after all, and he was being quite mean and snappy. "Sorry, I'm just in a state of shock at the moment."

"It's okay. I wasn't accusing you of drinking."

Well, you were, he wanted to blurt out. "I would appreciate your offer of assistance. You need to get to your friend and I don't want to keep you too long."

"We'd better get started in that case," said the woman. "The name's Arlene, by the way."

"I'm Peter McGough."

"Cool."

"Indeed."

"Right, we'd better get started."

"Well, I'd better love you and leave you," said Petey, when they'd finished. "Thank you so much, Arlene, I don't know what I would have done."

It was late morning and the day was beginning to heat up. Arlene had done most of the work, taking off the damaged wheel and screwing on the replacement. She told Petey she'd used to work as a mechanic and still carried a number of tools of the trade in the boot of her truck.

"It's okay. My pleasure, hun."

"Well, I'd better continue on my way and find a place where I can get a signal. My wife'll be worried sick."

"I'm sure she will. You'd better get a move on. It's fifty miles at least until you get anywhere near a signal spot."

"Okay." He let out a huff of air. "Right, well I'd better get going."

"Unless you wanted to come with me." She took a step closer to him. "My house has a good signal."

"Yes, that would be great."

"In that case, follow me. We're going back the way you came."

"What about your friend?"

"Oh, I'm sure a book can wait until another day. I'll just say I got caught in a traffic incident, which would be the truth." She smiled briefly, then regained her strange, silent composure. "Are you sure you want to come back with me?"

"Very sure." And he was. This was the chance he'd been waiting for. This was the opportunity to take that leap.

Arlene's house was like one typically seen in a 50s Western Movie: tall structure, dusty windows, a wooden patio complete with a rocking chair. The sound of horses could be heard. Petey caught sight of a stable in the distance.

He got out of the car and stretched. Damn, he needed to rest. How much sleep had he got last night? Not much. Clearly.

"You like it?" Arlene asked him, slamming the door of her truck shut.

"It's..." He couldn't pick out the words to describe the hand-carved wooden pillars that supported the roof over the patio, nor the beautiful porcelain plant pots that hosted such a variety of colours, nor the black horses galloping around in the field at the back. It was like a dream from a children's story.

"Haha, you like it, don't you?" She placed a cold hand on his wrist. "Come on in."

"Can I be a couple of minutes?" Her scratchy skin was making his brain spasm. "Need to phone the wife."

"Well, I'll be inside." She released him, like he'd been her prisoner. "Don't be too long."

"Yeah, everything's fine," he must have said for the millionth time.

But even his soothing words did not quell the worry in Sarah's voice. She was gibbering, hyperventilating, hyper-everything.

"Honestly, you need to calm down," he said firmly.

"Petey, I was worried as fuck last night!"

"I couldn't exactly do anything, could I? Christ, Sarah!"

"Are you okay now?"

"I'm fine. Look, you need to take a deep breath."

"How can you expect me to do that?!"

"Look, I'm going to be back in a few days. Sit tight until then, okay?"

"Okay." Sarah whistled as she breathed out. *"Okay."*

"Now, I need to get back on the road."

"Okay."

"I love you, Sarah."

"I love you too."

He hung up and found himself grabbing his case from the car. Why... What... the hell was he doing? He went through the wooden, age-old door.

Inside, the house wasn't quite what he expected. There were no gas lamps, no oil paintings, no cowboy-related items. Actually, the hallway and rooms were mostly empty. Only a chunky wooden table stood wonky in the – presumably – dining room. Two chairs and a television adorned the – most likely – lounge. He peeked into the kitchen: full of the necessary bits and pieces to live a healthy existence (including a bowl of apples), but lacking a sense of purpose.

"Arlene?" he called out. "Arlene? That's me finished on the phone. Sorry about that!"

He walked through the house. Every footstep felt like an intrusion. Why did it feel more uncomfortable to be the trespasser rather than the victim of such a waste-of-space loser?

A cuckoo clock jarred into life, making him clutch his heart. Made of brittle, splintering wood, it seemed to be the only thing of value in this house.

A back door. Open.

Placing his bag neatly at the side of the hallway, he stepped into the open air. So fresh and sweet. He made his way to the stable, where Arlene was busy petting one of the horses. She'd put on a long-sleeved shirt that made her look like a true farmhand. He went up to her. She must have heard his approach, because she turned, warmth in her eyes. There was no issue with the connection this time. They stopped before each other, fractions of a very long distance, and then their lips touched.

"I grew up here," Arlene said, arms outstretched, facing the ceiling. "I was born here. Right down where the dining table is. We were such a close family. My mom, my pa, my brothers, we were all so happy together. Funny how the years change everything, isn't it? They're all gone now, gone to the other side. Just me left. I was married once. Me and him lived here, my two daughters as well. When Gordon left me, taking the kids with him, I stayed. I wanted to look after the family home as best I could. But over the years, I've got poorer and poorer. I can barely afford to keep the ranch running. Which is why the house nearly empty. Amazing how you can start selling the small things, like that china ornament you don't want, then it escalates to pieces of furniture and family heirlooms."

"I'm sorry." Petey stroked her hip and kissed the lobe of her ear.

Arlene's bedroom was much like the rest of her house: empty, except for the bare essentials. Her clothes were dumped like rejected factory products in front of the wall opposite the bed. The walls themselves were peeling, like decaying skin.

"So, you're married?" Her question wasn't that much of a surprise, yet it still had bite.

"I am. Nearly four years."

"Are the two of you close?"

"We are. She's the love of my life."

"How'd you two meet?"

"It's a long story..." He took a deep breath, pulling Arlene closer. "Come on, let's have a cuddle for a bit."

She pushed him off, rolling over to face him with her hands folded over her breasts. "No, I want to hear it."

"I warn you, we'll be here for a while."

"I'm not doing anything today."

"Very well. Don't say I didn't warn you..." So, he told her. 1989, 1999, 2007, 2014. He talked about all he could remember. Only now, he became aware of how complex the story was, a true legend in itself, full of twists and turns, like a literary thriller, packed with bizarre characters.

However, he wasn't quite aware of how complex the story actually was. For instance, did he realise that the fat guy who'd called him a *baby killer* was so inspired by Petey's words during their drinking session at the brink of the new millennium that he went on to travel the whole of Africa? And subsequently got himself hacked to pieces in the Central African Republic, when he returned there in 2014 to visit a woman he'd befriended (and hoped to become boyfriend-girlfriend with)? For instance, did he know that Megan had become a brutal drug addict after the incident at the 2007 Edinburgh Book Festival? She'd died in an Edinburgh council estate in 2009, having overdosed on heroin.

When he got to the end of his little tale, Arlene sniggered, then pecked his left cheek. "Cool story. I know it's a longshot for me, but I believe it."

"Thank you."

"It wasn't a compliment. Now, tell me, why have you come out here, away from your wonderful wife?"

"Because I'm insecure. I've never really done anything with my life. I've never really taken any chances, never been spontaneous. Yet..." He knew what he had to say, but the words were even treasonous to think. "Yet... *she's* done all these things. She's backpacked most of the world. All I've done is sell fucking computers."

"You say that, Peter, but your computers have made a difference to many lives. Particularly young lives. How can you say that you've never done anything, when countless people owe their childhoods to you?"

"But I've never thrown myself into the unknown!"

"That's all relative. You say your wife has backpacked most of the world. But you said it yourself earlier, you travelled the world to sell computers. *You* are the one who's made a difference, not her. It is *your* name that kids *and* adults will remember, not hers."

"But all the same –"

"There is no but. Do you hear me?" She took his face in her hands. "You're a champion, Petey."

"No, I'm not. I let myself get hammered that night.

If I'd stayed sober, if I hadn't stayed with Yvonne, Nicola and Mary would be with me right now. I'm responsible for their deaths."

"Look, you're going to have to find a way to forgive yourself. I know it's not easy. I can't imagine what you went through. But you have to find a way. It may be five years, it may be twenty, but you have to pull yourself through this."

"I can't."

"Find strength."

"I don't know if I can."

"Go home to your wife, Petey. Go home to her. She's your rock."

Monday 8th October 2018

Petey flung his case into the boot and took a swig from his water bottle. It was going to be a fairly warm Autumn day. Blue skies, dusty air. He swivelled on his feet and wrapped Arlene in a hug.

"You look after yourself, okay?" she whispered. "Remember, be strong."

"You too."

"I'm happy I hit that bottle."

"Funny how things work out, isn't it?"

"I shall miss you." He kissed her, clutching her waist, then released.

"Take care," she said, voice breaking with emotion.

He flopped onto the driver's seat and started the engine. Taking one look back at Arlene, he released the brake, and then looked to his front. The car kicked up sand as he left the obscure little house behind.

What was spontaneity? A feeling? A philosophical idea? An ambition? A thought process? It was something you couldn't work towards. It also wasn't a gift, something that you were given at birth. It only came when you dropped your guard and allowed the world to fill you up. You had to stop being pretentious. You had to have faith in nature. Spontaneity came when you learned to embrace your personality, the things that made you up. He had embraced it now, with massive open arms.

He stayed the night in Seymour, back in that crappy motel. But he didn't need to walk the streets looking for adventure. He was alive, healthy, married to the love of his life.

He called Sarah just before dinner, apologising for his temper yesterday. He told her that he was coming home early. Dinner as soon as he got back, a nice fancy restaurant; his treat.

He was filled with stories. They choked his mind. Arlene, whoever she was, had set him ablaze. His imagination was brimming with electricity. He could write it down, explore it.

Before disappearing to the land of slumber, he checked the news. The usual worldwide nonsense. Not that he cared. Had he looked a little closer, he would have seen that Donny Bell had been released; but his fiery mind just didn't acknowledge it.

He would change his future. No longer would he be

afraid of his talents. He would transform himself into a better man, someone honourable, whatever it took.

Prediction

Los Angeles

Friday 7th June 2030

The mike burst into life with a cat-like screech. The baying audience, always eager for their next instalment, dulled into silence. A PA rushed along the front row, head ducked. The camera gave that wicked glint: you were going to get your fifteen minutes, whether you liked it or not.

Petey crossed his legs and fiddled with the tweed jacket (bought especially for this occasion). He smiled at the audience, many of whom had travelled for hours to get here. He could see library-cosy-thick-spectacles women; smart, business-like professionals; a few journalists (presumably so – they were rapidly noting things down); and the desperate stare of wannabe writers (all of whom would be trying to get advice from him at the end).

Sarah was at the back, face relaxed, sitting next to Alan Stanley and his still-attractive, still-working-as-a-fitness-instructor wife, Erin. They were all on the brink of old age now, teetering over the edge.

His interviewer, Greg Berry, checked the notes on his clipboard yet again. This event was being filmed for Berry's damned magazine and the man clearly didn't want to let his boss down.

"Okay, well thank you all for coming," said Greg, clearing his throat. He adjusted his blue-and-white striped tie. "I'm Greg Berry, Assistant Editor of the *Herd of Words Magazine*, and this marks seventeenth and final instalment in our *Interesting Discussions Series*. Over the past few months, we've had a variety of extraordinary literary guests, ranging from poets to screenwriters to novelists to graphic writers.

"I think our guest tonight needs no introduction. He is the author of the bestselling *Rick Elder* series, which has sold over eighty-million copies worldwide. In November this year, the latest novel in the series, *The Parson's Tears*, will be published. As you all no doubt know, there have been several film adaptations of the *Rick Elder* books and there has been the recent announcement of a new T.V. series. In addition, he has written a number of standalone thrillers, including *Firing At The Dark*, which was nominated for several awards and is due to be adapted into a movie next year. He is one of the most prolific and bestselling writers working in America today. Please give a round of applause for Peter McGough."

"Thank you!" said Petey, trying to be courteous. He had a flashback of 2007. A lifetime ago. But this time the audience were not a bunch of crackpots.

"I'm going to interview Peter for the next forty-five minutes and then I'll open it up to the audience in the last fifteen minutes," Greg announced. "I'm sure there will be a lot of questions from you folks.

"So, Peter, how does it feel to have completed the twentieth book in the *Rick Elder* series?"

"Amazing."

Audience laughter, nervous. Perfect timing.

"No, in all seriousness, it feels great. It's exhausting, but it's one hell of a personal achievement."

"It must be." Greg Berry consulted his clipboard. "So, it must be interesting to work with a constantly evolving character."

"It is."

"In your last *Rick Elder* novel, *The Shining Red*, Lieutenant Tricia Halbrook died. How did that make you feel, killing off one of the most iconic characters of the series? How do you think this will affect *The Parson's Tears* and all future *Rick Elder* books?"

"Well, first of all, Captain Rick Elder is, by his very nature, a loner. He exists on the edge of society. The fringes of the world. He's a good detective, risking his life to keep the residents of Los Angeles safe. But he needs Halbrook. They go well together. With her gone, he's now more alone than ever."

"A lot of readers were quite angry and disheartened at that. Are you worried about your future relationship with your readers?"

"Not really. I mean, whenever a new novel in the series is published, there's always a risk that my fans may get put off and go for another blockbusting author."

"Well, there's no chance of that tonight," said Greg, gesturing a hand to the audience.

There was a loud, high-pitched cheer the moment Petey entered the wine reception. He gave a wave and sat behind the small desk, piled high with copies of his books: the recent six volumes in the *Rick Elder* series. No, wait, there were two copies of *The Checkmate Game*, one of the early *Rick Elder* books. Surplus copies, most likely, which his publisher was determined to get rid of.

A small glass of wine had been provided for him, which he took gratefully. There was a line of red rope that shielded his little island from the crowd. Greg Berry took a seat next to him, quickly checking his watch. Sarah, Alan and Erin stood some distance away, like vultures waiting to pounce.

The book signing went well. No one wanted to chat too long; a few asked him for writing advice (which he was duly expected to give). He was done inside of a half-hour, with most of the books signed and sold. He got a refill on the wine and went to his wife and friends.

"Glad that's over!" he huffed, flinging an arm around Sarah's shoulders.

"It's not over yet," Alan told him. "You've still got at least an hour of mingling with this lot!"

"Tell me about it," Petey moaned. He saw a photographer dancing that sidestep pattern of impatience and desperation, trying to occupy himself with taking snaps of the attendees. "Fuck," he whispered. "Right, guys, I'd better go and get my photo taken."

"Have fun." Alan gave him a solid pat on the shoulder.

The photographer, a very friendly, down-to-earth Chinese bloke, bustled him into a corner and took at least twenty (maybe thirty?) photos, one after the other, a zigzag line of whirring and clicking. The man then moved Petey over to the signing table (where a bored-looking attendant had opened another box of *Rick Elder* books and was stacking them, his face like that of a scurvy sufferer). The photographer shooed him away, almost knocking a copy of *The Vision of Amethyst* off the top of a column, and proceeded to grab several shots of Petey posing in front of the table, to the left, to the right, and finally sitting down like a man on a severely delayed train, just wanting to get home.

Finally, after at least fifteen minutes, the photographer was done. He orbited around the reception, every working second and every spare second a photo opportunity of some kind.

Petey was just about to relax, when he was accosted by a group of fans, each eager for their little bit of fame with him. He flashed a pretend-desperate look to Sarah.

Her thick, auburn hair was beginning to show specks of grey. She wore glasses now, dark-rimmed. Her face seemed to be paling, just a tiny bit. Had she started to slump? Was she getting a little scruffy? He shouldn't have been thinking like this, but it was hard not to when you had to ban your wife from drinking red wine at book events in case she dribbled any down her top. She was the rock of his life, but it really felt like running his hand through sand on particular occasions.

Then came that familiar assault of words, fresh from a young woman who'd probably spent a hundred dollars on makeup for tonight: "Do you have any advice for new writers?"

"Christ, I thought that would never end," Petey moaned, his head falling back. "Damn."

"It did drag on a bit," said Sarah, eyes focused on the passing streets and cars. "When's your next book signing?"

"Next week I think." He could taste the acid tang of too much wine in the back of his throat. It wasn't an unpleasant feeling; just a nice cushy drunkenness. "Oh, fuck, I forgot to say goodbye to Greg."

"Ha, don't know why you're bothered." Sarah slapped his knee. "You're big enough to tell him to F.O. without losing so much as a single sale."

"Haha," he chided. "What are we going to do when we get home?"

"You're the writer. You think of something."

The taxi juddered as they turned a corner. The driver, blank-faced like he was on cocaine, whispered something to himself. They entered a highway and picked up speed. They were in an oyster, shielded from the real world.

Fireworks were exploding in the distance, coloured flashes of hope and wonder and jewels and love and fear.

"I love you," she said, interlocking her fingers with his.

"I love you too," he replied. "Do you remember when we first met and I said that to you? Stupid idiot kid that I was."

"Haha, yeah. Took me completely by surprise, so you did."

"It was a good surprise, though, wasn't it?"

"Yeah, indeed it was." She leaned on him and buried her scalp in his neck. "Indeed it was."

"We've been through one hell of a ride together, haven't we?"

"We have indeed."

"You know, through all the years, the one thing that has kept us together, despite the mistakes, despite the mishaps, is honesty."

"Honesty is what solved that legal thing with Georgina's brother," she remarked. "It got him to realise the truth of the matter."

"Yeah, but I'm talking about us. We've always been straight with one another. Even during the bleak times."

"We have indeed."

The word 'honesty' made Sarah uncomfortable. She had been a good wife to Petey, supported him at the beginning of his writing career, comforted him when he'd cried about his Nicola and Mary. As soon as they'd moved in together, she'd told him all about what happened in 2007 and why she had lied.

She had seen him comatose, delirious on the station floor. After checking on him, she had run away, terrified, a miserable coward.

But there was a bigger secret that she was keeping from him. It pained her even to admit it to herself. In January every year, she kept promising to reveal it to him, as part of her New Year Resolution. In December, she was kicking herself for her failure.

In truth, ever since it had happened, she had nursed it like a hidden wound. But seeing Petey settle things with Georgina's brother, sitting down with the broken man, apologising for what had happened, that had been the detonator for her guilt. *"It was my fault. I have no intention of blaming anyone else. It was my mistake. Ever since that day, my heart aches at the devastation I have caused you."*

It was simple: Petey deserved the truth. He had the right to know why, on the 19th of May 1993, whilst he'd been waiting on North Bridge, she had been a short distance away, hiding, too anxious to come forward.

Petey made them both tea when they got in. He stood in the kitchen, swaying a little, but happy. He flicked the model of a cuckoo, hung on the wall above the oven; it bounced like a flea. After preparing a small plate of chocolate biscuits, he loaded everything onto a small tray and carried it through to the lounge.

Sarah sat on one of their bright white sofas, reading a magazine.

"Ooh, just remembered, I've got a meeting with my editor tomorrow," she said, tossing the glossy thing on the transparent, stone-ornament-decorated coffee table.

"Cool, no worries. Is it in L.A.?"

"Yeah. We're just meeting for coffee. Should be home by lunch."

"Do you want a lift into town?"

"No. I'll get a cab. Besides, you won't be safe for driving."

"Oh, and when did you get so politically correct?" He landed the tray on the table, nudging a stone representation of an eagle to the side as he did so. He dropped down next to her and teased her neck.

"It's safety."

"Miss PC."

"At least I don't act like a grumpy old git."

"I may be fifty-eight..."

"...Soon to be fifty-nine, but go on..."

"...But I still have a lot of energy left in me."

"Oh, I bet you do."

"Enough to bore me to death?" she said, massaging his neck.

"How about we skip the tea and biscuits and I'll show you some real entertainment?"

"Knowing you, that's be a very long, very boring, very drawn-out, Fifties romantic movie." She flicked his ear playfully.

"I was in the mood for a lustful thriller," he suggested methodically.

"Well, come on then. Let's see what you've got."

Saturday 8th June 2030

She woke in the early hours with that horrid taste of nausea in the back of her mouth. Fumbling like a blind beggar, she reached for her glass of water and took a long gulp.

Petey was stretched out, face down, snoring gently. She loved him when he was like this, dead to the world.

There was a gentle pattering of rain; it drooled down the floor-to-ceiling windows that made up two sides of their bedroom. She went up to the glass and looked out onto their Japanese-style garden. It was a particular passion of Petey's; he'd been building it for the past five years, ordering the plants online and setting them up like a kid sets up an army of toys. He'd done a good job of it though: beautiful and ornate, it was like stepping into a foreign land, somewhere deep in the past, a world so far away.

And it always reminded her of secrets.

Petey murmured something in his sleep. She went over to him, reaching out a hand, stopping just before skin met skin. How could she be truly intimate with a man she was lying to? She returned to the window and pushed her palms against the pane.

The rain was her frustration. The plants were her nightmares. And the dark was the unknown.

Shortly after the taxi came for Sarah, Petey put on some coffee and fired up his computer.

His writing room was directly above the bedroom, also with floor-to-ceiling windows, giving him a most excellent view of his Japanese garden. The room itself was plain; a very important factor. He felt he could only write in the absence of complicatedness.

He took a couple of minutes to take in the leafy view, then dashed back through to the kitchen to retrieve a cup of the black stuff.

The screen desktop had a picture of the Alps as its background, dotted with numerous files and folders, manuscripts and notes, downloaded research articles, and snaps from his travels. The whole wretched thing was a mess that needed to be sorted. He'd been swearing that to himself for a year.

He opened the folder marked *The Indigo Blade*, the twenty-first *Rick Elder* novel, and resumed work. Elder was pursuing a drug dealer through the heart of Los Angeles. The dealer had just killed three witnesses to his latest crime and was wielding a gun. Two bystanders were shot as the dealer fired back at Elder. The chase was in the sweat-soaked heat of the day. Elder was a different character this time, now that he had lost Halbrook, a truly broken soul. All in all, it was a good scene; the perfect climax for the book. *The Indigo Blade* would no doubt go on to sell tens of thousands of copies in the first week.

Petey owed this new writing career to Arlene, that strange woman who lived by herself in that old house. Her words had inspired his words. Did she have all his books? Was she excited at the news of his first *Rick Elder* novel being translated to the small screen? Did she even know?

He had all the trimmings of life: a loving partner, first-class travel, regular backpacking experiences (he'd learned how to do that, finally), a writing career that most would kill for. He had a beautiful home, a hundred bottles of wine, friends, family.

Sarah's life was good too. Awareness Of Orange had grown, onwards and upwards. She had become a bigger celebrity than he. Her own writing career had led to her doing book signings and guest talks in places like New York, London, Buenos Aires, and Cape Town. She wrote about the fragility of the world, the vitality of preservation, the tyranny of certain governments who didn't care. She was a true environmentalist. She didn't need to walk around with a placard and shout abuse. She had the free nature of an independent woman, but she didn't need to brag about it. She was true to herself and to everyone else. It was very rare to see someone who wholly deserved their success, but she fitted into the category perfectly.

Petey just wrote cop thrillers. He fed the mass market with nonsensical, heart-pounding, adrenaline-pumping, trashy crap. He wasn't serious, however much he pretended to be. He tried so hard to make Rick Elder appear a troubled, deep-thinking detective, but the public just viewed him as a bloke who shot baddies. As hard as it was to admit, the truth did sting.

He closed down *The Indigo Blade* and opened up a password-protected file named *Prediction*. This was his attempt, maybe the last chance he would ever get, at changing his identity. This was a piece of serious literature. He'd only done fifty pages, but he was enjoying it more than his other works. An ill-fated romance between a lowly housewife and a sheriff during the American Gold Rush, it would be the novel that he was certain would label him as a *proper* writer.

There was only one obstacle. Would his publisher take it? He had a meeting with Bernard on the 12th of June, just before his book signing that evening. Bernard always had the mass market in mind. Publishing was business, nothing more. Fingers would be crossed. Petey had a dinner/meeting with Alan on the 11th of June, so there would be ample opportunity to get things from a legal perspective. It shouldn't matter, he knew, but in this business, you couldn't take chances.

Prediction wasn't working today. He was too stressed. Too knackered. He needed to feel carefree, reluctant to be part of the real world. As weird as it seemed, that's the way it was. After an hour of staring longingly at the screen, he packed it in, instead getting on with *The Indigo Blade*.

By the time Sarah returned in the early afternoon, he'd finished the chase scene. It wasn't his best, but, after careful revision, it would certainly impress readers and drive a few positive reviews.

"How did it go?" he asked, as she dumped her handbag in the hallway and slipped off her sunshades.

"Oh, fine." She sounded out of breath. "Jim seems happy with the edits. He'll be in touch with me about the publication date." She gave him a hug and pecked him on the lips. "How do you fancy going out for lunch?"

"Sounds good to me."

"Is that you?"

"Excuse me?"

"Your phone?"

"Oh, bollocks!" Petey raced back up to his office and yanked up his mobile on its sixth ring.

"Hi, Petey, it's Alan." The voice was soppy, as usual.

"Hi, mate. Everything okay?"

"Yeah, mate. I'm not going to be able to make dinner next week. I've been called to London on urgent business. I'm leaving tonight."

"When are you going to be back?"

"I don't know. Could be a week, could be a couple of days."

"What's happened? Should I be worried?"

"Oh, don't fret! It's a legal issue with your U.K. publisher, but nothing serious. It's to do with Russian translation rights."

"Well, can't they deal with this in a phone call?"

"Well, publishers are publishers. Anyway, mate, I

need to prepare a few bits and pieces. I'll email you when I get things concluded. Don't worry about it."

"That's what I pay you for! So I don't have to worry!" Petey joked.

"Haha. Right, I'll catch you later, mate."

"Oh, Christ," he stuttered, chucking the phone down.

"Is everything okay?" Sarah had wandered into the room.

"Not really. Alan's going to England for a bit. I'd hoped to see him before..." He couldn't reveal his literary intentions, not yet. "Before I finish the first draft of *The Indigo Blade*."

"You think you'll finish it in the next few days?"

"Hopefully. That's the plan."

"What's Alan going across the pond for?" She was sounding like a true American now.

"Oh, stuff to do with translation rights. There's been a bit of an issue. He told me not to worry. That's what he always says."

"Well, Alan will sort it." She tapped his cheek with her knuckle. "Right, you, Mr Wordsworth, lunchtime."

Against the sunset, Sarah walked alone, bare feet stroking the sand. It seemed as if the salty breeze coming from the sea was filled with the curses and taunts of a past she didn't want to bear, a heavy pendant that was sinking into the skin of her neck.

What would his reaction be? Anger? Disappointment? Would he kick her out, tell her he wanted nothing to do with her?

Two joggers passed her, giving mock salutes. She smiled back.

She couldn't stop thinking about 1993. May 19th. She was a coward to have treated him like that. Ignorance. She was an embarrassment. A failure. An imbecile. Georgina's death was her fault. She should never have promised to meet him.

But it wasn't just that. There was a whole string of things she'd done to hurt him over the years. Most not directly.

In 2021, Alan had turned up at their house, wanting a meeting with Petey on some random subject (since forgotten). She and the lawyer had sat waiting for Petey to come back from his shopping trip. The path of conversation had eventually led to disastrous relationships. Alan had mentioned his ex-wife, Irene, her breakdown in 1999 because of her father's infidelity. Sarah had known, without Alan even going into detail, that she'd been the one behind it. During her little sex trip to London in 1989, trying to earn money.

Guilt piled up on her shoulders like bricks.

"I'm sorry," she said out loud.

The sea heard her and replied with puff of wave-crashing mist.

Wednesday 12th June 2030

Any time he was going into a tense literary meeting (like his first lunch with his first agent), Petey always had a rum and coke. This time was no different. He downed it in five large gulps, attracting dodgy looks from people who didn't quite know who he was.

The restaurant itself was definitely for the established in life: movie stars, screenwriters, blockbusting authors, magnates, celebrity lawyers. The people who usually pissed on the poverty-stricken without even knowing it.

Bernard Erikson, noticeable by his dangerously slim figure and wet eyes, entered the restaurant, plonking himself in the booth.

"I'll have a glass of your finest wine," he commanded a waiter. His half-Swedish, half-American accent had the tendency to annoy people at literary events.

"Certainly, sir. Would you care for anything else, sir?"

It took a moment or two for Petey to realise that he was being addressed. "Oh, a Gin-And-Tonic, please. Best gin."

"Certainly, sir. Would you gentlemen like to see the menu?"

"Yes, please." Bernard popped his briefcase on the seat cushion next to him. "Actually, could you bring a bottle of your finest wine instead? And two glasses."

"So, what have you got for me?" Bernard didn't like to engage in business chat until the first of the alcohol had passed his lips.

Both men had placed their orders. Petey had ordered the lamb rack, whilst Bernard had opted for spaghetti.

"First of all, I need to ask, what's the problem with the translation rights?" Petey was aware he sounded like a desperate little child.

Their meals arrived. The waiter carefully put them down, not saying a single word. These two men were untouchable. You just didn't go near them. You pretended that they existed behind a sheet of glass.

"What problem?" said Bernard, sucking in a strand of spaghetti. Flecks of tomato sauce burst into the air.

"My lawyer said there was an issue with the Russian translation rights with my U.K. publisher."

"Not that I know of. I was talking with Jerry on the phone last night. According to him, everything is on schedule for... oh what is it? I struggle to picture all the *Rick Elder* titles in my head. You've done so many. Now, let's see the goods."

Petey opened the small non-leather briefcase nestled by his left foot and took out the manila folder containing the first ten pages of *The Indigo Blade*.

"Excellent," the publisher said, his tongue clicking, when he'd finished skimming through. "Excellent."

"Glad you like it."

"Your fans will adore this. Now, you said in your email there was something you wanted to show me. I'm presuming something other than the latest *Rick Elder*..." Bernard dabbed his red lips with a napkin. It came away with a lipstick kiss emblazoned on the silky fabric.

"Yes, indeed." Petey fumbled in the case for the pink folder and took it out, holding it like it was his own Declaration of Independence. It merely contained a one-page file that detailed the plan for *Prediction*. He was about to give it to Bernard, when the man's phone rang.

"Excuse me a moment." Bernard held it to his ear. "Hi, Wes. That's great, my friend, I look forward to it. No, not right now, I'm meeting with Peter. Yeah, Peter McGough. Okay, see ya. Have a good one." He put the device away. "Sorry about that. Anyways, before I take a look at that, I want to make a suggestion."

"Sure. Didn't you like the opening of *The Indigo Blade*?"

"Actually, I did. Very much. Slightly unusual for you, but hey ho. No, I want to talk to you about Halbrook." The man grimaced. "I want you to bring her back."

"What?"

"A lot of fans were disappointed at *The Shining Red*. Social media has been livid. I'm worried that *The Parson's Tears*, which will no doubt sell, I know, may lose you some favour among your fans."

"But I killed her off." Petey's mouth was so dry that he couldn't even panic properly.

"How did she die again?"

"She was shot six times by a corrupt cop." He'd said this flatly, to try and gently push Bernard away. But Mr Erikson, five times nominated for the *California Publisher of the Year Award*, was not moved an inch.

"Is there any way she could have faked her death?" he said.

"Not really."

"Maybe she had some of those blood capsule things, like you see in the movies. This –" He punctuated with his fingers. "– 'corrupt' cop could have been helping her."

"But –"

"Here's an idea. Just a potential storyline. Lieutenant Halbrook was having a secret affair with a man in Colombia. Over the years, they'd become close lovers. Like so close, they were husband and wife, in all but name. Halbrook, determined to be with him, knew she couldn't leave her family and just go be with this guy. So, instead she made a secret arrangement with this cop to fake her death. She also made deals with people in the morgue to put a Jane Doe in her place. Halbrook had obviously made friends with fake I.D. people over the years and she arranged for a fake passport, etcetera, etcetera. You put in a twist like that, my friend, you'll become an even bigger bigshot than you are now."

"The cop who killed Halbrook is executed just prior to the events of *The Parson's Tears*."

"Well, you're the writer! Think of something. I'm being serious about this. The guys and gals at the office think the same as well." Bernard started spooning down spaghetti again. "Now, what was it you wanted to show me?"

Petey stroked the folder with his thumb. "Oh, it's nothing. Just an idea for the next book in the series," he lied.

"Okay, well don't show it to me now. Let's get *The Parson's Tears* published and *The Indigo Blade* edited first. But I want Halbrook brought back for your next novel."

"Okay. I'll get on it."

"You will also note how I said 'your next novel', not 'your next *Rick Elder* novel'."

"What do you mean?" Petey knew where this was heading. He hung his head in resignation at his horrific fate.

"I was discussing things in some detail with everyone at the office." Bernard refilled his wine glass. "*Rick Elder* has become an international phenomenon. With this new T.V. series on the way, it has been the general consensus that... we don't want any more standalone thrillers. For the time being at least."

"What?"

"The guys and gals at the office think that... and I most certainly think so too... that you're suited solely to *Rick Elder*."

"But I've got so many ideas for standalones." Petey felt embarrassed, ashamed and disappointed, all rolled into one.

"I know you don't want to hear this. Believe me, your standalones are amazing. I can't wait for the movie of *Firing At The Dark*. But you have to understand that publishing isn't just about creativity and smiling faces at book events. It's a business. There are a lot of pressures on us these days. With the damn environmentalists threatening to have us shut down over the number of trees we slash down to print our books, well... you can understand, I'm sure."

"I'm married to one. Believe me, I understand."

"Oops. Forgot. No offence was intended." Bernard had finished his meal. Licking his lips, he reached for his wine glass and swallowed the lot in one. "Look, I need to get going. Got a meeting with one of our new authors. He's only twenty-one and he's being considered for this major prize for literary fiction. Can you believe it? Crazy shit. Anyways, shall we touch base tomorrow?"

"Sure."

Both men shook hands. Whistling, Bernard gathered his things and left the restaurant. He threw a coin in a pond of water by the entrance, took a sharp left turn, and vanished into the day.

Petey sat back down. Motionless. What had just happened? Had his dreams just been crushed? And who the hell was this twenty-one-year-old prick?

It occurred to him that he hadn't even touched his meal. He dug his fork in. He gulped down the wine and cursed when he saw that the bottle was half-empty. He raised his hand for another one.

By the time he left the restaurant, he was pretty drunk. He was stumbling around in hysterics, laughing at the thought of Bernard Erikson being found after an overdose of sleeping pills.

How he found his way home without causing a mess, he didn't know. Sarah helped him into the living room and forced him to lie down on the sofa.

"Bad meeting?" she asked.

"Yeah, you could say that," he slurred.

"Do you want a coffee or something?"

"Please. And a pint of water. I need to sober up for tonight. Pretty badly."

Sarah could sense something was wrong with Petey, even after the alcohol had largely worn off. She tried to coax him into talking, but he remained silent, gazing out the window. There wasn't a separation between them and the driver, so she concluded that this was the reason for his reluctance to talk about whatever was on his mind.

Tonight was yet another big night for him. Yet another book signing.

They were heading back into Los Angeles for this one. The evening was warm, full of hope, promise. It wouldn't be as major and full of pomp as the other literary events. No video cameras, no special guests. There might be some red rope, just to keep the baying crowds at bay.

When they arrived, Petey paid the driver and exchanged a long-forgotten, most likely one-sided joke with him. He took her hand and led her through the entrance of the bookstore, where a smiling bald man, Nathan Pilgrim, owner of the bookstore chain, shook them both warmly by the hand.

The shop itself was small, one that very easily filled up, even during the minor literary events. But tonight, on the first floor, the management had evidently worked even harder to make things work: bookshelves had been moved, expertly wheeled to the side; a drinks table had been stacked with cartons of cheap wine; plastic seats had been placed out in neat orderly rows with not one, but *two* aisles that led to the front. Two chairs with a varnished wooden table in between waited to provide the evening's entertainment. Finally, by the entrance to the authors' green room, a signing table; a cloth ordained with the well-respected symbol of the bookshop chain had been draped over the top. Just missing the customers.

"We've still got an hour," Nathan said. He'd obviously seen the look of horror on Petey's face. "Be back in a few moments."

"What is it?" she asked Petey, as Nathan headed into the green room. "Come on, tell me."

"Bernard wants me to bring Halbrook back."

"What? Is that all your little misery mood's about?"

"Not exactly. He's told me that they're going to stop publishing any future standalones. They just want *Rick Elder* books."

"Oh. Were you working on any standalone projects?"

"Yes. I was trying to write… a literary novel."

"Do you want to talk about it?"

"Tonight. After this fucking thing's over."

Nathan emerged from the green room. "Hi guys, got it all ready for you. Just had to check everything was in order. Do you want a glass of wine or something?"

"Yes, bring us in two glasses of white," said Sarah.

Petey held the sheet before his face, quickly

sweeping his eyes over the hungry, half-tipsy audience. His interviewer, Stacey Idler, of the *Zig-Zag Arts and Literature Magazine*, sat quite stupidly, her mouth one quarter open. Pretend eagerness, a common trait among editors these days...

"*The beach was as black as the night,*" he read. "*Elder walked along the sand, weapon drawn. Cars swished in the distance. His heart pounded. He readied himself for the fight.*

"*He caught sight of a figure, a silhouette against the streetlight pouring onto the beach. It was him. The killer. The psychopath who had brutally murdered five women and dismembered their bodies.*

"*Now this bastard was going to pay.*

"*Elder aimed the gun and slipped his finger around the trigger. This was it.*

"*Suddenly, hands grabbed his ankles. The next thing he knew, he was facedown. Someone was on top of him. He was trapped.*"

He lowered bundle of papers and sent a smile in the direction of Stacey Idler. The audience, very predictably, clapped.

"Thank you very much," said Stacey in her booming voice. "I myself can't wait for *The Parson's Tears* to come out. Thank you so much for bringing along this sample."

"Not a problem. Publisher's orders."

"I'm sure you're all aching with questions for Peter, so please put your hand up and a roving mike will be along in a second or two."

The first question came very quickly, followed by a rapid succession of enquiries into his writing process, favourite authors, particular wines, and his car. This was capped off by a very personal one about his private life, which he did his best to skirt around, but ultimately the customer didn't look satisfied.

"Thank you very much for your questions," said Stacey, checking her watch. "Unfortunately, we have now run out of time. I think *The Parson's Tears* will be an amazing read when it's released in November – not too long away. However, there are copies of Peter's other books available for purchase, and I'm sure that he will be more than happy to sign them for you. Please join with me in thanking Peter for coming along."

"Thank you," he said, nodding, as clapping sounded once again. He moved over to the signing table, where another glass of white had been carefully positioned. Were they trying to get him drunk?

There were handshakes; smiles; signing books (of course); requests for advice on submitting to agents and publishers (Oh God). It was actually quite a pleasant signing queue and when the end was in sight, he felt himself relax, basking in the warmth of his fans.

The last to come was a young woman – in her early twenties, by appearance. She had thick, straight, blonde hair that hung like a curtain. She was dressed in a shirt and jeans and carried a small, fabric handbag over her shoulder. She held out a copy of *The Curse*, the second *Rick Elder* novel.

"Didn't think anyone would be interested in the early stuff!" he joked, as held the pen out, poised.

"Can I ask something?" Her voice was pristine Australian.

"Sure. Do you want it signed for someone?"

"No, just for me. Philippa."

"No worries." He did as she asked and returned the book to her.

"Actually, could I invite you to something?"

Petey had been warned about this from his agent and publisher. Say no. No exceptions. "You're not supposed to contact me directly about literary events. Contact my publisher. They're the ones who organise everything."

"Oh, I didn't realise. It's for my student magazine." She looked hurt.

He was feeling sympathetic tonight, maybe as a result of the wine. "Alright, do you have a contact email or something?"

"I prepared this." She put down a slip of paper. "It's got my email and number, as well as details of the event."

"Thank you. I'll have to run it via my agent and publisher." He quickly skimmed the details. "Hmm. The Twenty-Second of June. That's a bit short notice. I'll see what I can do."

"Thank you." She reached out her hand to him.

"Not to worry." He took it. "Look after yourself."

She nodded in acknowledgement to the bemused Nathan and Sarah, and then stepped into an elevator that led to the ground floor. Just before the doors sealed, she flashed Petey a look of hope, as if she'd been waiting for this moment for years.

"Who was she?"

Petey didn't answer. He was still trying to recollect the name of the cheap box wine. It wasn't that bad. He might order some. Perfect for a movie night.

"Hmm?" he said at last.

"That woman at the end."

"Oh, I dunno. Philippa, she said her name was. You were there, my dear."

"Yes, I was."

The taxi went over a bump and Petey felt his stomach lurch.

"She should have contacted Bernard," Sarah went on. "It was completely inappropriate what she did."

"She didn't mean any harm," he said defensively. "She didn't know. Besides, it would be good for me to get out. The Twenty-Second... I can definitely work that."

"Well, I'm away in the Philippines then, so I won't be able to come along."

"What's this for?"

"Oh, it's the International Luther Conference."

"Oh, right!" He was mildly embarrassed at forgetting.

"Final preparations are still going on. They're still trying to put up the displays, can you believe it?"

"When are you flying out?"

"I'm heading out on the Twentieth, coming back on

the Twenty-Fourth." She took out her phone and began scrolling through various things. It lit up her face and made her look eighteen again. "Yep, back on the Twenty-Fourth."

"Fantastic. I don't have any events scheduled between now and the Twentieth, so we could maybe go away somewhere for a couple of days. Chillout."

"I'd like that, but I've got a lot of stuff to do for the conference."

"Okay."

"I also might go out tomorrow, to a café or something, have a final check on the manuscript."

"Why don't you work from home?"

"Because I need the fucking space!" she hissed at him. "Fuck, Petey, you're always breathing down my neck! Can't you just give me a bit of space?"

"I'm sorry, I just need a bit of space." She was crying.

"Hey..." He stroked her arm. "Are you all right?"

"No. When we get home, there's something I have to tell you."

Petey wasn't angry. The revelation had taken him by surprise, but whereas twenty years ago he might have snapped in rage, today he was mellow. He rested his head against the glass in their bedroom. His eyelids barely held the tears in.

"I'm sorry," she said for the seventh or eighth time. Hunched on the edge of their bed, her face was smothered by her hands.

"You knew I was studying at Edinburgh University,"

he half-whispered, half-said. "Why didn't you get a message to me? Let me know you had doubts about meeting?"

"I wouldn't have known how to."

"Oh, for pity's sake! You've travelled to every inch of the planet. I'm sure you'd have figured out how to get a message to me!"

"I was too scared."

"Scared of what?"

"We were both young, Petey. I didn't know who I was. I didn't know what I wanted. When I saw you, standing waiting for me, I panicked."

"Sarah, you are the love of my life." He turned away from the window and knelt before her, like a dreadful movie remake of his proposal. He pulled her hands from her face and pinned them to his chest. "You are the only thing in the world that matters. I have no family, apart from you. I trust you more than I trust myself. So, if you are lying to me, then where does that leave me? I want the truth, Sarah. I want the whole truth."

"I need a drink first."

They went downstairs to the dining room. Petey opened a bottle of red and poured them each a large glass. They sat on opposite sides of the dining table, eyes locked on one another.

Sarah took a swig, let out a sob, and began her story.

In 1989, after her encounter with Donny Bell in

Glasgow, during which she scarred him for life, she panicked. The sirens of police cars resonating through Glasgow City Centre forced her to take decisive action.

She fled to Glasgow Central Station and boarded a train to Edinburgh. When she arrived, she went about looking for another hostel, but with no success. She fled to the Old Town and spend the night huddled up in a small hollow in a wall.

The next morning, she made a decision to stay in Edinburgh for a few days. After successfully finding a cheap bed in a hostel, she ended up staying for two weeks. She did more sex work and managed to pocket nearly a thousand pounds.

Unfortunately, whilst having breakfast one morning, she overheard a conversation between two old ladies that a young man with blond hair had been viciously assaulted in Glasgow and the cops suspected that the assailant had fled to Edinburgh. Once again, she had to hurriedly get her things and run for a train.

She took one to London. Cuddled up in a cramped seat, she thought about what she needed to do. The cops would give up after a day or two. This certainty made her relax. She would hide in London for a month, do more sex work so she'd make enough money to go to America or somewhere for a bit.

But in the Lake District, the train broke down. After being stuck for an hour, Sarah, fearing for her life if any police boarded, used an emergency exit to escape from the carriage. She was able to sneak away without alerting anyone and soon found herself wandering through steep, rugged ground.

After walking for several hours, she came across a hamlet. She found a small hotel, but all the rooms were booked. She was left with no choice but to see if any of the local residents would put her up for the night. She was met by many rejections, including accusations of her being a tramp. Finally, she rapped on the door of a cottage located a short distance from the hamlet. It was answered by an elderly man with a fluffy, white beard.

"What do you want?" he asked.

"Do you have a spare room for the night?"

"I'm not a Bed-And-Breakfast, young lady. I suggest you go elsewhere."

"I could pay you two-hundred pounds in cash." She showed him.

The man thought about it for a minute or two and then agreed.

His home was untidy and dishevelled. Dogeared paperbacks, videotapes, an umbrella, fleeces and jumpers, and various other detritus were strewn about the passageway and living room. The place wasn't unclean or dirty, just very messily disorganised.

He was called Devlin Malice and he was a World War II veteran whose wife had passed away two years previously. They'd had one son who was living in Glasgow and who had started seeing a barmaid up there. Rumours were that they were both in love with each other.

Over a hot bowl of soup and a tin of lager, sitting in front of a roaring hearth, he told her about his wartime experiences.

"I saw a lot, maybe too much," he said, crossing his ankles, fingers netted together over his cardigan. "I saw death and destruction on an unimaginable scale. That's something you young people don't understand. You truly have no idea of what it was like back then..."

He'd been seen action right across the world, from France to the Horn of Africa. He had taken part in Operation Appearance on the 16th March 1941 and during the fight had been separated from his troops. An escaping group of Italian soldiers had stopped him from re-joining his men and he had been forced to flee inland, right into the depths of British Somaliland.

Of all the battles Devlin told her he'd fought in, Operation Appearance seemed the one he was most eager to talk about. He merely listed the others, occasionally including a few details such as the number of men killed, which side won, jokes the men told to each other. But he discussed Operation Appearance at length. Not the actual invasion – he just did a quick summary of that – but his journey through British Somaliland and the thing he found at its heart.

It was a story that intrigued Sarah, so much so that in 1992 she went to try and find it too. It was the reason why she was so fascinated by Africa, why she referenced it so much in her books, why at times she was simply unable to shut up about it. It would influence everything that was to follow.

Lieutenant Devlin Malice ran quickly from the scene of battle. Though he was a new officer to the army, he'd developed skills quickly, much more so than his fellow soldiers. It was dangerous to stay around: the priority was to get as far away as possible.

Gunfire billowed like wind over the sand. Shouts from the retreating Italian soldiers indicated they had seen him. After some sporadic firing, they quickly gave up. They had more important things on their minds.

For the rest of the day, Devlin continued running, not daring to turn the other away. It was highly likely that there were other fleeing enemies. Towards the evening, as fatigue overtook him, he allowed himself to rest.

With limited supplies of water and food, he forced himself to rest by a large boulder for the night. After getting barely any sleep, he spent the next day trudging along, exhausted to the brink of blacking out.

He was lost, with no map, and he didn't know which way he'd come. His footsteps had been eroded from the sand by a gentle breeze that had sung its sweet tune throughout the bitter night.

For the next few days, he wandered aimlessly, terrified of being found by the enemy, but petrified of being lost forever.

To block these horrific thoughts out, he pictured his schooldays, growing up in sunny Kent, together with his four brothers. He could taste the lemonade, served in the warmth of the afternoon in their garden, despite the heat of the day scorching his cheeks and mouth. He could hear the bell of the village school ringing away, as Mr Leighton shook it violently, his stern demeanour signalling the end of playtime. Memories could seem so much more vivid when you were caught in a situation like this.

On the sixth day, with his food gone and the water canteen empty, he resigned himself to ending things with his revolver. He was about to draw the weapon from the holster, when he spotted a small village in the distance. There was music, dancing and chanting emanating from the collection of thatched roofs. Keeping guard, he headed towards it.

There was some sort of tribal ceremony going on. Men dressed in strange, otherworldly clothes, feet bouncing off the ground in such a perfect, wonderfully orchestrated ensemble of movements, sang words that simply had no meaning to Devlin.

He entered the scene, aware that formidable eyes were turning on him. He didn't know how to address them. Did they speak English? He introduced himself and apologised for interrupting their assembly. He enquired as to whether they had any food and water they could spare, fully aware that he appeared like a pathetic, timid soul, and if they should turn hostile, there would be nothing he would be able to do about it.

The ceremony or whatever it was stopped. The eerie scene, that of this intense tribal gathering, spread through the centre of this tiny hamlet, dust and sand filling the air, was enough to make Devlin shake.

A man stepped forward, from deep within the spectating crowd, his bare feet like hooves. The fact that this man spoke perfect English wasn't the thing that scared Devlin; it was his calm demeanour, relaxed like that of a snake about to strike.

"Welcome," said the man. "Are you injured?"

"No, sir," answered Devlin. "I have been separated from my men and urgently require food and water."

"Ha ha ha," the man laughed. "Do you think this is a hotel?"

"I was not thinking that for a moment, sir."

"Ha! Come, my friend, watch our ceremony for a few minutes. Food and water will be brought to you."

So, Devlin watched the ceremony. The tribal dance, as frightening as it was, had an allure to it, an addiction. A thrill. Despite food and water being brought to him, he was transfixed by the intense, acrobatic display.

The man who'd spoken to him turned out to be the chief of the village. He was quite an interesting fellow, full of stories about his people.

But Devlin, in all truth, wasn't listening. He was looking at one of the dancers, a woman with narrow eyes locked on him. Even though she was moving in the wildest formation, legs striking the air like batons, she was able to stay on him. She spun and leapt with the grace of a ballet dancer, but the aggressiveness and rage of a warrior. When the dance was over, she wandered to a hut near the end of the village, casting one last glance at him before disappearing inside.

There was something about her that stayed with him.

That evening, he was invited to dine with the chief. The meal was tender, a true delicacy, something to be savoured, a taste of adventure. But the image of that woman lingered in his mind. Eventually, he asked the chief who she was.

"A mistake surely," the chief told him.

"I beg your pardon?"

"The dance you saw is only performed by men."

"I went to the hut she went into," Devlin told Sarah, a sadness falling off his tongue. "I searched the whole village. Not a trace. The chief thought I was mad. The next morning, a patrol found me and I was safe and sound. But I always wondered who she was. What if I had followed her into the hut?"

"You shouldn't think like that," said Sarah. "Maybe you were hallucinating. Don't forget, you were wandering the desert for days, dehydrated and starving."

"I know I wasn't hallucinating," said Devlin. "How can you accuse me like that?"

"I wasn't. It wasn't my intention to accuse you." She finished her meal and, unsure of the correct etiquette, placed the tray on the floor.

"No, you're right. It was a long time ago. I was a different man then. A young, naïve fool." He sighed. "Would you like a glass of whisky?"

They spend the night exchanging stories of their travels. As the hours passed, she became aware of how inexperienced with the world she was compared to this veteran. He had seen it all. The more he talked, the further he drove the knife of shame into her side.

Devlin showed her to a spare room and she had a good night's rest. She dreamt about that village. How she knew exactly what it looked like, down to the strands of straw on the ground, it was impossible to know, but she did. She was walking through it, a lonely traveller. And she saw the woman with the narrow eyes watching her closely, following her every move.

The next morning, after a hearty fried breakfast, he drove her to a nearby town where she would be able to get a bus south.

Just as she was getting out of the cranky four-wheel drive he owned, she asked him, "Will you ever go back? Try to find that village again? That woman?"

"No," he told her flatly. "I have a son who is in love with a woman. I may be a grandfather soon. What more do I need in life?"

"You should try to find her."

"I won't. And neither should you."

Those curt, strong words were a clear indication that she should leave. No sooner had she shut the door, when he took off, accelerating hard. As she watched his vehicle disappear around a corner, she felt a rush of excitement churn in her gut.

Devlin was a pretty bad liar. He'd seemed very evasive when she'd asked him about that woman. Why did she have the sneaking suspicion that there were a number of details he was leaving out?

Over the next year, she did a number of menial, dead-end jobs, and a lot of selling herself to rich gentlemen. She accumulated tens of thousands of pounds. After putting a lot into a number of savings accounts, she set her sights on Somaliland. She arrived there in the February of 1992.

She spent weeks travelling about the place. She was groped, robbed, threatened with a knife on a couple of occasions. She asked locals about this village, giving as many details as she could remember from Devlin's story. Her cover was that she was here to look for a village her grandfather had visited during the Second World War. There were a few people who were helpful, but most treated her with a vicious, cold hostility. Eventually, after several false leads, she arrived at what she believed was the village.

"What am I fucking doing here?" was all she could say when she stood in the stubbed ruins.

She thought about Devlin coming here. How had he coped with the strangeness of being utterly alone, stranded? But for her, there was nothing. In the broken shells of homes, she found nothing, only dust.

She stayed in Somaliland for another week, then gave up and went home. But the mysterious woman was always on her mind, like a cancer digging at her soul.

Over the next few months, she travelled, seeing as much of the world as she could. But around every corner, in every hostel, behind every window, the woman with the dark eyes was there, keeping an eye on her like a secret guardian angel.

In 1993, when she went to meet Petey in Edinburgh, the woman was there, in the background, telling her to run away. Stupidly, she listened.

"Well, that's one hell of a story," said Petey. "Why on Earth didn't you tell me that sooner?"

"I just didn't have the words right," Sarah said, whimpering.

"I was being sarcastic. Do you really think a story about some exotic dancer is really gonna make me less shocked?"

He didn't want to believe with beautifully-spun yarn she'd told him. Nothing about it made the remotest bit of sense.

"So, what's going to happen now?" she asked, fingering away more tears.

"What, do you think I'm going to chuck you out over something that happened years ago? I appreciate the honesty, but I don't know why you bothered to mention it."

"You're not going to kick me out?"

"Why would I do that?" He took her hands again. "Look, Nineteen-Ninety-Three was... well... a long time ago. It's in the past. What matters is the now."

"I swear to you, on my heart, that what I told you is true."

He sighed. "I believe you. I believe you."

Thursday 20th June 2030

"Wish I didn't have to go on this bloody thing," Sarah said miserably.

"Don't be like that." Petey steadied her by the shoulders. "This is a good thing for you. You'll do really well. Keep those buggers in line."

They were waiting outside the house for the taxi to pick Sarah up. The parking at LAX was such a nightmare these days that it was better for her to get a taxi there, instead of both of them having to make a rushed goodbye at the drop-off zone.

She laughed anxiously. "I'll email when I can."

"When you get home, we'll go out for a nice meal. Just the two of us. No fancy limos or paparazzi. Just a lovely meal, plus a nice bottle of wine."

The cab turned up and squeaked to a halt. The driver had some music playing low, his head bobbing to the beat. The man stepped out and put Sarah's bags in the trunk.

"When I come back, I want to meet with Bernard," she said. "Believe me, after I've had a chat with him, he'll drop his bullshit attitude and allow you to write whatever you want."

"Sounds like a plan."

The driver held the passenger door open.

"Well, see you in a few days," said Petey.

"I love you, Petey."

"I love you too." He kissed his wife lightly on the lips. She stroked his hip as she got inside the car. After the taxi left, he stood for a minute or two, breathing in the fresh sea air, and then went into his house. There was work to do.

That evening, he received an email from Alan, informing him that everything was *going well*. He replied, demanding to know *what* was happening, but didn't get a response. What the hell was going on? He emailed Erin to see if she knew. She answered within a few minutes, claiming she didn't know why her husband had jetted off to England.

Paranoia swept his mind like a forest fire. Alan was his most trusted friend. Everything he did had to have a reason behind it. Was Petey facing legal action? If there was something kicking off, then Alan would know about it damn quickly. That might explain his silence: he wouldn't want to alarm Petey needlessly if there was a chance that he could resolve it without any dust being kicked up.

Petey poured himself a glass of single malt to take his mind off things. Such an old trick, but it still worked. He watched some television and imagined what it would be like to be caught up in the floods in France, displayed across the screen like the deleted scenes from an indie movie. There were bigger problems in the world than his. He had money, resources, fame. Those poor souls swept away by the waters had nothing now.

When night settled and the lights of Malibu ignited like fireflies, Petey switched the television off and went for a walk. There were shouts and cries of joy emanating from bars and clubs. The world could be such a social place at times, when people didn't have their heads shoved in the wrong places. On a rooftop, a garden party was in full swing. Shortcut dresses, waistcoats with unbuttoned shirts. There would be no problem for him getting in there. He would merely walk up to the bouncers and they would know straightaway who he was. Such secret dwellings of joy and fun were no longer off-limits to him.

But for now, he was content. He could walk like a stranger through these revelling streets. It was like having a cellar full of the richest wines on Earth. Why the need to open all the bottles? Why not leave some of them to gather dust and remain sealed with their liquid joy?

There was a common misconception about Malibu, that it was a place reserved for celebrities, with exclusive parties and million-dollar homes. That was simply untrue. It was a place of self-discovery, where you could melt into the background and start again. That's what it had done for him anyway. Here, you could change for the better and make peace with your past. You could get over the pain of losing your wife and daughter. You could stroll along the beach in the evening light and feel a sense of hope for your future.

Most towns and cities had burnt-out men who walked alone. Not Malibu. It was a safe haven for the soul.

After walking for a good hour, the alcohol began

to wear off and his smile grew even bigger. He turned around, content to walk home and get an early night.

"Mr McGough!" a voice shouted.

He looked behind him to see Philippa. Wearing a sparkling diamond dress, she looked weirdly beautiful, with the appeal of a Greek goddess. She was swaying in the middle of the pavement, a curious look of inquisitiveness spreading across her lips. A glass of fizzy stuff was fastened to her fingers.

"I'm sorry, I didn't see you there!" he said. "How are you?"

"Yeah, I'm good. Busy, busy." She giggled. "What brings you out?"

"Oh, just stretching my legs. My wife's gone away for a few days, so I'm able to get a bit of peace and quiet."

"Sounds great."

"What about you? Didn't think Malibu would be your haunt!"

"Oh, a mate of mine's having a party here." She gestured with her head behind her to a bar. There were no drunks in it: just socialising and enjoyment. That was part of the beauty of Malibu: not everyone needed to get flat-out wasted.

"Cool. How are studies going?"

"Yeah, they're going all right. I'm not studying right now. I'm doing an internship over the summer with a newspaper."

"Oh, yes, sorry! Yes, I remember, you mentioned on the phone."

Philippa looked at the ground, then back up at him. "Do you want to join us? If it's not inappropriate, I mean?"

Petey shuffled indecisively. Was this a wise idea? He really should get back to his computer, do some more edits. But the temptation was here. What harm could it do? A beer or two?

"Yeah, I'd like that," he said finally.

Without warning, she slipped her free arm through his. "Excellent," she whispered. "Come and meet my friends."

She led him into the bar, bathed in blue light like an aquarium. Leather chairs, with tall occupants sipping the night away, melted into the varnished wooden floor. Spirits of all shapes and kinds ordained the wall behind the three bartenders. Cocktails flowed like multicoloured streams into funny-shaped glasses. Music was playing at just the right volume, a sweet melody that didn't have to make logical sense for it to be enjoyed.

Philippa's friends were gathered in a tight corner booth, empty drinks glasses piled like falling Roman columns. There were two men, one of whom looked like Petey in the early Nineties: wavy hair, blue shirt with the cuffs undone, and a cleanshaven face. The other guy was scruffier: a t-shirt with funky writing on, with shorts and sandals hanging loosely. He looked unwell, his sunburnt face covered in sweat and his eyes like pits. The third person present was a woman wearing an emerald dress. Her brown hair was tied in a ponytail and her nails were painted bright red. She nodded at Petey and Philippa in acknowledgement, then turned to the email or text she was currently tapping out on her phone.

"This is Peter McGough," Philippa announced. "We're doing the interview with him in a couple of days."

"Oh yes," said the scruffy guy. "I'm Owen, that's Cary over there. If she'll ever get off her phone, Wilma might just shake your hand." He was drunk... and Australian.

"Hi," said Cary. He was a Texan by the sounds of it.

"Sorry, just composing an email," said Wilma. "Be with you shortly."

Owen let out a belch and shifted along. "Come sit down, Peter."

"Shall I order drinks?" Petey asked.

"Actually, I've placed an order for a bottle of champagne," Philippa told him.

They both sat next to Cary. Owen launched into a rant about the rent prices in the city. Wilma finally got off her phone as the champagne arrived. Cary filled their glasses and raised a toast.

"To freedom of speech!" he declared.

"Here, here," muttered Owen.

Petey beamed at them all and took a long sip. He was used to the richest champagne, but this was all right. It didn't quite have the flare he was used to, but it still packed a punch.

"So, how's the writing going?" Philippa asked him.

The others were discussing some journalist Petey had never heard of. Apparently, they were having certain issues trying to access information on the Chinese Government's human rights record...

"Oh, it's going well," grumbled Petey. "Just doing a lot of editing at the moment. My publisher's pushing me a lot. Don't tell anyone this, but..." He moved closer to her and whispered, "He wants me to bring Lieutenant Halbrook back."

"What?"

"There's been an executive decision of sorts made in the office. They want her back. I don't have any creative control anymore. Plus, they're going to stop publishing my standalones."

"What?" She looked aghast, as though she had written *Rick Elder* herself. "What are you going to do about it?"

"What *can* I do? I'm trying to write this literary novel at the moment and I'd hoped that publishing it would be no bother, but... it's not going to happen now."

"It's not fair on you. How can they just do that?"

"They're a powerful publisher. I'm merely their product."

"Don't say that!" She stroked his hand. "You're more than that. You've got to learn to stand up for yourself. Be firm with them."

"I can't." The glass in his hand was a fountain of lost chances. "Publishing isn't just about printing stories, it's about money. All they care about is money."

"You've to stand your ground. I'm sorry, but there's no other way to say it."

Owen suddenly interrupted, his speech a slur of exaggerations. "Hey, guyseseses. You never giss what we're talkn bet!"

"I sold an article to a magazine!" Wilma declared, throwing her arms into the air. "Fuck! I did it!"

"She just got the email," explained Cary.

"Congratulations, Wilma," said Petey, not resisting Philippa's touch, not caring whether anyone saw them linking fingers. "This deserves a treat." He called over to one of the bartenders. "Three bottles of your finest champagne, please!" The young woman's hand felt like the skin of forbidden fruit. "I'm going to have a beer as well," he told his new friends. "All the drinks are on me tonight, so if you want something, just ask."

They reminded him of a group of lads he had met on an unplanned night out long ago in Edinburgh. But this time there would be no mistakes. This time he would not get bladdered and wind up at a dreary railway station. He was stronger now. He would not fall.

Friday 21st June 2030

It was around One A.M. by the time Owen, Cary and Wilma left in a cab. There were hugs and pats on the back. Owen drunkenly proclaimed his eagerness for the upcoming event. Promises of alcohol were made. As the night ended and the prospect of dawn came upon Malibu, more and more partygoers, drinkers and lovers left.

"One hell of a night," said Petey, letting out a yawn. "Jesus."

"It's just like a typical Australian evening out." Philippa leaned on him and sniffed the dead, moist air of the bar. "Typical. If you're ever there, I'll show you in person."

"When are you heading home?"

"End of next month. I've just been studying here in Los Angeles as part of an exchange thing, then I ended up with this internship. But my college magazine got in touch with me, wanting me to do a piece for them. They suggested you. Gonna miss this place though. In a few months, it's back to Sydney and probably a part-time job to fill the gap."

"You're more than welcome to come here and visit any time you want."

"Oh cheers, mate."

"Do you want me to fetch you a cab?"

She rolled her eyes up. "Nah, mate. Is the bar still open?"

"I think so."

"Well, order us another bottle of champagne then."

Waves gently lapped against the shore, kissing the sand. Dawn was imminent, an ever-encroaching sobering device.

"I shouldn't really be doing this," said Petey. "I am a married man."

"I'm probably going to get engaged soon." Philippa

brushed her lips against his neck. "So, we're both breaking the rules."

"Who's the lucky guy?"

"Guy, as it happens."

"What?"

"His name's Guy," she stressed playfully. "Guy Grisham."

"Cool name."

"Well, he's not exactly cool. Works as an assistant in a post office, for fuck's sake."

"Then why are you going out with him?" Why was he starting to feel desperate? He couldn't have this woman. That door was closed... forever. Sealed off.

"Because... I dunno." She stopped them both in their tracks, unlinked her arm and faced the ocean. "He's stable, he's faithful to me. I've been cheated on before and I can't really go through that again."

"He's lucky to have you."

"Oh, thanks. I just need to inject some life into the miserable sod."

"Why are you so unhappy?" he asked her. This was a question that Sarah once used to ask him, decades ago. Now he was the one saying it out loud, a proclamation of contradictions.

"I dunno, mate."

"What do you want to do? I could get you a cab, breakfast."

"Why?"

"Well, you're torn between flirting with me and trying to get away."

"I suppose so."

"Then what do you want to do?"

"Stay here until the sun comes up." She slumped down onto the sand and put her legs out straight.

Petey plonked himself down next to her and held her close to him. Half-asleep, her head slumped. He gently tilted her head onto his shoulder and looked back out to sea.

The sunrise crackled into life, a cool flame that reached the corners of the eyes. There was an element of grace to it, the way it filled up the ocean and the sand. Malibu changed from a scene of nightclubs, bars and cocktails into a montage of joggers stretching before their morning runs, shops and cafes opening their doors, and dogwalkers making sure their pets were properly exercised before the heat got too much. The silvery, free-flowing alcohol streams were gone, giving way to the rumbles of expensive cars starting up. The social bonding of the night evaporated, replaced by the intricate intrigue of a new day.

He dozed off quite unexpectantly. He was shaken awake by Philippa, who promptly dragged him to his feet.

"What the hell happened?" he stuttered.

"You dozed off, you lazy bastard."

"Bloody hell. Must be getting old."

"Any excuse," she joked. "Now, are you going to buy me breakfast or what?"

He didn't take Philippa home, instead ordering them both the unhealthiest, fattening, risk-of-getting-food-poisoning fry-up you could get in Malibu. He knew the owner of the establishment, Jose, who'd come up from Mexico twenty-five years ago, initially to study business management, but a newfound friend had made him try an American fried breakfast. Long story short, Jose had been hooked and decided to make a business of it.

"How can you eat this stuff?" said Philippa, with a playful act of disgust, when Jose had set their meals down. He only did one course: everything mashed together.

"Best hangover cure," Petey responded. "Can't beat it."

"It makes me nauseous."

"No, that's the alcohol. This stuff gives you all the vitamins and minerals and bollocks you need to restart your batteries."

"You're a typical Brit."

"Thanks. Why do you say that?"

She did a crude impersonation of him. "*All the vitamins and minerals and bollocks.*"

"Haha. Now eat up."

"Can I ask you a personal question?" She munched on some fried bacon and gingerly prodded her coffee mug with a pinkie.

"Sure."

"How much do you love your wife?" asked Philippa.

Petey's neck tightened. "With all my heart. She's the single most important thing that's ever happened to me."

"Oh, that's sweet."

"Thank you. Why do you ask?"

She ignored him. "So, what are you up to for the rest of the day?"

"Well, I've got some prep to do for tomorrow night. I'm looking forward to it."

"We're going out for drinks afterwards if you want to join us," she said, spooning some mushrooms into her mouth.

"Yeah, I'd like that."

For the rest of the morning, they talked about various things, from the new plight of the third world, to the latest thriller by Fletcher Pringle (often a rival to Petey in book sales). When they had finished their breakfasts, Petey called the student a cab. There was a rushed goodbye outside the café, reminiscent of clumsy farewells from decades past. For the second time in two days, Petey stood slightly helpless as a taxi sped off carrying someone he cared very dearly about.

Saturday 22nd June 2030

Petey chose the cinnamon aftershave for tonight. He splashed it on with the ridiculous nature of a water pistol with a broken nozzle. He was in a thousand-dollar suit, wearing a shirt of such fine nature that to see a movie star in one would be as rare as spotting a pink elephant in Antarctica. He was fully assembled ten minutes ahead of schedule. He skipped down to the lounge and poured himself a single malt.

Tonight was going to be good. It would be a break from the normal routine. No miserable-looking-I-am-so-desperate-to-be-successful-like-you readers queueing up like they were waiting for the gates of hell to welcome them inside.

The venue was a lecture theatre at the University of California, in the Ike Building. He hoped that all the seats were booked up. But not for his sake: as part of the agreement with the university, the organisers received two dollars for every ticket sold. Philippa might make a tidy little profit from it.

After finishing his drink, he quickly brushed his teeth and went outside. The taxi appeared on time and soon enough he was on the highway, trying not to imagine the evening ahead – that only spoiled things.

Arriving at the campus, he expected to be greeted by that ever-wonderful series of flashes called paparazzi, but there was just the black yellow of the university pathways. The driver took him right to the front door of the Ike Building. Petey paid the fare and stepped out, with the ginger nervousness of a fox dashing in front of headlights.

Why was the building empty? Puzzled and mildly alarmed, he stepped through the glass entrance. The Ike Building had been built last year, according to the university, as *a celebration of the remarkable education we offer*. But for a building that housed dozens of lecture theatres and a library, it was as silent as a tomb.

"Excuse me, sir, can I help you?" asked a gruff voice. A janitor, complete with a stained shirt, shambled towards him.

"Yes, I'm Peter McGough. I'm meant to be doing an event here with some students. But they don't seem to have turned up."

"Oh yes, I know now." The janitor coughed and spluttered. He spoke with a cigarette smoke-flavoured New York accent. "The event has been cancelled."

"That's impossible! I had confirmation in writing!" Of course, it made perfect sense. This whole thing was a ruse. A prank. They wanted to have their five minutes of foolery with a successful crime writer.

"I was informed last night," said the janitor. "I take it no one told you?"

Petey was about to launch into a rant, vowing to sue the university, when Owen opened one of the great glass doors.

"What the hell's going on?!" Petey yelled. "I can't believe this!" He stopped when he saw the tears collecting around the Aussie's eyes. "Is everything okay?"

"I'm sorry," said Owen. "It's Philippa."

"What, is she okay?"

"She was killed yesterday. As she was getting out of a taxi. The police think it was a mugging."

"Fuck."

"We cancelled the event out of respect for her. It fucking hurts so much! We didn't have any way to contact you directly. Philippa had all the contact details on her phone, which the cops have got. We emailed your publisher, but I'm guessing they didn't pass on the information."

"It's okay."

"Listen, I need to head off now. I'm flying home tomorrow. I don't think I can stay here any longer. She meant so much to us. She was so full of life." Owen sniffled like a baby. Was this what a broken man looked like? "You know, I don't think Philippa ever looked happier in the past few days. She was talking about you all the time."

"I'm sorry."

"Listen, I've got to go. I'm sorry. Take care of yourself." Owen stormed away.

Petey felt the tears crawl out. "Shit." His legs were trembling. What was that expression? Two left feet. The Ike Building felt even emptier now, as though it had swallowed his emotions.

He started walking around the campus. Were students saying things like, "Whoah, is that Peter McGough?" Did someone ask him to sign a book? He thought he might have put pen to paper and scrawled a signature.

At some point – he didn't know when – it could have been an hour later – he was in a cab, trundling through the city lights, on his way back to Malibu. Time didn't make any sense now. Philippa's death had shattered reality.

It probably wasn't a good idea, but he went for a

drink in the bar where they'd been. It was much quieter now, quite surprising for a Saturday night. He only stayed for one. The bitterness too much.

It still hadn't hit him. In the weeks and months ahead, he would find out the gruesome details of how Philippa had lain writhing on the pavement as blood spurted from her neck. But for now, all he could sense was loss. What had their relationship been? Romantic? Professional? Friendly? Overfriendly?

He went home after his drink, alone. The brokenness tore at his heart.

He poured himself a whisky that hours before had seemed so full of amber joy. Now it burned at his throat.

It was like standing at that bus stop, watching Sarah leave. He'd been abandoned, yet again, left to emotionally fend for himself.

Sunday 23rd June 2030

He spent the early hours of the morning lying awake in bed. A bed that seemed so big and empty was not a bed fit for a king, but one for a man thrown to the sharks of solitude. He didn't even get up to make himself coffee and toast. A morning run was the furthest thing from his mind. It would remind him too much of Philippa.

He turned instead to philosophy. The big ideas. Where do we come from? Where are we going? What does it mean to be human?

Those who travel in life, those who achieve great and wonderful things, sometimes find themselves facing an uncomfortable fact: that they have come further than they were ever destined to. They are like lost space probes, cast to the far side of space, far from home.

Monday 24th June 2030

When Sarah's taxi turned up, he nearly let tears overcome him, but he fought them back. He was going to live for the now.

He didn't mention Philippa. Sarah didn't need to know. He told her that the event went well and a large number of books were sold.

Over a light lunch, he suggested they might try an Italian tonight. She agreed, saying she'd had enough foreign food. A nice pizza between them. That would suit her down to the ground.

He called his publisher that afternoon, laying the law firmly down to Bernard: Lieutenant Halbrook would not be coming back and he, Petey, would be writing standalone thrillers, and there would be a literary novel coming out in the not-too-distant future. Or, he, Peter McGough, bestselling author of the Rick Elder series, would be finding a new publisher. This confidence surprised Petey, but even more so Bernard. The publisher informed him that the necessary arrangements would be made.

He spent the rest of the afternoon working on

Prediction. Philippa had inspired him, given him the emotional whirlwind. He knocked out five-thousand words like quicksand. He only stopped when Sarah called up him: "We need to start getting ready, dear!" He bounded down the stairs and gave his wife a long kiss.

"Someone's feeling extra cheerful tonight," she said teasingly.

The doorbell chimed.

"Oh, shit," he cursed. "I thought the cab wasn't picking us up until Seven?" Nevertheless, he whistled as he went to the door and opened it.

"It's good to see you," Alan croaked, pushing his way past Petey.

"Everything okay?" Petey asked.

"Fine." Alan dropped his briefcase and slung his jacket on the chrome coat stand in the hallway. "Just got back from the U.K."

"Perfect timing. Sarah and I are just about to head out to dinner. I'm sure we can get an extra place at the restaurant, if you want to join us."

"No, I won't be. In fact, if I were you, I'd cancel your reservation. Immediately." Alan picked up his brief-case and went through to the lounge. He perched on the edge of the sofa and rubbed fingers through his hair. "Can you get me a drink? I really need one."

"Is everything all right?" Petey said, pouring out a single measure of whisky. "Mate, you look like you've been in a train crash. Here, take this. You look like you need it."

"What events do you have lined up?" Alan was livid with stress. He looked unwashed, grubby, and hungover.

Sarah came into the room, fastening her earrings into place. "Hi Alan. Are things okay?"

"Will everyone please just stop asking me if I'm all right and just listen to me!" he shouted. "Please!" He chucked down the drink in one. "Right, can you please cancel your dinner reservation for tonight? Now!"

"Sure," said Petey. He took up the house phone and called the restaurant, making sure that he apologised for the inconvenience.

"Now, what events do you have lined up?" Alan said forcefully. "You know, book signings, etc."

"I don't know. About eight. I'm heading to Seattle next week for the first of them. Then the rest are in –"

"I don't need to know where they are! You need to email your publisher and agent and cancel your attendances."

"Okay, is this about the translation rights? I'm really confused, Alan."

But the lawyer steamed on, angrier by the second. "Do you have any holidays scheduled?"

"We're booked to go to Mauritius in a couple of months," said Sarah.

"You need to cancel. Get a refund. Try to get every penny in compensation that you can. I will help you. You also need to put this house on the market and move to lodgings. You need to sell everything that you don't need: jewellery, ornaments, you know what I mean; your cars as well."

"What the hell is this about?!" bellowed Petey. "Am I in legal trouble?"

"I'll explain after you've emailed your publisher and agent. It's really important that you do so! You also need to pack for a few nights. I've booked rooms in a small motel in the south of L.A. As soon as you've messaged your agent and publisher, cancelled Mauritius, I'll explain in full. We need to be gone from here by Nine, at the very latest. Every second we wait, it's going to be even more difficult to leave."

"Alan. I am not leaving; I am not emailing a single fucking soul until I know what the fuck is going on!"

"Are we in danger?" gasped Sarah.

"Alan, I want to know what's going on!" Petey shouted.

"Okay." Alan yawned and tapped the bridge of his nose with a forefinger. "Sit down. Both of you. Get me another drink. I suggest your pour yourselves a large one too. This is going to be one hell of a shock."

Alan Stanley needed three whiskies before he was ready to talk. Massaging his temples, he stretched his legs out and crossed his ankles. The lawyer had the appearance of a Mid-19th Century American farmer, admiring the day's handiwork with a glass of something at sunset. Petey and Sarah had pulled two armchairs in front of him; they held hands. She was scared witless, he realised.

"It's kind of hard to explain," said Alan. "It'll take a few minutes. Then we really need to leave."

"Just tell me what the problem is with the translation rights." Petey had encountered something like this before, five years ago. It was after the publication of a standalone thriller (he couldn't remember which one) and there was a legal issue or something with getting it translated into Portuguese. Oh, the many trials and tribulations of being an international blockbusting author, one could say.

"There's no problem with that. That was a small lie I told you, because if I told you what was really going on, you would panic. On the night of the Seventh of June, I received an email from the British police. I don't know why they informed me instead of you. Perhaps it was due to the background nature of how this has all come about. I don't know."

"What's happened?"

"Do you remember Nick?"

"What?"

"Nick." Alan nearly reached down for his briefcase, but stopped. He uncrossed his legs and hunched forward like he was at prayer. "The bully from school."

"What?"

"Guys, what I've got to tell you is... shall we say... a complicated story. That's why I've been in the U.K. for quite a bit. Well, firstly, firstly, I've managed to negotiate with the cops to hold things from the media for some time. But that levy could break at any second. Secondly, I wanted to get the full story, every nook and cranny of it. To make sure your defence is as full-proof as possible..."

"What do you mean, 'defence'?" Petey filled a glass to the brim, drinking it like water.

"Has she told you?" said Alan. "Has your good lady wife told you how she and Nick became lovers in Nineteen-Eighty-Nine?"

"Excuse me?"

"Oh, yes. When you two first met."

"That's impossible!" Petey shot back.

"No, it's true." Sarah's words were a lonely horse galloping across a plain. "That's why I was walking past your house. I'd been in Banbury, you know, seeing the sights, when I met him in a pub. We had a one-night fling. I told him that I wanted to end things, but he was very pushy. One day – the day you and I met – I was out walking, when I saw him following me. So, I took a detour and entered the lane where you lived. When you came out, telling me you loved me, it was the perfect opportunity to get shelter. I was a bit reluctant at first, but I could see him looking at us. He gave a massive shout. Animalistic almost."

"You mean, you used me."

"I promise you, Petey, everything I said to you on that day was truthful. You must understand, I had to hide from him. But I meant everything I said. I promise you that."

A deep cut opened between the two of them. Neither side knew what to do.

"When I left you the next day," she continued, "he

came up to me in a café, as I was about to leave Banbury, and he got very threatening."

"He wanted revenge," stated Alan. "And revenge was what he attempted. He was going to destroy the both of you, because you spurned him, Sarah. So, he wrote a letter, alleging that, you, Sarah, told him that Peter McGough raped you. He made it so nice and formal. Hand on his heart, that sort of stuff. The bastard intended to mail it to the police a few days after he wrote it. For safekeeping, he placed it under a pile of clothes in his bedroom. As we know, he was hit by that car. That letter stayed hidden for years. His good old mum kept his room as a shrine."

"Why now?" The reality hadn't sunk in for Petey... yet.

"Donny Bell," growled Alan. "When he was released from prison twelve years ago, he went about looking for revenge."

"Petey, my love, I'm so sorry," Sarah whispered.

"Let's just hear the facts, okay?" said Petey.

Alan continued, like he was presenting a lecture on the latest theories in evolutionary biology. "Mr Bell was able to use his connections to carry out thorough searches of your life, Peter, and yours, Sarah. Over the past decade and a bit, he has tried and failed to find

something that he could use against you. Finally, him and his *crew* did a few searches in Chipping Norton. Our schools, Peter. Primary and Secondary. Raided. They searched our childhood homes. Then Mr Bell found out about Nick, i.e., that he used to be a bully. Well, those bald-headed brutes armed with baseball bats raided Nick's home. Nick's mother, stupid woman, had never moved and had kept all of Nick's things. As soon as they found that note, well, that was a golden ticket to the revenge factory. Bell wasted no time in handing it to the cops. Which is why we need to leave. We need to prepare a statement of some kind as well."

"Oh, Alan, this is preposterous!" laughed Petey, though his subsequent chortling was forced. "It's a handwritten letter by a guy who used to bully us at school. I think you should go home, get a few hours of kip, then we'll have a talk about this in the morning. I don't know why you've wasted your time tonight. Sarah, call the restaurant again, let's see if we can get our reservation back."

"Peter, I'm warning you." When Alan was calm, that was when he was the scariest. "The police are about to issue an arrest warrant. They've called Nick's letter a valid piece of evidence. As far as they're concerned, in Nineteen-Eighty-Nine, you raped Sarah. We need to get our ball rolling, if we've any chance of getting through this."

"Let's just try to calm down," said Petey, skin pulsing with disbelief.

"And there's another problem as well. Donny Bell committed suicide last week, so we've already lost a potential line of defence in that we can't challenge his decision to invade Nick's home."

"What about the guys who helped him?"

"They've scarpered. They were all wearing masks and gloves. Very careful not to leave fingerprints or DNA around. Plus, there are still a few bent coppers who supported Bell back in the day."

Sarah sniffled, face matted with salty water. "Come on, Alan, we'll fight this. Let's go out to dinner tonight. Take our mind off things."

"No." This didn't come from Alan, now looking on the verge of collapsing, but from Petey. He refilled their glasses and trudged to the doorway. "No. Sarah, do as Alan asks. Cancel Mauritius. I'll take care of things with my publisher and agent. As soon as we've done the necessary bits and pieces, I want you to go with Alan to the motel. Do exactly as he says. I'll stay here."

"I strongly advise against that." Alan got up, comforting hand poised. "The media will tear you to shreds."

"I'm staying here and will wait for the police to arrest me." Petey looked sadly at them both, knowing his next words would render them speechless. "I'm going to plead guilty."

Sarah opened her mouth to scream. Nothing came out.

They were able to get a few minutes alone. Alan was waiting by the door, tapping his feet. Petey took her into the lounge and sat them both down.

"What the fuck are you doing?" she stammered. "What the fuck?"

"It's going to be okay." He stroked the small of her

back with the heel of his palm, the way she always liked it.

"Why are you doing this?"

"It sounds like the police are pretty adamant about things. If we try to contest the letter, they'll accuse you of making a false rape allegation. You'll lose everything. We both will. I know you don't want to do this, but what else can we do?"

"What about fighting it?"

"I won't let you do this." Though the tears clogged his throat, he remained firm. "I love you. I will always love you, whatever happens. This is difficult. This is very difficult. But I can't let you put everything you have at risk."

Alan came in, looking at his watch. "Guys, come on," he said. "Sarah, we need to leave."

"Go," Petey ordered her. "Go. Alan, inform the police that I am here and ready to be taken into custody."

"I'll do it enroute to the motel." Alan gently took Sarah by her shoulders. "Come on, Sarah. Let's go."

She never said another word to him. Nor did she even look at him. She was simply gone, bundled out of the house like a celebrity being evacuated from a riot at a rock concert.

He opened the bottle of single malt and dribbled another measure into his glass. He didn't let his lips touch the edge; he just held it in his hand. This house, this luxurious home, he would never see it again.

He didn't think about Sarah. It was strange, he wasn't feeling anything. He thought about Philippa, such a kind soul taken way too early, in a truly horrific manner. Somehow, the Australian had made his rich world sparkle with the jewels of life. He was glad he'd met her, spent time with her on the beach as the sun came up. That was what freedom meant.

He waited and waited. Every time a car went by, he envisaged a SWAT team storming in, laser dots sweeping the place. The hours passed like gifts.

When the police finally did arrive just before midnight, he was almost relieved. Just two cops and a set of flashing lights. He opened the door for them, inviting them in for coffee. Of course, the officers couldn't partake. He was a suspected criminal after all.

"Sarah," he said, as the cuffs were placed on his wrists and his rights were read. "Forgive me."

Reversal

Pentonville Prison, London

Wednesday 7th March 2035

He awoke, fresh from a dream in which he was walking along a tropical beach, to a fierce rapping on his cell door.

"Oh, for fuck's sake," he hissed. "Christ."

The hulk of metal sprung open and two screws came in.

"What the fuck do you want?" he snarled at them. "I don't have any contraband or shit."

"That's enough of that please, Mr McGough," said one of the prison officers. "Now, can you stand up please?"

The bed, dotted with springs, squealed like a pig as he shifted his weight and got to his feet. The prison officers spread his legs and gave him a quick body search. After they were both satisfied that he wasn't carrying any offensive weapons, drugs, or other nasty implements that could *undermine the security and peaceful nature of Pentonville Prison*, he was taken out the cell and led to visitation area.

The past twenty years had seen U.K. prisons become more like their American counterparts. That

British sense of 'eating porridge' was replaced by a sterile sense of perfection. Everything had to follow an extremely rigid order. No exceptions. If you were out of line, well that was too bad. And it wasn't just prisons and detention centres: the whole of Britain had become cleaner and more precise. Nothing was taken for granted anymore. It was on time and on target.

A senior prison official, evidently new to the job judging by his clean, ironed shirt, gave him strict instructions on what he could and could not say, that when time was up, IT WAS UP, and there was to be no physical contact between him and his visitor WHATSOEVER.

The visitation room, wonderfully painted over in white, was empty of other prisoners and their families. Metal tables and chairs, nailed to the floor like mock crucifixions, begged an audience from the unfortunate souls to wind up in this politically correct justice system. The senior official showed him to the nearest one.

He'd been informed of the visit three weeks ago. No information had been provided. Of course, he knew who it was. The question was, why would she want to see him?

He started pacing in tight circles, knuckles snapping. He risked a few glances at the door, hoping and not hoping that he would see her behind the small window. He shut his eyes and opened them again, trying to quell the butterflies.

Sarah appeared on the other side of the glass, grimacing. He straightened himself.

"How are you doing?" she asked, as a guard showed her inside.

"Okay," he said.

They stood before each other, on either side of the table, like two generals of opposing sides in an endless war meeting for the very first time. Aware of the watchful eyes of the guards and CCTV, he motioned for them both to sit.

"How's Rome?" It was important for him to kick their conversation off on the right track, otherwise they'd be sitting irritably all afternoon.

"It's good," she said. "The rent's a fucker –"

"Tone down the language, please!" said a voice over the intercom.

"– but I'm involved with a lot of projects at the moment and am earning quite a bit of money."

"Excellent, I'm really pleased for you!"

"How are you coping with prison?"

"Same old, same old." He'd be saying this in twenty years' time, trotting around his cell, riddled with dementia. "We're having this big inspection next week."

"Oh, right" She shifted grey strands of hair from her eyes. "But, things are okay here?"

"Oh, yeah, they're fine. I get treated well. Three square meals a day. T.V. Music."

"You've shown amazing strength in doing what you've done." Sarah took out a cigarette and was promptly yelled at over the intercom to put it away. "Never mind, eh."

"I still stand by my decision," he told her, seeing where this was leading. During the first few months of his sentence, she'd called him every week, begging him to change his mind. But as the days and weeks and months and years passed, she'd seemed to become accustomed to the situation.

"I know," she responded defensively. "I know. I actually came to say thank you. You were right. There was no way it could have worked."

"Exactly. I mean, with Alan Stanley dying from that heart attack a few weeks after my arrest..."

"Yeah, there's no way we would have been able to defend ourselves, not with him gone." She cleared her throat. "There's something else. It's... I'm... I'm tying the knot next week." He remembered vividly listening to her on the prison phone, how she was moving to Rome, all the bits and useless pieces of how she was relocating. In recent years, she had really developed this uncanny ability to bullshit. She was doing it yet again right now: "He's such a great guy. Owns a chain of bakeries across Italy. Really intelligent. Pedro is his name. We met last year at this environmental thingy. He said I should come visit one of his bakeries. There was this bottle of wine when I arrived. So sweet. Really cute guy. Then –"

"You don't have to go into details. I understand. I'm happy for you."

"Thanks. Well, I just came here to tell you that. I believe in honesty. I have to leave. Flight to catch."

"It's funny, it's like Nineteen Eighty-Nine again. You're about to go off somewhere, into the world, and I'm here, stranded." He smirked. "The ironies, eh? Only this time –"

"I can't listen to your monologing all day," she said, hoisting herself up. "Look after yourself, Petey. I mean it, take care."

With that, she left the room. A guard sealed the door behind her. Her footsteps died away, vanishing into an ether of lost hope, sadness and heartbreak.

That night, just before shutting his eyes, he took out his small folder of newspaper clippings. A small reminder of who he was, his former self. He'd been collecting them since the late Nineties, like a secret stash of roleplaying cards. With the light on, illuminating the scraps, he leafed through:

Tuesday 5th January 1999: Newton-M-Wren Praised by School Bosses

Saturday 7th April 2007: Newton-M-Wren CEO's Book on Artificial Intelligence Becomes a Bestseller

Thursday 23rd August 2007: Newton-M-Wren CEO's Wife and Daughter Killed in Car Crash

Thursday 19th June 2014: Former CEO and Environmentalist Both Praised by Police for Helping Jail Gangster Donny Bell

Monday 6th January 2020: Author's Debut Novel Is an Instant Hit

Wednesday 10th May 2023: Peter McGough Signs Major New Publishing Deal

Friday 4th October 2030: Novelist Peter McGough Jailed for Life After Pleading Guilty to Rape

It was always a comforting shiver to see how newspaper headlines made your life into a timeline.

This was his home now, his reality. He'd been wrong to make the comparison to Sarah: this wasn't Oxfordshire. Unlike in 1989, he wouldn't be going off into the world, going to study at university; no, he was caged like a rabid dog. He would die here, alone, with nothing.

In the years ahead, he would think about the decision he'd made, justifying to his brain that it had been the right and dutiful thing to do. But every day that passed would raise doubts, like strings falling across an expanse of the imagination.

This was his life sentence. Not just a prison for his heart and mind, but for his soul.

Extension

<u>**Wilma**</u>

-

Bangkok

Tuesday 1ˢᵗ February 2050

My arrival in Thailand, thanks to the very inconsiderate nature of the airline I was using, was late, sweaty, un-airconditioned, and unneeded.

I stormed off the plane, giving a curt grimace to the stewards who stood mischievously by the exit. Well, I wasn't exactly happy. Every minute delayed was a minute deprived of journalistic activities; as pompous as that sounded, it was the truth.

Fuck, it was my sixth visit to this country and every time the rain seemed to get a little harder. I could see the clouds raging with lightning and droplets from the bridge. I hated coming here, this miserable dump. Only the thought of writing my article kept me going.

Passport control was the same pathetic job it usually was: no one pointed you in the right direction; you were treated like you were mentally ill; the immigration officer would look at you like you were a potential terrorist. It could be compared with Heathrow in the aftermath of 9/11, except here no one bothered to speak English.

After surviving my wonderful experience with being shifted around from queue to queue like a drug smuggler arriving for a life sentence at a U.S. prison (and subsequently collecting my hold luggage like I'd been released from said prison on parole), I was finally on my way into Bangkok.

I had arranged to stay in this small, funky hotel – moderately pricey but you got your money's worth – located in the heart of the city. After checking in and unpacking, I took a quick shower and then set off, notepad clutched to my chest, to my first destination: the hotel where Peter McGough had stayed fifty years ago.

Why was I doing this? Because Peter McGough was innocent. By looking into his past, where he'd been, his travels, I was sure that I would find the evidence I needed.

I had met him once, only once, twenty years ago in Malibu. I'd been a young, ignorant girl back then, pratting around on my phone. He'd been sitting across from me, tall and graceful. How Philippa had fancied the pants off him...

But that was a long time ago. If I had any hope of succeeding, I had to stay focused, not get lost in the past.

My name is Wilma Penry. My mission was to set an innocent man free.

<u>**Iain**</u>

-

Glasgow

Tuesday 1ˢᵗ February 2050

"The truth is, I don't know," I was told by the extremely vulgar-looking agent.

"Well, I've put down a pretty good offer," I responded. "How can you possibly say that you don't know?"

"How can you expect me to guess other people's minds? If this other couple are serious about offering twice as much as the asking price, there's not exactly a thing I can do about that."

"I'm sorry." I'd gone too far. The agent was only doing his job.

Here I was, in Glasgow, this miserable dump, on a winter's morning at the halfway point of the 21ˢᵗ Century. I was trying to move my wife and I to Ohio. We'd got our eye on a nice little house, picturesque, all the trimmings. It was in Cleveland, not too far from the city centre, but enough to give us a sense of suburbia. This was something important, something neglected, especially in 2050.

My wife and I needed a new start. Our friend Herbert and his family would be there to look after us, help us to settle in. The Heywoods were good, caring people.

The agent folded a stack of notes and gazed at me

pitifully. "I'll be in touch, Iain," he said. He showed me out of the office and gave me a mildly hard pat on the shoulder.

Damn.

The rain, flowing like the tears of Roman Gods, continued its never-ending onslaught. I pulled the hood of my waterproof coat tight around my head and trod onwards through the rain.

Trongate was its usual busy self. Everyone was wet, miserable, dreaming of their next shot of alcohol. An outsider totally unfamiliar with the world of business, travelling here for the first time, could mistake the businesspeople scurrying around like rats for mourners at a state funeral. A taxi whooshed past, splashing the ground in front of me with a consignment of dirty rainwater.

I wasn't driving today, so stopped in The Cross Name for a quick pint. Oh, how this neglected pub could soothe the soul. I nodded at a few regulars – who'd most likely been drinking since opening time – and ordered a local ale they had on tap. Perfection sometimes came in such small amounts. I even forgot about the whole issue with the estate agent after a few sips.

I checked my phone, seeing what was happening in the world. There had been another attempted coup in South Africa, but they were happening so regularly across the world that it was the new normal.

"Ha," I muttered, seeing the next news item below. I was surprised that it was even on the website.

Peter McGough had tried to commit suicide... yet again. Would he ever stop being so self-pitying? The man was guilty, he should have just accepted things. I knew he was guilty. I'd met him once: forty-three years ago. The man whose drunk ramblings had led me to Olga. That wonderful misfortune didn't hide the fact that I hated him for lying to the public. He belonged in prison. He deserved to die there.

Wilma

-

Bangkok

Tuesday 1ˢᵗ February 2050

The hotel, in a severe state of crumbling, had the appearance of a jagged nightmare. How I'd been allowed to gain access, that was down to a miracle. The local mayor had apparently taken an interest in my journalistic career; 'enthused' was the rumour. I wandered inside, my camera deployed.

Was there evidence here? No, of course not. But I had learned over the course of my career that you had to get a feel for things. If you were trying to find out the truth, you had to walk where the truth had been. It seemed silly, but it was a necessity.

Dust caked the floor, reception desk, walls, well... everywhere. The hotel, once Mr Luxury with all the bells and whistles, was a corpse. I wanted to get out, run away – there was always that cowardly templation. But the room Peter McGough had stayed in was only a few flights up. 303.

I missed her. Philippa. Our friendship had been one of sheer closeness.

I tried to keep my eye on the goal, but it only made me think of her more. As I ascended the steps, my mind became loose, falling back, like a marble bouncing down an endless flight of stairs.

The first time I saw Philippa was during our induction day: Monday 3rd September 2029. I turned up at the Ike Building at the University of California, jetlagged as fuck. My flight from the U.K. had been delayed several hours. I was grumpy, lethargic, and a little unwell.

There were several students in the room, including Cary and Owen, who I would get to know in the coming months. I went around, putting on the best smile I had, my every word a struggle as I shook hands. Thinking I'd finished with the introductions, I breathed a small sigh of relief mixed with resignation, but then saw a girl standing by the window, fingers on the ledge like cobwebs.

"Hi," I said, going up to her.

"Oh, hi!" Australian, she had to be... She held out a slim arm to me.

"I'm Wilma," I told her.

"Philippa."

Neither of us got another word out, because our course directors came in, nasty-looking stacks of paper under their arms. It was going to be a lengthy induction lecture. I waved at Philippa and went to sit down. I suppose that I now regret the decision not to gesture her to seat herself next to me. The lecture began, dull and insensitive. I should have been paying attention, but I couldn't avoid putting my eyes in the direction of Philippa, just two rows in front. If I'd known that we would be having the adventure of our lives in the year ahead, I would have stared at her harder, but like every nervous foreign student, I didn't know what to do or what to say.

I spent a good hour in 303. Of course, I didn't find anything. But I felt closer to Peter McGough. He'd been here, right where I was standing.

"It'll be over soon," I said out loud. "Just keep it together."

I walked out of the hotel in a semi daze, like I'd gone out on a blitz the night before and was emerging from the consequential one-night stand hungover as fuck. I phoned for a taxi to take me to the conference centre.

There was an email from Owen. You may as well know: he was now my husband. He was worried about me, asking if I was getting along with my investigation okay. I was about to reply, when the taxi turned up.

It was funny, so obscure, how everyone seemed to be in a hurry when you looked out a taxi window. Whether they were children, old men with walking sticks, poverty-stricken mothers, they all seemed to be going at a hundred miles an hour. A rush to the grave.

When I arrived at the conference centre, I duly paid the fare to the driver and made my way inside. I'd been briefed by my editor that the building, whilst still operational, was beginning to fall into disrepair and was thus hazardous. I was meeting a contact here, someone who claimed they knew *a lot*. They had contacted me a few weeks ago, saying that they were desperate to help. No fee was requested. No expenses desired.

"Hello?" I called out, when I noticed the entrance doors were stuck. "Hello?" I rattled away, like a Victorian child locked out of school, fearful of being caned.

I'd been stood up. But I was to blame, seriously believing whoever it was: *another* fucking timewaster.

I readied myself to phone for another taxi, but then the entrance swung open. A man, very tall, heavily built, stepped out.

"Wilma Porter?" he questioned.

"Yes, that's me," I answered, irritated. "Porter is my maiden name. I'm Wilma Penry now." After marrying Owen, I had considered keeping Porter, but – foolishly, I admit now – now wrote articles and stories under the new name.

"Let's go," he said, holding the glass open. "We don't have all day."

Iain

-
Glasgow

Tuesday 1st February 2050

Of course, it had been way too early for a pint. Nine A.M. These days, licensing hours were far less strict. If you wanted alcohol, you could get it; any time you wanted. But it had made me groggy, slightly nauseous, and tired. The work of a bad pint? Or maybe I was drinking too much.

I arrived at my home in Rutherglen to find that my wife had gone out for the day. The note was sarcastic, unwelcoming, as if she knew I'd been out for a couple of drinks:

Gone shopping. Be back later. Full info with regards to Ohio when I'm back please.

There was nothing wrong with our relationship. Pauline had been a big support over the years. She was an open person, always willing to listen, no matter how ludicrous it was. But her patience was beginning to wear thin with me these days.

The wind was picking up, rumbling the walls of the house. It was old, over two hundred years at least. The stone was beginning to turn to dust. Even stroking a finger along its smooth surface would send flakes into the air.

The house would fall someday, as every house will. Looking around, I saw the beams cutting across the living room ceiling like fallen masts. How long had they been there, buried in the plaster like the corpses of saints?

Every home has its own personality. Mine   mine

and Pauline's – was no different. Our emotions, love-making, arguments, struggles, they were all absorbed into the wood and stone, hidden away like secret codes. Others had been here before us; others would come after we had left. But this building we called our home would one day fall down. Inevitability had a definite allure to it, like melted dark chocolate.

I made myself some tea and powered up the laptop in the living room. Flexing out on the sofa, I surfed the net a bit before going over our finances. Money wasn't the problem for us – it was organising it. We had fifteen separate accounts, a sensible precaution. After making sure everything was in order, I shut the computer down and started thinking about what I was going to say to Pauline. She was going to be very, very unhappy.

Darkness crept up outside, a neglected animal wanting revenge.

<u>Wilma</u>

\-

Bangkok

Tuesday 1st February 2050

"My father worked here," said the man, "many years ago. He was strong and muscly back then."

"Your father, he's the guy who warned Peter McGough about the protesters, isn't he?" I asked.

Our footsteps made thudding kisses as we moved deeper into the building.

"Yes, he is." The man's voice was soft, but with an edge of coldness in the undertone.

"Would it be possible for me to speak to him?"

"No, unfortunately he died five years ago. Heart attack."

"I'm sorry."

We were in a corridor, very tight-fitting, if such a term could be used. Had Peter come down here, all trussed up for the conference? Had he stood where I was now? Here? On this very spot?

"In here..." The man pointed at a doorway.

The conference hall. I walked inside and gazed around. Taking in the technical vista. Tables and chairs had been moved to the side, stacked carefully like square marbles. I snapped a few photos with my phone and made a couple of notes with the memo tool.

"Mind if I have a look around for a couple of minutes?" I said. "I won't be long."

"You won't find anything," the man replied from behind me.

"Well, I'd still like to take a good look, if you don't mind. I also want to get some more photos from around the rest of the conference centre. Thank you for your help by the way. I owe you one for this. Also —"

My tongue caught in my throat. Something metallic clicked into place and then I felt the icy muzzle of a gun on my neck.

<u>Kate</u>

-

Tacoma, Washington State, U.S.

Monday 7th March 2050

"I've been clean for over five years," I told the group. "Clean as a whistle."

There was silence. There always was. We don't believe you, girly.

The Support Group, as it was plainly known, was situated in a former basketball court. Holes spotted the floor, an indication of the neglect the gymnasium had endured. A light beamed down from above, like the forgotten God of Pestering.

"Care to elaborate?" said Marty, consulting his clipboard. He stroked his pointed beard with a pen and shuffled in his plastic chair.

"There's nothing more I need to say. I'm clean. I don't understand why I need to come here."

Marty let the clipboard leave his hands and slap the floor. "May I enlighten you? Three months ago, you assaulted a parking attendant."

"And I did my time."

"Yes, two weeks in a jail cell. You avoided a lengthy prison sentence in exchange for you attending these meetings. So, Katie, can you please elaborate?"

"Fine," I muttered. "I was born in San Diego and grew up there. I started using when I was sixteen. Weed at first, then I moved on to the bigger stuff. Parents found out and kicked me onto the streets. Travelled around the country a bit, selling my body, using crystal meth. Did heroin a few times as well. But in Two-Thousand-And-Eighteen, when I was hiding in a house in Seymour, I met this guy. Peter was his name. Nice guy. Cool guy. We got talking at this party I'd gate-crashed. We came back to the house and we had a good chat. Then he left me, walked out. But his kind words did inspire me to give up the drugs. For the next decade of my life, I did everything to quit. I succeeded a number of times, but quickly relapsed."

"It must've been painful," Gareth chimed in. Damn, he was so annoying. A recovering heroin addict, he looked like a failed audition for the lead role in a movie about drug users.

"It was." I mentally fast-forwarded to 2028. "Eventually, I got control. Got a job. Even ran a half marathon. Wrote a small eBook on my experience."

"That's good," said Marty, rolling his sleeves up. Fucking imbecile.

"But then, Peter... Peter McGough, you'll know him for the *Rick Elder* novels... he got put in prison for that crime. He was guilty as sin. I thought, as I watched the news report, hell, I'd stupidly allowed myself to get close to that bastard. I was thinking, had he raped me? I was high that night, so there was every possibility. What more's there to say? I started using again."

"Go on..." Marty sounded like an evil, cocky dummy. "And tone the language down, please."

"Eventually, I got the help I needed. Really good professional guys. They got me clean. That was six years ago. I'm here now. I'm clean. And I'm ready to move forward. With your help."

"That's good!" Marty boomed. "Now what do we say, everyone?"

"*We stand with you, we stand with you,*" came the chorus of the disenchanted and dispossessed.

I eyed them all irritably. James, Larry and Pita gave me looks of pity, misery and hopelessness. Larry was someone assigned to me my 'friend' whilst I was in the group. By 'friend', I mean supporter. Though he didn't appear to be much good at keeping a moral fibre: weariness, vomit-stained, ill, drained, were understatements about him.

"Thank you for your support," I said.

"That's what were here for," Marty answered. "Now, I think that wonderfully concludes tonight's meeting. It's been great to hear from you all. James, you need to keep writing your letters. Pita, continue having faith in God. Kerry, you have wonderful musical talent. Explore it. Now, what's our motto?"

We all chanted the words: "*Drugs are bad. Friends are good. People are human.*"

"That's cheered me up no end," I whispered under my breath, as people began to make their way out. Marty was pushing on ahead, always in a hurry.

Outside, in the particularly brisk air, I lit up a cigarette. Healthy lifestyles were forcibly encouraged these days, but no one really gave a shit. I hummed a tune to myself, realising that I was truly pissed off at my big mistake. I should never have mentioned Peter McGough. What would this group think of me now, being involved with that rapist?

I was about to leave, when the elderly woman who served us coffee patted me on the elbow and wished me a good night.

"Night to you too!" I called after her.

Surviving this session had been an achievement for me. Just another week until I returned to the patronising bunch or arseholes who were going nowhere in life. Hmm, they didn't have what I had: a shitload of money.

Wilma

-

Bangkok

Tuesday 22nd March 2050

"Why won't you let me go?" I asked. "I deserve to know!"

The guard merely put my meal down on the dressing table, gave me a meek smile, and walked back out, locking the door behind him.

"Fuck you," I hissed, half-hoping he would hear it, come back into the room, and beat me senseless. At least I would be free of this boredom.

I'd been kept hostage in this room for nearly two months, if I'd counted the number of days and nights correctly. It had all the necessities: bathroom with sink, dressing table where I could keep my clothes (which my captors had duly brought from my hotel), a comfy bed, a small dining table with two chairs, and a window (which I was told was bulletproof and sound-proof) that offered a fairly decent view of the city; I'd also been told that it was one-way glass, so no one would be able to see me waving for help.

I didn't know who my captors were, whether they were offering me for ransom or if this was a political statement of some kind. They fed me well, treated me like a guest; but in a way that's what made it more ter-rifying. Would I be here forever?

No, of course not. My husband would already know that something was off – after all, I hadn't been in contact. He was a journalist like me. We were all bonded together, all over the world. We always knew when one of us was kidnapped.

Of course, I had no way of monitoring the situa-tion. My captors had deprived me of television and in-ternet devices. I may as well have been locked inside a concrete bunker.

I tucked into the noodles. They were good ones this week, not like the tasteless crap I'd been served over the past fortnight. For a moment or two, I forgot about my imprisonment, enjoying the ecstatic emotions as-sociated with good foreign food.

If they only they would give me a book to read!

Or at least some paper and a pen! A chessboard! A colouring-in book! Anything to fill my brain and stop me withering away!

After finishing, I placed the tray by the door and rapped with my knuckles three times, then took five steps back, like I'd been taught to by my jailers. The metal cranked open and the unsmiling guard hoisted the assembly up into his arms. He slammed it shut and I heard the mechanism click back into place.

I fell onto the bed and yawned. I wasn't scared of this place anymore. Just bored. Just restless.

When the door opened again, I thought I'd forgotten to put the beaker of water on the tray with the spent noodles bowl. But it wasn't the guard who came in. An elderly man wearing a beige raincoat and corduroys entered. I couldn't tell if he was Thai or Malaysian or Chinese, but I was trying to restrain myself from jumping with joy: a new face!

"Apologies, Mrs Penry," he said. "I have some explaining to do."

"I think you do. You've kept me as a hostage for nearly two months. I think I deserve more than a fucking explanation!"

"Please, Mrs Penry," said the man. He seated himself at the dining table. "Please join me. I will tell you everything."

I did as he told me, my neck pulsing with rage.

"My name is Ray. I understand you've been doing a little digging around, a little investigating." His English was pristine, an educated accent. He took off his wafer-thin spectacles and rubbed them with a silk cloth.

"Yes, I have. Are you trying to stop me?" My journalistic bravado came to the fore. "You can't silence the truth, sir. Even if you put a bullet in the back of my head, someone else will come along. The truth will come out, I can promise you that."

"My dear woman, I have no such intention." Ray placed his glasses back over his ears. He called behind him, "Can we have some tea, please?" The guard promptly brought in two plain china cups, which he filled from a metal flask with an herbal liquid of some kind.

"What do you want?" I asked him, when the guard had left.

"I want to help."

"You know, you could have just taken me out for lunch. Not kidnapped me."

"I'm afraid I was on urgent business in Hong Kong. It lasted a number of weeks. I needed to ensure you wouldn't have left the country."

"You could have just asked me to stay."

"Couldn't take the chance you'd leave." Ray sipped his tea. "You journalists hop around like locusts. I want you to listen to what I have to say."

"There are plenty of ways to contact me. I have a very good email, which I respond to as soon as I can."

"You will like what I have to tell you."

"Am I free to go?"

Ray reached inside his coat and pulled out a passport. He slapped it down on the table. "Your bags and electronic devices are outside. As soon as you've heard what I have to say, you are free to go. You have my word."

"What do you want to tell me? Do you have information on Peter McGough?"

"Better than that. I met him. And I have something that will prove his innocence."

"Excuse me?" All notion of my kidnapping vanished. Now my journalistic inquisitiveness was back in full force.

"I was serving him and his first wife dinner on the brink of the new millennium. Fifty years ago."

"Tell me. Everything."

"There's a large backstory to it, necessary to put everything in context. We have to go back to the early Twentieth Century. It is a long story, so let us have our tea first. Then I will order in some strong coffee and tell you everything."

When the coffee was placed before us, served like we were royalty, Ray polished his spectacles again and thanked the guard for his services over the past few weeks.

"It's a beautiful day," he said, sipping his drink. "Before you leave Bangkok, you should take a walk around, admire the sights."

"I will," I said, with the attitude of a junkie-fuelled teenager in a geography classroom. I didn't think much of the tea. Too bitter. "I want to hear your story. I want to know everything."

"Very well. I knew you'd be eager. I shall begin..."

Atid Apichai was born in Bangkok, in Siam, in 1901. The youngest of three brothers, he was destined never to achieve much in life, as his older brothers would run the family business, which had existed for more than a century.

For the first five years of his life, Atid spent time with his mother, whilst his father instructed his older brothers in the ways of the world.

Atid married Hathai at the age of twenty. With no commitments and no obligations, he started a small farm in the north of the country and lived a peaceful life with his wife.

Sadly, on 5th June 1923, Atid's father, mother and brothers were murdered in a break-in at the family home. With nowhere to go, Atid decided to move his wife, who had just become pregnant, to England for a fresh start. They made immediate preparations and were soon on their way. They arrived in London on 1st November 1923 and set up a small silk business. Their son, Niran, was born two weeks after their arrival.

Atid Silk was popular with Londoners, and in no time at all, more shops sprung up across the capital. By 1928, Atid and Hathai were indeed living rich. With the addition of two daughters to their family, Mayuree and Pensri, they were a strong unit.

On 17th April 1930, they had another son, whom they called Montgomery. There was a reason for this: Atid wanted a son who could start a proper British family, someone who would be British in all but appearance. They gave him a surname too: Robertson. He would be free to start on his own, when he was of age, of course.

Tragically, devastation runs in families. In August 1939 - the specific date is not known – there was a major fire in the family home. Atid, Hathai, Mayuree and Pensri were killed mercifully quickly in their sleep by smoke inhalation. Fortunately, a quick-thinking passer-by called George Lilley, the great-grandfather of Dan Lilley, who was on business in London to buy shares in a cotton business, dashed in and saved Montgomery.

With no living family, but a hefty inheritance left for him, Montgomery was sent to live with a wealthy family in Yorkshire. He actually arrived, terrified to the bone, on the day the Second World War broke out.

This family, the Smiths, took good care of Montgomery and raised him in a kind and decent manner. Despite the food rationing, they made sure that they fed him as best they could and regularly took him on trips to nearby towns and the countryside. The Smiths and Montgomery, who was allowed to keep his surname, survived the War.

In 1948, when Montgomery turned eighteen, he was able to access his inheritance. Now that *Atid Silk* had gone out of business, he had no ties to Britain. Instead, he decided to return home, his true home.

It was chance, mere chance, that on the way to catch the ferry to France, he met his future wife, who was standing behind him in the ticket line at Dover Harbour. It was love at first sight, apparently anyway. Montgomery asked if she would like to have dinner, and when she said yes, he had a strange feeling that home was even further away now and yet even closer.

Her name was Ella and she too was on her way to the continent, with the intention of meeting a potential suitor her father had organised.

They had dinner at a small restaurant in Dover, one which had barely made it through the War, and by the end of the evening, they had both made the decision to stay in Britain.

They fell so deeply for one another and settled down to a quiet life. Montgomery launched a small publisher, Hope-Star-Dream, which would one day become one of the foremost publishers on the planet, with offices in London, New York, New Delhi, Sydney, Paris and Jakarta. Unfortunately, Montgomery died from tuberculosis in 1959 and never got to see how Hope-Star-Dream would one day publish the likes of many famous authors, including Peter McGough.

But the most important thing was that he and Ella had five children: Alfred, Michael, Eric, Jeremiah, and Kieran. They would all go on to live decent lives, with good careers, settling down and marrying. They never did anything remarkable, to be blunt; but they all helped grow Hope-Star-Dream from a small press into a major entity.

Nothing truly interesting happened until 1980 when Kieran and his wife, Dinah, had a son called Ray.

Throughout his life, Ray, despite the pressures of his family, constantly felt the need to return to his home, his true home. Listening to stories about Thailand, its beautiful sense of mystique, its myths and legends, he became evermore intrigued; to him, it was a painted veil of a billion colours.

Shortly he was due to attend university, Ray took a trip there, saving up the money from odd jobs he'd been doing for over a year. He loved it so much that he obtained a working visa and spent time working as a waiter in a restaurant.

On 30th December 1999, Peter McGough and several companions came into the restaurant for a meal. Ray was serving them that night. They didn't notice him, but he was there, an invisible character in a long-forgotten novel.

Ray became fascinated with them. So much so that he followed them back to their hotel and to the conference the next day. He saw Peter's interrupted speech and witnessed him meeting Sarah again. He followed them, keeping one step behind. That night, when they were having beers, at the brink of the new millennium, he secretly videoed them. Many years later, he would be blackmailed by Donny Bell into handing the tape over.

Ray left Thailand in March 2000, returning to the U.K. to take up a position in Hope-Star-Dream, quickly rising through the ranks to become the publisher's CEO. When Peter McGough's agent sent over a book about artificial intelligence, Ray was only too pleased to offer a contract. He believed in this talented man whose computers had revolutionised the world. Even when Newton-M-Wren when out of business, he stood by McGough, feeling his pain over the loss. When McGough submitted a crime novel to him, he snapped it up and made every effort to turn the man into a blockbusting author.

Now Peter McGough was the victim of a serious crime, which was why he, Ray, was determined to help.

"So, that's why you're keeping his books in print?" I asked.

"Yes," said Ray. "I believe in Peter McGough. I know that he is innocent."

"But you have proof too, you said."

"I do indeed."

"What is it?"

Ray refilled our coffee cups. It was never a surprise how quickly the black stuff drained. I'm a journalist, I know these things.

"A recording."

"What of?"

Ray flexed his hands and gave me a meek smile. Then he patted my elbow and said in a calm, matter-of-fact manner: "A recording of Donny Bell discussing with his gang the plan to take revenge on Peter McGough."

"Okay, if you have this recording, why the hell

haven't you released it? He could be out of prison to-morrow!"

"It's not that simple," said Ray. "I can't just release it myself. I need a team. I need people who have known Mr McGough over the course of his life. If there's a number of us, we sit down at a press conference, or something silly like that, and we announce to the world that Mr McGough is innocent. Then we show the video."

"That might carry some weight," I conceded. "Okay, you're right."

"I already have a few contacts trying to get this sorted, but you are a journalist. You know how to get through to people."

"That I do."

"I want you to operate from Bangkok. You will have use of an office, which has everything: computer, internet, notepads, pens, you name it. You will have all the resources you need. I will also use my contacts in the government to extend your visa for several months."

"Well, I'd better get started then. Take me to this office of yours. I'm going to contact several of my colleagues in London and New York. They'll get the ball rolling on this."

"But there's someone I want you to contact first of all, before anyone else. I have tried and several of my associates have also made attempts, but to no avail. I want you to get through to Sarah."

"Impossible," I said sharply. "She's lived a very isolated life since her second marriage broke up. She keeps an extremely low profile, to say the least."

"I want you to do it," Ray said firmly, like a disappointed parent seeing that their child hadn't done their homework.

"I'll do my best."

"That is all I ask."

Iain

-

Glasgow

Wednesday 23rd March 2050

As was usual these days, it was the rain that woke me up. Glancing at my illuminated analogue clock, I was reliably informed that it was just past Four A.M. Three hours until I had to rise out of my warm bed.

My wife was flat on her stomach, snoring lightly. I have to admit, this was when she was at her most beautiful. Vulnerable. Still. I reached out and stroked her back, feeling the warmth pass through her thin blouse to my palm.

The rain began to come harder. A river ran down the window, a meander crisscrossing like a constantly fluctuating parallax of dreams.

This feeling of security, of peace, had come about since the beginning of the month, when we'd successfully bought a house. Not the one we were after. This was somewhat smaller, but we would be close to our friends. That's what mattered.

Anyway, it would be better than here.

We had to get out.

I was counting down the days to our departure date: 2nd May. We would start the process of packing in the next few days. Cardboard boxes would be arriving soon. One whole morning would be spent physically assembling the things (which reminded me, I needed to buy some tape). Then it would be a case of labelling everything and ensuring that things were sealed up in an organised fashion.

A flash zapped through the stillness of our room. Followed by a swift boom. It would have been an incredible sight, if it wasn't such a normal occurrence these days. The world felt like it was dying, and thunderstorms were a symbol of the cancer that had spread across its surface.

I got up and gently slammed my fists against the glass.

"Everything okay, hun?" Pauline was stirring from her sleep.

"Yeah, it's okay."

"Rough out there?"

"You can say that again."

"It's going to be okay."

"I have a feeling it won't." I shouldn't have said this to Pauline, but sometimes words just like to play their own tune.

"It will. I promise. Now come back to bed."

I fell into her arms, burying my nose into her chest.

"I love you," I whispered.

"I love you too," came her reply.

Kate

-

Tacoma, Washington, U.S.

Monday 28th March 2050

"Thank you for a great session," said Marty, slapping his knees in the way he always did, a way which always pissed me off. "Now, people, what's our motto?"

We all hissed: "*Drugs are bad. Friends are good. People are human.*"

"I will see you all next week. Pita, I want you to continue working on your coping strategies. That was very good today. Keep it up, okay?"

I pushed out of the room. I was not in the mood to talk – such an understatement. I wanted one thing: to get back to my apartment, put my feet up, and neck down a few vodkas.

Larry was calling over to me, wanting me to come to his stupid brat party. Didn't he understand the meaning of the word 'no'?

I continued to the bus stop. There was a solid determination in me: don't get distracted. I would not be dragged down by this group of people. I was assigned here as punishment. I was complying with those terms. I was attending the meetings. I was leaving them. But I didn't have to bond emotionally with any-one. That wasn't part of the sentence.

"How are you?" said a welcome familiar voice.

Okay, maybe I was being a little harsh in dismissing everyone.

"Hi, how are you?" I asked. "Hardly seen you at the sessions lately!"

"Oh, I've been in the background, serving the cof-fee as usual." The coffee lady straightened her back as she came into the bus stop. "Certainly cold tonight," she remarked.

"You can say that again," I told her. "Damn!"

"I'm going to make this brief," she said. Her manner had changed, like wind switching direction. "Do you want to save Peter McGough?"

"What do you mean?"

"Do you want to save him? Yes or no?"

"Well, he's a guilty man."

"He's not," she told me firmly. "He is innocent. I will be outside your apartment on Friday. Nine-Thirty A.M. Make sure you have a suitcase packed."

"What do you mean?"

But she was walking off, shuffling away into the night. She was an old bat, a quiet woman. But I was sure that what she'd just said would have unnerved even the sturdiest of people.

Wilma

Bangkok

Tuesday 29th March 2050

It's always a funny experience: to be wanting to work for the person who has you kidnapped.

Here I was, in an office lent to me by Ray. Everything was in order: the visa extension had been processed; my long-term hotel booking had been secured. There was a strange comfort in all of this, a sense of something official.

Since properly starting a week ago, I'd constantly been on the emails. Ray had been pretty insistent on me contacting Sarah, so I'd sent messages to fellow journalists across the world, hoping that one of them might get through to her. As yet, she hadn't responded.

The office was only a few streets from my hotel in a disused apartment. As Ray had promised, there was internet access; food, water and coffee; notepads and other journalistic materials. There was a bathroom and a sofa, as well as a coffee table and a drinks cabinet. Very plush.

I started writing an email to a colleague in Baltimore, who was a recognised talent for getting through to reclusive people. John McGrath was a bit of a loose cannon, doing things his own way, something which had earned him a reputation that went in both directions. I didn't like him in all honesty, but I was down to my last chance. Everyone I'd messaged hadn't been able to help, or were too fearful.

My own attempts at contacting Sarah had also been fruitless. She had no legal representation, no contact address. All that existed were online forums where people claimed to have met her.

After I finished the email and sent it off, my mind wandered once again. I was back in my university days. I was with my husband before he became my husband. I was with Cary. I was with Philippa.

"How are you guys finding the course?" Owen said, in between mouthfuls of green vegetables. His attempts at becoming a fulltime vegan were failing spectacularly. (I'd caught him munching on a piece of fried chicken two days ago.) But the poor guy was giving it his best shot.

"Fine," murmured Cary, his head deep in a *Rick Elder* novel.

It was Tuesday 9th October 2029, just over a month into our course. We were having lunch in a small park just outside the campus. The autumn sun was out in full bloom, illuminating us like saints. We were sat on a small bench that was rapidly falling to pieces, smeared here and there with bird shit.

"When's this assignment got to be in for?" said Philippa. She was cross-legged next to me, studying one of the many textbooks we'd been given.

"Tomorrow," said Cary.

"Oh, shit, you're joking right?" When Philippa panicked, she panicked. "Fuck, fuck, fuck!" She leapt up, knocking over the cup of tomato soup mixed with spiral-shaped pasta. It slushed across the benchtop like an amateur crime scene.

"Christ, Philippa!" Owen snapped, reeling from the deadly orange splashes.

"Sorry, guys, gotta go!" Philippa snatched up the rest of her books and bag and dashed in the direction of the library.

"Stupid bitch," said Owen, digging his plastic fork back into the green stuff. "Why's she even on this fucking course? This is the third assignment she's been late for! She's so fucking disorganised!"

"Hey, watch it!" I protested.

"Yeah, well, it's a fucking fact." He gave up on his vegan meal and took it to a nearby bin, chucking it into oblivion. "I mean, just look at her grades!"

"Come on, we're only a few weeks into our course. She's probably got a lot on her mind, you know, moving here."

"Yeah, well, you know where I stand." He picked up his satchel and popped a cigarette between his lips. "Right, I need to do some prep work for this next assignment. Later, ma homies." Smoke billowed over his hair as he walked away.

"What are you up to the rest of the day?" I asked Cary, his eyes still stuck on the page.

"Nothing much," he barely responded. "Got a lot done at the weekend, so I might just chillout for a bit."

I was getting slowly but surely frustrated. This

course was dull as sin. There was no fun, no enthusiasm. My classmates drifted along like bowling balls. I'd been awarded a scholarship (thus not having to self-fund everything), but I couldn't help get rid of the sticky feeling that I was slowly but surely wasting my life.

"What do you do to chillout?" I asked, hoping and hoping that Cary would answer with something like, "I watch baseball and go to the movies." There was the possibility of socialising then.

"I watch Red Danger Fox."

"What's that?"

"*She* is quite simply beautiful."

"What do you mean?"

"My favourite porn artist."

"So, you watch porn in your spare time."

"Not just watch..."

"Oh, fuck." I sighed. "Listen, instead of watching Red Danger Fox, why don't you watch me instead?"

For the first time that day, Cary looked up from what he was reading.

I should have been more honest with myself: I loved intimacy, I loved sex, I loved pure, vicious, merciless fucking.

Lying on my stomach, burying my face into the pillow that reeked of cum. Yes, I was dead certain about that. The guy clearly liked jerking off into his pillow.

"Hey baby," hummed Cary, stroking my arse with his finger. Christ, there was life in him! "You enjoy that?"

"I did," I said. "Did you?"

"Of course."

"Way better than your porn star, then?"

"Certainly."

Twenty years from now, I'd probably regret fucking Cary, but for now I was pretty content.

His room was like a typical student's, one could suppose: posters, a computer, dirty socks, takeaway pizza boxes, spewed toiletries. He was filthy. Christ Almighty, how could men live like this?

I stayed until he'd drifted off to sleep. The second he was snoring, I quietly put my clothes back on and tiptoed out.

I was unsurprised to find that the campus was dark. Night had come for its song and dance. Drinkers and loud, deep, booming music. It was always conspicuous how an establishment famed for its 'academic excellence' suddenly changed into a party. That nasty feeling of missing out crept in like an infection. I went back to my room, grabbed a quick shower and got changed into a red flower summer dress. When I re-emerged into this butterfly display of beer and top-button-undone-shirts, my spirit lifted higher and higher. I wandered towards a group dancing around a speaker. Five guys, two women. No wait, three women. One was at the back of the group, dancing away like the end of the world. A dark woman with the look of infinity about her.

Someone handed me an opened bottle. I took a swig, then I took it all, one gulp. I suddenly had the burning beautiful wish to socialise, to become one with the party. Become fully human.

I was walking, falling, shifting. Springing, jumping for joy, yelling.

You could connect so easily. I started chatting with random guys. Did I kiss one?

I was feeling so funny. Lightheaded. I was staggering now. Two guys were leading me. Threatening tones in their voices. Where were they taking me? Oh, fuck. My drink. Spiked. Yeah, that was the term they once used for it. Spiked. Their fingers were digging into my armpits. They were laughing, cackling like witches.

"Let's make sure we're discreet about this, okay?"

"Totally!"

Someone was yelling. "Fuck off! Get away! Go away, or I'm calling campus security! I've recorded you! Fuck off now!"

Hands let go of me. I fell. Head smacking pavement.

Hands picked me up again.

I retched, throwing the shit up.

"There, there, let it all out," the gentle voice said.

Whoever it was began to lift me up and I guess I gazed into their eyes like a pathetic puppy.

"It's okay," said Philippa. "It's okay."

I didn't remember much about what happened next. It was just a blur of a blur. Images. A medical room. Orderlies. A drip connected to my forearm. Intimate examinations of my private parts. Shaking. More retching.

All through it, Philippa held my hand.

The next week did bring a sense of justice for me, but I was very unnerved. The two guys were expelled from the university and I was given a compensation payment of four-thousand dollars. I considered dropping out of my course, but Philippa persuaded me to stay.

I suppose that's what kicked off our friendship.

For the rest of 2029, we spent hour after hour together. As the days grew colder and the nights seemed to have a disturbed nature of their own, we moved from parks and outdoor bars to the library and cafes. We still hung around with Cary and Owen, of course, but Philippa and I began to have a friendship unlike any other. We got accused – in timid little whispers – of being a couple of lesbians.

Philippa's work got better. (As arrogant as it sounded, this was all down to me.) She started handing her assignments in on time; her marks and grades shot up; all in all, she seemed happier.

Our end-of-semester exams went well. All four of us got top grades. What else needs to be said?

On the last day, to celebrate, the four of us went to this plush restaurant in the heart of L.A. Really funky. It was Owen's treat, most likely in an attempt to woo me. We drank rich wine and ate like kings and queens. Though I was careful not to drink too much: I had an early flight home to England tomorrow. Christmas with my family was never ideal, but I suppose I owed it to them. Cary was flying home to Texas the day after.

Three days from now, Owen and Philippa were heading back to Australia.

After the meal, Philippa and I went for a walk. The city seemed to breathe next to us.

"You know, it's funny," she said, "but I'm glad I picked this course instead of the one back home."

"I'm glad too. If it hadn't been for you, I don't know what I would have done."

"I sure helped out."

There was something unsettling in her voice. Something deeply wrong.

"Can I talk to you about something?" she asked.

"Sure."

We passed two cops interviewing a stopped driver. One of them was holding a breathalyser. Stupid idiot.

"It's kinda hard for me to say." Philippa was strutting, looking down.

"Just say it. Is something bothering you?"

"Yeah. Listen – I want something more than friendship from you."

"Oh, I see. Well, I'm not really inclined that way."

But the truth is, I was. I wanted Philippa more than anything. I just didn't have the guts to say it. Too terrified of destroying my own image.

The two of us headed back to the campus, bid each other happy holidays, and parted ways.

A former mentor of mine, Professor Maria Pollock, who had delivered a series of guest lectures on an economics course that I had done alongside my degree back in the U.K., once said. "*Every moment is unique.*

Treasure it. Hold it. Never let it slide by." How many times she'd repeated it, I don't know. But it was so true.

Looking back, I wish hadn't just said Happy Christmas to Philippa. I should have hugged her, told her I wanted her. That moment was gone forever. It would never come again.

How many chances did I have in 2030 to make amends? Many. Every day, I promised that tomorrow I would tell her. When she died, I knew this chance was gone. I now bore a curse: What Might Have Been. What if I hadn't been such a bitch? What if I'd had the courage to take that step? Even just a small one?

Moments are like trees. Every branch, every twig, every piece of bark. When a tree is cut down, you may plant another of the same species, but it will never be the same. It will never have the same marks, the same arrangement of branches and twigs. When a moment is lost, it is lost. All future potential turns to dust.

I fought back tears, forcing myself to concentrate on the screen. It blinked.

John hadn't replied yet. That wasn't unusual. He often took his time. Despite his craziness, he did think carefully. He knew what to do and how he was going to do it. I'd first met him at a journalist's conference in Miami five years ago, when I was told I could still write decent articles. No, nothing romantic had happened between us, but over single malts, we'd gained an intimacy that lovers have – but without the physical contact.

I emailed Owen again, this time as his wife.

I put on some coffee. The hopelessness was setting in. This wasn't an ordinary difficult assignment, where the answers were always lurking somewhere. This one felt like all the doors had been sealed, a long time ago.

Iain

\-

Glasgow

Wednesday 30th March 2050

It rained with such never-ending bleakness that it seemed like I'd never known what dry sunshine felt like.

I really should have been helping Pauline out with the packing, but, after a long day's shift in the warehouse, my arms were sore and I was beat. Maybe she didn't realise this, but I was doing these extra shifts to get as much money as possible! For us!

I'd had issues getting home: diversions were in place due to the flooding. I was cold, wet, and badly in need of a hot shower.

Yet, I found this nonsensical comfort in staring out of the window. It couldn't be explained, yet the symmetry was unmistakable: both scenes before the window and behind the window were exactly the same: wet, cold, with a mild dose of hopelessness.

"That journalist who got kidnapped in Thailand is all right!" Pauline shouted up the stairs. "Turns out it was just a misunderstanding! Can you believe how crazy people go when a woman goes off on her own?"

"Oh, you're not starting one of your feminist rants again, are you?"

"I'm just making a pertinent point, matey."

"Oh, I know."

I sneaked into the shower. The crisp water pinched at my back and arms. I daydreamed about luxurious, clear blue tropical ocean, and white, silky sand.

Wilma

-

Bangkok

Thursday 31st March 2050

John finally replied, with a bang and a whimper. He always had a particular way of bursting on to the scene with a spiralling swarm of surprise.

I'll look into it. Leave things to me. J

Short and snappy.

Kate

-

Tacoma, Washington, U.S.

Friday 1st April 2050

The elderly coffee lady turned up at my apartment when she said she would: Nine-Thirty A.M. I invited her in and offered her some coffee, but she held up a palm.

"We need to be going," she said. "Do you have your bags packed and ready?"

"Yes."

"Well, get them."

I nipped into my bedroom and hoisted up my wheelie bag and rucksack.

"Come on!" the coffee lady demanded. "We need to go!"

"Just a second!" I hollered, dragging my hefty wheelie bag through the doorway. "Two seconds!"

"We don't have the time!"

"I'm coming!"

She opened my metallic apartment door for me. I moved my bag through and locked up behind us.

The stairway had an atmosphere of artificial facelessness, a void of voids. In fact, I'd say that it had the essence of containment, a prison for the lost and the daydreaming dead. Its white, chipped marble and broken concrete steps were a reminder of the decaying state of the world. It was easier to get cut off, to find yourself living in a lonely state of routine and inexperience.

The coffee lady inched her way down, with a surprising deal of strength. I felt embarrassed at the thought of helping her.

When we were outside, I did something I probably

should have done some time ago. I asked what her name was.

"My name's Arlene," she informed me.

"How do you know Peter McGough?"

"He came to my house once."

Iain

-

Glasgow

Friday 1ˢᵗ April 2050

The rain let up during the morning, but only for an hour. Enough time for me to wander onto the patio and stare up at the heavens as a tiny ray of sunshine poked through the clouds.

"Can't wait to leave this place," I said out loud.

It was my day off. My boss at the warehouse had *made* me take a holiday. Can you believe that?

I was a lucky man. My friends often told me that I was fortunate to have a loving, faithful wife. The beam of yellow seemed to indicate that. But it was also a suitable metaphor for how close I'd come to throwing it all away.

You know when you have that impulse? You know when you feel you have to risk everything by taking part in a stupid love affair? I did that three years ago.

Her name was Amelia.

I'd met her when I was working nightshifts at a bottling factory in Coatbridge. The work was shitty and the hours were long, but the pay was good. Pauline and I were desperate to save. We were opening account after account. That was the common-sense rule: don't keep all your chips in the same bag.

It was Six A.M. on a Saturday, the end of our shift. The siren blared and we workers stopped what we were doing. We marched out like prisoners and collected our payslips. A young woman with hair dyed red handed them out to us, eyes blank and unseeing. She was twenty, doing a small job that her father (the owner of the factory) had pushed her into. She looked uninterested, bored, in search of something she selfishly didn't deserve. Our eyes met as I walked out and we exchanged a grimace.

I didn't think of her for a few weeks. I saw her, yes, but I didn't register her. My mind was too busy with bank accounts, savings, emergency savings, emergency cash savings. (Pauline and I took no chances. Too many fraudsters out there, waiting for their chance to pounce.) It was only four weeks after the initial encounter that we exchanged words.

It was break hour. Pauline had made me cucumber sandwiches and a small flask of cheap coffee – very unappetising. But cheap. I was munching away in the rec room at a table on my own. The cucumber was dry and the coffee was sour. I watched my colleagues, gathered in a tight huddle at the next table, laugh at a joke. I was about to refill my cup when someone sat down next to me.

"Hi, I'm Amelia, don't believe we've met."

"Iain," I said, quickly adding the correct spelling.

"Haha," she laughed. "How long have you been working here?"

"Oh, about six months. Just trying to get every penny I can."

"Know the feeling. Saving up, are you?"

"Yep. I take it you are?"

"Yeah. Trying to get out of here as quickly as I can."

"Are you moving to America?" I asked.

"Not sure yet. Just plan to travel."

"Oh, where to?"

She leaned forward, whispering with silky, sweet breath: "Let's talk about this elsewhere. I don't want the others to know."

"Sure. Maybe when I'm finished? What time do you finish?"

"Same as you. I'll meet you out the back. By the bins."

Before I had a chance to say anything else, she tidied away the ruins of her meal into a small plastic box and scurried off. Astounded, mystified and deeply curious, I quickly finished my sandwiches and returned to the bottling line.

When the siren sang its monotonous wail, I waved a quick goodbye to everyone and hurried out to the bins. Sure enough, she was there, smoking a thin cigarette.

"Hey," she said, quickly eying my figure, up and down, like a yoyo.

"How was the rest of your shift?"

"Oh, same old, same old."

"Huh. Well, where are you travelling to?"

"I'm not going to tell you. Why should I?" She dropped the smouldering butt to the floor and snuffed it out with her heel. "Come on."

"Where are we going?"

"My flat."

"Um, I don't think that's a good idea."

"Why not?"

"Well, I'm a married man."

She choked on her own laughter. "Oh, come on, a quick fuck."

I hesitated, a schoolboy stranded on the dance-floor.

"Come on," she repeated.

"I dunno."

"Look, I'll put it to you simple. Technically, I am a higher-ranking worker than you, so I am within my rights to tell you to follow me."

Orders were orders, I suppose. So, I did.

Amelia led the way, her figure like a silhouette from a 1950s drama. Her phone rang and she answered in girly chat. Whatever the conversation was about, I couldn't give a shit. She put the device away just as we walked into Coatbridge Sunnyside station. The information screens were flickering, a symptom of how well-kept they were.

"You look like you've never been on a train before!" she teased, taking me on to the westbound platform.

"Haha. Where do you live?"

"Oh, Blairhill."

"Cool."

"I take it you don't use the train much?"

"No, there's no direct route to work. Far simpler to take the bus."

"Well, I've always been more of a train gal."

The train, croaking and grunting, pulled into the station. Amelia was first to board, not waiting (and not caring) for me to step inside. We sat across from each other. A table covered in takeaway detritus separated our two plains of existence.

"I hate this place," she said, brushing aside a plastic carton that once held fizzy drink. "I fucking do. It's a fucking shithole."

"Tell me about it."

The ticket examiner came by. Amelia showed him her return and I purchased a single.

"When are you planning to escape?" she asked me casually.

"Probably in a few years' time. We've got plenty of money, but we're trying to save as much as we can."

"How much money have you got saved up?"

"About half a million."

"Okay, Iain, you need to get the fuck out of here. You can keep saving and saving. Years and years. The sooner you get out of here, the better."

"When are you planning to leave, Amelia?"

"As soon as I can. Probably in the next few weeks. I've got my suitcases packed."

"Where do you think you'll go?"

"Not sure. Africa, probably. Not fully sure."

We fell silent. The train bumped and cracked like an old man's spine. When it stopped at Blairhill, Amelia was up. I hesitated.

"Come on," she said, as the doors opened. "What are you afraid of?"

"Oh, a lot of things."

We walked across the platform, stained security cameras focusing on our every move. Two skeletons departing a metal moving closet. Two loners in a night that belonged so especially to loners.

"Come on." Her impatience was growing like bamboo.

She ended up leading me to a small house, its walls an ever-present reminder of the decay of the world. She opened the front door like her home was a vault that contained the secret of all secrets. No sooner were we inside when our lips pressed together. That's what it was like: no offer of coffee, no vodka, no soft music. All that mattered were the covers. All that counted was us holding one another in the dark as the world churned outside.

That's how it was. Our little affair.

For the next two weeks, we snuck off together after my shift. The lie I told Pauline was that I was socialising with colleagues. Which was true, technically.

We made love like passionate teenagers, not a care in the world, not a care for the world. Though often the storms would often hurl their might against the glass, we held each other tight, skin on skin.

Once, when we were able to spend the night together (I had told Pauline that I was away for a team-building exercise in Aberdeen), we ended up having one of those talks. You know, the ones where you talk for hours and hours and hours. It started off as our respective favourite coffees, then somehow moved on to great works of literature we thought were *not* so, before miraculously finishing on interesting facts about the human genome. Afterwards, when our mouths were sore from all the talking, we looked into each other's eyes. I suppose that's when the sadness dawned on both of us.

"You know this can't go on," said Amelia.

"I suppose you're right. Pauline's smart. She'll realise before long."

"Absolutely."

"How do you know? You've never met my wife..."

"Hmm... that sounded slightly ominous. But get out as soon as you can." She sounded serious now. Very serious. "Okay?"

"I intend to."

I fell asleep shortly after, my head against the softness of her neck. I could hear, feel and smell her gentle, homely breathing. It contrasted – and I've found that life is full of contrasts – to what I woke up to the next morning: an empty bed. Amelia was gone.

In a frightened state of broken-hearted loss, I rushed around the house. Empty chests of drawers, empty shelves bearing ghosts of ornaments, empty kitchen, empty hallway.

After getting dressed, I finally accepted what was reality. Should I have kept tighter hold of her? No! She was free now. I had no right to control her. She was heading to the tropical world, where the air was warm and the oceans bore the heartbeat of life.

The next few weeks were a constant torment on my mind. I would walk past the places we'd walked, unable to stop seeing her. How could these pavements and pubs and parks and shops, which had once been so full of such a great joy, stand so icy and suffocating?

My work performance slipped and I received a warning. I managed to hang on by my fingernails, my character a chess piece teetering on the edge of a cliff.

My resolve gradually hardened. My time with Amelia had taught me to seize the moment. That's what I was going to do. I had to leave this place, go somewhere new, wherever it may be. I was going home... my real home.

I went back inside, nodding to the yellow liquorice strand coming from the clouds, and opened a bottle of cheap beer. I flexed out on the sofa, kicking off my slippers, and turned on the telly.

It was the usual carnage that greeted my eyes: war, famine, freak storms, disease outbreaks. It's just that they were so regular. This was 2050 after all. This was the now. To see some starving kid crying for his momma was as common as getting a bottle of cheap cider from the off-licence.

The beer tasted fuzzy and warm, but it made my head light and my muscles relax.

I was getting out of here. I'd be in America soon. There I'd be able to plan our next move, to anywhere in the world. Maybe I'd see her too, Amelia, on a mountaintop, or a desert island, or a far-flung place in the imagination.

Kate

-

Sunday 3rd April 2050

Of course, I had no idea where I was. Arlene had kept me updated with the progress of our journey and what day it was, but I didn't have any idea which way we were flying. The windows had been blocked with thick, black material.

There hadn't been any tremoring in my gut. I didn't feel in danger. Rather, I was bemused. I mean, how would you feel if an elderly woman who served coffee at support meetings for addicts suddenly whisked you off to some unknown destination in the world?

Arlene was sitting across from me. She'd peeled off her shoes and crossed her ankles. She was engrossed in a fashion magazine of some sort.

We were in a private jet, leather and carpeted interior; but not over-the-top: this wasn't the typical luxury,   you-fly-in-it-when-you've-made-your-first-billion airline.

"Tell me about when you met him," I said.

"Who would that be?"

"Peter McGough."

"Oh, it was a long time ago. I don't remember much." Arlene folded her magazine shut, straightened out her legs and looked at me with those watery eyes. "Twenty-Eighteen. October. Texas. I was driving along the highway and I saw this car. I stopped, asked if the driver was okay. Peter, his name was. He'd driven over a glass bottle or something. Tyre got busted. I sorted him out and took him back to my house. I guess you could say we got intimate that night."

"October Twenty-Eighteen?! Fuck, that's when I met him."

"I know. That's why we've brought you onboard."

Something twigged in my memory. "In the first *Rick Elder* novel, in the acknowledgements, McGough thanks someone who saved his life in October Twenty-Eighteen. He never named who it was."

"Highly likely it was me. But there's always a possibility it could have been you."

"Hmm."

"Right." She looked at her watch, scowled. "Right, we're landing in fifteen minutes. Buckle up."

Wilma

-

Bangkok

Sunday 3rd April 2050

I was in the middle of writing up my notes for the day when Ray barged in. Shining in a three-piece suit, he beckoned me over to him.

"Get your jacket, we're going on a little ride."

"Where to?"

"Just do it."

Annoyed, I picked up my handbag and coat and followed Ray down the stairs into the blinding sunshine. A car was waiting for us, engine humming away. The driver stepped out and held the rear passenger door open for me like I was a movie star in what was once Hollywood. Ray chatted with him for a few minutes, before getting into the front. The driver hit the accelerator hard and we lurched off.

"Hey, easy!" I yelled in protest.

"Sorry," said Ray. "Max is new to this line of work. He'll get used to it eventually."

"Where the hell are we going anyway?"

He didn't answer.

But he didn't need to. The drive must only have been twenty minutes in duration. We passed through the city and on to a highway, speeding up. Clouds were gathering and parting, parting and gathering, gathering and parting again, a never-ending dance of the predictable and the unpredictable. Shortly after joining the highway, we pulled off and entered a stark, bare single-track road. In the distance... an airfield.

We stopped at the gate and a heavyset security guard came forth, exchanging a nod with Ray. A white gate opened and we drove through.

A private jet sat a hundred feet or so away. Two people were gathered beside it: an old lady who looked like a rejected hunchback, and a woman who seemed like she'd crawled through the horrors of the First World War.

We drew to a stop in front of them.

Ray stepped out and exchanged a kiss on each cheek with the old lady. The younger woman appeared to have discovered what the true definition of a hangover was.

I didn't wait for Max to open my door for me. I threw it outwards, ensuring that everyone knew my discomfort.

Ray took me by the elbow. "Wilma, I would like you to meet Arlene Aitchison," he said proudly. "Arlene, this is Wilma Penry."

"It's good to meet you," I said, taking the elderly woman's skeletal, not-quite-there hand.

"It is an honour to meet you, Mrs Penry," she answered, her accent thick with that ever-so-dreadful Texas carpet drawl. Arlene turned to the junkie. "Kate —"

"Yep, Wilma, I heard. Great to meet you." Drug Girl shook my hand with a cocaine-infused fierceness.

"Now, that you're all acquainted, we should get to work," said Ray. "We have a busy few weeks ahead of us. Together, we are going to work to free Peter Mc-

Gough. Wilma, if it's okay, Kate will set up in your office with you. The two of you will be able to liaise at lot more closely. I've booked hotel rooms for you, Arlene and you, Kate."

"Thank you," said Arlene, her gratitude amplified by her own shameless personality.

Kate was unenthused. She raised a lip.

"Now, I don't want us working today," said Ray. "I've booked us in for dinner tonight. A nice little restaurant. I used to work there once, decades ago. But now I run it. Ah, the ironies of life."

"Sounds good to me!" shouted Kate. "Be good to eat some proper fucking food for once."

"Not so fast, young lady." Ray produced a small black bundle from his jacket. He unfolded it and removed a syringe.

"Christ, what the fuck?!" I blurted out.

"Of course not! What do you take me for?" He flicked the syringe with his forefinger and squeezed a faster-than-light jet out. "Inoculations. A whole bunch of them combined into one needle. We'd hoped to give them to her last week, but trying to get anything into the United States is like trying to walk to the moon." He stuck the needle into Kate's left arm and pushed down. "There, that should do it. It'll take a bit of time for it to come into effect, but use a bit of common sense and you'll be okay."

"Glad to know," was her response.

"Right, we need to get going! Max, let's head to the

hotel. I want to get these ladies checked in. Then, how about we go for afternoon cocktails?"

<u>Iain</u>

-

Glasgow

Tuesday 12th April 2050

After a long shift in the warehouse, I was looking forward to a break from the packing. I wanted to curl up with a glass of red and a film. An old British drama from the 1950s. As I stepped up to the front door, I pictured the sharp taste of the grapes and alcohol.

Instead I found Pauline on the sofa, head in her hands. When she saw me, she looked up and wiped away tears.

"You okay?" I said.

"Shop let me go."

"Oh, I'm so sorry. Let me get you a glass of wine."

"Why are you always fucking *drinking*!" she screamed, digging her nails into the fabric of the sofa. "Every time I see you, you're getting a glass or a bottle of something!"

"I didn't realise –"

"Oh, come on!" She sobbed and let out a sniffle. "Look, I'm fucking tired. I'm getting an early night."

"But, it's only Half-Six!"

"Look, you stay up as long as you want. Drink your fucking wine. Kill yourself for all I care."

"Whoa, that's enough!"

She tried to run past me, but I caught her by the arm and held her tight.

"It's all fucked!" she sobbed. "It's all well and truly fucked!"

"It's going to be okay. Soon we'll be gone from here. We'll be in America. Where our friends are."

"It's just, I can't fucking stay here any longer. I fucking hate it here!"

"Just a few more weeks, okay? Just think of lovely hot America. Just think."

"Promise me one thing."

"Anything."

"Promise me we'll never come back here."

"Of course!" I kissed the ridge of her nose. "We won't set foot here ever again for the rest of our lives!"

"You don't understand, babe. I don't ever want to come back. I want to forget about this place. I want it to be like we'd never lived here."

"I promise," I said, running my knuckles across her throat. "I promise."

"Then pour me a glass of wine."

The rain returned for its evening onslaught with divinity.

"To new futures," said Pauline, nodding her glass. Her third.

"To America," I said. "To our new home. To newfound friends. To a future without pain, without worry, without sadness."

The forest of sagging packing boxes, stacked up

like failed attempts at a city, seemed to resonate with how wrong the world was. You could see how messed up things were simply by taking a quick peep through the window. It wasn't natural rain, refreshing for the garden: there was a sadistic, bullying nature about it. It knew you were alone. It knew you were helpless. And it was there to make sure that you never forgot.

"What are we going to do when we get to America?" she said.

"I dunno. First thing's first, when we arrive, I'm going to open a bottle of wine, sit on our new balcony and watch the sun go down."

"Do you miss her?"

"Who?"

"You know who I'm talking about. *Her.*"

Yes, I knew. Pauline often hinted at her when she had a drink or two in her gut. It made me gag when she did this, such a dirty attitude to have, digging up something that shouldn't have concerned us.

"Olga died decades ago," I said, already aching with the tension. "Forty years."

"Do you miss her?"

"Of course I miss her. But she doesn't conquer my every thought. I've accepted what happened. And I've moved on. I'm a new man. We're going to America in a few weeks. That's the priority. A month and a bit from now, we'll be unpacked, with our friends, where the rain doesn't fall like meteorites. We'll be like a happy couple in a fairy-tale. There'll be no one and nothing to keep us apart."

"I just have this fear we'll be stuck in this place. Something'll happen in the next week or two that'll leave us stranded here."

"Why do you think that?" I took the wine from her hands (fearful of spilling it on the sofa that we were spending money on to move it to America) and positioned it on the table behind the arm.

"You know when you have a premonition that something will go very, very wrong?"

"Well, I get that all the time. But we'll be together. If something viciously catastrophic happens, we'll get through it, together."

"It's so bad out there." Pauline turned her head, an owl with worry on its mind, towards the storm, then faced me again.

"It's not going to be long until we're basking in the warmth of an American sunset."

"Not long." Her face twinkled. "Can I have my wine back?"

Kate

-

Bangkok

Wednesday 13th April 2050

The beauty about being a junkie was that you were invisible. No one bothered you. Left to your own devices, you could do anything, within reason. You could be who you wanted to be, within reason. You could travel anywhere in the world, *definitely* within reason. You could sit all day long and take anything you wanted, and no one would give a fuck. Just a shame I got in trouble with the law.

Now I was in a place where my movements were strictly dictated by this guy, Ray, whoever the fuck he was. He had a rule for everything. He knew about me and my drugs, as well as the methods I used to buy them. When not working with Wilma, I was confined to my hotel room. Two burly-looking Asian men stood guard outside.

I shouldn't have agreed to this. All I did was help Wilma out with the filing, photocopying, emails, and a bunch of other so-fucking-bad-I-want-to-cut-myself-stupid stuff. The only noteworthy thing I'd done was to tell Wilma about the day I met Peter McGough.

I was a pet to them. A little helper.

But to be reasonable, Wilma was all right. Though she mostly ignored me, she wasn't too unkind. Unlike Ray and Arlene, who constantly found ways to have a dig at me, Wilma always gave me a smile.

Maybe I was being a bit blinkered. After all, this wasn't about me. This was an assignment... to reverse a terrible miscarriage of justice.

Today, in the late evening, I reassured myself of that. Well, there was nothing else to do with my time, apart from reassure myself.

Humming with a stringy resolve, I picked up a do-geared hardback I'd bought two days ago from a sec-ond-hand shop and resumed reading. You couldn't beat *Rick Elder*. Especially when he was running down a street, trying to catch a killer. Simple, unputdownable, plotless entertainment.

The door opened and Ray came in.

"How about you fucking knock?" I shouted at him. "Fucking hell, man!"

"You need to come with me immediately. We're having an urgent meeting." Ray checked something on his phone and then waved for me to get up. "Come on."

"What's going on?"

"Wilma has just received a message. Sarah is travelling over here to meet us."

"What?"

"She's arriving tomorrow. We have a lot of things to discuss."

Wilma

-

Bangkok

Thursday 14th April 2050

The silver, red line-patterned jet touched the runway with a soft thud, smoke billowing from the wheels. The craft slowed down, turned off the main strip and headed towards us. Guards – Ray's militaristic men – dashed forth and secured the wheels. The engines powered down and a door began to swing open, like a white petal.

"Let's be respectful," said Ray. "Remember, she's been through a lot."

Arlene and Junkie Girl stiffened.

A man in a suit and tie, plastic link into his ear, made his way out of the plane and down the steps. He looked about him and then nodded up the staircase.

Like a ghost, a pale ghoul, a woman in a white shirt emerged from the interior and started downwards. She had a frail composure, devoid of personality, hope, whatever remained after decades of worrying too much.

"Hi," she said, making her way to me. "Wilma Penry, right? I've heard a lot about you." She held out her hand.

"It's good to meet you," I said, taking it. "Mrs, Miss...?"

"Just call me Sarah." She coughed hoarsely. "You are Ray, right? And you must be Arlene. Heard you fucked Peter some time ago. We'll need to have a good long chat about that. And you are...?"

"Kate," said Junkie Girl.

"Don't know who the hell you are. Did you come to one of Peter's book events or something?"

"No, they met in Twenty-Eighteen," said Ray. "In Texas."

"I wasn't asking you!" Sarah barked.

"I apologise." Ray bowed his head.

"The lady can answer the questions without your assistance."

"We met in Seymour, Texas," Kate said assertively.

"I was a really bad addict in those days. Constantly taking any kind of shit I could lay my hands on. I met Peter totally by chance. But he did a good thing. He changed my life. We didn't get intimate or anything, nothing romantic at all. In fact –"

"It's okay, I believe you." Sarah peeked behind her and nodded at her security man. "We should get going. I've booked myself into the same hotel as the rest of you. We will dine there tonight and go over the plan."

"Please, I have a car waiting for you." Ray extended his arm towards the limousine, like a salesman hoping to please a client.

"My security detail will be taking me." Unimpressed. "We have our own vehicle. Sorry, Ray, but trust is a very expensive commodity these days. You're a rich bloke, but you can't afford me."

Ray came across as being quite self-conscious; he goggled at the floor for a few moments before elevating his eyes back up to Sarah.

"Well, I look forward to later," he said. "There are many questions I must ask. There is a private function room in the hotel that we can use for dinner."

"Then get it sorted. My detail will get me checked in, and then they will get in touch with you with regards to dinner. Can't be too careful."

"Of course not. I have my own security detail. Right there in the front of the car."

"You've got one hell of a reputation, Ray. I mean that. I'm of the age now where I know a true rumour from a story cooked up because some idiot wants the attention."

"I think that's the world in general, Sarah. The world is coming apart at the seams, but in a good way: the liars are being exposed, little by little."

Sarah's security guard stepped forward. "We should make a move, ma'am. We are in an exposed position here."

"Of course, Connor." She exhaled. "Right, guys, you'd better get going. I will see you later."

Ray did not look happy as we entered the city. Evidently embarrassed from the charade at the airfield, he'd poured himself a whisky from a small bottle on the drinks shelf. Arlene tried to talk, but he brushed her off like a coalminer removes coal dust. You could see the cogs whirring in his brain. You could hear them.

It was Kate who broke the quiet trauma that Ray seemed adamant to share with us. Sitting next to him on the rear-facing seats, it would be impossible for him to avoid her. "What is our plan of action for the next two or three weeks?" she demanded from me.

"Well, I'd kinda figured that we wouldn't be getting Sarah," I said, casting yet another silent *Thank you!* to John, "so I'm going to have a lot less work to do than I thought. With Sarah on our side and maybe a few of Peter McGough's friends, former colleagues and acquaintances, realistically all we need to do is host a conference with the media and show Ray's film."

"What film?" said Ray.

"The one that shows the gangsters setting up the plan to frame McGough."

"I know what you're talking about. It doesn't exist."

"Excuse me?"

"I lied to you."

"What?"

I didn't know what to think. "May I have an explanation?" I demanded.

"I expected Sarah to be more into it." Ray was like a child with their hand in their mouth. "We wouldn't need to resort to the film. Her words would carry weight. I seriously didn't think she'd behave the way she has."

"You've gambled everything on Sarah!" I shouted. "Fuck! I was doing everything perfectly! My investigation was producing results! I've wasted the past... fucking... I dunno how many weeks... on this shambles!"

"I think we all need to calm down," said Arlene. She was sat by me, eyes looking blankly in the direction of travel. "Ray knew what he was doing."

"You mean *you* were in on this as well?"

"Yes."

We plonked our way through the city, moving past shops that sold every kind of curiosity known to mankind. A loudmouthed bossy lady was sweeping debris up, shouting at a group of boys, presumably in getting them to help her. A group of sporty-looking, professional cyclists were zooming past us, faces out of breath. Typical 2050 Bangkok, I suppose.

My decision had been made. "Tonight, at dinner, I'm going to tell Sarah what I've found so far on my travels. Tomorrow, I'm going to book myself on the first flight back to London. I will continue my own investigation in *my own* way."

"Fine by me," said Ray, reaching for the bottle of whisky.

"I'm sorry that you will be leaving us," said Arlene. "Very sorry indeed."

"Well, I'm not," I responded.

The bottle split apart in Ray's hands, splintering, and coating him with the amber fluid.

"What the fuck?!" he yelled.

"Jesus fuck," said Kate. "It's all over me too!"

"Whoever supplied this whisky, I'm suing their ass!" Ray wrung his hands.

I felt a breeze on my shoulder. Looked round. A small hole in my door. Bullet-sized.

There was an almighty pop as glass shattered. Daylight streamed in. More glass breaking. Gunfire. The puff-puff of silencers.

Kate's right eye was bleeding. She slumped forward, slipping off the leather.

One of the guards in the front turned around to face us. "Stay down!" he roared. We did exactly what he said. "Stay down! Francis, put your foot down!"

Loud raindrops slammed into us. Whoever our attackers were, they were organised.

Ray was reaching into his jacket. He produced a small revolver, glinting like a fake diamond. Silver.

Russian-female-villain type. He leaned up on his knees aiming out of the car. His head turned to red dust. Straight through the forehead. The gun fell from his hands. I heart it strike the outside of the car.

"Stay calm!" the driver told us. "There's nothing to be afraid of! We've trained for this!"

More gunfire. More concentrated. Rapid. Screams.

The car was spinning out of control. The chassis squeaked as we rolled from side to side. Then we hit something. A stall, judging by the strange and wonderful fruit that flooded through the ruined windows. Then we smashed into something hard. I felt myself get flung forward, somersaulting into Ray's body. Then there was... stillness.

"You okay?" I asked Arlene.

"Yeah, fine." She had been rolled next to me by the force of the impact. "Fuck, I think I've cracked a rib."

"We need to move!" Where was this confidence coming from? Probably survival mode.

I opened the door and carefully swung my legs out. People were gathering, confused, scared. I stood up and helped Arlene. Ruined sticks of wood were piled across the place like matchsticks. What a waste of fruit! It was as far as the eye could see. Whoever's store this was, their business was over. The car had gone into a small garage, the metal door bent beyond recognition.

"Shit!" Arlene cried, wincing. "I need to get to the hospital! I –" She clutched at her throat, eyes livid.

Blood poured between her fingers like blackberry waf-fle mix.

I let her go and stepped back.

Four men were approaching us. No. Wait. Teenagers. Shorts and t-shirts, laughing innocently. Silencers protruded from their hands like mutated limbs. This was it. They aimed their weapons.

Then a thought came to me. I could still survive.

I rushed to the driver's door, yanked it open, and jumped inside, face buried in the crotch of the pas-senger guard.

The teenagers were firing at the car.

The guard's weapon was on the floor by his foot. I picked it up. Kill or be killed.

One of the kids poked his sneering face through. It turned to horror as I pointed the weapon and pulled the trigger. My ears screamed with the bang. I'd fired an automatic pistol once, years ago, with Philippa, when we were students, when we were almost lovers.

I kicked the teen's body away, emerging to face my attackers, like a forgotten female superhero. One of them fired at me and I shot back. Two kids stum-bled as my shaking accuracy brought them down. The last one standing fired a shot. I heard it skim by me. Maybe I shouldn't have been using the weapon one-handed. But it was too late for that now. I pulled the trigger, launching bullet after bullet after bullet until the magazine was empty. He fell as the bullets made contact with him.

"Yes!" I yelled, letting the gun drop. "That'll fucking teach you!"

Why was everyone looking at me in horror? Why was a parent covering their daughter's eyes? Why did they look so concerned? A man stepped out, telling me to relax. What the...?

Hmm, maybe they had seen that I was no innocent.

I knew something serious was wrong when I felt my left hand throb. Must have been that last bullet. I didn't want to look, because I knew what I'd find. Tears were in my eyes. Inevitability was always such a bastard. I held my hand up before me, sobbing with shock. My left forefinger was gone, knocked clean off, leaving a bloody stump.

I fell down, praying that it wasn't true. But it was. I was mutilated.

I didn't care about Peter McGough now. I just wanted to sleep and give up on everything. I was ruined. Things were over for me now. My life was done. I wanted to die from this injury. I wanted Philippa. I wanted to hold her and never let go.

Iain

-

Glasgow

Sunday 1st May 2050

"It'll be fine," I reassured Pauline for the tenth time. "Okay?"

"You know, I almost don't want to leave this house." She yawned and stretched out.

Our house was stripped down to the bone. The boxes had been shipped out last week, sailing away to our new home. Our peaceful new home.

This was the last night in our old lives. Tomorrow we were moving on. We were cuddled up in an old duvet, pillows and covers, which we were leaving behind. Who would move in here when we were gone? A young couple looking for a new opportunity? A lonely man with no heart?

"Well, my dear, goodnight," I said.

"Goodnight," she said, switching off the bedside light.

I snuggled down into my pillow, thinking about what lay in store for us on the morrow. I knew what I would dream about tonight: only hope.

Monday 2nd May 2050

We left the house at precisely 09:13, according to my digital watch. Our suitcases in tow, we headed to the taxi rank. There were always taxis there, so there hadn't been a need to call for one. Sure enough, when we turned the corner, neither of us glancing back, there were several cars, lying there like batteries.

Pauline led the way to the nearest one. "To the airport please," she said.

Myself and the driver put the cases in the boot, then we were on our way.

"I'm going to miss this place," she said. "Really. Truly."

"I thought you wanted to put it out of your mind."

"I wish I could," she said. "I really wish I could. But that's not possible. So, the only other option is to cherish the memories."

"But we're going to make new ones," I said.

"Indeed, we will."

If someone walking past looked in our direction, they would just see a couple. But I hoped they'd see much more: two people starting afresh, in a new country, with new opportunities, ready to let go of all the pain that was the past.

<u>Wilma</u>

-

Bangkok

Monday 2nd May 2050

"I don't feel like eating," I told the nurse. "Seriously, I'm fucking mutilated beyond belief. Look at me!"

The nurse, who must have been straight out of school, cursed aggressively at me, then wandered off.

I held up my bandaged hand, redressed with a fresh tang. It still throbbed, but every day I was shot up with painkillers. I was dreading taking them off, and being greeted with a first-class view of my mangled hand.

The doctor had come in yesterday to discuss a prosthetic finger, but I'd told him to shove it. I'd asked him about replacements, actual living replacements which had been developed a few years ago, but he didn't seem to know about them. Arrogant, self-centred prick. He'd even had the guts to accuse me of wasting hospital resources! Apparently, according to Dr Amudee, I should only have been in for a couple of nights, four at the most; but my constant and fuck-I-feel-so-sorry-for-myself wailing had guilt-tripped the hospital into keeping me on. Never mind that there were other patients, many of whom had severe, life-threatening injuries, Wilma Penry, world-renowned journalist, had to be kept and cared for!

I started sobbing, the fifth time in two days. There was no doubt that I seemed like a malignant little cunt. Such a filthy word to use. Cunt. Cunt this. Cunt that. Politically incorrect. Such a politically incorrect cunt... minus a finger.

Then *she* came in.

Sarah had visited me three times so far, clearly shaken by my ordeal. Now she had a look of persistent groaning about her.

"Time you got out of here, Wilma Penry." She edged alongside my bed and sat down on a small stool. "Quite honestly, I'm getting pretty sick of this. Sorry you lost a finger. Worse things happen in India. You're moving out of here today. If you refuse, my two security men will drag you out by your toes. They're waiting just outside the ward. With orders."

"Oh, just cut to the fucking chase, will you?"

"We've found the organisation responsible."

"Make sure you slice their left forefingers off. Wait, did you say...?"

"Yes. I did. They call themselves the Domino Cartel. They're an international criminal group, much like the Italian Mafia. They had ties to Donny Bell at one point. My belief is that they were trying to stop you from exposing Bell, just in case they were exposed too."

"Well, they don't need to worry. The fucking film doesn't exist."

"I know that. I think they knew it too. But, I guess, they couldn't afford to take the chance. But..." She raised her left hand... just to have a dig at me. "But, they picked the wrong people to do it. Stupid teenagers. Suppose they'd hoped it would look like an armed robbery. They've left themselves with an open wound. They're running, hiding away. But we need to act fast."

"I honestly don't care. I just want the vodka."

Sara ignored me. "We're having a news conference. A week today. At the conference centre; you know which one I'm talking about. Media from all over the world will be there. I've ensured it."

"What are we going to say?"

"What evidence to you have?"

"Smidgens. Not even proper evidence."

"Present it anyway." She smiled... yet again. Fuck, I hated that. "I will present my own little piece. Let me guarantee, it will change everything. Peter will be a free man."

"I hope you're right." I'd given up the will to argue. "You'd better be. I've given a lot to this. Both mentally and... and... physically."

"I need to go now. The guards want to keep me secure."

"Going back to the hotel?"

"Indeed." She gave me a stare of pity. "It'll be okay, darling," she said, walking to the exit of the ward. She tilted her head back. "It's just a finger."

Monday 9th May 2050

I stood on the steps, facing the tall, swooning, intimidating conference centre like a Victorian orphan turning up for their first day at a workhouse. Peter McGough – this was a blooming fact – had once had his feet on this spot over fifty years ago. Half a century. Some things just stood the test of time, a gift and a curse of nature.

I forced myself to look down at my left hand. No point getting miserable about it and crying my eyes out. That's the way the world turned.

The media hadn't arrived yet and wouldn't do so for several hours. The conference had been scheduled for Two P.M., to give everyone time to digest their lunch. It was currently just after Nine in the morning. Oh, I loved to be organised... that journalistic trait.

Philippa's voice spoke in my head. *"Good luck, babe."* And I reached out for her hand like I *really* wish

I'd done many years ago. Regret had the unique characteristic of tasting sweet and bitter at the same time.

Sarah and I took our seats in the main hall a few minutes before the allotted time. Members of the media were doing their final preparations. Sarah's two security guards were standing either side of the table, doing their utmost to look formidable. *Don't try to take us down.*

We were in the main hall. According to Sarah, decades before, she and Peter were here, in the prime of their youth. I think she believed that she was back in those days: her eyes fluttered and scanned, like a kid with a toffee apple at a fairground.

There was no fanfare. No one clapped their hands. No one called out for everyone to be quiet. In fact, Sarah merely started when her phone showed Two P.M. If some of the reporters weren't ready, then that was there problem.

"Thank you all for coming. I know many of you have travelled great distances, across countries and continents. I really appreciate it.

"As you all know, twenty years ago, my ex-husband, Peter McGough, former CEO of Newton-M-Wren and subsequent bestselling author of the *Rick Elder* novels, was convicted of rape. I want to make it absolutely clear to you that the allegation is completely untrue. I have the evidence to prove it."

There was some murmuring.

"I am now going to hand over to investigative journalist Wilma Penry, whom, as you are probably aware, was injured in an attack by an organisation that had connections to the criminals behind Peter McGough's wrongful imprisonment."

There was a little bit of clapping – something I knew I'd never be able to do again, not without me (and everybody else) seeing the stump.

"Thank you," I said, clearing my throat. My suit felt itchy and hot. And a size too small. "I have spent some time investigating, travelling all over the world. I want to tell you about my travels and what I have found..."

I was going back in time, falling through a web of memories.

Truth be told, ever since I had heard the news that Peter McGough had been charged with historical rape, I had doubted it. At the time, I was deep in the throes of grief over Philippa's death and passively watched the unfolding reports on the telly, whilst sealed up under my bedcovers. It was only several months later, when I returned home to England, that I began to think about Peter's case in much more detail.

Grief, depression and regret tend to do strange things to people. And I was no exception. Peter Mc-Gough was a distraction, an embolism in my brain, a tender, star-crossed lover for my liver.

Christmas 2030 was downright miserable. My parents, who are fans of having the entire family round for the big day, became worried and, I found out much later, did consider at one point referring me to a psychiatrist.

In January 2031 I started working for a small newspaper in West London. I rented a small apartment close by, my life becoming like that of a socially trapped factory worker's. Quickly though, I found it harder and harder to concentrate. Not because of Philippa; no, it was Peter. Obsessions always have the knack of developing easily and before I long I had photos and newspaper clippings pasted along my bedroom wall, like an assassin gathering intelligence on their target. I only wanted this as a little hobby, but it crawled into my everyday life like cockroaches infesting a one-star restaurant.

In the summer of 2031, I took my holiday in Malibu. My parents and my friends thought I was off my rocker going back there. *"Are you sure you want to be doing this? There's a lot of pain there!"* They were right as well. I went back to that bar, the one where the five of us had sat, a happy memory consigned to the ash heap of the imagination.

But I was an investigative journalist now (by my own admission anyway). I was here to *find things out.* I went to Peter McGough's former home – currently in the state of being demolished. I found out later that this was about ensuring *a healthy change in society.* That fucking word... *healthy...* always had a sinister connotation when used in this context.

There was nothing to be found in the soon-to-be-ruins, so I moved on to the city. I trod through the places where Philippa and I had walked. If I had known two years ago that I would feel such a cold stab of burning emotions, would I never have taken the course? What would you do to escape the pain of loss?

I asked questions of several bookstore managers. They had all hosted events for Peter McGough, but all of them knew nothing that would help me – well, all of them, except one: Mr Nathan Pilgrim. He was not just the owner of a bookstore, but CEO of the chain of which it was part of.

"It was the Twelfth of June, Twenty-Thirty," he told me, over a glass of cold beer amidst the heat of the urban, drug-blitzed day. We were in a lowkey, unair-conditioned bar next to a very busy road. "Beautiful evening. Peter McGough was doing a book event with Stacey Idler, don't know whether you know her or not. I'll put you two guys in touch. She probably saw more than I did, because her mouth dropped open with shock. But anyway, he was doing his reading. I was standing at the back, just watching. I suppose a business owner always takes pride in his charges. We were about halfway through the event, when I saw something that startled me. Out the corner of my eye, I saw a woman, a – please pardon any accidental racism – black woman dancing. She was as dark as coal. You should have seen the expression on Stacey Idler's face! She was actually panicking with terror!"

"Do you know who she was? This dancer?" I asked.

"No idea. And that's the funny thing! When I turned to face her, she was gone! Honestly! Like she'd been a figure in my imagination, jumping up and down!"

"How can that be possible?"

"Don't ask me! I suggest you get in contact with Stacey Idler. She can tell you more than I can. Here..." He took out a business card from his jacket, along with a silvery ballpoint pen. "Look, I'm going to write you out her email. She doesn't like phone calls."

"Cool, well I'm in L.A. for another three days, so –"

"No, she lives in Auckland, with the Kiwis. She's a literary agent now. Hence the reason, she doesn't take calls. I'll drop her a message later to let her know you're going to be emailing her. I've got your email, so I'll send that to her as well. Just in case she thinks you're an amateur writer and casts you down to the slush pile."

"Thank you, Nathan. Are there any more details you can give me on this dancer?"

"I've told you everything I know."

"Okay. I really appreciate you taking time out of your day for this."

"Not a problem. I'm really shocked about Mc-Gough. Can't believe he did what he did. And at eighteen too? Funny how these things always come back to bite you in the ass."

Nathan Pilgrim left after that, giving me one of those silent, in-a-hurry waves. Apart from receiving a message from him confirming that Stacey Idler was awaiting my email, I never saw or heard from him again. He died five years later from a self-inflicted gunshot wound, brought about by, according to a leaked coroner's report, *five years of severe depression and anxiety.*

I emailed Stacey Idler the day after meeting Nathan, having worked out exactly what I was going to say. When she responded, it was in a jolly tone, if such a thing could be said about an email. She was *very* eager to meet me, as soon as humanly possible.

When I got back to London, I made arrangements with my boss, Kelly Bunton. There was no point lying. I told her that investigating the case of Peter Mc-Gough would be extremely beneficial to the paper. After much negotiating, she agreed, and before I knew it the paper had booked flights to New Zealand.

I was never much good with long-haul flights and when I arrived in Auckland, on 3rd September 2031, I was in a great deal of discomfort, my legs feeling like they had been waxed in concrete.

I met Stacey Idler at a coffee shop in the city, and I will say this to you, she looked a complete and utter mess. Overweight, struggling to make eye contact, breathing fast, pale skin. It was as though she had narrowly escaped a car crash in the Antarctic.

"Yeah, she looked pretty scary," Stacey conceded, as our coffee was delivered. "That's why I moved out here, to the end of the world. I'm now a literary agent, pure and simple. I make other people's dreams come true." She hiccupped. "Sorry."

"It's okay. Can you tell me everything you know about this dancer?"

"Only like she was something from the nightmare of nightmares. You know when you have one of those? And when you wake up? And when you're not sure if it was a nightmare at all? You're never sure what to think."

"What did she look like? Any tattoos? Markings?"

"No, she was just black. Like those African tribeswomen you used to see in old films."

"What was she wearing?"

"A traditional dress of some kind. I can't remember much. How do you think this will help your investigation?"

"Well..." I probably should have thought this through. I knew, of course, but I didn't quite know how to form the words. "Peter McGough, when he ran Newton-M-Wren, well, he had a lot of contacts in Africa. He used to go out there quite a bit. I'm thinking that this woman, whoever she is, may know a few things."

"Are you planning to travel there?"

"No. It's not safe at the moment. Civil wars raging all over the place. I'm going to dig up some of these old contacts and see if they know who this woman is. Don't worry, I always protect my sources."

"Thank you." Stacey finished her coffee. "Listen, I've got some advice for you. Be careful. Whoever did this to Peter McGough, they're really bad people."

"You sound like you know Peter McGough is innocent."

"He is."

"How do you know?"

She paused, breathing in, looking around her. "A few weeks after McGough was arrested, I was having a drink with someone in a bar. I blurted out that I had seen this strange woman at Peter McGough's book event. Two days after that, I woke up to find two men in my bedroom. They said that they were from Donny Bell's lot and they were laughing and sneering. They said they were proud of putting McGough in prison, and if I mentioned anything about this dancer or what they'd told me to anyone, they'd hunt me down and rape me and cut me up."

"Bloody hell. Are you okay?"

"Not really. But he's innocent. There, I've told you everything I know. I'm sorry." She sniffled tears.

"It's okay, you don't have to apologise. I'd be exactly the same if I'd been through what you've suffered."

"No, I meant I'm sorry for what I'm about to do. I'm sorry that you're going to be in police interviews for the next few days."

"What...?"

Stacey stood up and walked out of the café, striding confidently across the car park to the highway.

"Don't!" I yelled.

Too late.

Stacey stepped with her arms outstretched into the road. A truck, pelting like a boulder, screeched as the driver applied the brakes. Metal made contact with flesh. A child started crying. The whole world seemed to trip.

I ran out of the café, heart pounding like a dynamo. Horrified at the sight of the blood, my stomach lurched.

"Fuck!" someone howled. The driver of the truck. His face was an orange mess. "Oh fuck! You stupid bitch! You stupid little cunt!" He started kicking one of the wheels, a hammer striking a bell. He went harder and faster, suddenly yelping. He fell over, clutching his foot. He must have broken something.

As Stacey had promised, I was interviewed by the police for a number of days – I can't remember how many exactly. When I was released, I found out that they had contacted Kelly Bunton; her response to this whole affair was to pull away my support.

Two days before my flight, I went out for a drink in this nightclub in Auckland. I'm not sure how long I stayed, because one drink quickly led to another. Music pulsed against my eardrums. I danced and I moved like I'd never moved before.

I saw her across the dancefloor and I can honestly say that I fell deeply in love. Blonde hair, golden dress. Just like Philippa. I went to her – very unattractive in my thin cardigan, jeans and brown boots – and to my surprise she looked up and moved towards me.

We spent the night dancing, kissing and groping, before discreetly leaving the nightclub. We were both drunk out of her heads and fell about in each other's arms.

I was revelling in the moment so much that I nearly missed her, a woman, an African tribal woman, dancing in the streetlight. My heart skipped several beats. She truly was the stuff of nightmares. Her eyes were focused on me, burrowing into my own.

"Hey," said my newfound friend, biting at my neck.

I looked away from the dancer for less than a second, then glanced back to where she'd been under the flickering streetlamp. Only the dancing light remained. A can cluttered down the pavement. A homeless drunk zigzagged by a bin, swearing about something.

"Sorry," I said. "Thought I saw something."

"Well, you're going to see something else now..."

I don't remember anything else with any clarity.

The next morning, after carefully prising myself from the woman's sticky sheets, spinning around from the alcohol still in my system, I ventured back towards my hotel. I was truly scared now.

I stayed in my room until I had to go to the airport. Fast food went down my gullet like coal down a chute. By the time I left, the bed and table were in such a state that I actually empathised with the cleaning team.

I knew that I was never going to New Zealand again. As I looked out at the disappearing landmass, the plane clawing upwards, I sensed that my investigation was over. Dead in the water.

Back in London, Kelly Bunton was crystal clear that I was to spend no more of the paper's time and money on it. I was to get on with my real job, or face prompt dismissal. What could I do?

A few weeks later, I heard from Owen, who wanted to meet me for lunch. He was doing very, very well for himself: editor of a magazine, company car, two-bedroom house. He asked me out, wondering if I'd come back to Australia with him. So, I did. He got me a job at his magazine, well-paid, with *eight* weeks holiday a year. He proposed only three months into our relationship. We were married on the Gold Coast in 2032, with our complete package of respective extended families.

Life was good for us. We settled down, did some travelling, talked about having a child but never got around to it; we're actually quite happy we didn't.

Peter McGough, quite shamefully I now admit, became a forgotten soul. Banished from my thoughts like an evil prince.

It was in 2045 that a bizarre set of circumstances and, at the risk of making it sound like a turn-the-page-rapidly-thriller, fates not only reignited my belief in McGough, but gave me an extremely vital piece of evidence that would prove his innocence. Not only that, but I found out more about this exotic tribal dancer.

In January of 2045 – 15th, according to my diary – I was at a literature festival in Perth. I was there to interview a debut novelist, Norris Pace, 23, before he went into his big event. From New Zealand, he was represented by the Stacey Idler Literary Agency (set up in memory of the aforementioned (they prided themselves on launching careers)). We sat in one of those garden cafes that you often get, burning in the Australian winter, and talked about his seven-hundred-page novel *Kissing The Yellow Sap*, a tale of forbidden love between a maid and her master in Auckland in the late 1800s. Exciting stuff. Pace went on and on, going into so much detail about how he had "been influenced by so many great writers" who were way better than him. Obnoxious little cu –

When we wrapped things up and he was led away by a festival attendant to a tent where three hundred people were packed together like sardines, I went to the festival bar (wonderfully airconditioned with leather chairs and wooden tables, where, according to the festival guide, *you could sit, relax, and read*) to get myself a cold lager. Well-earned.

But not so, according to a grumpy-miserable-looking bar attendant, his tiresome and tireless eyes scanning me like I was a newly-discovered marine specimen from the bottom of the Indian Ocean.

"Can I see your ticket stubs?" he asked me.

"Excuse me?"

"How many events have you been to today?"

"Not that it's any of your business, but I haven't been to any. I work for a magazine. Just been interviewing a writer."

"Well, you have to go to a minimum of one event before you can purchase an alcoholic beverage."

"Is that a joke?"

"I'm afraid not. Festival policy."

"What kind of a policy is that?"

"It's to ensure fair custom, since you are not charged an entry fee."

"I don't understand. Why can't you just let me buy a pint of lager?"

"It's our policy. As I said, to ensure fair custom."

"You know what? I'm going to find another place. One where they don't employ idiots like you."

"I'm sorry to hear that. If you have any complaints —"

But I was gone before that ignominious arsehole could say another word. This was the last time I was ever coming to this festival. Owen could send some other poor fucker next year!

"Shit! I'm so sorry!" a man shouted at me.

"Fuck!" I screamed, as I felt burning down my front. "Jesus fucking Christ!"

The man, shorts and t-shirt (and American), had bumped into me and spilt his coffee down my legs. What kind of wanker has a coffee in the middle of the day!

"Look at me!" I bellowed. "You fucking dickhead!" Well, that was me banned from the festival for life.

A consoling student volunteer put an arm around me and walked me away. I was given a festival uniform and the sincerest apologies. But I told them to shove their apology and to change their policies. Then, looking like an overgrown student, I started to make my way out.

I was nearly at the entrance, when I was nabbed by a concerned and very sunburnt man.

"Could you tell me where the Horatio Tent is please?" he asked. Scottish. Brilliant.

"Oh, I'm not working for the festival. Sorry, I know I'm in the uniform. Some fuckwit just poured a pint of coffee over me."

"Oops. Hold on, you're Wilma Penry, right? I subscribe to your magazine. Listen, could we maybe have a talk after my event? I know I'm a bit out of line with my etiquette. I know it's not the way it's done."

"I can give you my card."

"Ah, okay. Or I could buy you a beer afterwards."

"Well, you have to go to an event to buy an alcoholic beverage and the tickets cost and arm and a leg."

"That's no bother. I'm sure I could swing a bit of weight." Sweat trickled down his temple. "I'm Mark, by the way, Mark Crook."

I shook his hand.

With his big, bald, domed head, he had the appearance of an escaped Victorian prisoner. He wore a faded pink shirt with baggy tan-coloured trousers – completely out of place.

"I've written a book about my grandfather's time working on the railways in Scotland," he told me, as we wandered through the literary village.

"Oh, that's really cool." I took the copy of *Tracks of Time: A Railway Man's Journey* that he handed to me and quickly leafed through it.

"My grandad worked from the beginning of the

Nineteen-Sixties to the end of the Nineteen-Eighties. Nearly thirty years."

"Wow, that's incredible."

We bumped into a staff member, who answered Mark's enquiry with acute professionalism and directed us towards the Horatio Tent. He paid for a ticket for me – probably to guilt-trip me into interviewing him – and I promised him I'd meet him afterwards in the garden café.

Less than half of the plastic chairs were full. Judging by the bearded, specky, geeky composition that happened to make up most of the audience, I knew that I wouldn't be too far out of place.

Mark Crook entered with a guy I vaguely recognised from the literary scene. I think one of my colleagues had done an interview with him once; he edited a railway magazine of some sort.

The event was actually more interesting than I thought. Mark certainly knew his stuff, detailing how his grandfather had started working the railways at nineteen, before retiring in 1989. There were so many little stories and anecdotes. Funny little situations, traditions, quotes of a time long gone. Don't worry, I didn't fall asleep. I even asked a question at the end.

When we met in the garden after, he took me straight to the bar. I was a little bit desperate to make a snide comment to Mr Policy, but his shift had clearly finished. A jolly woman with red hair and enormous tits served beer like a broken oil well. Mark got us a couple of pints and we found a reclusive table neatly tucked away in the corner.

"Good event?" he asked, as if testing whether I'd been paying attention.

"Very good," I replied. "Your grandfather sounds a really interesting human being."

"I love your word choice. All you professional writers say the same, particularly when you sign books. Which reminds me..." He raised a fresh copy of *Tracks of Time* from a plastic carrier bag at his side and scrawled his signature with a black, felt-tip pen. "Happy reading."

"Thank you! I'll enjoy perusing through this."

"I'm sure you will."

"Well, we could do the interview now, if you wanted?" I offered. "I've got my notepad and things."

"Oh!" He sounded startled.

"Sorry, my mistake."

"No, it's okay. I just get a bit presumptuous sometimes. I just wanted to say hello properly and get to know you. If it's okay, we could do the interview over the phone next week?"

"Of course. That would be better actually. It'll give me time to read the book. Oh, bloody hell..." I lifted my pint. "Congratulations on the book!"

"Thank you!"

Our glasses clinked.

The cold beer hitting my parched throat made me want to puff with relief.

"Can I just check something with you, Mark?"

"Sure."

"You said earlier, and again in the event, your grandfather started working for the railways at the beginning of the Sixties, when he was nineteen, but retired in Nineteen-Eighty-Nine. He wouldn't have even been fifty."

Mark's face twitched, beer spilling over his lips. A fleck of beer froth made contact with his shirt.

"Doesn't make sense, does it?" he said. "You're not the first person to pick up on that. In the book, I've written that it was due to an injury."

"But that's not the truth, is it?"

"Nah, it isn't."

"I apologise, I shouldn't be asking."

"No – it's okay. Someone'll find out one of these days. I'd rather it was you." He took a long gulp of beer. "Listen, there's a restaurant down the road. Have you had dinner yet?"

"Not yet."

"Well, I'll buy you a steak and another pint. I'd rather get away from here. I've heard that word tends to travel fast in the literary communities."

"You make it sound like quite a tale."

"It is." He finished his beer and slapped the leather of the chair. "But I didn't want it in the book. You won't mention it, will you?"

"Not a word will pass my lips, unless you want me to."

I drank the rest of my beer as quickly as I could and then followed Mark out of the festival village.

"What forced your grandfather to leave his job?" I asked.

"Mental illness."

"Look, if it's too personal, I'm okay if you don't want to talk about it," I said, stepping over a hole in the pavement. Fucking safety hazard.

"It's quite all right. Here we are..."

A yellow, glittering, flickering sign scratched back of my eyeballs: *Sandy's Steak Shack*. The restaurant was perfect for our little chat. Candlelit. Soft music. No other customers. Attentive staff who left us alone.

Mark, at his insistence, ordered us two medium-rare steaks and a local ale.

"It's good stuff," he explained, as amber pints were delivered. "The wife absolutely loves it. When we come on holiday here, she always insists on it."

Our respective gazes touched.

"Okay," he said, "I am going to tell you the story, the *real* story of what happened to my grandad. But I want you to know that Aiden was a hardworking man. He was never lazy. Always respectful. He was a decent, honest human being."

I nodded.

"Okay, here goes..."

Aiden Crook was born on 13th March 1943 in Glasgow, the youngest of six children. He grew up in a small tenement in the Gorbals. To say the least, he had an impoverished childhood, despite his father working long hours in many menial jobs. Each of his three brothers and two sisters were all put to work as soon as they were able, and Aiden was no exception. By the time he was nineteen, he had worked in a shop, a dairy farm, a butcher, and a pub.

On his nineteenth birthday, at a small party organised by his frail mother and father – attended by his brothers and their wives, and his sisters and their husbands – he made a conscious decision to try and escape this life. A plan of running away to the bottom ends of Earth began to form in the recesses of his imagination. It wouldn't be hard: save up a few pennies, head south on a train. But at a quiet drink down the local a few weeks later, he met a young lady who would one day become his wife.

With a committed relationship and a new home, he started looking for a new job and found one as a ticket inspector. He started work on 12th June 1962.

Over the years, amidst the pressure of his job and providing for his son, he became accustomed to the fact that, bar the occasional holiday, he would be stuck in Glasgow for the rest of his life. He made peace with it. In time, he began to enjoy it.

But the yearning for adventure and something new never goes away. It might be beaten down, it might be buried, but it is always there, hiding away. Often, with many people who have this *condition*, it goes to the grave; but sometimes, it can be awoken like a sleeping monster under the bed. Whether such a trigger can be viewed as good or bad luck depends on your perspective.

On 8th August 1989, Aiden Crook was working the London to Glasgow train. As it pulled into Glasgow Central, he saw a sleeping woman with ginger hair. He proceeded to rouse her from her sleep, angrily telling her: "Come on, it's not a hotel!"

He didn't think anything of this woman for several weeks, but on 21st September, he woke up in the early hours, sweat choking him. He realised then and there that he had been living a lie. That woman, curled up on the train, had been living the life of her dreams – he just knew it! He also was a traveller by nature! All his life, he had been told what to do! No more!

Over the next week, as the trauma of his awakening took hold, Aiden's colleagues became more and more concerned. After an incident in which he got horribly drunk during a shift, his boss made the decision to make him take an early retirement, "for the good of everyone".

This only freed him more.

On 1st November, he walked out of the family home with a thick wad of cash and jetted off to South America, returning many years later (and badly in need of a place to live) in the summer of 2007. Of course, his son refused to let him anywhere near his now ex-wife and told him never to come back.

He wandered around Glasgow for a few days, ending up at Blairhill station. That was when he saw a drunk man staggering about, someone he recognised as Peter McGough. And who was this helping him?

Why, the woman he had seen on the train all those years ago!

It is not known fully what happened next. Six weeks later, Aiden was found hanging in a hotel room in Pretoria. A single note that declared *I'm sorry* was placed neatly on the table.

"I'm so sorry," I said.

"Don't be," said Mark. "These things happen. And I believe that you know who this woman is, don't you?"

"Yes." Blood squelched through my ears. My mouth was dry. "Sarah."

"Do you know where she is?"

"No one knows where she is. She's been off the radar for over ten years. Her environmental company's gone down the spout. There are rumours that she's changed her name, but I don't know. You don't forget a face like hers."

"Exactly."

"How did it affect your father, if I may ask?"

"He's still fuming about it after all these years. It's made him a very angry and bitter man. He and my mum got divorced a few years ago." Mark looked blankly at his drink and then sighed. "That's all there is to it."

It was clear he wanted to draw a line under things now. He told me some more tales about his grandfather, funny little stories, things you wouldn't expect to hear from a railway man. I put on my pretend-interested-face. My mind was racing with questions.

Would all this help prove McGough's innocence? Or would it only help to frame him further?

We said goodnight with a firm handshake and went to our respective hotels, promising one another that we would keep in touch.

When I returned home the next day, I emailed Mark to arrange a time for our interview. It was conducted a week letter and led to a successful article in the magazine; a series of award nominations subsequently came our way.

Over the next year, Mark and I became close friends. One memory that will always stay with me is having him and his wife visit us at our seaside home on the Gold Coast. We drank dark red wine and munched on lamb in the heat of the evening, the sound of waves licking at the sand. Yes, the four of us were aware of the problems in the world: the flooding, outbreaks of war, but that didn't stop us from basking in the warmth of love and friendship, as pathetically romantic as that sounded.

"I've read your book, Mark," said Owen, refilling our glasses. "Mighty impressive read, if I may say so."

"Glad you liked it. Miriam's been such a supportive influence." Mark drunkenly held out his hand to his half-Scottish, half-Chinese wife. "I love you, babe."

"Haha, I know that," said Miriam, resting her head on his shoulder.

"There were times I nearly gave up."

"That's what all writers say!" laughed Owen. "Who was that guy we did that thing with when we were students?" he asked me, joshing. "You know, when we were in America? Where we *met*?"

"Oh, yeah," I said. "Peter McGough."

"Peter McGough!" Owen shouted. "My God, to think we let him buy us drinks...!"

Mark and I stared into each other's eyes, slightly alarmed at where the conversation was turning to. You can't stop a freight train with a verbal protest.

"I used to love his *Rick Elder* novels," said Miriam. "Binge read them when I was a student in Edinburgh."

"Have you read his standalone stuff?" Owen blabbed on.

"Not so good." Mark's wife was shaking her head. "Actually, have you read his book on artificial intelligence?"

"Couldn't get past the first chapter. He's so pessimistic about everything."

"After what he did to that girl, no wonder! Maybe he felt the shame that only a rapist could feel."

"Do you any of you think that he may actually be innocent?" I blurted out. Stupid, stupid, stupid.

"How so?" Miriam questioned. "Don't forget, he pleaded guilty."

"Don't you think it's funny that it came out after decades? That this guy who used to bully him at school wrote a note alleging the rape and yet he got killed straight after writing it? And yet, somehow, it is discovered by gangsters hellbent on getting even with McGough?"

"I'll correct you on one thing, Wilma, there was

clear evidence it was a genuine accident that killed Nick Yard. There was a good documentary that came out shortly after this conviction. A police detective showed detailed evidence of the accident."

"You can't believe everything you see on the telly," I countered.

"The note was also examined by a handwriting specialist. The prosecution ordered it. They compared it to some of Nick Yard's school books. One-hundred percent match."

"Well, you can't hide from the fact that it was gangsters who found it..."

"Ladies, please!" snapped Mark. "We're trying to eat dinner!"

"Sorry." Miriam looked embarrassed. "But you can see my point."

We finished our meal and wine in a degree of bored and anxious stalemate, one that only comes when you are so mentally exhausted you don't know what to say next, for fear of igniting conflict. Owen and I took the dishes into the kitchen and began the process of giving them a quick rinse.

"That was a pretty stupid thing to do!" said Owen. "I know you like being this justice campaigner, but you shouldn't have started an argument like that!"

"Excuse *me*, but you're the one who mentioned McGough in the first place!"

"These people are our guests *and* our clients."

"I realise that. Okay, babe, I'm sorry. Let's keep shtum."

"Agreed." Poor Owen. I'd just deprived him of his argument.

Miriam's scream was like a dog yelping for its owner.

"What the hell...?" Owen stammered.

I followed him outside to the decking. Mark was on the floor, writhing. He'd knocked his own chair over; it lay in the sand like a gigantic stick insect. His eyes were as wide as white pebbles.

"He just keeled over!" cried Miriam.

Owen was kneeling over him. "Oh, fuck! Miriam, get an ambulance! Now!" He started pushing down on Mark's chest.

"Oh no," I said. "Is he...?"

"He's had a heart attack," said my husband. "Oh, no, no." He pushed harder and gave him the kiss of life, no inhibitions.

"Mark, are you okay?" I said.

"Of course he's not fucking okay!" Owen yelled. "Come on, Mark, fucking breathe! Breathe, you cunt! Fucking breathe!"

I heard Miriam's frantic sobs from the house: "Yeah... he just fell to the floor! ... I dunno! ... We need an ambulance now!"

It was way past too late. Everyone knew that. Mark was a goner. Boom. By the time the ambulance arrived, Owen was sitting with a whisky, cradling his right hand, and I was cuddling Miriam. Boom.

Funerals are never easy things to go to. Flying across time zones, particularly at our age, really does your body in. At the funeral in Edinburgh, we were respectful mourners, decent and honourable, shaking hands, telling everyone how much we enjoyed getting to know Mark and how he would be missed terribly. A bad mistake. We didn't actually say *we* would miss Mark. Being professional has its upsides... and its severe downsides, particularly with old ladies who are proud to be stoic, stay-at-home, normal folk, instead of travelling the world like Owen and I. Oh yes, we did get some dodgy looks at the wake.

When we returned to Australia, there was a letter waiting for me. Now, bear in mind that this was five weeks after Mark's death, so there was plenty of time for it to arrive. That evening, jetlagged as fuck, with a glass of white, I began to read. It had been written by Mark (I knew his sloppy handwriting like the map of the world), and he had arranged for it to be sent to me in the event of his death.

Dear Wilma,

If you are reading this, it is because I am dead. I know that sounds a bit cheesy, but what do you know? I'm a bullshit guy who writes bullshit about the railways. I have arranged in my Last Will & Testament for this letter to be sent to you.

As you know, my grandfather was an insecure man. I'm not trying to make excuses for him over the way he treated my grandmother and my father, I would never do such a thing; but I believe that there is more of a mystery to Aiden Crook than meets the eye.

In our phone calls and meet-ups, you and I have certainly exchanged a lot of stories. You quite clearly believe in Peter McGough's innocence, and I want to help.

You have mentioned on several occasions your trip in 2031 to Malibu and Los Angeles. What really struck me was your description of this dancer, who you believe has connections to the criminals behind Peter McGough's framing. It struck me, because I have met her also.

She is a hypnotist. Her name is Alison Charm – whether that's her real name or not, I don't know. She regularly tours the world. I saw her in 2023 in London at a show when I was there on business. She's a complicated individual. I went to meet her afterwards and she gave me a look of such disturbed intentions that I nearly cried out in panic. I fled from the theatre, actually pretty damn scared for my life.

When I was writing the book, there was an obvious bulk of research to do. My grandfather kept a diary – can you believe that?! He recorded many detailed notes. Then I found something so creepy I nearly jacked the whole thing in. I have lost count of the number of times I wanted to tell you about it (and also my own experience) after you mentioned to me that you had not only seen her, but you knew of someone who had. I suppose I was too scared. I hope what I detail below will not scare you.

In 1981, my grandfather, Aiden Crook, was sent down to Dover to assist a team of railway engineers in translocating a car several miles down the track. It was a difficult operation, because of the age of the car, and they had requested Aiden purely because he had experience in that area.

The job actually took three hours instead of the seven estimated. The jollity between the men was so great that they went out for dinner at a local restaurant, most likely to have their shot at pretending they were rich. My grandfather left the restaurant early, citing the desire for an early night in anticipation of the long journey back to Glasgow on the morrow.

He was walking by the docks when he saw something that made his blood run as cold as the English Channel. This dancer – exactly as you have described, Wilma – was doing her moves by one of the ferries. Even from the long distance, he could tell that she was staring right at him. My grandfather panicked and ran to his hotel.

This is as much as I can gather from his diary pages. But as far as I know, it is the truth.

I've just been too afraid to mention this to anyone, but with my health failing, I've taken the decision to write everything down. I have stashed my grandfather's diaries in a secure box in the Central City Bank in the Cayman Islands. I know that they are safe there. You will be receiving access codes in due course.

Now that I am gone, the onus is on you to use these diaries in your investigation.

Find who this dancer is. Prove Peter McGough's innocence.

Warmest Regards,

Mark

"Shite," I cursed. "Fuck."

"What is it?" asked Owen, coming out onto the decking. Casual stroll, unbuttoned shirt, half-empty glass of white.

I handed him the letter.

"Well, you're not investigating it," he told me, after reading it. "We've certainly had enough problems with this wretched thing."

"It can't hurt to take a peek."

"No, I'm being serious. You're not going anywhere near it. Write about the next big debut novelist. A big motherfucking interview. I don't fucking know."

"How about you watch your language around me?" I hissed.

"What, am I getting too aggressive for you?"

"A little!"

"Well, you're a journalist, you should be used to the abuse."

"I'm also your wife!"

"And as my wife..." He indicated his crotch. "...You have a job to do."

"I think you should sober up, matey!"

I'd never seen Owen lose it before, but I know I never wanted to again. He dropped his glass of wine, where it smashed apart on the floor like a politically incorrect historical figure's statue being torn down by politically correct students, and grabbed me by the throat, yanking me out of the chair like a doll. With his other hand, he slapped me across the mouth.

"You bastard!" I screamed. "Why'd you fucking do that?!"

"Get into the fucking bedroom," he snarled. "Get in there and tear off your knickers. You're going to be my wife tonight, whether you like it or not."

"You've lost your fucking mind, haven't you? Owen! Please!"

"I don't fucking care! Do it! Move! Bedroom! Now!"

"No!"

"You will." Menace danced in his tone. He inched closer to me, wine breath penetrating my nostrils. "You will."

"No."

"You understand I'll have to make you."

"Please."

He placed a hand on my shoulder, moving a finger up to my neck. He pulled me to him and started licking the lobe of my ear.

"Please." I was flashing my puppy face at him. "Please."

"Go on, you know you want to."

"Not like this. Not while you're pissed."

He slumped forward. I caught him, his lips sucking at the crook of my armpit.

"Come on, I'll get you to bed."

I helped him through to the bedroom and threw the covers over him. If he choked on vomit in his sleep, good. Two empty wine bottles hugged each other on the living room carpet. I slept on the couch, silently tearful, hoping that the pain wouldn't flood into my dreams.

His first words to me in the morning were: "I am so, so sorry." He staggered out meekly from the bedroom, dabbing his eyes with the sleeve of his shirt.

I told him to sit in the kitchen whilst I made us both a cup of black coffee. When we were facing opposite each other, me angry, him I-don't-know-what, I stated what I needed to. I'm proud of how I said it, though looking back, I'd have used slightly better words.

"What you did to me last night was evil. You assaulted me, sexually assaulted me, and attempted to rape me. I'm not sure what was going through your mind and to be honest, I don't want to know. I know you were drunk. I want to put it behind us, because I know that's not you, but I never want it to happen again. Am I understood?"

"Yes."

"And another thing: I am going to continue my investigation, and you're going to give me all the resources I need. Clear?"

"Yes."

"Now, we have to be getting on with things. This is a new start."

"Wilma," he stuttered. "Oh, Wilma, I'm –"

"You're forgiven."

No one likes to be violated, but for me it was an excellent thing. Not only did I have the full resources of the magazine, but Owen, no doubt in a pathetic attempt at an apology, rustled support from several of his colleagues in Asia. Basically, along with my contacts such as John McGrath, I had an army.

Three weeks after Owen and I signed our new agreement, I received a letter from Mark Crook's solicitor containing the access codes. Owen arranged the first flight to the Cayman Islands, no problem for him at all.

Yet again, I was crossing time zones; yet again, I was flying to new frontiers. Globetrotting can be so underrated at times. People say nonsense like: "Well, I wouldn't fancy being cramped up in a steel tube." Well, I say that's part of the fun. You never know who you're going to meet. Damn, I miss my backpacking days!

The trip was booked for three days. Go in, collect the diaries, get home, with a bit of relaxation in-between. But things got complicated very quickly. I found myself caught up in a very dangerous situation. Nothing like what I endured in Bangkok, but it still had that element of peril that threatens to send you home in several pieces.

I landed at Owen Roberts International Airport on 2nd April 2046, ready for my little mission. After a taxi ride – very proficiently carried out – to the hotel, and a hasty check-in, I made my way to the Central City Bank. I suppose I was being stupid in thinking things would be simple, that I would hand over the access codes, get shown by a very secret agent-type figure down to the basement, go through a series of circular metal doors, watch Mr Secret Agent open a small safe and hand me the diaries, then walk back out, exchange a decent handshake with the manager, and return to the hotel for cocktails.

Ah, if only…

"Identification, please," said the fake-American-accent manager, his cigarette-flavoured breath clumsily masked with cinnamon aftershave.

I handed over my passport.

"Mrs Penry, the famous journalist," said the manager, twiddling with his spectacles. "What interests you in the Cayman Islands? I can assure you all our activities are perfectly legal."

"Don't worry. I am here to retrieve something from the Central City Bank. The property of Mark Crook, who has recently passed away."

"It was tragic news, I was sorry to hear that. Do you have the access codes?"

"Yes, of course." I handed the manila folder over to him.

"Is this to obtain his collection of pocket watches?"

"No, I'm here to collect a set of diaries."

He rolled through the paperwork, grimacing. "Okay, okay, okay." He typed something into the desk computer and frowned.

"Is there a problem?"

"I'm just puzzled as to why you want access."

"Well, it's none of your business."

"These are part of a deceased person's property.

We do take serious precautions to those trying to gain access, even if they've been given the codes by the deceased."

"He left these diaries to *me*," I said, clearly sounding exhausted, because weary rich eyes swung my way with looks of disapproval. "You've got the access codes there. What more do you need?"

"We have to make sure that whoever accesses these artefacts has legitimate reason to do so."

"I have every legitimate reason imaginable. Mark Crook left instructions for me to take these diaries. Please, sir, I need access."

The manager stiffened and adjusted his jacket sleeve collars. "I will need to confer with my colleagues." He handed the folder back to me. "Please come back tomorrow."

"What, that's it? Are you having a joke?"

"Bank security is not a laughing matter."

Why did he remind me so much of that bartender at that wretched literary festival?

"I don't believe this," I cursed. I walked out, humiliated, severely pissed off, and wanting a cup of tea.

It was starting to rain when I left the bank. Why, oh why, didn't I bring a wretched raincoat? Or even an umbrella? Thunder boomed. The sky was going dark grey, swirling like a witch's spell. Ignoring it, as most modern journalists tend to do, I walked hurriedly back to the hotel.

That night, after a hot shower and a whisky from the minibar, I went down to the hotel restaurant.

American food was for me tonight. I ordered a tender juicy hamburger and a half-bottle of house red. I sat at a small table shrouded in dead red light, enveloped by soft jazz music coming from hidden speakers. Like all hotel eateries, it had an artificial sense of comfort. There were a few couples dotted about, oblivious to everything else except each other.

I was jolted from a daydream about my backpacking days by a waiter popping a cork. My sparkly, transparent, dishwasher-cleaned glass opened its mouth and filled with grape red.

"Thank you," I said. "Just what the doctor ordered."

He didn't get my joke. "Enjoy, ma'am," he said, putting the bottle down. "Let me know if you need anything else."

"Of course."

He bowed his head and began to walk away, then suddenly turned back. "One other thing, ma'am, we may ask you to leave as soon as you have finished your meal, as we have a VIP dining here tonight."

"And whom might that be?"

"Alison Charm," he said. "Thank you for your cooperation, ma'am."

"Excuse me?" I called after him, but he didn't seem to hear.

What the hell?

"What the fuck did you put in this wine?" I half-laughed, half-spluttered.

When my hamburger came, I thought I wouldn't be able to take a single bite, but found I had one hell of a ravishing appetite, munching away like a dog. When the waiter returned to collect my empty plate, he gave me a gentle verbal nudge that I was to clear out of the area.

"Sure thing," I said, a little drunk.

"Just move to one of the tables near to the door."

"That will not be necessary, sir," said a deep voice, one I'd had a split hope to one day hear. Behind me.

"Very well," said the waiter.

I dared not turn.

A presence, a disturbing entity, something that divided the air, came past me like a ghost and sat at a table three away from mine, accompanied by two suited, husky security guards.

"So, am I going to get some answers?" I said.

"What answers?" Alison Charm boomed.

"Who the hell are you?"

"Perhaps we should have a formal introduction, get to know each other?" she said, as the waiter filled her glass. She took a tiny, unthinkably minuscule sip, and winked at me.

"How the hell, how the bloody hell are you doing this?" I screeched.

"You mean, be all over the world?" she laughed. "I'll tell you this: I am everywhere. And I haven't aged a day since I turned twenty."

"Stop talking in riddles."

"Share a glass of wine with me. Maybe a couple."

I moved to her table. She sprinkled the red stuff into a new, vibrant, untouched glass.

Looking at Alison Charm, I felt an uncomfortable-yet-interesting sensation rising in my belly. She was young, a teenager with the gift of money. Her eyes were like little black holes, drawing me in.

"How do you do it?" I asked.

"I'm not alone. My family has helped out over the years."

"What's your involvement with the framing of Peter McGough?"

"That wasn't me, that was my sister."

"You mean, there's two of you."

"As I said, my family has helped out. Let me explain. I know who you are, Wilma Penry, and I know that you want answers. Ask and you shall receive. That is why I am here. I have travelled all the way to the Cayman Islands to provide you with the information you seek."

"I want to know everything. There's going to be a major fucking article on this, I promise you that."

"Well, you'd better let me start..." She gave a picture-perfect grin.

"Ready when you are."

For 1910, the Miltons were a typically average British upper-class family living in Chelsea, London. With a hardworking husband, Joseph, and a caring mother, Beatrice, the Miltons were a respected family, well-liked by their neighbours, a number of influential figures in British politics, businessmen across the length and breadth of the country. Yet they were not frequently talked about to the point that they became celebrities. They were talked about just enough that they were able to enjoy a healthy, rich lifestyle.

Joseph Milton owned a chain of packing factories around the country, with potential hopes for expanding abroad. Indeed, it would be one of these foreign ventures that led to the whole affair.

Beatrice Milton, for her time, was a very independent woman, who was a published poet. She held a number of positions in various social clubs across London.

There were two children: Matthew and Katherine, aged ten and twelve, respectively. They did not go on to live remarkable lives, so we shall not discuss anything else about them. Their lives were productive, oh yes. As a matter of fact, Matthew Milton Salts is still very popular a century and a half later... But the story is digressing.

We should concern ourselves with what happened in June 1910 when Joseph Milton went to San Francisco. In fact, Joseph Milton is a very unremarkable character himself, but his trip was very significant. After the whole trip was over, he would simple disappear back into the ether, a vanishing act of the decades.

He arrived on 1st June 1910 and signed a series of agreements over the next few days that would increase the links between his packing factory chain and an American one, the end result being a truly global affair of magnificent proportions.

On 10th June 1910, the day before he set off for the

East Coast to catch a ship back to England, he had a few drinks in a bar he'd taken a liking to. Many great men like him sat there, eyes on their spirits. It was nearly closing time when he spotted a woman nearby, sipping – presumably – a gin drink of some sort.

"What is a young lady like yourself doing in a place like this?" he enquired.

"Excuse me...?"

Obviously, if Mr Milton had asked this question in 2018, a lawsuit would be swiftly coming his way. But this is 1910, don't forget!

"I mean, this bar I believe is only reserved for gentlemen," he said.

The woman, with her white shirt, tweed trousers, and deeply uninterested face, did not respond. She simply stared at the book she was reading, twirling the glass in her hand.

"I say, did you hear me?" he croaked.

"I heard you indeed." Calm English accent. "I can assure you that there is no issue at all with me being here."

"Where are you from?"

"Buckinghamshire, as a matter of fact. I was born in Eighteen-Ninety. My father moved myself and my mother out when I was but three years old. My name is Eleanor Rinehart, by the way."

Gradually their conversation shifted into that or a cordial flow. They found, despite their vastly different attitudes, that they had a lot in common: both were owners of small business empires (Eleanor Rinehart was in the toy trade, specialising in dolls; she was in San Francisco to attend the opening of a new toyshop); both liked gin; and both were bored of life, wanting something better, something more extraordinary.

Alcohol began to flow a little bit too fast and these two respectable people found themselves getting closer together. In an act of chaos and despicability, they went to Joseph Milton's hotel room and made love. It was something that they both regretted the next morning, as they disappeared their separate ways.

For the rest of his life, Mr Joseph Milton, no matter how many awards and pats on the back in the brandy club he received, would always be troubled by what he had done. It ended up making him have a stroke in the summer of 1935, right outside his factory in Bolton, keeling over and smacking his head off a china plant pot, a scene that traumatised one of the factory boys for the rest of his days.

Meanwhile, for Eleanor Rinehart, things got very difficult. Nine months later, at her home in San Diego, she gave birth to a reasonably healthy baby. However, she died from the strain of childbirth. Considering the fact that the baby was ebony and Eleanor as a white middle-class lady, it was no wonder that her close friends and family – and indeed, society in general – shivered with condemnation.

The baby was given to an orphanage in San Francisco and was allocated a careless name by an uncaring nurse with too much time on her hands. Alison Charm grew up, excelling in dancing and aerobics. A travelling circus reached out for her, begging for her to be a part and offering her some juicy money. She went all over the world for various competitions. She socialised after the shows, mostly in the men-only bars. She was adored by the patrons, who always wanted to touch her on the arm, and she touched back. To put it bluntly, she slept around, repeatedly getting pregnant. And this was where a disturbing curse appeared, probably a punishment for Joseph and Eleanor's affair:

The babies were all identical. All the same. And they all took the name Alison Charm.

"Interesting story," I said. "I mean, I don't believe a word of it, but cracking entertainment nonetheless."

"Is that what you truly think?" she taunted. "Tomorrow, when you collect those diaries, think of what I've said."

"I'm sure I will."

"Goodnight," she said. She got up and stroked my shoulder, a touch that felt like burning rubber.

There was nothing I could do but watch her go. This woman, whose demeanour told a thousand stories and hid a million more, just strode off. An impossible woman who told a tale so extravagant and nonsensical, ludicrous yet sane.

The next day I did indeed pick up the diaries and before I knew it, I was on the plane home. There was nothing in the pages, except for the details on this mysterious woman. It only confirmed Charm's story. This family of lust and intrigue spanned the generations like a string of pearls.

Australia welcomed me like a long-lost relative, never quite sure whether to punch them or kiss them. After the champagne and nibbles, I resumed work on my investigation, even more driven by the desire to set Peter McGough free.

"As you can see, I've paid a hefty price," I said to the audience, holding up my wounded hand.

"What you're doing takes courage," said Sarah. "Guts."

To my surprise, a couple of members of the media started clapping, followed by ravenous applause. A geeky-looking Oxbridge toff wiped a tear from his cheek. A senior, weary, veiny-hand-sort woman with too much makeup, scrawled something on her notepad, cussing.

"I will be releasing all of my evidence to you," I informed them. "Sarah...?"

"Thank you." She waited for the wave of skin slapping together to die down. "Thank you, all. As you no doubt know, Peter McGough was... *is* the love of my life. I have evidence, that I do, which proves he is innocent of the wicked crime of raping me. But this evidence isn't scientific or legal or any other sort of nonsense like that..." She cleared her throat. "I'm going to tell you a story. The story of he and I, all we went through together. This is my evidence, a tale told from the heart of a woman's love for the man of her dreams. It begins, not on a beach, not on a cruising holiday, not at a romantic restaurant, but on a summer's day in Oxfordshire, England, in Nineteen-Eighty-Nine..."

At first, I was almost bitter, angry that this old lady was telling a longwinded story of a love affair (when she should have been presenting *evidence*!), but as I listened, I started to understand why. It was a mix of fates and fortunes, blended together in such an intricate fashion that making sense of it required certain talents, skills that you can only learn after having pursued the one you love.

I needn't have said anything earlier. This example of two people's love for one another would reverberate around the world, making people see the truth.

But would it be enough to make the justice system see? Time would only tell.

I listened, not trying to understand, but just hear. I let the story tell itself, spill its secrets.

I had to keep faith. I had to hope that this was enough. I had to keep a sense of ground, a sense of justice, if there was any such thing.

Terminus

London

Tuesday 4th April 2051

The cell door opened with a soft scrape.

"You're free to go," said the gruff voice of Hawkins – aka The Hawk – who had been less a screw and more of a friend these past four years.

Petey stood up, his aged body a mere instrument that ticked along. Picking up the rucksack Pentonville had assigned him for his release, he patted Hawkins on the shoulder and wandered out at a leisurely pace.

"I'm going to miss our poker games," said the guard, locking the cell door. "Actually, you're going to be missed a great deal. You're not just a number to us, Mr McGough."

"Thank you for your kind words, sir."

"I always knew you were innocent. You've never struck me as the guilty sort." Hawkins barked out a clearing of the throat and opened the door into the administration section. "We'll soon have you on your way, mate."

"Is she here? Sarah?"

"Yes. As soon as we have you processed, we'll take

you to her. We've got some procedures to get through as well."

"What?"

"Sorry, mate, should have told you: we've got a bit of a media circus outside."

"Didn't think I was that popular."

"Mate, have you been watching the news? Everyone's excited about this!"

"I haven't been watching the telly that much."

Hawkins signed a clipboard, his scrawl like that of a lonely, long-forgotten monk's. He smiled at Petey and then showed him into a small room. The prison governor was there, Mrs Melinda Peach, her expression as grim as it had ever been. With grey hair dyed blonde and badly ironed formal clothes, she looked like a go-it-alone-career-woman of the olden days.

"We've prepared some clothes for you," said Mrs Peach. "Hope the size is right. Thank you, Mr Hawkins, that will be all. I need to chat with Mr McGough." She handed a carrier bag to Petey: basic suit, shirt, trousers, underpants, socks, and shoes.

"I can't leave you alone in here with him, ma'am," said The Hawk. "Policy."

"Damn it, Mr Hawkins, the man is innocent!"

"Until he signs the release forms, prison regulations still apply."

"Just go, will you?! We've got a camera pointing down on us. If he tries to strangle me, I'm sure help will come."

When The Hawk had left, Petey said, "He's quite a character, isn't he?"

"He is indeed. He's a hardworking bloke, I'll give him that. Very professional."

"You said you wanted to chat with me?"

"Yes, I did. Um, I just wanted to say sorry for everything you've been through."

"You don't need to say that. You've been a good governor these past five years." Two decades of cells and bars had taught him to think and act like a guilty man. "I'm indebted to you."

"You don't recognise me, do you?" Mrs Peach motioned for him to sit down.

"Should I?"

"We met once. Decades ago." She scraped out the chair on the opposite side of the table from him and lowered herself down, an uncomfortable reminder of his induction into Pentonville. *You're a sick, perverted rapist, Mr McGough, and you shall be treated as such.*

"I don't recall."

"You drove up to my house. I was a kid at the time. Very young."

"Where was this? *When* was this?"

"Just after the Scottish Independence Referendum of Twenty-Fourteen. My mother was Yvonne."

"I remember that." Visions came back to him in a flood. He was driving south that day, to his new future. He had stopped in Blairhill, just for a bit.

"I'm your daughter. I'll probably lose my job for saying this, so don't tell anyone."

"Oh my."

Surprises, shocks, they were all in store for him today.

"Well..." he stammered.

"That's why I took this job. As soon as the opening was available, you know, after Mr Marvis died, I applied. I couldn't say anything to you about it, not while you were guilty according to the law."

"That's why I've been treated like gentry since you arrived, isn't it?"

"Yep."

"Well, I don't know how to put this, but shall we hug?"

"Dad, I'd love that. But there's a security camera in here. It doesn't record audio, but if someone sees us hugging, well..."

"Yes, you'd lose your job."

"You know I'd love to hug you, Dad."

"Of course. How is your mother?"

"Um, she passed away a long time ago."

"Was she happy?" He knew it was too personal a question as soon as he asked it, but it was too late now.

"She was," said Mrs Peach. "She married a farmer; can you believe it? They were very happy together. I was happy too."

"Are you angry at me?"

"I'll be honest, yes." The governor scratched the table with her thumbnail. "Apart from your little five-second visit in Twenty-Fourteen, I never saw you until

I arrived at this wretched prison. Why didn't you keep in contact with my mother? Why didn't you use your wealth to support us?"

"I had financial issues, as you very well know."

"After you'd made your millions with your novels, you should have supported us. My mother held us both together. She would starve herself when we had very little money, so I could get an education."

"I'm sorry."

"Are you?" Pause. "Okay, look, I'll leave the room for a bit, give you time to get changed. Then we'll get the forms signed and get you on your way." She got up to go.

"Melinda..."

"No, I'm not interested. What happened to you was wrong. I'm not saying that what those bastards did wasn't significant, nor am I trying to dampen the magnitude of losing your wife and daughter. But you were a lousy excuse of a father to me. My mother needed you. We both needed you. You left us."

"Maybe we could meet, talk."

"Maybe not. I'm leaving you the way you left my mother and I. Mr Hawkins and two other prison officers will be in with the forms in a few minutes. Get changed. I never want to see you again." She slammed the door with a jolt, swearing.

He remembered that day as though it were the rusty-hinged table in front of him. Stupid thing, driving over to Blairhill like that. What was he thinking?

He changed over to the smart clothes. The feeling

of the fabric was truly alien, a horrid-mixed-with-pleasurable sensation. When he was done, Mr Hawkins returned along with the two other promised staff members. The forms were signed and hands were shaken.

"Just walk out the room, turn right," informed The Hawk. "At the end of the corridor, at the left, you'll find a small waiting room. Sarah is there. When you're ready, another prison officer will show you to the carpark."

"Thank you, my friend." Petey held out his hand, which The Hawk promptly shook.

"Best of luck."

Petey left the world he'd known for the past two decades and started towards the open. Every footstep felt like climbing a mountain. Every muscle tore at itself. He walked determined, but he was limping – the result of a vigilante who had tried to murder him six years ago, failing to suffocate him, but successfully crushing his left ankle with a brick.

He almost didn't want to turn left. The façade he had been living with for twenty years would dissolve like salt in rain. But he stood straight and breathed in, striding with confidence to the door of the waiting room and pulling it open like a mime artist does an old trick.

There she was. Older. Greyer. Still beautiful. Tender.

"Hi," he said.

He prayed that she would give a sly, curt, I-really-don't-want-to-be-here response. But she didn't. He wasn't going to be disappointed today!

"Hey," she replied, walking towards him, swiftly wrapping him in a tight hug. "I've missed you."

"Missed you too." He held her like he had the first time they'd met.

"Have you been okay? I mean, have they been treating you okay?"

"Not exactly five-star, but it's been alright. I love you, Sarah."

"I know. I love you too." She wiped away tears. "I've always loved you."

"Let's get this media thing done, shall we? Then we'll get out of here."

"Sounds good to me." Sarah took his hand. "I've got a hotel sorted out for us. We'll stay there for a couple of nights, before flying to Italy."

"How are you coping? Your husband?"

"I'm fine, honestly. It was quick and merciful, considering it was a stroke."

"You know, if you're not ready for this, I understand."

"I am." She squeezed harder. "I am. Things are going to be okay."

They stopped at the translucent door, a filter that kept the dreams from the nightmares. The press was gathered like a group of adolescent Late-Noughties schoolkids, ready to launch their hormones and fake feelings on to the unsuspecting passer-by.

"You ready?" he said to her.

"I've always been ready."

And he pushed the door open, emerging into the light.

"Thank you!" he said, as flash after flash after flash exploded in the back of his eyeballs. He was back to being business-like, as if he was on the stand at a Newton-M-Wren event. "Thank you!" he called out again. "Members of the media, thank you!"

"How does it feel to be free?" a fat bearded man called out, perspiration flicking from his eyebrows.

More shouts sprung up like a chain reaction:

"Do you feel any ill will towards Donny Bell?"

"How have you coped?"

"Are you planning legal action?"

Eventually, a police officer – one of many standing in a semicircle in front of Petey and Sarah – yelled for the members of media to "step well back!".

"I have a few things I'd like to say," announced Petey, taking the prepared statement from Sarah. They had been working on it for weeks, exchanging it back and forth like a yoyo with absolute determination. *"The past twenty years have been traumatic for me, my friends and Sarah. It is thanks to them that I am walking out of here a free man. I have lost my literary career, my self-respect, my dignity, my pride, and, for most of it, my partner. I am indebted to Wilma Penry and her colleagues for their astounding investigations, the hundreds of thousands of supporters who marched in cities across the world after the Bangkok News Conference, and, without a doubt, the love of my life, Sarah. I will be releasing a written statement to the media in due course and no further comment will be made at this time. Thank you."*

A policeman showed them to the left of the shrieking crowd to a black car, shiny new. He opened the rear door for them and they clambered in. Petey, quite undignified, shuffled across and clipped on his seatbelt.

"Thanks," Sarah told the officer as the door was slammed. "Driver, please get us out of here. To the hotel, if you please."

"It's over, it's all over," he cried, as the prison – well, his home – left them behind.

"It's the past now. We're going to move on from this, you hear me? We'll be at the hotel soon enough. You'll get showered, changed, another new set of clothes, then we'll move on."

"Is there any chance... later... you know...?"

"Haha," she laughed. "I'm sure we can find a spare few minutes."

Petey hugged the bathrobe tighter as he ventured on to the balcony. Shimmering London flickered before his eyes in its routine of car headlamps, streetlights illuminating both posh and murky areas, and the pulsing of distant discos and never-ending sex-fuelled get-togethers.

He swindled the glass of whisky in his left hand and tried to loosen himself up. How long had it been since he'd just looked out on a cityscape, no concerns about tomorrow, no woes or fears? During his early travels promoting Newton-M-Wren, he had done a lot of it; a young, cocky fool he was back in those days.

The past twenty years hung over him like an ice-pick, ready to stab this past into him. It only felt like yesterday that he had been in their house in Malibu, ready to head out to dinner. Alan Stanley's face that night wasn't easy to pass into the recesses of the mind.

Wilma Penry, the tireless journalist. Only two weeks ago! Travelled to Galway, had a few pints, then took a bus to the Cliffs of Moher, followed by a jump into the sea. He hadn't talked about it with Sarah yet, but that was an omen on the horizon.

The two of them were going out tomorrow to stretch their legs. It had been so many years since he'd walked more than a few feet without having to ask permission or get questioned on his movements.

Donny Bell was dead, very thankfully. A withered, bitter old man. But he had won.

Petey sipped his whisky, arms locked over the metal railing, knees shaking.

Was that a couple bickering below? Something petty and totally, utterly insignificant.

After he'd finished his drink, he went back to bed, next to the sleeping Sarah. She stirred as he pulled back the covers and slipped underneath.

"You okay?" she murmured.

"Yeah, I'm fine. Needed a little nightcap."

"Like you always do."

He curled up next to her and, for the first time in twenty years, felt safe.

Wednesday 5th April 2051

"Time for breakfast, you lazy lump!" she shouted, jumping on top of him.

"See you've still got some energy," he groaned happily.

"I might be old, but I'm still a kid inside!"

"Oh, I've noticed..."

"Right, come on..." She got off him and yanked the covers away. "Prick!"

He stumbled towards the bathroom, narrowly missing a pillow playfully lobbed at his head.

"Watch it, you!" he cried out.

The shower felt – in the absence of fancy terms – nice. Fresh. Free. No dirty soap. No having to watch out for predators. The water was maybe a little bit too hot, but he wasn't complaining: the broken glass nature of the jet stripped away the skin he'd built up in prison. This was freedom. This was the removal of tyranny.

At breakfast, another alien feeling came along: that of being able to stride along a buffet. He'd done it so many times in posh hotels around the world, oh so many years ago! Now sending in a metallic tool to pick up a croissant from the slush pile of pastries, or sliding a piece of bread into the rolling toaster thing, or jostling with other businessmen for the orange juice jug, or pouring coffee into a semi-clean china mug (whilst getting needle-pricked by the splashes of hot liquid), felt like a dance he'd long forgotten how to do or a piece of music his fingers no longer knew how to play.

Sitting opposite Sarah, he tried to look like he belonged. He could tell she knew exactly how he was feeling. The croissants – warm, crispy and juicy – slid over his tongue like a compressed octopus. The coffee was tepid. The toast looked dry and mutilated.

"You okay?" she asked.

"This breakfast is too much... Never got this much when I was in prison. I guess I just need time adjusting."

"If you want, we could go to a restaurant."

"No, honestly, I'm fine. I just need a bit of time getting things together."

"Sure. Also, forgot to mention, our flight's at Nine A.M. tomorrow."

The relief at getting out of England made Petey's stomach gurgle. "Excellent. Well, we'll have to make a day of it today."

"What do you fancy doing?"

"Well, a pub lunch for starters. Not being funny about that. Do you know how many years I've been waiting for a pint of English ale and some fish and chips?"

She smirked.

"And when we've done that," he continued, marvelling at how his mildly sarcastic humorous speech was resurrecting itself after two decades of silence, "I want to go to Covent Garden for a very posh dinner."

"I'm sure that can be arranged..." She blew him a kiss and gripped his hands in her own with a surprising fierceness. "I've missed you."

"Missed you too." He knew she was hurt. He started caressing her knuckles. That's what she liked. It was their secret thing. Something no one knew.

The pub was a few hundred years old – and independent – which made it good enough for Petey's tastes. They went in, like two budgeting students, and placed their orders with the landlord: a bald, red-faced fellow, with his shirtsleeves drawn up like wrapping paper.

The ale tasted sickly sweet and the fish and chips that gorgeous yellow sharpness. Sarah was having lasagne and a glass of red, as though she was already anticipating their posh-posh-posh dinner tonight.

"I was sorry to hear about Wilma," he said, placing the greasy fork down onto the now-empty plate. "She was a good person."

"She couldn't live the way she was, deformed like that."

"Did they get the guys who shot the car up?"

"Oh yeah, there's been a massive worldwide police operation. Hundreds arrested. Courts in thirteen different countries are being prepared."

"Wow."

"There won't be any need for you to give evidence in any of the trials, so don't worry about that."

"Who was she, this dancer?"

"You mean Alison Charm?"

"Yeah, that's her."

Sarah sipped her wine. "She was an interesting... I don't think *person* is the right word to use.

"When I was working on setting you free, I did a lot of research into Donny Bell. He had many connections, including to a criminal group called... oh what was it... The Runners. Silly name, I know, but their origins can be traced back to the early Nineteenth Century, deep in Africa. It's really hard to find any information on them; they're so well-hidden. You wouldn't believe the methods I had to use to dig things up. From what I found out, they were set up as a sort of revenge crime sect over the slave trade. They deal in drugs, most notably hallucinogens. The Runners are extremely widespread."

"So, you're saying everyone who saw Alison Charm had been poisoned by this lot?"

"I don't have the proof to make that declaration."

Petey glanced around him. "It would certainly make a lot of sense. I wonder how many people had their drinks spiked. But how did different people see the *same* person?"

"I don't know." Sarah fumbled with her fork. "But maybe this is a conversation for another time. Let's have the day off."

"You're quite right," he said. "So, do you fancy a walk after this?"

They fed pigeons in Trafalgar Square for a good hour or so, breadcrumbs tossed like dead skin.

A photographer was snapping away, stepping back, changing position, snapping away again. His camera was aimed at the iconic Nelson's Column. It was crumbling to pieces, the result of decades of neglect.

Rain hung above like a threatening bully, ready to pounce like a tiger. A plane flew low, descending to London City Airport. Two youths kicked a glass bottle in a game of pretend football.

"That was a good lunch," he remarked. "Fish was a tad on the cold side, but it was good nonetheless."

"Do you ever think about life?" she said, getting so serious that her skin turned into fractured china. "You know, regrets, things you wish you'd done?"

"Sometimes. I suppose I wish I'd been more carefree. More open. Travelled more. But I've done a lot of incredible stuff. And I've loved you. My life is complete."

"I have one regret." She tipped her paper bag and emptied the last of her breadcrumbs. Pigeons flocked to her ankles and swept the lot up like miniature vacuum cleaners. "I lied to you about something. May Nineteenth, Nineteen-Ninety-Three. What I told you twenty years ago was the truth, but I never told you about what happened after."

"It's okay. This is water under the bridge. You don't have to tell me."

"Please, I insist. Maybe it'll clarify a number of

things. Maybe it'll help you understand me a lot more."

She began and he listened. She was right: it made sense. It was as though life itself were a puzzle box of mystery games and riddles, and her story provided the key to understanding it. Complexity disappeared and yet reappeared at the same time, a shifting entity of knowing and unknowing.

When she finished, he smiled, taking her hand. "Thank you for your honesty," he said.

"Shall we go and stretch our legs a bit more?"

"Sounds good to me."

"You know, it's funny, but there's something I've always wanted to do. It's a bit obscure and probably not good for OAPs like us. What do you say to walking from Westminster to Canary Wharf?"

"Ha!" Petey scrambled out the last of his bread-crumbs and threw them at the birds. "What, you're being serious?"

"Yeah, why not?"

"I've got my formal shoes on. It's a bit drizzly today. I don't want them to fall apart."

The Thames was pockmarked with raindrops. A small cargo ship boomed its horn, a sound that hundreds of years ago, would have once petrified a posh gentleman (who had inherited his father's business): confronting him with the realisation that the world was built on sweat and blood. A balloon, on its way to the heavens, skimmed over the water, swashed around by the wind.

Petey and Sarah squelched as they walked past a set of tight-fitting apartments, eyes set on the giant metropolis of Canary Wharf. Their hands, locked together like a vice, showed them as truly happy. What more could be said?

"Let's stop for a moment," she said, unlinking their fingers. She crossed to a railing that lined the walkway and rested her elbows on the metal.

He went up to her and cuddled her to him. "You okay?"

"Yeah, fine. Just want to stop for a moment."

"Feet hurting?"

"You could say that."

They became silent, huddled together in the cool breeze – unseasonable. The activity on the river pounded on like a thousand hammers striking a thousand anvils.

"We'll start over when we get to Italy," she said eventually. "It's a new life, for the both of us."

"For the both of us," Petey repeated. He shut his eyes, maybe for too short a time.

-

Epilogue:
Transference

Edinburgh

Wednesday 19th May 1993

Walking out of the cramped bed-and-breakfast, she yawned and started her journey through the Old Town.

Well, she'd promised him, hadn't she? This date, this very date. Two O'Clock in the afternoon. She kept the oaths she made, however difficult they made her feel. She wandered through the crowds of this place like she'd walked through the packed markets of Calcutta – when was that, two years ago? Time did fly when you travelled!

A stressed-out, red-faced, pug-nosed businessman yelled into his mobile. Something about this major deal that was coming up. The other side wasn't playing ball. The market was a bit dodgy.

She kept her promises. Today, she was holding herself to herself. She was her own judge.

She turned into this place, Fleshmarket Close. She'd come down it before, back in 1989, when she'd been on the run. Actually, was this where she'd slept rough? Yeah: right by the bins.

It was only Half-Past One – enough time for a

quick drink. At the bottom of Fleshmarket Close, she spied a small pub, cigarette smoke floating out like a ghost. She went in. Men – the typical trench coat sort – eyed her and looked back down at their drinks.

"Half a lager, please," she said to the drained-looking barmaid, who was currently stubbing out a fag on a bent ashtray.

"Sure thing."

When the drink was served in an unwashed, purple lipstick-stained glass, she took it into a dark and dingy corner, caressing it as though it would channel her thoughts.

She was doing the right thing. Of that she was certain. No doubt the poor boy would have arrived early, anxiously checking his watch. Stupid little bugger.

After finishing her drink, she left the pub and made her way towards the bridge.

Doubts crisscrossed her mind like a spider's web. Would he really be there? He was probably engaged to be married and currently having champagne with his soon-to-be father-in-law. They would be laughing about the things that a man and his future wife's father typically tend to laugh about – it was a bonding process where very few words were actually uttered.

"Fancy a drink, darlin'?" A drunken man, with a dirty greying beard, reeking of whisky, had stumbled up to her. In one, (surprisingly, given his condition) swift move, he grabbed her crotch.

"Piss off!" she yelled, shoving him away.

"Aye, fuck it!" he shouted, trudging on his way.

Loser.

She found herself walking slower, the minutes on her watch counting down. She should hurry, if she didn't want to miss him. Nah, he wouldn't be there. Her muscles twitched: too little exercise; she should get on the bike more.

Edinburgh North Bridge was up ahead, a path to the unknown. Why was she afraid? Was she going to be executed by having her heart broken? Utter tosh! Oh God, that was an expression *he* would use...!

She stopped her fast pace and dropped to a shuffle, edging out of the safety of the Old Town.

The bridge was packed with tourists, postcard-sellers, balloonists, a couple of policemen, tramps, the black and white business crowd, and a huge variety of other people; a chocolate box of humanity. Wait, wasn't the Fringe in August?

She shielded her eyes from the sun and scanned the bridge. She must have appeared like a poster girl from a Soviet propaganda campaign, hand above her eyes, looking victorious.

Wait, was that him? Shit, it was! Standing on the bridge! Exactly as she'd instructed him to!

"You bastard you," she laughed.

He was older, with a small beard, and a more determined look about him.

She was about to walk, her fears melted away, when a hand grabbed her elbow.

"You!" she stuttered.

"You love him, don't you?" said the dancer. Dressed

casually, in a t-shirt and jeans, she could pass for any-one, a typical passer-by.

"What d'you mean?"

"You've always loved him. Yet you don't have the courage to admit it."

"Stay away from me."

"I can, if you want. Or you could come with me. Experience what you've never fully understood. Let me show you new frontiers. Then, one day, when you're ready, you'll be able to properly love him."

As much as Sarah was repulsed by these words, she found her resolve slipping. She wasn't ready for him.

Oh, the poor boy. Glancing every few seconds at his watch, no doubt wondering if all these years had been a waste.

But she wasn't ready for him.

She let the dancer, whoever she was, lead her away. They set off to the Old Town, barely talking, invisible amongst the crowd. Just as they were about to leave the bridge, she looked back, seeing him with his hands clasping the wall. She silently promised that she would see him again someday, when she was a better person. But now, she had to travel, properly this time.

The two strangers, from vastly different back-grounds, disappeared into the nest of cobbled streets, ready for new adventures, new horizons, and maybe, just maybe, a little bit of hope.

Acknowledgements

This story began with an idea and quickly expanded into something greater than I ever imagined.

Without the intense support of a number of people and organisations, this project would never have taken off.

Balloch Writers Open Mic, Round Lemon, SubdriftNYC, Dove Tales, The Edinburgh International Book Festival, Write Here, Jean Rafferty, Ray Evans, and Noel Boyd.

Lastly, without a shred of doubt, my immediate family and friends.

Harrison Hickman
July, 2021

Notes

Front cover image designed using Canva.

Harrison Hickman was born in Oxfordshire in 1992.

His other books include The Cyclops Invigilation and Lifecycle: Twelve Stories.

His novel Set In Stone was entered for the Rubery Book Award.